LOVE AND FOLLY

LOVE AND FOLLY

Sheila Simonson

Walker and Company
New York

F I C

First published in the United States of America in 1988 by the Walker Publishing Company, Inc.

Published simultaneously in Canada by Thomas Allen & Son Canada, Limited, Markham, Ontario.

Library of Congress Cataloging-in-Publication Data

Simonson, Sheila, 1941–
  Love and folly / Sheila Simonson.
  ISBN 0-8027-1018-2
  I. Title
PS3569.I48766L6   1988   813'.54—dc 19   87-35194

Printed in the United States of America

10 9 8 7 6 5 4 3 2 1

*This book is for my husband, Mickey,
with love and friendship.*

1820

". . . if there is a more foolish year in English history, I do not know of it."—J. B. Priestley

Prologue: New Year's morning, 1820.

THEIR SISTER, LADY Clanross, sent Jean and Maggie to bed after supper.

At least it felt that way, though the supper had been an elegant midnight dissipation of salmon and lobster patties and champagne, with the orchestra playing Ancient Musick and county guests telling the girls how handsome they looked. Maggie and Jean had stretched their permission to attend Elizabeth's New Year's gala until the clock struck one. Then Elizabeth sent them upstairs, rather an anticlimax.

It was their first ball. They were seventeen years old and would turn eighteen midway through the Season, their long-anticipated come-out. Elizabeth had sent for Mme. Dulac from Lincoln to rig them out especially for this night, and Clanross himself had led Jean onto the floor—after the ceremonial first dance in which he had been obliged to squire the Duchess of Cope, who was fat and fifty.

Jean had danced the first dance, very properly, with their cousin Willoughby Conway-Gore, and Maggie had danced with Johnny Dyott, but Jean hadn't felt properly *launched* until she romped through the boulanger with her tall brother-in-law, Clanross. In that second dance Maggie had been stuck with red-faced Charles Wharton of neighbour-

1

ing Hazeldell, but she didn't object. Johnny had given her confidence. He always did.

Now, drooping over the balcony as the guests drifted back into the brilliantly lit ballroom, Jean fetched a huge sigh. "I could have danced forever. Until dawn, anyway."

Maggie yawned.

"I felt light as air, Mag. I floated from one partner to another like . . . like thistledown." Having called up the simile—it came from one of Mme. D'Arblay's novels—she gave a small bounce.

Maggie pulled her filmy stole closer. "You didn't mis-step? I trod on Clanross's foot in the Roger de Coverly. He said it didn't signify. Did you really drink two glasses of champagne? I had one, but Johnny brought me lemonade with supper."

"You're not firm enough, Maggie. I simply told Cousin Willoughby I wanted wine and he was very obliging." Jean peered over the rail. The orchestra were tuning their instruments.

"I thought better not." Maggie stifled another yawn with her gloved hand. Both girls wore elbow-length gloves of the palest blue, a gift of the earl, who had friends in Paris. Their gowns, though superficially similar in their gauzy overdresses and high corsages, had been cut to strikingly different designs. That was Jean's idea.

They were identical twins, so alike their close kin sometimes confused them, and with the added disadvantage of flaming red hair, they were bound to be visible. Jean wanted to make sure no one treated them as interchangeable dolls. They would dress for contrast throughout the Season, she had decided one frosty morning, planning. She would wear one colour, like a theme or favour, Maggie another. That way no one would have an excuse to confuse one for the other. Maggie could have blue, Jean had added, magnanimous.

When Elizabeth supported the notion, Maggie acquiesced. She knew herself to be foolishly shy, but more than once that long New Year's evening she had wished she could hide in her twin-ness. Her gown, a confection of silver spider gauze over a slim frost-blue crepe, she thought perfect, far nicer than Jean's pink rosebuds over white. But Maggie was not at all sure she enjoyed being *singular*. That was Jean's aim.

Maggie shivered a little, though for once it was quite warm, the heat from hundreds of wax tapers, three fireplaces, and upwards of two hundred Lincolnshire gentry overcoming even the endemic chill of Brecon.

Her twin straightened and turned to her. "I daresay we shall have to trot off to bed . . ."

"Oh, yes!" Maggie was sleepy.

". . . but I wish we needn't. They're going to waltz again. How I wish I could have waltzed with Tom."

Maggie's eyes narrowed. She knew Jean had cherished a *tendre* for their brother-in-law, the earl, since they were silly girls of fifteen, but Jean rarely slipped into Christian-name moonings over Clanross these days.

"Just once."

She sounded so defensive Maggie touched her arm lightly. "You'll waltz with him a hundred times before the Season is over. And I'll waltz with Johnny Dyott. I don't step on *his* toes."

"Oh, Mag, wasn't it splendid? And just think, months of balls and ridottos . . . what is it, Maggie? I thought you were having a good time. Do say you enjoyed it."

"Of course I did, sister. I'm only a trifle hagged. It *was* splendid."

Jean made a wide gesture with one gloved hand. "D'you say so? Then let's waltz!"

"What?"

"Here. You and I. They can't see us. Come, Mag, a dare."

Strictly speaking, they ought not waltz in publick until the Patronesses of Almack's approved their Ton, but Jean's eyes glinted with challenge. After a moment Maggie gave a small choke of laughter. "Oh, very well, Jeanie. But you lead."

Below in the ballroom, Johnny Dyott eased his shoulders against the silk-hung wall and watched the earl and Lady Clanross take the floor. They danced well together, he thought, though a trifle stiffly. Johnny was a master of the waltz, among his other talents. With the countess's young sisters packed betimes off to bed, he saw no lady he wished to partner other than Bella Conway-Gore perhaps. She was a notable exponent of the art.

The musick swelled and so did the company, swaying and swooping in the dance that very high sticklers still regarded as fast. Fortunately, like the Conway twins, the high sticklers had retired from the scene. The floor was left to enthusiasts. Johnny let his vision blur and watched the sweep of colours. A successful affair. Should ease his lordship's way with the county notables . . .

A flash of white at the top of his view caught his attention. What was it? He squinted. Above, on the long gallery overlooking the ballroom, Lady Jean and Lady Margaret Conway were waltzing together. They were so high up and so far away he could not distinguish between them, though his romantic fancy had always told him he would know Lady Jean. He watched, careful not to stare too obviously—for he didn't wish to call attention to what was a minor lapse of conduct—until the music swirled to a close.

Like flames, he thought, flames dancing against the night.

=1=

THE KING WAS dead.

Johnny Dyott clutched the strap and hung on as the top-heavy accommodation coach rattled out of the yard of the Angel Inn, lurched past St. Clement Danes, and headed west through the muffled clangour of London bells. It seemed to Johnny that the bells had not ceased since the old King's death, long awaited, was announced the evening before. Johnny had fallen asleep to their tolling.

It was Sunday, and now the bells of Wren's church—of all Wren's churches—summoned the faithful to morning service.

The coach jolted once more on the icy cobbles, slowed momentarily, and began to pick up speed as the wheels found purchase. Johnny leaned back and closed his eyes. He was a little subject to carriage sickness.

Sunday, the thirtieth of January, in the year of grace 1820. Snow blew with a thin rattle against the windows of the coach. Sunday. He ought not travel on the sabbath. Johnny's father, dean of Lincoln cathedral, had always been a strict sabbatarian. Ordinarily, Johnny would have deferred his journey another day out of respect for his father's opinions, but the thought of stopping longer in London, a strange London transformed by funereal gloom and suppressed excitement, had been suddenly insupportable.

He had awakened early, roused by the bells, and thrown his belongings into the portmanteau before the maid brought his hot water. She was red-nosed with weeping and ready to tell him her exact sentiments when she first heard the dreadful tidings, but Johnny cut her short and asked her to summon a footman to carry his traps down to the foyer. He meant to leave directly after breakfast. The maid was almost as dismayed at his resolve as his father would have been, though for less pious reasons, but, like all of the Conway servants, she was far too well-trained to demur. When Johnny pressed a generous vail upon her she even summoned a smile.

Owing to Lord Clanross's habit of rising before six, breakfast in the Conway town house was served at the unfashionably early hour of eight. The family were not yet in residence after the Christmas holiday, though Clanross himself had returned to town the week before for a debate in the Lords. He had brought Johnny and his political secretary, Captain Greene, with him.

The night before, the night of the king's death, Clanross had dined at the house of his brother-in-law and political agent, Featherstonehaugh, the M.P. The earl had taken Greene, not Johnny, with him, and Johnny was feeling ill used. He had hoped for a word alone with Clanross in the breakfast room, but, to add to his chagrin, he found Barney Greene at table before him making steady inroads on a sirloin of beef. Clanross was not yet come down.

Greene, a grizzled, stolid gentleman of forty, looked up as Johnny entered and mumbled a brief good day before returning his attention to the roast beef and mustard. He ate with the same single-minded despatch with which he attacked the earl's political correspondence. Johnny envied him the importance of his work.

"You've heard the news, I take it." Greene swallowed a draught of ale.

"That His Majesty died last evening? Yes."

Greene made an impatient noise. "The election."

Johnny's hand stopped with a spoonful of buttered eggs midway between the chafing dish and his plate. He felt his ears go hot. Why hadn't that occurred to him? The king was dead. Parliament would be dissolved and an election called for. As Lord Clanross had the disposal of several safe seats and some influence in the outcome of other, contested seats, Greene would be plunged at once into the business of politicking.

Johnny filled his plate at random, his mind racing. He listened with half an ear as Greene prosed on about the Conway interest. Perhaps Clanross would find some use for an energetic *young* man in the coming campaign. More than anything, Johnny wanted to be about the nation's business, though he knew he was unqualified and wholly inexperienced in political matters.

Clanross had hired him as a private secretary, someone to help him deal with his scientific papers, his numerous charities, and the wide personal correspondence inevitable in his position. Johnny had accepted the post with eagerness and gratitude that Clanross should remember a very green ensign whose brief, inglorious presence in his company had ended seven years before. But despite his gratitude and eagerness, Johnny had in his secret heart hoped that the earl would entrust him with a publick mission. So far that had not happened, but it could. It might.

Scarcely had Johnny seated himself and poured a cup of the very strong coffee Clanross favoured when the earl entered the breakfast room.

Then in his thirty-eighth year, the Earl of Clanross was a tall man with serious grey eyes and a thatch of thick, greying hair. It never ceased to surprise Johnny, who had known him as plain Captain Conway, that he looked the earl—or rather, for most earls were elderly, goutish, and decrepit, that Clanross looked as an earl ought to look, upright and distinguished. He dressed with a neat propriety that accorded better with his lean height than the extreme of fashion would have done, and he carried himself like a soldier.

That his military erectness owed more to a back injury he had taken in the Peninsula than to a disposition to stiffness Johnny was beginning to understand after three months in the Conway household. At eighteen, Ensign Dyott had hero-worshipped Captain Conway with all the foolish enthusiasm of his years. Now, at five and twenty, Johnny found that he liked the earl, a different and altogether more comfortable sentiment. Nevertheless Johnny was still a little in awe of his employer.

Clanross greeted Barney Greene and smiled at Johnny. "Waite tells me you've decided to leave for Winchester this morning." He cut a slice of sirloin and seated himself.

"I thought to." Johnny hesitated. "My lord . . . er, Clanross, if the king's death alters things . . ."

Clanross was pouring a cup of coffee. His eyes gleamed with amusement, but he said gravely, "It's bound to, you know. Especially for Prinny."

Johnny flushed. "I know . . . I meant . . . what with the election and so on if you've a more urgent use for my services . . ." He trailed off, incoherent with hope and embarrassment.

Clanross took a reflective sip of coffee. "I can think of few things more urgent than helping Richard Falk."

"Yes, but a novelist . . ."

"He won't require you to spin fantasies for him, Johnny, but his disability makes copying slow work. I daresay he'll set you to straightening the Canadian correspondence. Bookkeeping was never Colonel Falk's strong point." He sipped again. "He's done yeoman work as secretary, though. I should have foreseen he'd throw himself into that business. Richard never does anything by halves."

The Canadian "business" was a charity Clanross had organized—and funded—five years before when the government decided to grant officers lands in Upper Canada in lieu of prize money and arrears of pay. By then it was evident that discharged soldiers from the Peninsular Army would have great difficulty finding work. The economy was in a postwar shambles, unemployed weavers and mill workers rioted in the north, and veterans of many years' service were left to beg their way from town to town, desperate for bread and employment.

That the situation was bitterly unfair Clanross had pointed out in the Lords more than once, but the debt-ridden government were unwilling to increase taxes in a time when landlords suffered from declining rents and the Poor Law burdened the conscientious with further outlay.

Many of the less affluent officers had emigrated to Upper Canada themselves. But wealthier officers with no real need for the grants and no wish to transport their families to a wilderness, could be persuaded to assign their holdings to the use of discharged veterans. Some, like Clanross and his friend, Lord Bevis, donated their land grants to the project outright and made substantial gifts of money as well. Others, less affluent or less generous, were willing to help settle the men and their families as tenants.

It was a useful scheme, but it was complicated enough to require the services of Clanross's solicitors and at least one bookkeeper. Colonel Falk did not keep the books, but as secretary he had the considerable chore of writing cajoling, placatory, and grateful letters to contributors. He also kept a journal of the charity's transactions and provided emigrants with letters of introduction, testimonials of good character, and, alas, in some cases, pleas for leniency addressed to the colonial officials when beneficiaries indulged in feckless misbehaviour.

"Shouldn't have said Falk was the charitable type myself," Barney Greene mumbled around a mouthful of toast. "Had the reputation of a care-for-nobody."

"Appearances can be deceiving." There was ice in Clanross's tone. Greene's eyes dropped to his plate and he mumbled something apologetic.

Clanross turned back to Johnny. "The success of the project has been Colonel Falk's doing. Bevis and I lend our names, but he does the work. I never intended . . . well, that is by the by. The point is Richard needs your assistance, Johnny, and needs it now. I'll rub along without you for a fortnight or so. Do your best for him. He's my oldest friend." He sawed a bit of beef and daubed it with mustard. "You'll like Mrs. Falk. Charming woman. Have you taken a room at the Pelican?"

"Yes."

"Excellent. I don't want you to burden the household. What with my godson's illness and a new infant, Emily Falk will have her hands full."

"Yes, my lord." Johnny addressed his cold coffee and congealed eggs with a gloom he hoped was not obvious. It all sounded so domestic and trivial. "I'll do my possible. Does Lady Clanross come to town next week as planned?"

Clanross gave a wry smile. "She will be cast down, I daresay, but I fear the girls' come-out must be put off."

At that sally, Johnny smiled, too. Lady Clanross had spent Christmas bemoaning the necessity of removing to town to present her twin sisters to society. An astronomer of some note, her ladyship had lately caused the Chacton works to cast a very large mirror for her new reflecting telescope, and she longed to oversee its installation in the small observatory Clanross had built for her at Brecon. But if spring was the season for astronomical discovery, it was also the Season.

Lady Jean and Lady Margaret Conway would turn eighteen in May and they were determined to come out. Christmas had seen them aflutter with plans for new gowns and new sensations—theatre parties and routs and balls, balls, balls. At their insistence, their dancing master had called up all the gentlemen in the household including Johnny as auxiliary troops, and the long gallery echoed with dancing musick throughout the holiday.

Clanross had married the eldest daughter of his predecessor, a remote cousin. Lady Clanross's sisters, with wealth, birth and striking good looks in their favour, meant to take the Ton by storm. It was an enthusiasm neither the countess nor her husband shared, but they were inclined to indulge the girls.

Johnny was a little in love with the fiery and impetuous Lady Jean, and he had listened with melancholy amusement as the twins' eagerness wore down their elders' resistance. He also taught Lady Margaret the *pas de Zephyr*.

The girls were young. They could have waited a year to make their appearance on the marriage mart and no harm done, but when they put their minds to a course of action it was well-nigh impossible to resist them. It looked as if the king's death would throw a rub in their way. Johnny wondered how they would surmount the barrier of a year of national mourning. If he had been a gambling man he would have laid odds on their ingenuity.

Barney Greene, his plate of sirloin demolished, wiped his mouth on the heavy damask napkin and rose from the table. "The letter for Mr. Kilbride in Dublin?"

Clanross grimaced. "Finish that one first, then try the address to the Holton freeholders. A formality. Say all that's proper." Holton was a pocket borough. Clanross disapproved of pocket boroughs. He had inherited three.

Greene bowed and left the room.

Clanross ate in silence for some minutes. He looked underslept—the Featherstonehaugh dinner must have run late. Johnny finished his own meal and sat still, wondering if he ought to break in on his employer's thoughts. But it was now or never.

"My lord . . ."

Clanross started and looked at him, frowning. Johnny knew he did not like to be addressed by his style, having come to the title late and unexpectedly, but he said in kindly enough tones, "What is it, Johnny? I've a letter for Richard—more business, I fear—and another for Emily. Shall you carry the post for me?"

"Yes, sir." Johnny drew a breath. "If you could make use of me in the canvassing, Clanross, or in anything of that nature, I'd be glad of the experience."

The grey eyes narrowed. "Are you interested in politicks?"

11

"Of all things, my lord."

Clanross sighed and rubbed his forehead. "I envy you. I often think there's nothing I detest so much as politicks and politicians."

Johnny gaped. "But . . ."

"I know. I'm inconsistent. What are they calling me now, Radical Tom? Or is it Mad Conway?"

Johnny flushed and dropped his eyes. "But sir, if you dislike it . . ."

"Why bother?" Clanross rose, half his meat untouched. "I'm stuck with it, am I not? At least until we abolish the House of Lords."

Johnny stared.

"Too Radical for you? Never mind, Johnny. I shan't corrupt the youth of Britain with my more extreme ideas. There'll be work enough and to spare before the election. They'll delay the funeral as much as a fortnight—safe enough in this weather." Clanross's nose wrinkled. "Time for the crowned heads to assemble."

"I daresay."

"Meanwhile do your best by Richard and I'll see what I can find for you on the hustings."

"I. . . th-thank you, my lord."

"Come along, if you want to save the expense of a hack. And keep your ear to the ground whilst you're in Winchester. Who knows, you may find stirrings of discontent even in happy Hampshire."

Confused but heartened, Johnny rose, too, and went in search of his gear.

Clanross deposited him at the Angel in good time to pay the fare before the coach left for Winchester at ten. Then the bells began to toll again and Johnny's elation leaked away in the chill air.

The coach had begun to bowl along at a smart clip. Johnny opened his eyes to find a tight-mouthed clerk regarding him with disapproval. Probably fancies I shot the cat last night, Johnny reflected. I might have done, if anyone had asked me to.

"Ah," said the red-faced corn chandler who sat beside the clerk. "King's dead then, poor old gentleman. 'Tis a sad day."

"We shall not see his like again," the tight-mouthed clerk said piously. "He was a moral man."

The plump woman beside Johnny agreed, the black plume on her bonnet nodding sycophantically. "Not like some I could name."

"Aye," the corn chandler echoed. He shifted his heavy thighs. "Not like some."

They were thinking of Prinny, of course. The fat, dissolute, charming Prince Regent was now George IV. Hard to imagine Prinny as King of England. George III had been king through Johnny's twenty-five years. Even Johnny's father remembered no other monarch, and the venerable dean recalled the days of powder and patch, of knee breeches and hoops and style, when ladies wore silk the colour of Marie Antoinette's hair and gentlemen carried swordsticks. What if the king had been old and mad for almost as long as Johnny could remember? He had been king—and he had been a moral man.

"Time for a change, then," the corn chandler muttered. "Past time."

" 'O wind,' " Johnny intoned, quoting a line from a poem his friend, Hogg, had sent him lately in manuscript. Was it Byron or that fellow Shelley? " 'O wind, if Winter comes can Spring be far behind?' "

Everyone stared at him.

The king is dead. Long live the king.

No one was going to say anything further. The acts suspending habeas corpus and making open criticism of the government a capital crime were still in force and only that August mounted troops had ridden down unarmed citizens in the streets of Manchester. Whatever people might be thinking, they would keep their thoughts to themselves among strangers. Perilous times.

And I, Johnny mused, his melancholy deepening, am journeying to Winchester to help Colonel Falk scribble a novel. A noble endeavour. He leaned back again, closed his eyes, and tried to imagine the scene at Brecon when the Conway sisters discovered they were not, after all, to make their come-out. He rather thought Lady Jean would swear.

2

". . . so it's true, after all. The king is dead."

"Hellfire and damnation!"

Elizabeth Conway winced. "Really, Jean."

Jean's twin, Margaret, plucked a macaroon from the tea tray. "It's a great pity, Jean, but I daresay His Majesty didn't die to spite us." She nibbled the confection.

Jean sniffed.

A year ago, Elizabeth reflected, Maggie would have munched and Jean would have thrown something at her. *It is just possible that my sisters are growing up.* She reached again for her husband's brief letter. "Three months of deep mourning . . ."

Jean plumped down on the sofa beside Elizabeth and peered at the neat script. "Then in April we can put off our black ribbands and make our come-out."

"April will be taken up with electioneering." Elizabeth folded the letter again lest Jean see the private joke with which Tom had closed, an allusion to her new telescope. No point in adding fuel to Jean's fire. "The new Parliament are to take their seats on the twenty-fifth. After that, I daresay the leaders of the Ton will begin to entertain privately, but you cannot be presented this year, so what is the point? At least I don't think there will be a court levee. Prinny has never had a great regard for the proprieties, but even he . . .well, we shall see. Tom means to come home as soon as he can."

"Oh, good." Maggie dusted the crumbs daintily from

her fingers. "Una's healing nicely, but I'll want Clanross's opinion." Una was Maggie's Irish setter, a gift from Clanross, and a recent mother. The birth had been attended by complications.

It was Elizabeth's private belief that Maggie felt more enthusiasm for Una's puppies than she had felt at the prospect of a London Season, but Maggie was a good-natured girl and where Jean led her twin would follow. Whither Jean, seething beside her, would direct her frustrated energies, Elizabeth did not venture to imagine. She said cautiously, "Should you care to make your come-out in half mourning, Jeanie?"

Jean sniffed. Her small-boned fists clenched on her lap, and her flame-red hair crackled with indignation. "It's so unfair. Anne even promised in her last letter to take us to Mme. Thérèse."

Lady Anne Featherstonehaugh, their second sister, was a modish political hostess and awake to the highest kick of fashion, which Elizabeth knew *she* was not. That Anne had agreed to see to the girls' gowns was Elizabeth's doing and she was about to tell Jean so when the girl rounded on her.

"You don't care, Elizabeth. You're happy!"

"Do you accuse me of rejoicing at His Majesty's demise? Believe me, I'm not so lost to propriety."

"You know what I mean," Jean muttered, sullen. "Your blasted telescope."

Elizabeth looked at her from the corner of her eye. "Perhaps it's fortunate you won't be going about in society after all. Your language would make a grenadier blush."

Jean burst into tears.

Elizabeth and Maggie exchanged alarmed glances. Jean was not the crying kind. As she patted her sister's quivering shoulders and murmured soothing phrases, Elizabeth groped for some scheme of action to divert Jean's mind from her troubles, but nothing presented itself.

In truth, Elizabeth was rather shaken by the strength of Jean's disappointment. She tried to remember her own feelings when, twelve years before, she had prepared to make her debut in society. Her stepmother, Jean and Maggie's mother, was alive then, and their father as well. 1808—the height, or depth, of the war. The ballrooms had been full of uniforms. A dashing and rather exciting time, jollier, Elizabeth thought ruefully, than the present, in spite of alarums and excursions.

Her mind strayed to her husband, as it often did when he was gone; and she wondered what Tom had been doing in 1808. Probably sitting in winter quarters in Portugal, scratching his fleabites and rehearsing for regimental theatricals when he was not on outpost duty. Tom seldom reminisced about his military service, and when he did his recollections were apt to focus on fleas and fandangoes.

Oh Tom, come soon, she pleaded silently. I need you. Jean needs you.

As if in response to her prayer, the door opened. Elizabeth's pulse quickened. She gave Jean a squeeze and sat up. It was not Tom—only Nurse bringing the babies for their aunts to inspect and approve. Still, the diversion was welcome.

Maggie jumped to her feet and ran to capture the Honourable Richard Conway who had escaped Nurse's grasp and was waddling, petticoats already adroop, in the direction of the briskly burning fire. Nurse set Lord Brecon on his unsteady pins and straightened his skirts with a cluck. "There now, wasn't Master Dickon all clean and tidy for his mama, and now look at him." Maggie had rescued the baby from the coal scuttle. "I beg your pardon, Lady Clanross. He's too quick for me, that one."

Elizabeth smiled and held out her arms to Brecon who staggered solemnly over to her. "Mama," he said experimentally.

She gave him a hug. "That's right, darling. Just keep practising and you'll have it down pat any day now."

Beside her Jean gave a watery giggle. Brecon had caused some consternation over Christmas by calling all female persons above a certain age mama. At the time Elizabeth had been less amused than her sisters, but she was glad now that the baby had diverted his aunt from her self-absorbed gloom. "Will you go to Auntie Jean, then, Ba?"

Lord Brecon gave an assenting bounce and was duly handed over. Dickon, on Maggie's knee, crowed with delight as she began to tickle his round person, and the atmosphere lightened appreciably.

Elizabeth's sons, like her sisters, were twins, though the boys did not look much alike. It was some consolation to her that she had produced not one but two heirs to the earldom at the first try. Among them, her father's wives had borne eight daughters and no sons, which was why Tom was Lord Clanross.

In another sense the boys were a fortunate gift. As with Maggie's Una, the birth had been attended by complications. When she woke at last from a high fever, a week after she had begun labour, the physician had informed Elizabeth that she would bear no other children. In the weeks—nay, months—of melancholic reflection that followed, Elizabeth had clung to the fact that at least she had given Tom an heir.

She could not help feeling that she had failed him, even so. Tom had been orphaned young and had lost his own twin sister to the same illness that had killed his mother. While he cared not a whit about securing the succession, Elizabeth thought he needed a large family and she had wanted to give him many children, daughters as well as sons.

Elizabeth's barrenness was a grief to her, but it was a grief she kept to herself. Tom had never spoken of it. Indeed she sometimes wondered whether he had been told. However, his affection for the boys was unqualified. And, she thought, half sad, half amused, if she had not given him daughters, at least she had given him a raft of sisters.

Besides Jean and Maggie, who were great favourites with him, there were Anne in London and Kitty in Scotland,

Elizabeth's full sisters. And, in the Dower House down the gentle hill upon which the palace of Brecon sat in icy neoclassical splendour, where they were attended in great comfort by the redoubtable governess, Miss Bluestone, resided the three other Conway daughters. Fanny, Georgy, and Caro, Jean and Maggie's full sisters, were still in the schoolroom. Quite a population of Conway females. And they will all have to be presented, Elizabeth thought. Perhaps Tom and I should emigrate to Upper Canada before the evil day arrives.

She watched her sons and her sisters romping on the Turkey carpet and wished Tom would come. Parliament would be dissolved at once, he had said in his letter. The Whigs were hopeful that Prinny would bring them in at last. Tom was less sanguine and less enthralled by the current Whig leadership. The questions he considered most urgent—the want of work, the price of bread, Catholic emancipation to placate turbulent Ireland, redistribution of Parliamentary seats—were not likely to receive much attention even from the Whigs, if, as rumour had it, Prinny intended to divorce Queen Caroline.

On what grounds? Elizabeth wondered. Infidelity? But Prinny was famous—or notorious—for a series of plump mistresses, not to mention his morganatic wife, Mrs. Fitzherbert. Surely he would not be so brass-faced as to sue for divorce on the grounds of his wife's amatory adventures. What then? And if he does bring a bill of divorcement, will the queen countersue for divorce on the grounds of bigamy?

A divorce was bound to be a political matter. The parties would take sides, not on the truth or falsehood of the evidence, but on the basis of the advantages to be gained from taking one position or the other. Precisely the sort of false dilemma to produce rioting in the streets, as if there were not already enough civil disorder.

Elizabeth sighed.

"Do look, Lizzie, Brecon can dance!" Jean was laughing

heartily as the heir, looking pleased with himself, wobbled up and down a few times on his still uncertain legs. They gave way. He sat down hard and began to wail. Jean picked him up. Dickon, closely attended by his Aunt Margaret, was exploring the wainscoting. He had acquired a fine coating of dust. I must speak to the maid, Elizabeth thought absently as she rose to take her sobbing child from Jean.

"Good God, what's this, a donnybrook?"

"Clanross!" Jean and Maggie.

"My lord." The nurse.

"Oh, Tom, thank God you are come." Elizabeth ran to her husband. He enveloped her and the heir in a large, rather wet hug—he wore riding gear—and smiled at Maggie and Dickon.

"That's a fine greeting. What's the matter, my lady?"

She blinked, momentarily confused. Now Tom was home *nothing* was the matter. "Prinny cannot possibly divorce the queen. He has no grounds."

The earl's eyebrows shot up to his hairline and he grinned down at her. "And what has that to do with me and thee?"

Elizabeth flushed and laughed. "Nothing. Not a thing. Did you ride? You're wet with snow."

"And mud," Clanross agreed amiably, bending to kiss her cheek. "I'm growing too old for winter manoeuvres."

"But the carriage . . ."

"I left it in Grantham and hired a nag. It was faster than the carriage. Otherwise I should have had to put up for the night in Chacton." He had taken Brecon from her and was nibbling the fingers the baby poked in his mouth. "Very tasty, Ba."

"Papa!" Dickon beamed expectantly from Maggie's arms so Clanross took him, too, and they made a circuit of the withdrawing room, his lordship with a giggling infant on each arm. It was all very silly and happy, and Elizabeth, perversely, felt a strong urge to break into tears. My turn.

After dinner she and Clanross retired to their suite. Elizabeth had had an antechamber made into a cosy sitting room when she had finally agreed to live at Brecon—it was a splendid house but far from homely—and some of their pleasantest times had been spent there, remote from family and guests and servants with a warm fire crackling on the hearth.

"Shall you have to go back to town soon?" Elizabeth snuggled close and began playing idly with his watchfob.

"I left Barney Greene at the house. He can send for me if I'm needed. I've a week at least, Elizabeth." He pulled her closer still. "A reprieve, but I fear the next months will require my absence from Brecon more often than I like."

They spoke idly of absent friends. After a time Elizabeth murmured, "Did you send Johnny Dyott to your friend in Hampshire?"

"Yes. He rode down on Sunday."

"Sunday!"

"Perhaps he is beginning to kick over the traces at last. He won't take holy orders, will he?"

"I don't think so. He has come that far. His father will be distressed, but really, Johnny would chafe at the confinement of a parish." Elizabeth hesitated. "Have you considered that he might do well in politicks? He is a personable young man . . ."

"And a Tory by temperament, if not conviction."

"Does that matter?"

Tom said slowly, "The thing is, he has ideals, and I'd be loathe to disillusion him so young."

"He's twenty-five. Not a youth."

"Except in his own mind."

That was true. In many ways Johnny Dyott was an estimable young man, but there was in his make-up a core of indecisiveness and deference that made him seem much younger than he was. She wondered why it should be so— an overbearing father?

Tom sighed. "Richard will keep him occupied."

"I daresay." Elizabeth was not well acquainted with Colonel Falk, though he was Dickon's godfather. She had met few of Tom's military friends. Sometimes she felt as if Tom were deliberately excluding her from that part of his life, for he kept up the friendships. He didn't intrude his old companions on her company. She hoped he did not imagine she was reluctant to welcome them. Almost she asked him, but it would be easier to change the subject.

He did it for her. "I've found a librarian."

She straightened. "At last!" The Brecon library was in dire need of professional scrutiny. Tiresome Latin sermons by seventeenth century divines jostled family papers and rare incunabula, and no one knew what was where. "Who is he?"

"Owen Davies."

"Davies . . ." She pictured an ancient Welsh gnome.

"The rector's youngest."

"Good God, not the boy with spots!" Dimly she recalled a callow undergraduate sitting beside the rector's prim wife in the earl's Brecon church.

"He has been down from Oxford two years now and wants work. His scholarship is excellent . . ."

". . . but what?" She heard the reservation in his voice.

He gave her shoulders a left-handed squeeze and his voice lightened with amusement. "But he tells me he's a poet. I hope his muse will allow him a few hours a day to catalogue the books."

"Lord, a poet. The woods are full of them. It is all Byron's fault." Elizabeth's mind turned to more urgent matters. "What am I to do with the twins?"

"The boys? I thought they looked exceptionally frisky."

"I meant my sisters. Jean was in tears this afternoon . . ."

He frowned. "Good God, why?"

"She's determined to make her come-out, king or no king. It's an idée fixe. And you know how she creates when she's thwarted."

Tom laughed. "I daresay she's laying diabolical plots."

"It is no laughing matter, Tom. She's capable of embroiling herself in a real scandal—and relishing the melodrama. If only Maggie were a stronger character. Jean listens to Maggie."

Tom gave her shoulders another squeeze and rose to mend the fire. "Don't fret yourself, my dear. If worse comes to worst you can ship Jean off to Scotland."

"She would probably foment a rebellion."

He laid the poker back in its place and turned, smiling. "That would enliven Lady Kinnaird's drawing room."

At that Elizabeth had to smile, too. Her other married sister, Kitty, was a dull woman. Dull and peevish. "Better Kitty's drawing room than mine."

"And how did Maggie greet the dreadful tidings?"

Elizabeth laughed. "Maggie is so much more temperate than Jean. She accepts things as they are." In spite of herself, a note of censure crept into her voice. Elizabeth herself was not of a placid disposition and she sometimes thought Maggie a slow-top.

Tom leaned on the mantel. "That's not always a bad quality, you know."

Elizabeth flushed. It was a little uncomfortable when he read her mind. "No, but she is so sluggish."

"I shouldn't say Maggie was sluggish. Merely she has the capacity to be happy. That's a gift Jean doesn't share, poor child. If Maggie were to fall in love she would live happily ever after. Jean would aim for *Romeo and Juliet*."

"Then let us hope her reach exceeds her grasp."

A slow smile lit his grey eyes. "Speaking of reaching and grasping, Lady Clanross, should we not adjourn to the nuptial couch? I didn't ride that cross-gaited tooth-rattler all the way from Grantham to chat about your sisters."

"Uxorious man." Elizabeth found she was smiling, too.

"Hist! You can't be asleep, Maggie!"

"Mnnn." Maggie blinked her eyes open.

"What are we going to do?"

"Do?"

"I won't wait a whole year to make my come-out."

"Mm, no." The dying embers of the fire came into brief focus. Maggie snuggled closer to her sister.

"We'll have to do something."

Maggie thought. "Probably."

"What, daff-head?"

"I d'know," Maggie said sleepily, "but don't worry so."

"Why not?" Jean wriggled.

"Because you'll think of something, sister." She shut her eyes and drifted. "You always do."

It was possible that Jean said something in reply, but if she did Maggie didn't hear her.

═3═

THE OLD KING was dead.

He might have chosen better weather for it, Emily Falk reflected, peering out the window of her small withdrawing room. The bells of the cathedral had finally stopped tolling.

What was keeping Richard? A gust of wind rattled the pane in the tall sash window. Emily let the heavy curtain fall across the shadows of the lamplit street and retreated to her fire, shivering and glad that she was not out in the cold.

With a sigh she picked up her knitting—prosaic grey wool. Keeping the boys in stockings was one of the duller domestic chores. The dullness suited Emily's frame of mind. Grey wool, grey weather, grey mood. She turned the heel with absent competence and brooded on life's overall greyness.

I wouldn't mind so much if I were home at Wellfield. Her needles clicked. She thought of the spacious manor house as she had seen it at Christmas with the furniture shrouded in holland covers, the carpets rolled, and the bare hallways echoing. Wellfield was a house that needed to be lived in. It's not fair, she thought, rebellious. I should be at home, we should all be at home. But Wellfield was not her husband's home and that was that. Richard had leased the house in Winchester that September and moved his family before Michaelmas, and though she understood his reasons and tried to put on a cheerful face, Emily could not overcome her homesickness. The trouble with town life was that there was nothing to do.

That was nonsense, of course. She dropped a stitch, ripped out the row and began again. In a household containing four servants and four children—five when her son, Matthew Foster, was at home as he had been all the weekend—there was always something to do, but Emily was used to a much larger scope. She had run her son's estate since her first husband's death, leaving most of the domestic chores to her servants. Now she missed her tenants, her cows, and her ledgers.

I'm dull, she thought with melancholy satisfaction, dull and dreary.

At that point her sense of humour—or her sense of justice—caught up with her. I always thought I could be happy with Richard anywhere—in a cottage, on the high seas, on a desert isle. And here I am complaining to myself because he has moved me a few miles from my native ground to a well-appointed town house not a quarter mile from my son's school.

She pictured herself with Richard on a desert isle. The idea had merit. A tropical isle with no snowstorms or cathedral bells or gossiping ladies. But, her less romantic self retorted, you would not be alone with Richard on a desert isle. You would be on a desert isle with Richard, Matt, Amy, Tommy, little Henry, Sally, Mrs. Harry, Phillida, McGrath, and Peggy. And possibly Aunt Fan and Papa. And it would be a deal less comfortable than Winchester, even Winchester in winter.

If we were still at Wellfield I should see Matt only during the holidays instead of every Saturday and Sunday, and I should have the burden of Amy's education, too. Her needles clicked with fierce energy. Richard has done very well by me. He was right to force the move. I'm ungrateful.

But I want to go home. In spite of herself, she sniffled. She let the mass of wool drop to her lap and fumbled in the sleeve of her gown for a handkerchief.

The clock struck the half hour. Startled out of her mood of self-pity, Emily jumped up. Her knitting fell to the floor, as she again went to the window. Where was Richard? He had walked with Matt the quarter mile to Winchester College, no great distance and on well-lit streets. Perhaps they had quarrelled again. Matt had been unnaturally civil all day.

Her breath fogged the window and she scrubbed at the pane with her wool sleeve. Richard cannot have gone for one of his walks in this weather. But if Matt cut up at him again . . . Her stomach knotted. Richard's usual response to Matt's resentments was a retreat to cool civility, but the boy tried his temper, and when Richard was in a temper he walked. Miles, sometimes. But not in the teeth of a winter gale, Emily's practical self advised her. Probably he has stopped by the Wilbrahams for a look at the major's maps.

This commonsense explanation soothed her, and she picked up her knitting and resumed her station by the fire. Scarcely had she completed the heel, however, when she heard a pounding at the front door. Forgot his key, she thought, relieved and tolerant. The pounding continued. After a frowning moment she set the stocking on the worktable and rose.

When she reached the first-floor hallway she heard McGrath grumbling his way up from the kitchen. Sometimes McGrath drank a little too much gin a little too early. He had been Richard's batman and was unsuited temperamentally to the role of butler. Emily leaned on the cherry wood bannister and peered down at the foyer. McGrath's balding head passed below her. He was shrugging into his frock coat. The pounding became a tattoo and she heard McGrath swear as he reached the door.

"Jaysus, hold yer horses . . . what is it, sor?" The truculence vanished in mid-sentence. He sounded alarmed.

Emily grasped her skirts with one hand and the railing with the other and began to descend the stairs rather more

27

rapidly than was wise. What in the world? McGrath had disappeared outside leaving the door ajar.

As Emily reached the landing halfway down Phillida erupted from the direction of the kitchen followed closely by Mrs. Harry with a saucepan and spoon in her hand. When Phillida saw her mistress she slid to a stop and Mrs. Harry bumped into her.

"Drat you, Phillida, if ever I saw such a clumsy wench. What is it, ma'am?"

"I've no idea . . ." Emily broke off, staring as the door shoved open and McGrath and her husband entered bearing the limp form of a man. Phillida shrieked.

"Be still," Emily commanded, darting down the last steps. "Good God, Richard, set him down. Your arm . . ."

Richard and McGrath laid the young man, he looked very young and very still, on the bare polished wood. "Careful of that leg," Richard muttered. "I think it's broken."

McGrath grunted and straightened the caped greatcoat, easing the boy's head down.

"Who is he?" Emily croaked.

Richard rose, grimacing. "I've no idea. He was lying on the pavement by the street lamp." He rubbed his right arm. He had been wounded in the shoulder at Waterloo and the joint had anchylosed. Though he could raise the forearm as far as his waist, he was not able to lift anything heavier than a pen without considerable pain. "Blankets, Phillida. At once." He jerked his head and the maid clattered off, still exclaiming.

"Brandy, sir?" Mrs. Harry gestured with the saucepan.

Richard frowned. "Spirits of ammonia, I think. He's unconscious and I've no idea how long he's been lying there. There's no one in the street."

"Then you'll need smelling salts *and* brandy, sir." Mrs. Harry stumped off toward the pantry.

"McGrath should go for the surgeon." Emily knelt and touched the still face. It was cold as marble. "Is he dead?"

She heard Richard draw a long breath. "I don't think so. He groaned when we lifted him. Oh, there you are, Jerry."

Emily turned. McGrath had evidently retrieved Richard's hat and stick from the street. Now he stood in the door, his eyes on Richard.

"Will you fetch the sawbones? Take my greatcoat. No time to go for yours." Richard was fumbling at the buttons. "It's damned cold out."

McGrath helped him out of the heavy garment and threw it over his own shoulders. "I'm off then."

Richard closed the door behind his servant and leaned against it.

"Are you all right?"

"Yes."

"Where were you?"

"Walking. Don't move that leg."

Emily nodded. She undid the large, brass buttons of the fashionable driving coat and loosened the neat cravat. The right glove came off easily. The other resisted her. When she removed it at last, she began chafing the boy's hands. "He's very cold. Do you think we ought to carry him to the parlour? We could build a fire . . ."

"Better not move him yet . . . ah, Phillida."

The maid dropped a mountain of pillows and blankets on the floor. "Oh, the poor gentleman, is he dead? Oh, dear . . ." She sounded as if she were working herself up to a fit of tears.

Emily said sharply, "He's merely unconscious. Help me slip that pillow beneath his head . . . yes, that one. Carefully, Phillida." She sat back on her heels. "The coat is wet, Richard. Phil and I can remove it."

"Very well, but be careful." He knelt, too. "I think he whacked his head on the cobbles."

By the time Mrs. Harry had returned with the vial of smelling salts they had contrived to remove the man's greatcoat without jarring him too much and had swathed him in the blankets. Emily felt his head and discovered in the crisp brown hair a bump the size of a plover's egg. There was no bleeding, however.

She held the spirits of ammonia under his nose. After a still moment he turned his head and groaned weakly.

"That's the dandy," Richard said, and, to Emily, "Try it again."

This time the man sneezed and blinked his eyes. He mumbled something.

"Brandy, sir." Mrs. Harry had poured a generous dollop in a wide glass. She handed it to Richard and bent, slipping a broad hand under the man's head.

"Careful of that goose egg." Hastily Emily placed another pillow beneath him.

He choked on the brandy, most of which spilled on his shirt. "Wha . . .?"

She made soothing noises. "A little sip more . . ."

This time he swallowed and his eyes blinked open.

"You've fallen and cracked your head," Richard said. He handed Emily the glass. "But you're quite safe and we've sent for a surgeon for your leg."

"Mmmn."

"Can you tell us your name, sir?"

"Mmmn . . . ah . . . Johnny."

"Johnny what?"

"Dy . . ."

"No," Richard said firmly, "you're not going to die."

"Not die," the man mumbled. He blinked, considering. "Dyott."

"Johnny Dyott . . ." Richard rocked back on his heels and looked at Emily. "I'm damned. Isn't that the name of Tom's secretary?"

Emily stared. "I think so . . . yes."

Richard snorted. "A great help *he's* going to be."

"Hush, Richard, he'll hear you."

Richard stood up and ran his hand through his hair which the wind had already thoroughly disordered. He was grinning. "Not a bit of it, my dear, he's out like a snuffed candle."

Emily swabbed the slopped brandy with a cloth Mrs. Harry had thoughtfully provided. Richard had not been best pleased when he heard she had writ Tom of his need for a copyist. She said crossly. "I don't think it's funny, precisely."

Richard gave her a hand up. "Funny as a crutch."

Living with a satirist had its drawbacks.

Johnny woke. Someone was watching him. Why?

He lay very still and brooded. Where was he? London? No. He had reached Winchester, walked to the quiet inn near the cathedral, inspected the room the landlord had readied against his coming. He had seen his gear disposed and bespoken dinner at seven. Then he had gone down to the ordinary and drunk a glass of hot punch to take the chill off.

The long coach ride had left him numb with cold, aching with it. He had drunk his punch by the fire. Then what?

He opened one eye cautiously, expecting to see the low, black-beamed ceiling of his room at the inn. Instead a clean expanse of white plaster stretched above him, and, at the edge of his vision, a plain moulding. Both eyes wide, he lowered his chin and gawked round him.

He had never seen the room before. It appeared to be a study. The walls were hung with a grey striped paper and the window to the right of his bed was covered with a heavy blue velvet curtain. It must be day—broad day—because even with the curtain closed he could see plainly enough. But that couldn't be right. Vaguely he recalled darkness and blown snow.

He stared, trying to make sense of his surroundings. There was a fire on the hearth. A modest writing desk, no doubt to make room for the bed he lay on, had been shoved back uncomfortably near a set of glass-fronted bookshelves. A stack of papers and a standish showed that the desk had been used recently, though the candle in its pewter holder was unlit. Johnny's head began to ache. Where in the world . . .

He caught a flicker of motion in the corner of his eye and turned his head on the pillows.

A small boy, perhaps six or seven years old, regarded him solemnly from the door. Johnny stared back, wondering if he had run mad. The child—he was thin with straight black hair and large, unwinking black eyes—looked like any one of hundreds of Spanish and Portuguese urchins he had seen in the line of march, and been haunted by since.

"Who are you?"

The child continued to watch him silently.

Johnny fought back panic, forcing his mind to take in the fact that the boy was not ragged, dirty, or shoeless. In fact, he was dressed unexceptionably in nankeens, a white ruffled shirt, and a neat blue coat with brass buttons. He wore white stockings and black kid slippers, and someone skilled had trimmed his straight, blue-black hair. The child was not a refugee from Johnny's nightmares.

Johnny took a breath. "What's your name?"

Again the boy did not answer. After a moment, he turned and scampered off in a decidedly un-ghostlike fashion.

Johnny found he had been holding his breath. He exhaled and, thinking to sit up, twisted to the left. A shaft of pain shot up his right leg. He gasped aloud and sank back against the pillows. His head whirled as much from bewilderment as from the ache in his leg. What had happened to him?

"Awake, I see, and feeling the pangs."

Johnny turned his head. "Where am I?"

The man in the doorway was in shirtsleeves but his dress otherwise indicated that he was an ordinary English gentleman. Not a Portuguese muleteer or a Spanish priest.

"I'm Richard Falk." The stranger surveyed Johnny with quizzical hazel eyes. "You fell in front of the right house."

"But . . . oh." Memory flooded back. "I set out to find your house. I meant to call if you were at home, leave my card. I must have slipped on the cobbles."

"So we deduced. When we discovered you in possession of your purse and watchfob we concluded you weren't the victim of footpads."

"I wonder how I came to be so clumsy . . ." Johnny's voice trailed. "I only drank one glass."

Falk's smile was wry but not unkind. "I daresay you hit a patch of ice. You've broken your leg."

"Oh, no!"

"Yes. The shinbone. Neatish break, nothing fancy. But you had a bad bout of fever from lying out in the cold. The surgeon thinks you'll be up in a month."

"A month!" Johnny groaned.

The election. All the preliminaries would have been set in train within the month. He had meant to be at Clanross's side well before March. What curst luck. He reopened his eyes to find Colonel Falk watching him with a slight frown.

"Kicking against the prods? I fancy you're hungry, but let's make you comfortable first."

Johnny was surprised to find that he was hungry. Other even more urgent needs were also beginning to press. To his embarrassment Falk attended to them with despatch and no comment.

Presently, when Johnny was feeling more the thing and had been propped in a half-upright position, he said haltingly, "I'm grateful to you, sir, but oughtn't you to leave sickroom chores to your servants . . ."

Falk handed him a facecloth. "I thought I was uncommon deft for a one-handed paperhanger."

"I didn't mean . . ."

"Scrub."

Johnny scrubbed, hoping his face did not betray the extent of his humiliation. His beard prickled.

"My man, McGrath," Falk mused, "is just now escorting my daughter to her school and the housekeeper to the fishmonger's. His wife, who is the children's nurse, is upstairs with the baby and Harry. The baby is colicky and Harry has a cold. Phillida—that's the housemaid—is paring something, and, in any case, she would drop a basin on you or fall across your leg. Phillida is a trifle awkward. We do not permit her to enter sickrooms. So I rather think you're stuck with me. Unless you'd like me to summon Emily? My wife," he added, removing the cloth and handing Johnny a comb. "She's fixing your tray."

"I beg your pardon, sir. I've been a great deal of trouble to you."

"You've caused us some anxiety, I'll allow. And I'm glad you've come out of the fever. Even with the splint in place, we had the devil of a time keeping your leg still. Especially, for some reason, at four in the morning."

"Good God, how long was I out?"

"Three days. And nights."

Johnny shut his eyes, mortified. "You'll be wishing me in Jericho."

"Not at all. I wish you right where you are. When you're feeling more the thing, I mean to put you to work."

"Even so . . ."

"Come, Dyott, it was an accident."

Johnny bit his lip. "I know, but . . ."

Falk smiled at him. "Only fancy what I'd be thinking if you'd taken a notion to break your right *arm*."

In spite of his embarrassment, Johnny had to return the smile.

Falk tidied the cloth away. A china pitcher and basin sat on the low chest of drawers by the head of the bed. "We'll rig a lap desk for you . . ."

"Clanross!" Johnny interrupted, appalled.

"I've writ Tom. And we found your traps at the Pelican."

"How?"

Falk had finished tidying the basin. He sat on a straight-back chair near the door. "I sent McGrath round to all the likely inns. And then to the unlikely ones. Did you know that the Pelican is a den of piety? Country curates and rural deans. No one else uses it."

Johnny felt his cheeks flame. He was blushing like a maiden, and why not? The whole situation was damnably embarrassing. "My father is dean of Lincoln cathedral . . ."

"And he recommended the Pelican. I see. All our mysteries cleared up." Falk looked mildly disappointed.

Not quite. "There was a boy."

Falk's eyebrows rose.

"When I woke. A little boy. He looked Spanish."

"My son Tommy. His mother was Spanish." He rose and went to the desk.

Johnny digested that. "I spoke to him but he didn't answer. I thought I was dreaming. When he vanished . . ."

"Tommy does not hear."

"He's deaf? Good God, I heard he'd been ill. He is Lord Clanross's godson, is he not? I am sorry."

Falk was fiddling with the standish. "I posted him to warn me when you woke."

"Does he not speak?"

Falk straightened the pile of papers on the desk. "He does, but not often. I think being unable to hear his own voice confuses him."

Johnny turned that over in his mind. "I daresay it must be frightening for him."

"Yes."

"How long . . ."

Falk looked up. He was frowning painfully. "The children—all of them but the baby who was newborn—fell ill in July. It was just measles. My wife was still rather weak and I didn't like to expose her or the infant, so I kept Emily from the sickroom. The McGraths and I nursed them. We were more anxious for Matt than for Tommy at first. Matt ran a high fever." He straightened and went to the bookcase, opening the glass front. After a moment he closed it again without removing a book. When they recovered we found that Tommy had lost his hearing."

"I'm sorry," Johnny repeated, troubled by the older man's contained distress. "Measles!"

Falk gave a short, unmirthful laugh. "That's what's so stupid. If it had been smallpox or scarlet fever or something more threatening . . ."

He was afraid he might have done something to prevent his son's deafness, Johnny thought. What an appalling burden. He groped for something to say. Phrases about God's will his father surely would have found efficacious entered his mind—and stuck in his throat. Nothing, he thought grimly, will induce me to become a clergyman.

After a moment Falk left off his restless pacing and resumed his seat by the door. "I have been teaching Tommy his letters. He could read a little and write his name before he fell ill. I thought if he could read and write with ease . . ."

"That he might not lose his grasp of language? I see."

Falk took a deep breath. "He does very well, and he's beginning to understand what is said by watching the speaker's mouth. That is very encouraging, but I wish he would speak more often. His speech has lost something of clarity."

"Still, if he understands . . ." Johnny's voice trailed. "I see why you need help with your correspondence," he burst out. "Your work must have been seriously interrupted."

Falk smiled a little. "That is one way of putting it. I've kept up with the correspondence relating to Tom's charity, but I'm behindhand with my blasted history. My publisher is squawking."

"History? I thought you were a novelist, sir."

"I am, by preference. Murray asked me to write a three-volume history of Marlborough's campaigns. In a moment of mental aberration, I agreed."

Johnny felt his spirits rise. He had balked at wasting his

time over a mere novel, but a history was a more respectable undertaking. "Surely you must find such work more gratifying . . ."

"Must I?" Falk rubbed his forehead.

"To be dealing with so important an event as the War of the Spanish Succession! Marlborough! Blenheim!"

"Malplaquet! Close order drill! Lady Marlborough!" Falk was mocking him. "Frankly, I find it all exceedingly dull."

Johnny stared.

"I am a satirist, not an historian, but the climate for satire is not healthy these days. The thought of spending months in durance vile for taking the odd jab at Lord Liverpool gives one pause." Falk's mouth twisted in a wry grimace. "My publisher fancied he—and I—would be safer rehearsing pointless marches and countermarches where the outcome was known and the politicians safely dead. It appears that the publick have a boundless thirst for dead campaigns. I cannot imagine why."

"I see," said Johnny, though he didn't, precisely. "But a history . . ."

"I daresay mine will be the two hundredth recapitulation of the battle of Blenheim," Falk said flatly. "The only positive consequence of publishing three fusty volumes of the stuff will be their effect on my overdraught."

"I cannot believe that, sir."

Falk's mouth relaxed in a grin. "You will when you've copied a few chapters."

"My word, it's early days to be speaking of copying, Richard." A lady in a lace cap and striped spencer appeared in the doorway. She carried a tray, and she had brown curls and merry blue eyes.

Falk had risen. He said dryly, "Mrs. Falk. Dyott. If you were in any doubt."

She advanced with the tray held before her like a guerdon. "Do help the boy up, Richard. Two more pillows, I think. How do you do, Mr. Dyott? You must call me Emily because I fully intend to call you Johnny . . ."

Her gentle chatter washed over Johnny, very soothing. Falk's ministrations were less soothing—the leg ached abominably—but in the end Johnny squirmed to a position that would make feeding himself possible. The effort left him limp. Colonel Falk took his leave. Johnny ate. Emily Falk watched him critically.

When he had finished she removed the tray, set it on the chair, and swept up a few errant crumbs of toast. The beef broth had been excellent.

"Better?"

"Much. Thank you . . ."

She smiled. "But your leg is hurting again and you have a strong desire for solitude. I shall leave you in peace, but first you must take a glass of the apothecary's vile potion. It is mostly laudanum, I fancy, and should ease the pain."

Johnny considered protesting. Laudanum would also put him to sleep. He did not like to be quacked, but he felt quite exhausted, suddenly, and the leg did hurt. "Very well, ma'am."

"Emily," she corrected gently. She measured a spoonful of medicine from a small brown bottle into a glass of water. The water turned milky. "I am glad to see you awake at last." Johnny drank the potion.

She beamed at him. "There. That should make you more comfortable in a trice."

Johnny blinked. "Thank you . . ." But she had disappeared as suddenly as she had come. The Falk family did a good line in vanishing acts, he thought rather crossly. Prestidigitous. Presently he drowsed off with visions of Blenheim and Peninsular urchins floating in his fuddled head. Clanross was saying something earnest about Reform. Johnny strained to understand his point but couldn't help thinking how odd his employer looked in a long curled wig.

=4=

Jean stared at the young man and her heart thumped in her throat. For a shaming moment she thought she might faint.

Owen Davies was beautiful. Why had no one said how beautiful he was? Not above the middle height, he was proportioned like a marble Mercury, but he moved with the grace of some sleek cat of the mountains. He wore Hessians, and his primrose inexpressibles clung to his thighs, moulding the long muscles. The conventional bottle green coat and grey waistcoat did little to tame the wild abandon of the carelessly knotted kerchief he wore in place of a cravat. His fair hair hung long and tousled, with just enough curl to tip under where it met his collar, and his mouth was exquisitely carved, mobile and sensitive. Though he affected no jewellery, his agate green eyes glowed with a light of their own.

". . . Lady Jean Conway," Elizabeth was saying. "My sister."

Jean's hand floated up of its own accord. When Mr. Davies touched her fingertips her arm tingled to the shoulder with electrical warmth.

He bent over her hand, brushing her knuckles with his lips. As he straightened, he met her eyes. A wordless message passed between them. Then he was making his bow to Maggie and the sensation passed. But Jean knew her life had been transformed.

Owen Davies. A librarian? Nonsense. He was a poet,

with the soul of a poet in his speaking eyes and all the wild music of Wales in his light tenor voice. He was murmuring civil phrases to the others—Maggie, Miss Bluestone, Cecy Wharton who had come from Hazeldell to take tea—but Jean heard only the music of his voice, not the sense.

Stiffly she reseated herself on the sofa and watched as the party reassembled with Mr. Davies on Elizabeth's right, a place of honour he assumed with no unbecoming hesitation. He accepted a glass of sherry from the tray Fisher offered, and sat sipping and listening, with a faint curl of his sculpted mouth, a faint droop of his eyelids, as Elizabeth spoke of his parents.

The Davieses of Earl's Brecon could not be his parents, not the catarrhal rector and his prim wife. So splendid a creature must have sprung from another race entirely. Jean had been rereading McPherson's *Oisin*. Vague images of the riders of the wind, the pale, unearthly Sidhe, flickered in her mind's eye. A changeling? Perhaps that was not the right term. A figure certainly from another time, his alabaster skin still tinged from exposure to the chill air outside and his hair touched by the snow-laden wind.

Jean shivered deliciously.

". . . and you must take your mama a packet of my tisane of birch leaves. She asked for it when I last saw her," Miss Bluestone was saying with dreadful, prosy cheer. "I meant to send it by Jem any time this sennight but I kept forgetting. I daresay your father is feeling more the thing by now, however."

"Yes," Mr. Davies said, eyes half-lidded. "I believe Papa goes on very well, ma'am, but you must pardon me. I've told my parents I must be about my work. They cannot expect me to call on them often."

Jean sat straighter, listening now to meaning as well as sound. So he would stay at Brecon. Elizabeth had not been sure.

Elizabeth smiled. "Clanross won't expect you to keep your nose to the grindstone day and night, Mr. Davies."

"You misunderstand me. I mean my *work*. My poetry," he added when Elizabeth cocked her head quizzically.

"Do you write sonnets?" Maggie interposed.

Oh, Maggie. Jean quivered.

He looked at her twin. "Rarely, Lady Margaret. My métier is the ode. And the satirical ballad, though that, I fear, I pen merely for my own amusement these days."

"Why? Won't anyone buy your ballads?"

Jean went hot, then cold. Maggie had a prosaic soul, Miss Bluestone had been forced to concede that when the twins were still in her schoolroom, but even Maggie ought to know better than to speak of buying and selling to a poet.

Davies favoured Jean's twin with a slight, sad smile. "A bookseller, do you mean? They tell me my poetry is caviar to the general." The sculpted lips took a wry twist. "I don't even think of a commercial publisher, Lady Margaret. My odes circulate in manuscript. Some friends were kind enough to have a volume of my political verses published privately, however. That is the safe course these days." His lip curled again at the word "safe" and he took a sip of sherry as if to counter a bad taste.

Elizabeth raised an eyebrow. "I take it your sentiments are, er, radical."

"I am a neo-Pantisocrat," he said simply. "Anathema to Liverpool and that lot."

Miss Bluestone leaned forward, her fichu bobbing. "Do you mean, sir, that your work is seditious?"

The brilliant eyes blazed. "I recognise no nation but humanity, ma'am, and there my loyalties lie. If that be sedition, well, I am ready to suffer the penalty."

Jean thought he looked magnificent. She let her breath out in a long trembling sigh. Miss Bluestone blinked.

Cecilia Wharton, who had been nibbling obliviously at a slice of currant cake, broke the silence. "I like this very well, Elizabeth, upon my word. There is so little I can eat these days without discomfort. Pray tell Mrs. Smollet I must have the receipt." Mrs. Wharton was in an interesting condition for the third time and large as a house.

Elizabeth smiled at her. "You shall have it if it's not one of her mother's. *Those* receipts she refuses to part with. Mr. Davies, I can see that your presence will enliven our company. Perhaps you'll be kind enough to read us your work one of these evenings. We're all fond of poetry, especially Jean."

Oh, Elizabeth. Jean shrank into her bones, but Davies cast her a look so eloquent of hope and uncertainty that she contrived a smile for him. "I love poetry of all things."

"Wordsworth, I daresay."

What was the right reply? Hang Wordsworth. Jean cleared her throat. "I . . . often . . . prefer the older poets."

He frowned. "Carewe?"

"Herrick, sometimes, and Campion."

His eyes lit. " 'Follow your saint, follow with accents sweet. Haste thee, sad notes, fall at her flying feet . . .' "

Jean gulped. "Yes, indeed. And Spenser."

He set his sherry glass on the tray and leaned toward her. "*The Amoretti?*"

"And *The Faerie Queen.*" She groped in her memory. "*The Shepherd's Calendar.*"

"Certainly I'll read for you. It will be a great pleasure," he murmured, and she was sure he spoke to her alone.

Elizabeth placed her teacup on the tray with a rattle. "Splendid. Jean and Maggie, if you will show Mr. Davies the library I'll see to his room. Cecy, Miss Bluestone, I know you too well to stand on ceremony. Pray make yourselves cozy by the fire. I must just have a word with my housekeeper."

"Don't forget the receipt." Cecilia was cutting herself another slice of the cake.

"To be sure. I'll be with you again in a trice." Elizabeth sounded crisp, almost angry, but in what cause Jean knew not.

Jean stared and Elizabeth stared back, unsmiling.

42

Maggie jumped up. "The book room is gothick, Mr. Davies. You'll love it. Come on, Jean."

Jean rose and so perforce did Mr. Davies. He took a polite farewell of Miss Bluestone and Mrs. Wharton, and then they were free of tisanes and currant cake. And of Elizabeth's mood, whatever it might signify.

Maggie seemed wholly unconscious of Jean's heightened sensibility as the three young people traversed the long gallery to the library. She was giving Mr. Davies a house-keeper's tour, pointing out ancestral portraits and bits of classical marble as they went, and her cheerful chatter sounded like the tweedling of a bagpipe to Jean's sensitive ears.

Jean hoped Mr. Davies would not despise her twin. He was being polite but so attuned was Jean to his mood she could sense his impatience. For the first time in her life she wished her sister elsewhere. Her disloyalty clogged her throat so that she could not have spoken to save her life.

When they finally entered the vast gloomy book room even Maggie fell silent.

The architecture of Brecon was Palladian. To seventeenth-century taste had been added eighteenth-century wealth, and the effects were grand—or grandiose. Marble doorways and vast, richly ornamented plasterwork ceilings, a recent one by Angelica Kauffman, showed in brilliant contrast to walls hung in intense silks, green and watered blue and rose. Miles of parquet shone beneath narrow, Wilton carpets. But the library, panelled in dark wood and crammed with bookcases and tables heavy enough to sink a poet's heart, was a Jacobean throwback.

Though the huge room was skylit and further illumined by tall sash windows, the light came from the north. The library always seemed dark to Jean and rather menacing. It smelt of leather and ancient snuff and decaying book glue. The faint scent of decay tickled Jean's nose and made her eyes heavy. Books jammed the tall shelves and the glass-fronted cases, overflowing onto tables and, indeed, every flat surface. Thanks to Miss Bluestone Jean was well read, but it seemed to her that the weight of words in the Brecon library dragged at one's soul.

Davies strode to the refectory table that stood before the hearth and touched the huge globe of the world that reposed there in its mahogany stand. "A magnificent room."

Jean's apprehension lightened. She felt almost giddy. "It's a large collection. My grandfather added to it."

"He was a famous collector. Is that Hakluyt?" He moved to the unlit hearth and ran a hand along the open shelf beside it.

"In the original edition." Jean fished in her reticule for a handkerchief. "Here. You've smudged your cuff."

He took the square of lawn as if it were the favour of some medieval princess. "Thank you, my lady. Shall you help me with my book list? I'm a hopelessly impractical fellow in dire need of rescue. Yes, I think you are going to take pity on me."

"I'd like to be useful." Jean winced at the stiff propriety of her own words but he held her eyes, returning the crumpled handkerchief. His smile faded to something more intense as, greatly daring, she tucked it in her bosom.

"I should like it of all things," Jean half whispered.

"Only fancy, Jean, I've found *The Monk*!" Maggie was still near the doorway. "It was here all the time. What a hum. We needn't have sent to Lincoln after all."

Miss Bluestone had interdicted Mr. Lewis's gothick tale, so Jean and Maggie obtained it from Piersall's Circulating Library by stealth and took turns reading it to each other. Reading *The Monk* in a whisper late at night by the light of flickering candles had added to their delicious terror. Now Maggie flipped the pages, announcing the edition was inscribed to their mother by the author. Her voice squeaked.

"We enjoyed the book when we were younger," Jean

heard herself say. They had first read *The Monk* in November. "Do you have a scheme for the library, sir?"

"I'll use the system my tutor worked out for the collection Lord Edgware donated to the Bodley. Lord Clanross approves."

Jean had no idea what system he was referring to, but it seemed unlikely to include gothick novels. "Clanross and my sister Elizabeth receive a great many scientific journals."

His nose wrinkled. "I daresay. I shall have them bound."

"You'd best ask Lizzie first."

Jean jumped.

Maggie had materialised at the poet's elbow. "She likes to have the journals to hand. For her correspondence, you know."

"I believe Lady Clanross uses a telescope."

"Lizzie," said Maggie, rather pink in the face, "is an astronomer. Her instrument is one of the finest in the nation."

"Indeed," Davies murmured, his eyes heavy-lidded. "I'd like to see it."

"I daresay she'll show it you if you ask her nicely." Maggie's chin went up.

Jean wanted to sink into the carpet. Everyone in the neighbourhood knew of Lizzie's spy glass. Why was Maggie so fierce about it? Mr. Davies had said nothing disparaging.

Jean shifted from one slipper-clad foot to the other. "Clanross says my grandfather had a catalogue made."

"His lordship gave me a copy, but it was never completed. The collection has doubled since your grandfather's death." Davies ran his hand through his hair so that it stood up in gold tufts. He smiled charmingly at Maggie. "It seems I have a heavy task ahead of me. Shall you help, too, Lady Margaret?"

Jean felt a stab of jealousy.

He turned his gaze back to her and again the smile faded.

His eyes bespoke her. "Lady Jean has already been kind enough to offer her assistance."

Jean trembled.

Maggie said baldly, "To be sure. We've nothing to do until we go to London in April. Cause one of the footmen to go over the books with an oiled cloth first, however, or we'll all be covered in dust."

"Yes," said the poet absently.

He held Jean's gaze, and they spoke volumes together without saying a word.

"What think you of the poet?" Elizabeth asked.

Miss Bluestone smoothed the cuffs of her sober grey gown. "Mrs. Davies says he is greatly improved. His father has high hopes of him."

Cecilia Wharton had gone off in her husband's carriage, and the two ladies sat alone in the withdrawing room over the remains of the interrupted tea. The fire crackled as a gust of wind shook the windowpanes.

"I can't approve his manners," Elizabeth said bluntly. "He's full of himself."

Miss Bluestone's eyes twinkled. "All young gentlemen of three and twenty are full of themselves."

Elizabeth's tension eased. "True. At least Johnny Dyott contrives to conceal his self-absorption."

"But Mr. Dyott is unusual, and several years older than this sprig."

"Johnny unusual?" Elizabeth smiled. "You must find our captive poet commonplace indeed."

"It's certainly the fashion to play at being a poet these days. He may have a genuine gift, but I cannot like his neckcloth."

"Byron has a great deal to answer for." Elizabeth hesitated. "I think Jean is taken with young Davies."

Miss Bluestone's eyebrows rose. "Indeed? That would not be at all suitable."

Elizabeth shrugged. "Oh, the connexion is respectable

enough. And though Jean has her share of step-mama's fortune, the boy doesn't strike me as mercenary. I don't fear for Jean's establishment, merely for her heart."

"She has been losing it regularly these past three years."

"True." Elizabeth spread her hands. "But she was not then of an age to act on her impulses. Now she fancies herself grown up. She's not up to snuff, Miss Bluestone. I've been remiss. I meant to prepare the girls, but the past year . . ." She rose and began to pace before the fire. She had spent the past year recovering from childbirth. It had not been in her power to give children's balls and breakfasts and musicales suitable to the entertainment of very young ladies, and for a sixmonth before the boys' birth she and Tom had been in Italy. At least the Christmas season had provided Jean and Maggie with a few social encounters.

Miss Bluestone had taken out her workbasket and was mending a lace scarf. "Jean and Margaret will do very well. Do not alarm yourself needlessly, Lady Clanross."

Elizabeth flung herself onto the sofa. "Very well, ma'am. I shan't start at shadows, but I wish Tom's librarian were a trifle less intense." She looked at Miss Bluestone. "And a trifle less like the statue of a Greek god."

"You could remove the girls to the Dower House again."

For three years Jean and Margaret had lived under Miss Bluestone's care in the Brecon Dower House. They had been invited to move to Brecon itself as a token of their new maturity—and to relieve that modest household of overcrowding. Three other schoolroom misses, Miss Bluestone, and four servants inhabited Elizabeth's old home; and it was not a large house.

"It's kind of you to offer," Elizabeth said with a sigh, "but they would be deeply offended. And Jean, at least, would perceive my motives. I'll simply have to keep a close eye on them—and the poet. Thank God for Maggie's common sense."

"You mustn't neglect your telescope, my lady." Miss

Bluestone folded the scarf and bestowed it in the small basket.

Elizabeth smiled at her. "I shan't. The weather is far too cold to permit me to work at it now, but I do wish Johnny Dyott had not broken his leg. *He* would keep Master Davies in line. Johnny has a *tendre* for Jean."

"And Margaret has a *tendre* for *him*."

Elizabeth stared.

Miss Bluestone inspected the torn flounce of a petticoat.

"Does she indeed?" Elizabeth began to laugh. "Perhaps it's as well Johnny is stuck in Hampshire. I've no desire to enact *A Midsummer Night's Dream* in my drawing room—Maggie pursuing Johnny, Johnny pursuing Jean, Jean in love with the poet, and Mr. Davies in love with himself."

Miss Bluestone set a deft stitch. "Perhaps you have noticed, my lady, that these small affairs of the heart are comic to observers but the stuff of tragedy to the participants."

Though there was no censure in the governess's mild voice, Elizabeth flushed. She had spent a miserable summer in the not-distant past mooning over Tom, and Miss Bluestone had comforted her.

Elizabeth bit her lip. "I shan't laugh at them. At least not in their presence."

Miss Bluestone smiled. "I place too much reliance on your good sense to apprehend any such blunder on your part, my lady."

Nevertheless, Elizabeth was troubled. She had found Owen Davies ill mannered, conceited, and thoroughly charming. He was a double for the statue of Apollo Belvedere she had seen in the papal collection—clothed, of course. She wished Davies were still a callow undergraduate afflicted with spots.

For Jean the first days of Owen Davies's residence at Brecon spellt pure enchantment, though she hugged her feelings to herself. The only flaw in the reverberating crystal of her delight was her failure to confide in Maggie. Always before, she had poured out her sentiments to her sympathetic twin and Maggie had always entered into her feelings exactly. There was no reason for Jean to keep her passion from Maggie, but such was the intensity of her emotion she *could* not speak of it.

Every morning after breakfast the two girls met with the poet in the newly dusted bookroom. He was an exacting taskmaster, keeping them to their chores until midday.

Because Jean wrote a clearer hand—so he said but she thought he meant to keep her near him—she made a list of the books Maggie fetched to the larger of the two refectory tables. The poet examined each tome, taking note of its author and contents, the probable date of its publication, though a surprising number of works contained no date, and the condition of its binding. Sometimes he would lose himself in the work as a stack of calf-bound volumes mounted on the green baize.

He read snatches of poetry aloud. Some of the works were in Latin, which the twins had studied briefly, or in Greek. They knew no Greek but Jean thought his voice conveyed all the music of the Aegean and she could have listened forever as he recited the long mellifluous lines of Homer's *Odyssey*. He read from Chapman's English translation of Homer, too, but when he read in Greek Jean could concentrate on the beauty of his voice and dream unhindered.

When he forgot to replace the books in the order Maggie had brought them from the shelf, they would have a game of hunt-the-fox, chasing after the elusive volumes amid much laughter. He teased Maggie, who had warmed to him, but it seemed to Jean that when he read, he read for her alone.

They took their nuncheons with Elizabeth, of course, and made up the numbers of Elizabeth's quiet dinner parties in the evening. A few months before that would have seemed an enormous treat, but Jean was growing rather blasé about small social privileges. The February weather was foul—snowing and blustery. Often enough Elizabeth seated only Mr. Davies, Jean, Maggie, and herself at dinner. Miss Bluestone rarely ventured from the Dower House in the icy wind and no one came to visit from farther away than Earl's Brecon.

Once Elizabeth sent her carriage for Mr. Davies's parents, but the evening went slowly, all parties stiff with constraint. It was clear that the Davieses regarded their son with baffled admiration. His feelings were less clear.

The Sunday after he arrived, a snow-laden gale blew in off the North Sea. No one went to church, and they were quite without guests at dinner so Elizabeth persuaded the poet to read from his works.

Jean knew she was incapable of judging the quality of his poetry. His voice rang so sweet in her ears that he might have read a list of dirty linen and still transported her. She knew that and it didn't trouble her. He read from his odes, and he touched on all the proper subjects—mutability, nature, the sublime. She thought his tropes particularly elegant, but she might have said the same had he recited Crabbe or Thompson. He seemed to prefer the Spenserian stanzo.

It was after this session, when their abigail had gone and they had scrambled into their nightclothes in the chill of their room, that Maggie finally forced her twin's confidence.

Jean tucked her red curls into her nightcap and leapt into the warmed sheets.

Maggie stood on one bare foot before the sea-coal fire. "You're mad for Owen Davies, aren't you?"

"What?"

Maggie cat-footed across the polished boards and jumped into her side of the four-poster. "You're in love with Owen Davies." She snuffed the candle and the room darkened, the only light a dancing red glow cast by the fire on the hearth.

"What if I am?"

"I don't know." Maggie's voice was muffled. She had yanked the eiderdown up to her chin. "I just wondered."

"He has a beautiful voice."

Maggie said nothing.

"He does, Mag. And he's so . . . so beautiful." Jean felt her cheeks go hot and was glad of the darkness.

"D'you think so?"

Jean sat up. "Do not you?" She squinted down at her twin.

"He's good-looking, and I like working with him in the bookroom, but he's not very organised."

Jean groaned and flopped back against the pillows. "What does that signify?"

"Nothing. *Are* you in love?"

"Yes . . . oh, yes, Maggie—fathoms deep."

"*As You Like It*," Maggie said drowsily. "That's all right, then. I thought you were but you didn't *say*."

"Oh, Maggie, I'm sorry. It was so strange, as if something constrained me to keep my sentiments to myself. But I do love him. His voice is like . . . like an aeolian harp." Jean had never heard an aeolian harp, but she wanted to. "And his eyes!"

Relieved to have the ear of her lifelong confidante once more, Jean spoke at length of the poet's brilliance, beauty, and charm. It was only as she began to evaluate the quality of his verse that she realised her sister had fallen asleep.

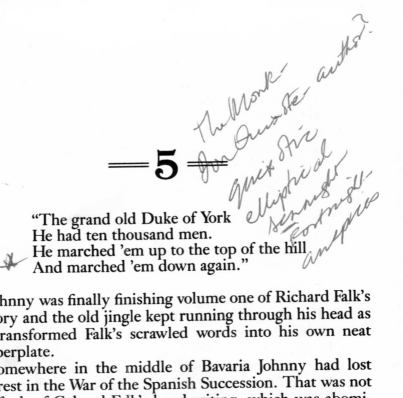

"The grand old Duke of York
He had ten thousand men.
He marched 'em up to the top of the hill
And marched 'em down again."

Johnny was finally finishing volume one of Richard Falk's history and the old jingle kept running through his head as he transformed Falk's scrawled words into his own neat copperplate.

Somewhere in the middle of Bavaria Johnny had lost interest in the War of the Spanish Succession. That was not the fault of Colonel Falk's handwriting, which was abominable, nor yet of his prose, which was lucid. Perhaps if Johnny had been reading neatly printed folio pages at his usual breakneck pace, his enthusiasm would not have flagged, but there was something about syllable by syllable transcription of dead bivouacks, dead skirmishes, dead battles, that rendered them very dead indeed.

"Oh, when you're up you're up,
And when you're down you're down,
And when you're only halfway up
You're neither up nor down," he sang mournfully.

"It can't be that bad."
Johnny finished the last scrolled letter, sanded the sheet, and regarded his hostess solemnly.

Emily Falk set a nuncheon tray on a chair by his daybed. "What a beautiful hand you write. Richard's publisher will have palpitations." She peered over his shoulder. "You're finished!"

Johnny flexed his fingers and grinned. "Absolutely. Except for Volumes Two and Three."

"Murray will have to be satisfied with Volume One for the time being. You need a holiday." She flitted to the foot of the daybed and twitched the eiderdown over his legs. "Richard will be delighted."

"*Aux anges,*" he said dryly. "In transports."

She looked at him, blue eyes serious. "He will be enormously relieved, Johnny, and grateful to you."

Johnny sighed. "And he'll say, 'Handsome work, Dyott. Pity it's such tripe.' "

"Is it?"

"Of course not. It's clear and accurate and gracefully expressed."

Her face fell. "Oh, dear."

"It will probably run through two printings in a quarter." He wasn't sure what he'd said wrong. He hadn't meant to intimate he found the history dull. Its dullness was probably an illusion. "Really, ma'am, it's a solid piece of historical writing."

She looked as if she might burst into tears.

Alarmed, he struggled to a more upright posture. "I *like* it," he lied, gasping because he had jarred his splinted leg.

Emily Falk sniffed and gave him a watery smile. "It's kind of you to say so, Johnny. Now, let's move the manuscript out of the way so you can eat in peace." She squared the sheets of foolscap and carried the neat stack to Falk's desk. Falk had gone off for the day to see his sister.

"I wish you'd tell me what I said wrong." Johnny handed Mrs. Falk standish and pen and watched as she tidied the lap desk that also served him as a table.

"It wasn't what you said." She handed him a warm,

damp cloth from her tray and he swabbed the inkstains from his hands. "I was just remembering Don Alfonso."

"Is that Colonel Falk's novel?"

She gave an exasperated cluck. "You're an ignorant jack-anapes and don't deserve Mrs. Harry's burnt sugar custard. Richard has writ five novels dealing with the adventures of Don Alfonso." She arranged his cutlery and served him boiled chicken, fresh sliced bread, and preserved cherries, placing the custard and a glass of white wine whey—the last a medicinal draught—artistically on the tray. She was neat-fingered and her place settings always looked good enough to eat.

"I ought to read them one of these days." He spread the heavy linen napkin over his chest.

"Not until you've finished copying the history."

"Why not?" He cut a bite of savoury chicken.

"Because the contrast would throw you into the glooms. It's bad enough having Richard in a green-and-yellow melancholy. *Two* gloomy men I refuse to abide."

Johnny chewed. "I know Colonel Falk prefers the novels . . ."

"Anyone with a sense of humour and a modicum of intelligence prefers the novels. I do wish he hadn't agreed to write this dreary history . . ." She broke off, biting her lip. "It can't be helped. Richard will return around four in a foul mood. We might as well prepare the manuscript. If he doesn't want to send Volume One off today he can always undo the parcel."

She whisked out the door, and Johnny fell upon the chicken. It was excellent, as usual.

Richard did indeed return at four and, while his mood was not precisely foul, he did look gloomy. His mother was ill.

"How is she?" Emily had spent an hour in the nursery and had just retired to the withdrawing room to collect her wits.

"Sarah says failing."

"Oh, my dear, I'm so sorry."

He shrugged. "*Anno domini.*"

"For the love of God, Richard."

"Do you want me to mouth conventional phrases? I do not know my mother, Emily, by her choice, and I have no intention of pretending to sentiments I don't feel. I'm sorry she's ill. Robert has the gout. I'm sorry for that, too, but there's nothing I can do to amend either condition."

Emily blew her nose. "Allow me a conventional sniffle. I liked her grace on the one occasion I met her, and I am *very* sorry for Sarah's distress."

"There is that," he agreed wearily. "Sarah sends you her best. She'll call on you when the roads are passable. Has the post come?"

"Yes. Three for Johnny, one perfumed, another from Tom. Go find out the latest Town gossip."

"Gossip! Lord Clanross is a leader of the opposition, ma'am, not a mere gabblemonger. Show a little respect."

"He hates it, doesn't he?"

Richard considered. "Tom regards politicks with the same enthusiasm I feel for three-volume histories. Hatred is too passionate a word."

Emily said seriously, "Why don't you give it up, my dear? You should be writing what you wish to write."

Reserve closed Richard's face like a shutter. "Perhaps I'll take up sonnets. 'Fair matron,' " he declaimed, hand on his breast, " 'when I gaze upon thy face

" 'Adust with flour like a bannock bun . . .' "

"Do I have flour on my nose again?" Distracted Emily made for the kitchen where Mrs. Harry assured her she was neat as wax and did the colonel fancy a bit of cod with the roast veal?

"Drat the colonel," Emily said crossly. She was worried. Sooner or later Richard would have to sort out his feelings toward his mother. He might pretend indifference but the anger beneath the mask had been smouldering for twenty-five years. It prevented him meeting her grace halfway. Though Emily understood his reasons, she thought he would find pride a sorry comfort when his mother had gone beyond earthly reconciliation. Richard was on good terms with his half-sister, Sarah, but that was more Sarah's doing than his. Sarah's and Emily's. Emily wished God had given men common sense.

After dinner, when the children were abed and Richard writing, Emily kept Johnny company for a while.

"Lady Clanross writ me a long letter," he confided.

A pity. Emily had rather hoped the perfumed letter was from an amour. "Are her ladyship and her sisters well?"

Johnny's brow clouded. "Very well, I believe."

"But . . .?"

"Clanross has sent Owen Davies to Brecon," he blurted. "To catalogue the library. You've probably not heard of Davies, sir."

Richard looked up from his letter. "Can't say I have."

Johnny drew a breath. "I was at university with him. He's a poet."

Mercy, thought Emily. How improvident of Tom. "A good poet?"

"Clever enough," Johnny said glumly. "A mad Radical and full of nonsensical quirks. He was rusticated once for writing a parody of the chancellor's peroration, and he despises what he calls the medieval trappings of rank."

"Heavens, then what is he doing in the employ of an earl?"

Richard gave a muffled snort of laughter. "*Tom* despises the medieval trappings of rank." He bent back to his work.

"I daresay it suits Tom's sense of humour to keep a Leveller at Brecon," Emily said severely, "but how uncomfortable for Lady Clanross."

"Her ladyship don't mind that." Johnny wriggled. His leg hurt worse at night for some reason. "Davies can be devilish charming with the ladies. He's a good scholar," he added in a palpable effort to be fair-minded.

Emily brooded. Charming with the ladies? Perhaps Tom had taken leave of his senses. "And the young ladies are seventeen?"

"They turn eighteen in May."

"Lord, I don't envy the countess."

Johnny looked miserable but said nothing.

Emily's soft heart melted. "It won't be long before you'll be using a stick, Johnny. A fortnight, the surgeon said."

"Her ladyship kindly suggested I convalesce at Brecon."

I daresay she did. Emily suppressed a smile. Johnny was so obviously *safe*. The answer to a beleaguered chaperone's prayers.

"She . . . they're so young!" Johnny flushed at the revealing pronoun lapse and avoided Emily's eyes.

Clearly "she" did not refer to Lady Clanross. Emily wondered which of the twins had captured Johnny's fancy, but she forebore to prod further.

Presently Richard finished the letter he was writing his publisher and joined them. He was never an effusive man, but she was pleased that he contrived to praise Johnny's work on the first volume without sounding unnatural, and that he distracted the younger man from his melancholy by soliciting Johnny's opinion of the field at Malplaquet. Soon they were off on a discussion of troop deployment. Johnny's countenance became almost animated as they quarrelled over the ideal placement of skirmishers. Dull, masculine stuff but safely emotionless. Richard had occasional moments of tact.

On the eighteenth, Elizabeth received a letter from her husband with an account of the King's funeral.

 ". . . the day was so cold I shouldn't wonder if
 half the peerage caught their deaths. The latest
 mot, unkind but bearing the stamp of truth, con-

57

cerns the Duke of Clarence. As you know, the Duke of Kent was buried a few days before the king. Clarence is reputed to have said, as Kent's cortege were forming, 'We made a bungling business of the queen's funeral. However, we shall have a rehearsal today, so I hope we shall manage the king's better.' What it is to have an hereditary monarchy. H. R. H. was right. The business went without a hitch in a procession of frozen royalty and congealed nobility, but it was a damnably long ceremony. I rode with Dunarvon. He looks very ill.

"Your sister Anne keeps me *au courant* of the latest political gossip. Parliament will dissolve on the first of March (hurrah!) and the new Parliament will take their seats on the 25th of April (fie!). At least the campaigning won't last forever. I mean to depute everything possible to Featherstonehaugh and Barney Greene. Anne insists that the ministers have talked his new majesty out of a divorce. I hope so. If not, the government will bring a Bill of Pains and Penalties (lovely phrase— sounds as if they mean to put the queen to the rack), and we shall have what amounts to a trial in the Lords. That will mean London for me all summer, so let us hope Anne is right.

"I shall come home alone on the second. Johnny writes that his leg will keep him in Hampshire until mid-March. How does the Poet? How do you, my lady?

"My best love to the boys, Jean, Maggie, Fanny, Georgy, Caro, Miss B, and the telescope—and even better love to you.

"Your funereal spouse,
"Tom"

Assured at the first hasty perusal that she would see Tom within a fortnight, Elizabeth reread the letter. After dinner she read an edited version to her sisters and Owen Davies.

She rather thought she had given the poet fuel for political outrage. He looked pensive and excused himself from a hand of whist. To write, probably.

They were used to Davies's company. Elizabeth was beginning to like him, so long as he didn't read more than three stanzoes at a sitting. She suspected he hid shyness behind his peculiar manners, but he had no small talk and no interest in the natural sciences. Elizabeth had never shone at small talk either and had no interest in political theory, his obsession, so there were often gaps in the conversation.

Jean seemed content to gaze on her idol in uncharacteristic silence. It was Maggie who filled the silences with light chatter. Elizabeth had cause to be grateful to her little sister. Perhaps Maggie would grow from forthright girlhood to civil womanhood without going through the silly stage at all: a consummation devoutly to be wished.

The weather eased briefly, then lowered again with fitful flurries until Friday, when it began to snow in dead earnest. Elizabeth, Jean, and Maggie were standing with the omnipresent poet looking out the withdrawing room windows at swirls of eiderdown. As the snow began to blot out the carefully sculpted landscaping that spread down the long flat slope below the house, a carriage hove into view. So thick was the blown snow that the vehicle had nearly reached the entrance before they made out the Conway arms on the door panels.

Jean pointed and gave a small shriek and Elizabeth's heart started hammering. It was only the twenty-sixth. Tom would not come before the second at the earliest. Something must be amiss.

Maggie squinted. "It's Clanross. He has Captain Greene with him."

Elizabeth hitched up her shawl and made for the door. "I'll have to give orders," she called over her shoulder.

She knew she ought to await Tom decorously in the withdrawing room. Her step-mamma's strictures on unseemly displays of affection still held weight with Elizabeth, and she knew she was setting Jean and Maggie a deplorable example. Still, she wanted to see Tom.

She flew down the long, marble flight to the vast foyer as the butler and a footman contrived to open the door. Elizabeth did not envy the footman. The wind was blowing direct from Norway. As she reached the hall, Tom's man Sims, muffled to the ears, entered on a blast of chill air, followed by Barney and Tom. They were divested of their storm gear in swift order and Tom, spying her, strode over and enveloped her in a large, chilly, and very publick embrace. Tom had never met Elizabeth's late stepmother.

"What is it, Tom?" Dishevelled but not displeased, she pulled away.

"I'll explain in a few minutes, my dear. Is Owen Davies about?"

"Upstairs in the withdrawing room with the girls."

"Good." Tom sounded grim but turned and began instructing the butler to see to a double ration of rum for the coachman and Sims.

"Aye, that's the ticket," said Sims. "Cor, I wasn't 'arf glad to see the old pile loom up. A close run thing, me lady, but th'major would push on."

Sims had been Tom's bâtman and was outspoken, but he rarely slipped into calling his master by the old rank these days. Elizabeth deduced that he had wanted to stop at Chacton. "Never mind, Sims, you're here in one piece."

Sims felt his nose. "I ain't so sure, me lady."

Barney Greene stood shivering behind Tom, Mrs. Smollet bustled out to receive her orders, the footman slammed in laden with portmanteaux, and Fisher tried to hustle Sims to the kitchen for his noggin of rum. It was quite a mob scene but eventually Elizabeth sorted everyone out. She led Tom upstairs with Barney, still shivering, and the butler trailing behind. Both gentlemen made for the fire when they reached the withdrawing room. Fisher plied them with brandy whilst Owen Davies and the twins watched in wide-eyed silence.

At last everyone was seated once more and Tom, standing before the fire with one foot on the fender and a glass of brandy in his hand, had their full attention.

"What is it?" Elizabeth prompted. "What has happened?"

He frowned down at the glass. "A plot to assassinate the Cabinet was uncovered Thursday. There was a skirmish in Cato Street between the Runners and the conspirators, and the guards were called out. Some of the ringleaders of the plot escaped, and one at least was killed. Most of them have been rounded up. They meant to blow up Lord Harrowby's house whilst the Cabinet members dined."

"Good God," Elizabeth muttered into the stunned silence.

Lord Harrowby's house in Grosvenor Square lay within sight of the Conway town house. Tom had been living in a powder keg. Elizabeth felt sick.

"How I wish I'd been there!" Owen Davies was very pale.

Tom regarded him for an unsmiling moment. The poet's eyes dropped. "You may thank your stars you were safe in my book room, Davies. It was a stupid, wrong-headed business, and it has probably set the cause of Reform back ten years."

Owen bit his lip. "But if it had succeeded . . ."

Barney Greene growled in his throat.

Tom set his glass on the mantel. "Do you fancy you'd have had your revolution? Don't be a fool, Davies. If the ministers had been killed they'd have been replaced at once, and you may imagine the repression their successors would have exercised in the name of self-defence. It's bad enough as it is. The group was riddled with informers, a practice such conduct justifies. Respectable opinion was against the government after Peterloo. It will now reverse. Mark my words, Englishmen do not like violent threats against Parliament, however unrepresentative it may be. The government are now clapping every known agitator in prison, confiscating pamphlets, and stiffening enforcement of the sedition laws. Publick opinion will support them."

"Sheep!"

"If by sheep you mean the Publick, I think they show good sense. Blood in the streets may sound animating in the safe precincts of a college, but there is nothing ennobling about it."

Davies said between clenched teeth, "Was there not blood in the streets of Manchester?"

"Yes, and if that colonel of fencibles had had the wit of a peahen he'd never have ordered his men out into the crowd. Don't fancy these fatheads in Cato Street were heroes, Davies. They were fools and knaves and deserve the fate that awaits them."

The twins had been watching this exchange with their hands clasped in identical attitudes of horror, Jean pale as snow, Maggie flushed.

"Did you come home to warn Owen?" Jean burst out.

Tom glanced at Elizabeth and smiled slightly. "I came home because I wanted to come home." He sighed. "And to warn Davies. You would be well advised to lie low for a sixmonth, Davies. That pamphlet your friends published . . ."

"It was privately printed," Davies said angrily.

"Be that as it may, the Runners have come by a copy."

"Oh, no!" Jean whispered.

Davies twisted his hands. "How?"

"I don't know. An informer, perhaps."

"Not among my friends."

". . . or perhaps one of your friends was careless," Tom went on. "You need have no immediate apprehension for your safety, but I'd avoid sending out any work that might be construed as sedition. Including lampoons on Lady Conyngham's girth."

Davies blushed—as well he might. Prinny's mistresses

were all substantial ladies. Hardly an original subject for satire.

Elizabeth felt a twinge of sympathy. Davies's political poems were full of bloodthirsty images and clarion calls. The association would do Tom no political good at all, but the boy was young. As she watched her sisters, her inclination to sympathy faded. Maggie looked worried. Jean—lips parted, wide eyes fixed on Davies—looked as if she had seen a fearful vision.

6

Rumours of the conspiracy to kill the ministers at a banquet shot through the countryside ahead of the worst snowstorm in a decade. It was two days before the mail coach broke through drifts on the London road to bring Winchester reassuring news of the plotters' capture. There was much bustle in the garrison, but it was Emily's opinion that any stray revolutionary would be too cold to move, far less throw bombs.

The newspapers Richard and Johnny pored over were full of the most alarming ideas. Johnny chafed at his inaction. Emily suspected her husband was saving the more outlandish details of the hysteria for his next satire, which, he said sardonically, would probably see print sometime around mid-century at the rate the government was restricting the press. Prinny—no one could remember to call him King—had offered a thousand-pound reward for the apprehension of a caricaturist.

That fact and confirmation of the more lurid events of the Cato Street affair came in a letter Tom writ Richard from Brecon. The catalogue of books in the Brecon library went on apace and Lady Jean and Lady Margaret were assisting the poet in his labours. That announcement galvanised Johnny. Although he had taken only a few tottering steps with the aid of crutches, he announced he was healed and meant to depart for Brecon the next morning. It took Emily's pleas and his own weakness to convince him that laming himself in the cause of chivalry was an extreme course and that Clanross's presence at Brecon would keep the poet in bounds.

As the week-end wore on, Johnny's moods ranged from champing impatience to flat despair until even Emily, who entered into his feeling with the utmost sympathy, wanted to shake him. He was copying Volume Two with savage speed and considerably less elegance than Volume One.

On Tuesday, the surgeon replaced Johnny's clumsy splint with a contraption of canvas and whalebone that kept the bone immobile so long as Johnny did not put his full weight on the limb. He learned to manoeuvre on his crutches and dined at table like a Christian. His temper improved, but his desire to leave did not abate.

So heartened was Emily by her patient's progress that she gave a small dinner party in his honour with Richard's friends, the Wilbrahams, and their daughter as guests. Miss Wilbraham was an amiable girl, popular with the subalterns in garrison, and Major Wilbraham and his wife, though unfashionable, were easy, unaffected people. Though the gentlemen showed a tendency to lay out battle plans on the napiery, Emily's dinner went smoothly. Afterwards, Miss Wilbraham sang one too many Italian airs. She accompanied herself on the lute and looked classical.

Emily fancied she had succeeded in diverting Johnny from his obsession with the Brecon ladies for a few hours. She sent him off to his bed, for he looked pale. Then, because McGrath was a trifle elevated, she and Richard saw their guests out. A groom in Sir Robert Wilson's livery strode up with a message as Richard was about to close the door against the icy wind. Emily's heart sank. She took the shivering lad belowstairs for a tot of McGrath's rum, tipped him, and sent him off to the hostelry Sir Robert patronised.

Richard was still in the foyer, frowning at the letter, when she returned.

She touched his arm. "My dear . . ."

"I'll come up shortly, Emily." He spoke with his usual calm, but she felt the tension in his arm.

"I'll give Mrs. Harry my orders and await you upstairs." When she went to their bedchamber, she donned her nightclothes and sat for a time at her vanity, brushing her short curls and trying not to think the worst.

The Dowager Duchess of Newsham had suffered grave illnesses twice since Emily married Richard. Both times Richard's half sister, Lady Sarah, had tried to effect a reconciliation between her mother and Richard, who was the fruit of the dowager's affair with Lord Powys. Both times Richard had refused to visit the ailing woman. His obduracy puzzled Emily as much as it appalled her, for he was not a spiteful man. Although his half brother, the present Duke of Newsham, had done Richard great harm, Richard had taken no steps to avenge himself, even when an opportunity presented. Why he should rebuff the dowager so coldly when he treated the duke with forebearance Emily could not imagine.

Emily had thought her grace charming, and she knew the duchess felt some interest in Richard's well-being and considerable concern for her grandchildren. After Harry's christening three years earlier Emily had writ her unacknowledged mother-in-law a note describing the child, who was named for her own father. She sent it off without considering Richard's reaction. When she told him what she had done he was furious.

"Don't you see how your letter could be construed?" he'd demanded.

Emily began to lose *her* temper. "Enlighten me."

"The duchess comes of a powerful family—the Tyrells, I mean, not the Ffoukes. Your little note will look as if you are currying favour for your son."

Emily gaped. "Your mind is poisoned."

"That may be, but I've good reason to know how that order of society conducts itself to importunate outsiders. Harry does not need the duchess's patronage."

"I see." She drew a breath. "If that's how you feel, I'm sorry, Richard. I meant no such thing."

"I know you didn't," he said gruffly.

They did not discuss the matter again, but though Emily could see a certain warped logic in his viewpoint she was unconvinced. The Dowager Duchess of Newsham, however exalted her rank, had a grandparent's interest in grandchildren. Emily's own father doated on his grandchildren, including his infant namesake, and she did not see why the dowager should be immune to the universal fascination with the future.

Now sitting at her dressing table, Emily brooded over the puzzle of unmotherly mothers and unfilial sons. When the chill in the air penetrated her thick robe, she added a reckless shovel of seacoal to the fire instead of climbing into bed. She had no intention of retiring until Richard chose to explain the letter.

She fetched a volume of poetry from her nightstand and composed herself to read, but the words floated on the page and the candle flame flickered in the draughts. Finally, when she had reread Mr. Coleridge's apostrophe to Mont Blanc for the fifth time she heard her husband's footsteps in the hall.

She turned as he entered. "What is it, Richard?"

"Another summons."

"Then she's alive." Relief surged through her.

"Yes. Or was when Sarah writ."

"I'm glad . . ."

"Will you advise me? I don't know what's right." He made a clumsy gesture.

She turned back to the mirror, puzzled, trying to think what she might say. She toyed with her brush. "Right in general or right for you, Richard?"

"I don't know." He drew a ragged breath. "Sarah is a sentimentalist. I assume . . ."

Light dawned. Emily sat up straight, her eyes on his reflected face. "You assume Sarah has badgered your mother into sending for you."

He rubbed his forehead. "I may be wrong but I've no

reason to think otherwise." His eyes were dark with very old pain.

She drew a deep breath. "You should go to her, Richard."

"Very well. Robert's carriage is waiting at the Mitre." He looked up at her and spoke more naturally. "He sent from London. The duchess is at his town house, it seems. I'll leave at noon. I might as well take Dyott with me."

"What of the copying?"

"Dyott wants to leave us. The election, I daresay."

"Oh, Richard, *not* the election. He is brooding over the young ladies at Brecon and their resident Poet. He has forgot the election." She was relieved when Richard's mouth quirked in a smile.

He came to her and touched her nape, rubbing the warm skin. "I'm glad you see these things, Emily. I don't." He kissed her cheek. "Come to bed. It's very late."

The carriage jounced over a frozen rut and Johnny's death grip on the strap tightened.

"Hurt?" Colonel Falk leaned forward and flipped the travelling rug back over Johnny's outstretched legs.

"It's bearable." Johnny's breath came in a gasp of steam. The air was icy. He was sitting sidewise on the well-padded seat with both legs across it. Though the position was more comfortable than facing forward with bent knees, it rendered every jolt perilous. He felt he might roll off onto the floor at any moment, his leg hurt abominably, and his arm ached from gripping the strap. The motion of the carriage was beginning to make him queasy.

"Shall I direct the coachman to drive slower?"

"No, thank you, sir." Johnny swiped at his damp brow with his free hand. Colonel Falk leaned back against the squabs and resumed his frowning contemplation of the frigid landscape. He had been silent for the most part since their journey began and if his mother were ill it was no wonder.

Nevertheless Johnny felt impelled to apologise. "I'm sorry to leave you with so much copying undone, sir."

Falk shrugged. "It doesn't matter."

"Shall you include a map of the action before Maastricht?" The carriage heaved. Johnny grabbed for the strap.

"I may chuck the whole thing."

Johnny stared but Colonel Falk was still looking out the window. "After all that work?"

Falk turned with apparent reluctance. "No amount of labour is going to redeem the book, Dyott. It's rubbish."

"You keep saying that. I don't see it. I've read far worse."

Perversely, the direct contradiction seemed to cheer Falk. "That's hardly a commendation. You're right, though. I exaggerate. It's a clear enough account with no particular merit other than clarity. I've come close to publishing work I was ashamed of before, but this is the first time I've hated what I was writing whilst I was writing it." He pulled the flaps of his greatcoat over his knees and regarded Johnny with quizzical hazel eyes. "Tom said you were with his company."

The change of subject startled Johnny. "Er, only for a sixmonth. I kept falling ill." In the Peninsula, Johnny had succumbed to ague, dysentery, boils, ague, pleurisy, and ague, in that order. He had passed the Vittoria campaign groaning in the baggage train.

"You must have joined after Tom exchanged from the Rifles or I'd remember you."

"It was 1813."

"If you were in the field half a year you know how to value military glory."

"I beg your pardon?"

"It's a load of misery and a pack of lies," Falk said with the air of a dominie who has a slow scholar on his hands. "History compounds the lies."

Johnny felt as if he were being tossed in a blanket. Surely Falk understood glory? He was a hero of Waterloo.

"Historians are liars?"

Falk smiled. "All writers are liars. Historians just don't admit it."

Johnny brooded. The coach swayed. When Colonel Falk continued to regard him quizzically, Johnny muttered, "I don't agree. The truth exists and a writer should at least try to find it."

"You may be right, but how?"

"I don't know! *I'm* not a writer. And where is the profit in bootless philosophizing?" Johnny burst out, goaded beyond his usual deference to his elders.

Falk cocked an eyebrow. "For five minutes at least you forgot the pain in your leg, so it can't have been a dead loss."

Johnny stared. "That's true, sir, but I now have a pain in my head as well."

Colonel Falk laughed. "I beg your pardon, Dyott. I'm a vile physician, am I not? I daresay I shall finish my three-volume lie. My overdraught admits of no other solution. Your labour will not go for nothing. Do you mean to canvas for Tom's candidates? Emily tells me you've an interest in Reform."

Relieved, Johnny spoke of the election and his desire to enter the world of Whig politicks. Falk refrained from further Berkeleyan questioning and Johnny forgot his resentment.

At Clapham they changed horses. It was dark and snowing again when the carriage pulled into Grosvenor Square and halted before the Conway house. From the number of windows alight with candles Johnny supposed Clanross had returned from Brecon. The butler answered the coachman's imperious knocking, and when Johnny had winced his way out of the carriage, he entered once more into the light of common sense. He made his farewells with more haste than courtesy and stumped upstairs on his crutches.

He went to bed at eight after tucking into a snug dinner. Clanross and Barney Greene had gone off to separate political dinners and neither was expected until late, so

Johnny retired with a clear conscience. He slept for several hours, then drowsed as the ache in his leg dictated. The bell clock on the mantel had chimed eleven when he heard a soft knock at his door.

"Come in," he called sleepily.

Clanross entered, shielding a candle. "I thought you might be wakeful. Waite says you appeared at the door this afternoon in a private carriage. Why the devil did you risk crocking your leg up? There's nothing urgent for you here."

Johnny rose on one elbow, nightcap awry. "Colonel Falk had the use of a carriage—someone named Wilson sent it—so he thought I might as well come to town with him."

"Wilson . . ."

"I believe Colonel Falk's mother is ill."

Clanross set the candle on the mantel and sank into the chair beside the hearth. "The duchess died this morning."

Johnny's jaw dropped. "Duchess?"

"The Dowager Duchess of Newsham," Clanross said precisely. "Richard's mother. If she sent for him he arrived too late."

"But . . ." Johnny's head whirled.

"I daresay you know nothing of that ancient scandal— why should you? Richard would not speak of it." He stared at the toes of his pumps—he was still rigged out for a formal dinner. "Blast! Sir Robert Wilson's carriage. Then Richard is probably stopping with his sister in Cavendish Square. I'll call on him in the morning." He rose and stood looking down at Johnny. "What am I going to do with you?"

Johnny swallowed his confusion. "Lady Clanross said I might convalesce at Brecon. If you don't dislike it, my lord."

Clanross's eyes narrowed. "Brecon? Excellent." A smiled tugged at his mouth. "You can keep a weather eye on the seditious librarian."

"But the election . . ."

"Anyone may go about polling freeholders. You, my man, can keep Lady Jean and Lady Margaret in check, a far more difficult task."

"But . . ."

"Prevent them from setting up a liberty pole on the village green, Dyott, or building bombs in the wine cellar, that sort of thing. On no account is Lady Clanross's telescope platform to be used as a rallying point for rick-burners."

"I shall do my possible." Johnny's spirits rose.

Clanross took the candle. "Good night. Rest the leg for a few days and I'll send you to Brecon in the carriage."

=7=

WHEN HIS TOWN carriage pulled up before Sir Robert Wilson's portico next morning, Tom saw that the hatchments were already in place. A black crepe bow hung on the door. He directed his man to take a turn of the Square. When he knocked, Wilson's butler answered at once.

Tom handed the man his card. "Pray convey my condolences to Lady Wilson and your master. I'd like a word with Colonel Falk, if he's up." It was half past nine, too early for such a call.

"I believe Colonel Falk is at work in the library." The man took Tom's hat and greatcoat. "If you will be so kind as to wait in the blue salon, my lord . . ."

"Show me to the book room," Tom interrupted. "Richard won't stand on ceremony."

The butler looked doubtful but led Tom up an elegant flight of stairs and down a long darkened corridor. In the distance a housemaid scurried from sight. The man entered a half-open door. "Lord Clanross to see you, sir." Tom was at the butler's heels.

Richard stood at a sort of *prie dieu*. He had apparently been writing or copying. He abandoned his pen and held out his good hand. "I thought you were snowbound in Lincolnshire. Mind the ink."

Tom clasped his friend's hand with both his own. "I came . . . that is, I'm sorry, Richard."

"Thank you," Richard said without expression.

The butler made a discreet noise. Both men had forgot

his presence. "Do you desire me to bring coffee or tea, sir?"

"Coffee." Richard nodded his dismissal. "Thank you."

When the door closed Richard gestured to an armchair and pulled another for himself. Both men sat.

"I fear you must have come too late," Tom ventured.

"We were both too late." Richard rubbed the chair arm. "The duchess and I."

Tom searched his friend's face. It was haggard but composed, the eyes veiled. "I wish you will come to me."

"I ought to make myself available to Sarah," Richard said quietly. "She's cut up—low from nursing my mother through the last illness. Robert and I go on comfortably, you know."

Tom expelled a sigh of relief. So Richard was on speaking terms with at least one of his kin. "I hope your children are well."

"They were when I left."

"And Emily?"

Richard's mouth relaxed. "Emily is herself, thank God, though she dislikes living in town."

"She's still homesick?"

"She doesn't complain, but I fancy she's bored."

The previous summer they had raked over Richard's reasons for removing from his stepson's estate, and Tom had been unable to fault his friend's logic. Richard could not afford to let another estate, nor even another country house. Though neither Emily nor Richard regarded the move with enthusiasm, it seemed the only answer. As Matt was enrolled for Winchester College, Winchester was the obvious place in which to take a house.

"Are you back in young Matthew's graces yet?" Tom asked.

Richard grimaced. "Intermittently. He's a stiff-rumped young devil but he doesn't want for sense. Amy likes her school."

74

"I wish I might see young Amy. Pretty as she can stare, I daresay."

A shadow crossed Richard's face. "I'm told she favours the duchess."

Tom cleared his throat. "And my godson?"

"Tommy is reading well."

"But his hearing is gone."

Richard nodded.

"I'm sorry," Tom said again.

"I daresay your boys have reached the waddling stage," Richard said tactfully.

Relieved, Tom gave him an account of Lord Brecon and the Honourable Richard Conway. Presently his mind turned to Johnny Dyott. "I thought he still had work to do for you, Richard. He hasn't copied the whole manuscript yet, has he?"

"He can't copy what isn't finished. Let be, Tom. Emily thinks he's taken with one of your sisters-in-law."

"Lord, so he scents a rival." Tom started to laugh aloud, then broke off guiltily. "I beg your pardon. They're minxes, you know, and clever as paint. I thought Johnny had taken their measure at Christmas but he is at the susceptible age, after all. Did Emily say which twin he fancies?"

A gleam of humour lit Richard's eyes. "Perhaps he's in love with both."

Tom chuckled. "I ought to commission you to write it all up."

At that point the butler entered with coffee. He was followed almost at once by Sir Robert Wilson, who seemed flustered to find an earl in his bookroom at the breakfast hour.

When Tom took his leave he thought Richard looked less drawn. He extracted his friends's promise to dine later in the week. He was troubled for Richard and concerned about the Duke of Newsham's response when that nobleman discovered his half brother in Sir Robert's house. Newsham hated Richard.

The following Wednesday, as Tom was rigging himself out for yet another interminable political dinner, Richard appeared in his dressing room. That is, the butler scratched at the door, Sims went to confer, there was much muttering, which Tom tried to ignore, and Sims admitted Richard to the presence. Sometimes Tom yearned for the bad old days when life was simpler and a friend might poke his head through the tent flap without ceremony.

When Richard entered, Tom rose, abandoning the silver knife with which he had been paring his nails. "Good God, is something amiss?"

Richard looked dazed. He gave his head a shake. "I need your advice."

Tom caught Sims's eye. Brandy, he mouthed, and for once Sims slid from the room without comment.

"What is it? Sit down, man. You look as if you've been overrun by a troop of *cuirassiers*."

Richard gave a short laugh. "I feel it." He groped for the nearest chair and sat. "It seems the dowager left me a fortune."

Richard's tone of voice was so much at odds with the tenor of his message that Tom did not immediately grasp what he had said. When he did, he stared. "I'm glad she showed so much good sense. My felicitations, Richard, and why the devil are you sunk in gloom?"

Richard said through his teeth, "When your predecessor died and you came into the earldom did you rejoice?"

When Tom succeeded to the earldom of Clanross he was under a death sentence. A chunk of metal was pressing against his spine. There had been no cause for rejoicing. That had come later, much later. Apart from his right arm, Richard was in the pink of good health. Tom didn't see a parallel and said so.

Richard ran his trembling hand over his face. "I don't

know whether to accept the legacy and risk a suit in chancery, or refuse it. I don't even know if I *can* refuse it."

"Probably not. And you shouldn't. You have Tommy's future to think of. A deaf child does not have easy prospects," Tom said bluntly. "You know that. It's driven you to write what you despise and to move your family to uncomfortably tight quarters. I daresay you'd have contrived something for Tommy eventually, Richard, but at what cost to Emily and your other children? You've every right to your mother's bequest, and, if the duchess's lawyers advised her properly, Newsham will have no grounds for a suit. Use her gift to secure Tommy's future."

"Gift? I'm not talking of a few thousand pounds," Richard said with something like despair. "It seems her grace collected terraces."

"I don't follow you."

"A genteel sum was settled on her when she married Newsham and she also had a small inheritance from her mother. She invested it all."

"I see," Tom said slowly.

"I don't think you do. I've had it explained to me by her man of business. Four hours it took him and that was after he read the will." Richard took a gulp of air. "After the duke's death, the dowager lived retired. Her expenses were modest. She inherited a manor in Yorkshire from her mother and she sat there, when she wasn't travelling to Harrowgate or Bath or Scarborough or Cheltenham, and *accumulated* properties. Her man of affairs said she made a game of it."

"Good God."

"My mother," said Richard with dangerous calm, "was a genius at what I believe Yorkshiremen call 'addling her brass.' She owned villas in St. John's Wood, and crescents and terraces in nearly every spa she visited—and in several she didn't, notably Worthing. None of it is slum property, none of it is rural, none of it touches on a manor belonging to the Ffouke estate. Where she couldn't purchase a freehold outright she took a ninety-year lease. She transformed her dower into an empire."

That was too much for Tom. He buried his head in his hands and laughed. When he composed himself he found Richard scowling at him. "My dear idiot, it's perfectly clear she was playing a vast joke on Newsham. I'll lay odds she left your half brother the original sum his father settled on her."

"To the farthing."

"And some respectable token to each of her other children."

"She left her jewellery to Sarah. The dowager's admirers seem to have expressed their devotion in diamonds. And she left fifty pounds apiece to the others. 'For mourning rings.' " Richard's mouth twitched at the corners.

"She must have enjoyed herself," Tom murmured, eyeing him.

To his relief, Richard grinned. It was a reluctant grin but quite genuine. "All right, so it's comical."

"Do you grudge her her joke?"

"I mightn't if I didn't feel I was the butt of it."

Tom said cautiously, "I'd lay odds the duchess had an eye on young Amy."

Richard frowned. Amy was his daughter by his first marriage. What was she now, ten? It hardly seemed possible.

"The fact is," Tom went on, "*you* were the only one of her grace's children the patriarchy didn't provide for. So she left you property with no traditional ties. Free property. Property that wasn't bound to parental descent. She was a genius. What's more she was a wit. I wish I'd known her."

Richard shut his eyes. "So do I."

Tom said in the silence his clumsiness had created, "I daresay no one knew her, Richard, but I begin to understand your feelings." He fingered the silver knife. "She couldn't give you what you needed, so she gave you what she *could* give. Wealth. It's a poor substitute for affection . . ."

"It's a dangerous substitute," Richard said without opening his eyes.

Before Tom could ask him to explain himself Sims barged in with the brandy decanter. Sims regarded Richard as a type of *bandito* and was apt to indulge in barely veiled criticisms, so Tom was relieved when his man left the room.

He poured two substantial dollops of brandy, handed one glass to Richard, and raised his own. "To the Dowager Duchess of Newsham."

"No," said Richard. "To Barbara Tyrell. Whoever she was."

"Elizabeth! Johnny is come home!" Maggie burst into the nursery as Lord Brecon emerged from his bath.

"Waw woo," said her nephew, who was growing more eloquent by the day. "Mama."

Elizabeth took his linen-swaddled lordship, still wet and wriggling like a trout, from Nurse, and sat on the nursery rocker. "Is he really, Maggie? His leg must be very much improved." She began patting Brecon dry.

Maggie danced across the room. "Yes, he's using a stick already and says he'll be able to ride again within the month. And only fancy!" She perched on a hassock by the screen Nurse had erected to cut draughts and beamed at Elizabeth.

"Only fancy what?" Elizabeth smiled at her. Brecon squirmed. Dickon splashed in the copper bath by the fire whilst Nurse hovered.

"He's wearing trousers!"

"Ah . . . splendid," said Elizabeth cautiously. Brecon had twined his pink fingers into the lace that edged her sleeve. "No, Ba. Don't eat. Trousers. Er, has Johnny taken to open collars and spotted neckerchiefs, as well?"

Maggie grinned. "No, he looks very dashing, though. He brought you a letter from Clanross."

"Good." Elizabeth would have preferred Clanross himself to any number of letters but she supposed he would come within the week. She gave her son a small jounce. He gurgled happily. "Has Mrs. Smollet seen to Johnny's room?"

"I gave her her orders." Maggie blushed. She was an unassuming girl. "I hope you don't think me encroaching."

"Nonsense, darling, it's good practice for you. You will be running your own house one of these days, after all. Bring me the baby's napkin and gown, will you?"

Maggie complied, her thoughts clearly still on Johnny. She folded and fastened the soft diapered cloth in place whilst Elizabeth held Brecon for her. He submitted to the tiny vest and petticoats with fair grace.

Dickon, still in the bath, crowed and splashed harder. Nurse clucked over him. Maggie took Brecon from her sister.

Elizabeth rose. "I daresay Jean and Owen are still in the bookroom."

"Oh, yes, but they'll come out for tea. Johnny brought me . . . us a book, Colonel Falk's novel. Have you read it?"

"Heavens, no." Elizabeth drifted to Nurse's side and touched Dickon's damp brown curls. He gave her a wide grin that revealed his pearly, but still sparse milk teeth.

"Barf."

"Yes, darling. Very wet, too."

Dickon splashed hugely.

"Adone do," nurse scolded. "Lookee now, Master Dickon, if you've not splashed her ladyship's gown."

"Hush. it will dry." Elizabeth plucked her dripping son from the water and thrust him into the soft towel Nurse held out to her. Dickon let out a startled wail. His attitude toward baths was Roman. He would have preferred to stay in his *calidarium* forever.

"Johnny says it's a very amusing satire, but perhaps not quite delicate."

Elizabeth took Dickon and towel in her arms and resumed her station at the rocker. "There, there, darling, all good things must come to an end. Well, Maggie, you've grown up now. You be the judge. If the book makes you blush you needn't finish it. Will Johnny come to the withdrawing room or take his tea in his own room?"

"He'll join us. He really ought to rest his leg, though." Maggie hid her pink face in Brecon's hair.

She does have a *tendre* for Johnny, Elizabeth thought, resigned. Ah, well. She towelled Dickon thoroughly, tickling him when he showed a disposition to grizzle.

Presently Nurse and her aide-de-camp, a wide-eyed young girl from the village, removed the babies with a promise to display them in the withdrawing room when they had been fed, and Elizabeth and Maggie left the warm nursery for the draughty second floor corridor.

"Did Johnny keep Tom's letter by him?"

"He gave it to Fisher. Elizabeth . . ."

"What is it, my dear?" Elizabeth lifted her skirt and grasped the bannister.

Maggie slipped down the stair ahead of her. "I'm glad Johnny's back. Now we shall go on very comfortably." And she danced off, leaving Elizabeth to descend to the first floor hall in a thoughtful mood.

Had Maggie been feeling uncomfortable for some reason? For the obvious reason? Owen Davies. I ought to put a stop to those long sessions in the book room, Elizabeth reflected, uneasy. But how? I cannot change my tune for no reason. So far Owen has not shown any obvious partiality for one twin over the other nor is his manner—at least in my presence—unduly warm. Still . . . She resolved to have a private talk with Johnny Dyott.

By the time he had drunk tea with the Brecon house party, it was clear to Johnny that Jean was in love with Owen Davies. There could be no doubt, though neither Jean nor Owen said or did anything a less acute observer would notice. Johnny, however, was unhappily aware of every breath Lady Jean respired. Her sighs—and her glowing glances—were directed at the poet. At least Maggie seemed unaffected.

As usual, Lady Clanross was gracious to Johnny, singling him out and questioning him with every appearance of interest about his health and his stay with the Falks. He thought he made a fair show of answering the kindly questions. He had no desire to make his jealousy a subject for talk, so he spoke with more animation than he felt and even, under Maggie's bright gaze, enlivened his account with anecdotes of the Falk children, whom he was beginning to miss. He also missed Emily. He had been able to confide in Emily.

After the tea things had been cleared away, Nurse brought in the babies and Davies excused himself. Johnny watched the poet's graceful exit with resentment. Davies did everything gracefully. Johnny's stiff leg and the embarrassing loose trousers made him feel like a Mohawk.

He admired the Heir and Dickon, who had sprouted new teeth since the New Year, and watched glumly as Jean and Maggie romped with their nephews. Nymphs and cupids. It was a charming scene spoilt only by Johnny's sense of being left out. Why had he not made a push to attach Lady Jean's interest before he left?

He knew why not. She was too young. He was her equal on paper, perhaps, being respectably descended, but in fact her birth and fortune placed her well above his touch. And she was his employer's ward and sister. Clanross would surely feel resentment if Johnny took advantage of the association with Jean and Maggie his work had made possible. They were the daughters of an earl and could look higher than the younger son of a dean. Now if the government were to make his father a bishop . . .

"An amusing thought? Penny for it," Lady Clanross said amiably.

Johnny felt himself flush. "I was watching Dickon," he lied. "Have you been able to use your telescope, ma'am?'

"No, it's been too cold for my blood. However, the thaw has set in. Perhaps I'll have time for an evening or two of stargazing before we go to town. I was used to begin my systematic observations in March. Johnny, I wonder if I may have a word with you before dinner. Come to my dressing room."

"Certainly, my lady." He eyed her curiously but she had returned her attention to her sons who were performing a sort of pas de deux on the withdrawing room carpet.

A starched-up abigail showed Johnny into Lady Clanross's dressing room half an hour before they ought to have descended for dinner. Though great ladies had been receiving gentlemen in their private suites for ages Johnny felt some discomfort at his intrusion. Lady Clanross wore a gown of wine-coloured velvet, cut rather high, with vandyked sleeves that showed a froth of Belgian lace at the wrist. Her maid was dressing her hair.

"Thank you, Dobbins." Her ladyship untied the strings of the short muslin cape that had protected her own whilst her hair was being done.

The abigail gave the glossy chestnut curls a final, critical touch with the comb and twitched the muslin off. "Your jewellery, madam."

"Ah, what does it matter? The garnet set . . ." Lady Clanross gave an impatient wave of her hand. "Johnny, I am glad you've come, and I daresay I don't have to point out why."

"Er . . ."

The maid placed a rather old-fashioned garnet necklace about her mistress's neck and gave a sniff.

"Yes, thank you, Dobbins. You may go."

The abigail whisked from the room, every muscle alert with disdain.

Lady Clanross sighed. "She keeps trying to turn me into a fashionable lady. I sympathise with her, but what can I do? The leopard cannot change her spots. For heaven's sake, sit down, Johnny. I don't want you to damage your leg out of mere politeness."

Johnny, who by then felt exceedingly uncomfortable, sat on the nearest chair.

"Jean has taken a fancy to Owen Davies. I have no objection to that so long as she doesn't throw her cap over the windmill and do something foolish."

Johnny had every objection to Lady Jean's *tendre* but he couldn't very well say so.

Lady Clanross watched him in her pier glass. "She is very young."

He cleared his throat. "Yes."

"I'd like you to keep an eye on her."

Johnny felt his discomfort turn to righteous wrath. "It is no part of my work to be spying on Lady Jean, ma'am."

Lady Clanross turned to face him, her eyes narrowed. After a moment, she said slowly, "I beg your pardon, Johnny. I expressed myself incautiously."

"But that's what you want me to do."

She frowned. "I wish I could deny it absolutely. I'm responsible for Jean's conduct—and Maggie's, of course. They are young and necessarily naive. Your friend, Davies . . ."

"Owen Davies and I were up at Oxford together," Johnny said precisely. "We did not sit in one another's pockets."

"Yes, I see."

He wondered what she saw.

Finally, she went on, "Well, I've no desire to turn you into an informer. Nevertheless, Jean is vulnerable because she's seventeen and gently reared. Her disposition is adventurous. I sympathise with that. My own temperament is neither tame nor conventional. Still, you will allow that a young lady must stay within very strict bounds or she's made to pay—as a young man would not be—for quite natural excesses of high spirits."

"Well, yes, but . . ."

"Do you suppose young ladies find the constrictions they live under agreeable?"

Johnny felt his anger leak away. "No, but Lady Jean . . ."

"Jean," said her sister dispassionately, "would have rowed Bonnie Prince Charlie across the Irish Sea in an open boat if she had been born a hundred years ago. That is her natural inclination, and not for the sake of his bonny blue eyes. For the sake of sheer adventure."

"But Owen is not Charles Stewart."

"And Jean is not a fool. I know. But she is looking for a hero, and I rather think she has found one. I'd be criminally negligent if I didn't take precautions."

Johnny let out a breath that was compounded of pure frustration. "Owen isn't a bounder."

"If he had been he would have departed weeks ago, Clanross or no Clanross. Owen is an idealist, and like most idealists he's willing to sacrifice himself and everyone about him to his goals. I don't think Jean should be his burnt offering."

'If you put it that way," Johnny said sullenly.

"If I put it that way it's because I'm thinking of Jean's future, not his. I don't know what her future may be, but it shouldn't include social ostracism at seventeen."

"You have all the heavy guns, Lady Clanross."

A smile touched her mouth. "Do you see me as a division of artillery?"

Thrown into confusion, Johnny could only stare.

She turned back to her looking glass, patted her coiffure, and rose. "I don't want to turn you into a spy, Johnny. However, I thought you might take your work—Tom gave you lashings of work, I daresay . . ."

"I have a great deal of correspondence to catch up on."

"Splendid. I thought you might take your work to the book room. You needn't report to me or betray confidences. I am counting on your mere presence to moderate Jean's transports."

That was a lowering thought. "You want a chaperon."

"If that is a more acceptable term than spy, so be it."

Their eyes locked.

"Very well," Johnny said heavily. "I'll take my letters to the book room, ma'am. I understand your apprehension."

"I'm sorry, Johnny, and I thank you."

He struggled to his feet. "There's not much Owen can do here in a political way. London's the centre of conspiracies these days." He cleared his throat. "Ma'am . . ."

"What is it?"

He said stiffly, feeling as if he had descended to a very low level of discourse but compelled to speak, nevertheless, by his upbringing, "I must apologise for my informal costume."

She regarded his loose trousers gravely. "I think you may take your forgiveness for granted."

"I should not like to appear *slack*."

She smoothed the flounces on her sleeves, avoiding his eyes. "My stepmother was a very high stickler. She always refused to admit men in pantaloons to her salon. Knee breeches, preferably black silk—that was her style—and she desired her guests to powder their hair. I am far less nice in my tastes. I think you look very well in trousers."

"It's the contraption the surgeon rigged in place of the splint. If I wear knee breeches or pantaloons I look as if I have gout."

She gave him a gamine grin that reminded him of Lady Jean. "No one could possibly accuse you of being goutish, Johnny. Maggie said you looked dashing."

He blushed but he was not entirely displeased.

=8=

By the time she received a letter from her husband informing her that he was coming back to Winchester at last, Emily was in the high fidgets.

Richard writ that there was a legacy. She had expected no less. Somthing to put by for the children's education. Very thoughtful of her grace. Perhaps Richard would now think better of his mother. *How* Richard was thinking of his mother was the crux of Emily's suspense, next to which learning the details of the legacy paled to insignificance.

Since she had first heard of Richard's unhappy childhood, Emily had felt his ambivalence. Richard's father, Lord Powys, had been killed by his mother's husband, the Duke of Newsham, in a duel that took place three months before Richard was born. Powys's family had made no move to acknowledge the boy. He had grown up belonging nowhere. It was a wonder he had made himself into so definite a personality.

It was not surprising that Richard wanted to live apart from his family. He kept even his half sister Sarah, who was fond of him, at arm's length. As far as Emily could tell, he had tried to avoid thinking of the duchess at all. Emily fancied he could not be entirely indifferent, and she hoped he had not tried to fool himself about so primal a feeling as that of a son for a mother.

She heard the coachman's rap and Phillida's quick scuffle as the maid answered the door. Impatient as she had been, Emily sat frozen in her place. She was not sure she knew what to say now Richard was come. She set her teacup down and gave herself a shake. Foolishness. He was her husband, and she loved him. She would say what was right.

By the time she reached the foyer he had dispatched Sir Robert's servants and was asking Phillida about the children.

"Richard . . ." Emily felt her throat close.

He frowned up at her with the same uncertainty in his eyes she had seen when she first agreed to marry him.

She ran to him. "Oh, my dear, I'm so glad you're home."

He held her tight for a long moment as if to be sure she were solid. When she finally pulled back, she was weeping a little but she directed the gawping Phillida to bring another cup to the drawing room and led her husband upstairs.

Richard drank a cup of tea and heard a full report of the children's accomplishments in his absence, and he began to look less harried. He said little beyond what he had already writ.

Presently Emily's stock of anecdotes ran down and she looked at him. "Well, Richard, how is it with you?"

He rubbed his forehead. "Well enough. Sarah is feeling more like herself. She sends you her love."

"I'm glad of it," she said mechanically. Blast Sarah.

He toyed with the cup. "Emily, there is no way I can delay telling you this any longer. My mother left me a great deal of property. I'm afraid it is going to change things . . ."

"She what?"

"A fortune," he said in tones that were a little too dispassionate.

A veil of red dropped before Emily's eyes. She had not believed that an angry person literally saw red. "Damn her!" She burst into tears.

Emily was not given to nerve storms or, indeed, to cursing. Even as she wept her outburst puzzled her. A shocking thing to have said. Richard comforted her, and she let herself be soothed, and apologised when she found her voice. The outward signs of her fury abated. She blew her nose and tidied her gown.

They went upstairs to the nursery and saw the babies. Tommy read his father two stories when he had stopped frisking about asking for gifts from town. Amy came home from her day school and was kissed and catechised. A large and very beautiful globe of the world was borne upstairs by McGrath, who grumbled and smelt of gin.

Richard was a gift-giver by temperament. What he chose was almost always the very thing, as far as his children were concerned. Emily thought it a kind of native tact. She wished his mother had been imbued with it. Her anger flared again, and again she bit it back.

Eventually they left the children and Peggy McGrath to the globe and dinner, and retired to dress for their own meal which they took rather early now Johnny was gone.

They dined in fragile silence. Emily's fury smouldered. It was she who had always tried to conciliate, to interpret the duchess charitably to Richard. Now she felt no charity at all.

It was not that she objected to wealth per se. She was not so quixotic. It would be a blessing not to have to pinch and scrape to assure Tommy's future. The duchess might have achieved that end by leaving Richard a few thousand pounds. That would not have been insulting. But a fortune . . .

Richard was not careless with words. If he said fortune he meant fortune. Their lives must be changed by such wealth—out of all compass. Emily feared what the changes would be, but most of all she feared for Richard's peace of mind.

To a remarkable degree for a man of his blood, Richard Falk was a self-made man. He had been cut off from the Ffouke family and his mother at twelve and shoved into the army at fifteen. Anything he achieved thereafter had been by his own efforts, for he heard nothing from his mother and had nothing of her, except, ironically, a statement that he was illegitimate, in the years that followed. He made his own life apart.

Now, when he could have no human relationship with his mother, she had chosen to shower him with favour—and favour of the sort he would find most baffling. Richard's experience of great wealth had been wholly negative. He was no Leveller and did not despise the modest prosperity of Emily's family, but he had excellent reason to mistrust the power of wealth. His half brother, Newsham, had used it to persecute him.

And so, wholly unprepared, Richard had had similar wealth thrust upon him. Emily thought he must be frightened and oppressed, and she was powerless to comfort him.

They retired early in near silence and lay for a time side by side. Finally Emily said, "I'm civil now. I think you'd better explain."

She did not interrupt as he outlined the nature of the estate the duchess had bequeathed him. He spoke dryly, almost like a man of law.

When he finished she lay staring at the canopy, turning the bizarre legacy over in her mind. "It's far too much."

"Yes. I directed her grace's man of business—he is now my man of business—to seek probate. As the will is publick record, or will be shortly, you may expect speculation from your acquaintances and importunities from tradesmen when the news reaches Winchester."

He sounded grim.

"My father . . ."

"I must write Sir Henry. Perhaps you ought to go to him for a time, Emily."

"And leave you here alone? I should say not!" She propped herself on one elbow and squinted at him in the darkness. "I wonder you would suggest such a thing."

He gave a muffled snort of laughter and pulled her to him. "Ah, God, Emily, promise me *you* won't change."

She touched his face. "Why should I? I married you for better or worse, as I recall."

"You do understand that wealth of this order is not an unmixed blessing?"

"The idea freezes my marrow. I'm a plain country-woman."

He kissed her fingers. "A countrywoman perhaps. Plain, no. I didn't bring you a gift, Emily. It wasn't for lack of thought."

"You may buy me a blue velvet bonnet. With swansdown trim."

He laughed shakily. "I love you."

"*Two* blue velvet bonnets." She wriggled against him. "And I shall buy you a stickpin with an amber head to match your eyes. There, we've disposed of your wealth. I'm glad you're home, Richard. I turn crotchety and no-tional the minute you go out the door. It is probably advancing age."

He was able to reassure her that there was life in her old bones yet.

The idea that she was now the wife of a very wealthy man began to sink in gradually over the next few days.

It rained for a week, thawing the last patches of snow that had lain like pale shadows under the Brecon beeches. Now a freshening March wind dried the footpaths and everyone could escape the prison of the house. The four young people went for a walk—only as far as the lake because the sky promised blustering showers—but the air that whipped against Maggie's cheeks held out a hint of spring warmth.

She matched her steps to Johnny Dyott's slow pace, though her impulse was to run like a colt down to the lakeside. Jean and Owen had already gained the water's edge where tame ducks bobbed among the reeds. The dogs—Jean's setter and Maggie's red bitch, Una, frisked and yipped at the ducks. It was a day for running wild.

"Shall you ride tomorrow, Maggie?" Jean, optimistic of good weather, was planning a horseback tour of the grounds, so Johnny's question sounded wistful to Maggie. The surgeon had forbidden him to ride.

She tore her gaze from her sister and the poet, and smiled at him. "I thought to, but I'm no horsewoman. Perhaps Jem will ride off Joybell's quirks before I have to mount her."

" 'Joybell.' " Johnny shook his head.

Maggie flushed. "At the time it seemed like the right name. We had just come here from Scotland, Jean and I. We were only thirteen and, well, joyful. Glad to be here," she added, anxious to clarify herself. "And not in fusty Lochnald with Kitty. Elizabeth said we might name our mounts." She grinned. "I daresay my choice involved a touch of magic."

"Like calling the fates the kindly ones?" Johnny leaned on his stick. "Are you afraid of horses?"

"No, but I am afraid of falling off."

He laughed, and they resumed their slow progress. "I take it your sister has no such apprehensions."

"No, and she can drive the gig like a coachman, too. Jean is much braver than me." Maggie swallowed the lump in her throat. It was beginning to wear on her that both gentlemen found Jean interesting. Maggie had no desire for the poet's homage, but she wished she could do something—leap a three-barred gate, perhaps—to merit *Johnny's* interest. But Joybell would balk at the gate. *And so would I,* Maggie reflected ruefully.

A gust of wind tossed the black ribbands of her bonnet. Johnny clutched at his hat brim. Jean and the poet had already reached the arch of the graceful bridge that spanned the lake at its narrowest point. They were deep in conversation. The poet's fair hair ruffled in the wind and he was gesturing with his right hand. Reciting again?

Yipping and panting, the two red setters left off teasing

the ducks and bounded back up the slope. Maggie took a breath. "No! Down, Una. Bad dog, Tom!"

"Why is he called Tom?"

"Clanross gave us the dogs for our fifteenth birthday, so Jean called hers after him. That was when she was in love with Clanross," Maggie said absently. Then she heard her words. She bit her lip and wished she hadn't mentioned her twin's calf love. She felt too comfortable talking to Johnny.

Johnny said nothing.

Maggie watched the two dogs whirl off, chasing each other across the spongy turf. After a moment, she bent and flicked mud from the skirt of her grey pelisse. "You heard from my brother-in-law yesterday, didn't you? How does the election go?"

Johnny swung into motion. "Well enough, except in Minchampton. They've been polling three days and that seat is hotly contested." He reached a stone bench at the lakeside and sank onto it. "I wish I might help with the canvassing."

"I wish you might, too," Maggie said with shameless untruth. She was glad he was at Brecon. "Do you mean to try for a parliamentary career some day?"

He gave a short laugh. "I'd like to."

"Why should you not?"

"I've no experience." He dug the tip of his stick into the damp gravel. "Clanross did say he would find something for me on the hustings, but that was before I broke my blasted shin."

Maggie sat beside him. "There will be other elections."

"Not for years," Johnny said glumly. "I'm twenty-five and no farther along than I was when I came down from Oxford."

"Surely that's not . . ." Maggie bit her lip again. What did she know of politicks? He would be thinking her a thrusting sort of female.

"Not what, Maggie?"

She faced him, hot with embarrassment. "Not entirely true. You have Clanross's interest."

"But I'm his *private* secretary. Barney Greene deals with political matters."

"That's true now, but in a year or so things will be different. Mr. Greene talks of retiring to his manor, and I daresay there will be a by-election, and . . ."

Johnny was smiling at her. "You have it all planned out."

"I'm s-sorry, Johnny. It's just that I'm interested."

"That's kind in you, Lady Margaret."

She looked away, sure she had offended him. He had been calling her Maggie all morning.

Jean and Owen had crossed the length of the bridge and were now coming back. They stopped again in mid-span and the poet flung out his arm in a gesture that embraced the grounds and the house, and all he surveyed, probably.

"I wonder what he is declaiming now?" Johnny murmured.

"He is writing an anthem for the ploughmen of England."

Johnny made a rude noise in his throat.

"It's very stirring." Maggie felt obliged to champion her sister's beloved. "So far. He has completed stanzo three."

"Good luck to him."

"Do you not like poetry?"

"I like it well enough. I used to write it. I was up at Oxford with a chap who wrote wild inflammatory verse. He and Owen egged one another on. Then old Shelley was sent down for writing an atheistical pamphlet or some such nonsense."

"Why was it nonsense? Was it badly written?"

After a pause, Johnny said, "I daresay I'm envious. It's been years since I felt so strongly in a cause."

Maggie cocked her head at him. "You speak as if you were as old as Barney Greene."

He didn't smile. "Sometimes I think I am."

"When did you feel that way?"

"I beg your pardon?"

"As Owen feels and your atheistical friend."

He jabbed at the gravel. "When I was sixteen I was wild to defeat Napoleon. Preferably in single combat."

"You went out to the Peninsula, did you not? That must have been an adventure."

He gave a snort. "Oh, yes, a grand adventure. My father thought I was too young, but I pleaded and threatened to enlist in a line regiment, so he bought me a pair of colours. I thought I'd be a colonel in no time, all medals and side-whiskers."

Maggie smiled.

He looked at her and his mouth twitched. "I *was* a cawker. I went to the Peninsula before my seventeenth birthday. I spent the entire voyage seasick at the rail of the ship. I should have read that as an omen."

"Clanross claims he is always seasick."

"Not on land," Johnny rejoined. "I fell ill the day we disembarked, and I stayed ill off and on the entire six months I was with the regiment. I was no use to anyone."

"You couldn't help that," Maggie said reasonably. "I daresay you tried to do your duty."

"Oh, yes, I tried." He gave a sigh. "In the end—after Vittoria—my colonel told me to take myself home. I never so much as drew my sword on duty."

"You were in my brother's company, were you not?"

"Yes, and he was all that was kind, but there's no room on campaign for malingering seventeen-year-old ensigns."

"Malingering!"

He grimaced. "I felt like a Belem Ranger. That's what the troops called men who were always reporting in sick. The main hospital was in Belem. So I sailed for home with my tail between my legs like a whipped cur. And sold out, and went to university as I ought to have done in the first place. My father was right. He usually is."

"I think you had to try," Maggie ventured.

"Perhaps." He stood up. "I believe Davies has finally run

out of strophes. Shall we rejoin your sister?" He pointed with his stick. Jean gave a wave from the near end of the bridge. Her cheeks were bright from the brisk wind.

Maggie rose. The ornamental bench was rather clammy. "You had to try," she repeated, stubborn in Johnny's defence. She brushed at the damp spot on her pelisse.

He glanced at her, frowning a little. "Yes. And I'm not sorry I did, but I've lost my enthusiasm for causes. And that would make me a doubtful asset in Parliament."

"Not if you did your duty. My sister Anne's husband is a member of Parliament. He works very hard. Anne says he does a great deal of good, and *he* doesn't write revolutionary verse."

Johnny laughed. "That's encouraging. Your sister is a famous political hostess, is she not? Clanross once took me to her salon."

"Anne loves politicks. Elizabeth calls her the Muse of the Radicals."

He was still smiling. "Should you like to be a famous hostess, Maggie?"

Maggie felt her cheeks go hot. "Jean would do much better than I . . ."

"Now what is this? I daresay you would do splendidly. You oughtn't to defer to Lady Jean in everything, you know."

"If that isn't a case of the pot calling the kettle black! You've spent the past half hour telling me how you can't do things. You *can* take up politicks. You *can* stand for Parliament," Maggie cried, vexed. "You can do anything you put your mind to. After all, you taught *me* to dance!"

Johnny laughed aloud. "And if I can do that I can do anything?"

Maggie knew her face was as red as her hair. "*I* think so."

He shifted the stick to his left hand. "Let us make a pact, Lady Margaret. If you won't always be telling me how much braver and cleverer your sister is, I shan't say my political hopes are a lost cause." He held out his gloved hand.

"Done." They shook hands solemnly.

"What are you doing? Laying a bet?" Jean had come within hailing distance. "Wait till you hear what Owen has writ!"

"Have you finished your anthem, Owen?" Maggie retied her mourning ribbands. "Do say it for us."

The poet's green eyes flashed. "So Dyott may compare me unfavourably to Byron? No, I thank you. I like an appreciative audience."

Johnny's lip curled. "Do you mean a captive audience?"

"By God . . ."

Johnny raised an eyebrow.

The poet turned away grumbling under his breath. Jean glowered. Maggie knew they would all hear the poem after dinner.

In the interests of peace, she intervened. "Isn't that rain I feel on my face? Let's go in." An obliging gust spattered them with raindrops. She led the way thankfully.

=9=

"PAPA!" EMILY HOPED her dismay was not writ on her face.

"Answering your own door again, eh? Very bad Ton, Emma."

"I'm sorry, Papa. I was in the hall."

Sir Henry Mayne removed his round hat, shook the rain from it, and gave Emily a hearty kiss on the cheek. "Well, slyboots, where's the heir?"

Emily took his hat, gloves, and sopping greatcoat and handed them to Phillida who had lurched into the foyer with her usual grace. "The heir?" Emily echoed, stalling for time. "If you mean Matthew he is at his school."

"Matthew? What the devil has young Matt to do with anything?" Sir Henry rubbed his hands. "I mean your husband, my gel, and well you know it."

"Richard is at work on his history. Pray come up to the withdrawing room, Papa. You must be starved with cold."

"Not at all. Spring in the air."

"But your horses . . ."

"Left the carriage at the Mitre. Took a room there."

"You might have had the guest chamber here. Mr. Dyott has gone up to Town and we've room to spare."

Sir Henry rocked back on his sturdy bootheels. "Nonsense. In this poky house?" It had not suited him to see his daughter reduced to living in a town, and he made no bones about despising the house. "Doesn't Richard write in that chamber?"

"Well, yes, but . . ."

"No need to put him to the trouble of moving his gear. I'll be snug enough at the Mitre."

Emily grasped the newell. "I shan't insist that you sleep here, but you *will* take dinner."

Sir Henry followed her. "Certainly. Mean to have a strait talk with your husband."

"Phillida, refreshment for Sir Henry, if you please."

The maid curtseyed from the foot of the stair. She was goggle-eyed with curiosity.

Like Papa, Emily thought sourly. She led her father up to the salon, in which a fire of seacoal burned. That was a luxury she did not usually permit herself in daytime, but she had been mending linens and could not sew at her usual rate with cold-stiffened fingers. Her work candles flickered as she and her father entered the room.

Sir Henry looked round with a contemptuous snort but seated himself without comment. When she had seen him comfortable over a glass of sherry, she said, "I'll fetch Richard. He writ you Saturday, did he not?"

"Yes, yes. Came as soon as I might. Sick cow." Sir Henry was noted for his stock-breeding experiments.

"I trust all is well now?"

"Yes. Your aunt sends her best. Laid up with the lumbago. Meant to come, but I told her she was better off in bed."

"My word, yes."

"You're looking a trifle hagged, my dear. Too much excitement?"

"Papa!"

"How are the brats?"

"Very well," Emily muttered. "Sally's cutting a tooth."

Sir Henry took a satisfied sip of sherry. "Forward for her age, ain't she."

"Fractious for her age. Peggy and I were up half the night. I'll tell Richard you've come." Emily fled. There was no point in asking her father to be tactful. Tact was a concept foreign to Sir Henry's character.

When she entered Richard's improvised study, he looked up, scowling. "Don't tell me. Amy has broken out in hives and Mrs. Harry has run off with the verger. At this rate Marlborough will never retire from the field."

"I beg your pardon, my dear. My father is come."

He grimaced and set his pen on the standish. "I thought I heard the knocker. Sufficient unto the day is the evil thereof." Catching her eye he said ruefully, "It's not your fault, Emily. He was bound to bestir himself if only to give me the benefit of his counsel."

"I hope he hasn't taken another chill." Sir Henry had suffered a frightening bout of pleurisy in December.

Richard shoved the chair back and twitched his cravat, which was rumpled. There was ink on his cuff again. "I'll lay odds he's been overseeing the calving, chill or no chill."

Emily sighed. "True. He is stopping at the Mitre."

He frowned. "He knows he's welcome to stay here."

"My dear, don't strain at a gnat. Do you *want* Papa walking the floor with Sally—and jibing at McGrath and roaring at Phillida? Come, let us get it over with." She slipped back into the hall and Richard followed. A muffled wail from the direction of the nursery told her that Sally's tooth had not broken through. The baby would be wanting to nurse soon.

Sir Henry rose when they entered and uttered several platitudes designed to satisfy the proprieties. He had never met the Duchess of Newsham but he was her contemporary and had known of her scandalous life even before Richard swam into his ken. "Ramshackle" was one of his kindlier judgements of the duchess's manner of living.

Richard responded to Sir Henry's condolences with cool civility. When he had seen Emily seated, he poured himself a glass of sherry left-handed and took up a defensive post before the fire. He inquired after Sir Henry's prize milch cows and was rewarded with a moving account of Bossy's maternal sufferings. Richard's interest in milch cows was minimal and Sir Henry knew it. He was a man who faced facts. With uncommon good sense, he drew his sad tale to a close.

"Well, my boy," he said at last, "I was obliged to you for your letter."

Richard inclined his head.

"It's an ill wind that blows nobody good. Have you filed for probate?"

"I asked the duchess's solicitor to do so."

Sir Henry pursed his lips. "Reliable man?"

"He appears to be. I have asked him to continue to manage the business of the estate."

"Is that prudent? No wish to offend you, Richard, but your experience of these matters ain't wide."

"That is precisely why I asked Chalmers to continue."

"Chalmers, eh? Chalmers, Rutland, and Morris." Sir Henry nodded. "What bank?"

"Coutts."

"Yes, yes, that should hold you. At least until the will is proven. Can't be too careful, you know."

Richard took a swallow of the sherry. "I asked Tom Conway to give me a letter to his man."

Sir Henry's eyes brightened. "Aye, that's the ticket. Clanross's affairs have always been well regulated."

"Not when he was an ensign."

Sir Henry scowled at this unbecoming sign of levity. "I meant the Conway estate." Money matters were *serious* matters.

Richard watched him, eyes wary.

Emily had also been watching her father. Now she reached for a damask tablecloth that wanted darning and took up her needle. At least Richard was not in one of his wild satirical moods. Perhaps he *wanted* her father's advice. As she listened to Sir Henry prying the details of the duchess's legacy from her husband, she considered the possibility.

In ordinary circumstances, Richard was a self-possessed man, no more inclined to ask for advice than for help. But her father was right. Richard had no experience of wealth. To the contrary. That was Emily's chief resentment against the duchess. If her grace had intended to turn her son into a nabob all along, at least she might have given him advance warning of his coming transformation.

It did not surprise Emily that Richard had discussed his legacy with Clanross. They were old friends, after all, and used to propping one another up. But Tom's relationship with Richard was not fatherly, could not be. And if Sir Henry could stand in that role so much the better.

". . . all very irregular," Sir Henry was saying, "but welcome news nonetheless. What do you mean to do now, my boy?"

Emily's ears pricked.

"Finish the third volume of my blasted history," Richard said coolly. "I have an obligation to Murray."

After a dangerous moment, Sir Henry chose to be amused. He laughed heartily, finished his sherry at a gulp, and took the refill Richard offered. "Well, well, in future you may scribble away to your heart's content. No harm in that."

"Papa!" Emily jabbed her finger with the needle, sucked at the wound, and glowered. "Richard does not 'scribble.' He has published one novel, seen his Spanish satires reprinted, and completed two volumes of the history since Waterloo . . ."

"Left-handed, too," Richard interjected with a wry grin. "Let be, Emily. The point is, sir, the will cannot be proved in less than a year and meanwhile life must go on."

Emily subsided, still seething. As far as Sir Henry was concerned, writing was no profession for a gentleman. Neither, of course, were the church, the law, the army, the navy, politicks, or the foreign ministry. Gentleman and farmer were synonymous terms in her father's lexicon.

"You will be looking about for an estate. A landed estate," Sir Henry said predictably.

"Shall I?" Richard's eyebrows took on the satirical twist. He sipped his sherry.

Sir Henry sat up straight. "You cannot mean to confine Emily to a town when there's no longer any need to do so."

"I had in mind one of the more fashionable spas." Richard, Emily perceived, was beginning to enjoy himself. "Cheltenham" he murmured, a devilish glint in his hazel eyes. "Bath. Brighton. I believe my mother acquired some very handsome properties."

Sir Henry gave an impatient wave of his free hand. "I daresay. But your permanent residence . . ."

"Scarborough," Richard murmured. "Harrowgate."

"My daughter," said Sir Henry sternly, "will be properly established in a house of her own or I shall know why."

Emily set the tablecloth aside as a lost cause.

Her movement caught her father's eye. "We've not heard your opinion, Emily."

"I was content to live at Wellfield, and I am content to live here."

Richard's eyebrows rose.

Their eyes locked and Emily flushed. At least I *tried* to content myself, she thought mutinously. "I'd like a larger house." In firmer tones, she added, "But where he chooses to live is Richard's business, Papa, and I shall go with him. I daresay Bath would be very agreeable." Bath sounded appalling, but she did not mean to give her father the satisfaction of knowing she concurred in his opinion.

"Of course," Richard murmured, "there is always London."

Emily and Sir Henry stared at him, aghast.

He smiled. "Early days to be making plans, Sir Henry."

Emily's father cleared his throat. "True. I'll look about me for suitable estates, however, if you've no objection."

"None." Richard set his glass on the tray.

"Meanwhile," Sir Henry persisted, "I think you and Emma should come to me. Children miss their ponies. Frances wants company."

Richard straightened and rubbed his right arm, frowning into the air.

"Oh, Papa, you know we cannot live under the same roof. I beg your pardon but you must see it is impossible."

"No, I don't see it. You're cramped and crowded, you miss your old neighbours," he cleared his throat again, "and I miss the lot of you. I kicked up a dust when Richard insisted on moving you to Winchester, and I daresay I said a few provoking words. You were right to assert your independence, my boy, and I knew it, but there's no need to be stiff-rumped about it now. Bring your family to Mayne Hall until you've made up your mind."

Emily was moved. Her father rarely admitted a fault. He had said more than a few provoking words, he had said a few *unforgivable* words, but she did miss the old neighbourhood and she did miss her kin, including her father.

At last Richard said slowly, "I can't impose on your good nature indefinitely, Sir Henry, but I shall have to spend considerable time in Town over the next few months. I dislike leaving Emily alone."

"I'm not alone," Emily protested. "God knows."

Richard regarded her, unsmiling. "If you have no fixed objection, Emily, I'd feel easier in my mind knowing you were all at Mayne Hall. Newsham . . ."

Emily drew a sharp breath. "Yes, I see. Very well, my dear, since Papa is so kind as to offer."

Sir Henry beamed. Clearly he had not expected to win his way, and he entered at once into enthusiastic plans for his daughter's removal to her ancestral home, ignoring the reference to Richard's half brother. Emily could not ignore it, however. Newsham's malice was real and had once posed a danger to the children, not to mention Richard himself. If Richard expected trouble . . .

"Men of Britain, loose the plough.
"Lay the Norman tyrant low!"

Owen Davies's clarion tones broke and he finished the verse in a half whisper, "Liberty in every blow!"

Jean raised clasped hands to her mouth. "Oh . . . oh, Owen, how splendid!"

He ran ink-stained fingers through his tousled hair. "I'm not entirely satisfied with the rhyme. Do you think the last line is strong enough?"

"Yes, yes, I do. It's perfect." It occurred to Jean to wonder if one could reasonably refer to Prinny as Norman. He was descended from the Electress Sophia of Hanover, after all, and wasn't she a German? But that was a minor point. "Norman tyrant" was probably some sort of trope.

Owen laid the sheaf of manuscript aside and rose. He began pacing before the book room fire. "If only I were in London. How I envy you, Lady Jean."

Jean and Maggie were to travel to London a good fortnight before they had thought they would, for the king meant to hold a levee in May and Elizabeth had decided they might as well make their come-out after all. That meant choosing and fitting their court dresses and selecting the gowns and fripperies Jean had been anticipating for at least two years. Now that the moment was come she had lost her enthusiasm for shallow feminine pleasures. She burned to aid Owen's cause.

"It is not safe for you to go," she murmured.

"No." Dejection overcame him and he flung himself onto a straight-backed chair. "What is the use of writing verses no one will ever read?"

She ached for him. "I thought your friend Carrington . . ."

"Oh, Carrington would see them printed up. But how am I to get the manuscript to London? I cannot entrust it to the mail."

Jean's heart began to thump. "*I'll* take the manuscript to your friend. I should have thought of it sooner."

"I cannot allow it, Lady Jean. The danger is too great." But Owen looked hopeful. The green eyes lit.

"Who would suspect an earl's daughter of smuggling Radical poetry into London?"

He seemed struck with the truth of her observation. "Who indeed?"

She jumped to her feet. "I *shall* do it. What is your friend's direction?"

"In Greek Street. It is near Soho Square, I believe."

"Hist!" Jean interrupted, nodding at the door. Johnny Dyott had just entered, leaning on his cane.

"What are you two up to?" he drawled. "More conspiracies?"

"We are working on the catalogue," Jean said with dignity. Why must Johnny always be lurking? Maggie was confined to her bed with a cold, and Jean had thought to have time alone with Owen at last.

"Splendid." Johnny laid a sheaf of papers on the longer refectory table and pulled the standish to him. "About time."

Owen said dangerously, "Do you accuse me of dereliction . . ."

"Nothing of the sort." Johnny mended his pen. "Happy to see you both so industrious." He bent to his correspondence.

Owen glowered.

"Here's the missing edition of Catullus," Jean said brightly. "I knew it would turn up." And in a low voice, "We shall speak of this later, Owen."

He nodded and took the slim, leather-bound book from her. His eyes spoke volumes.

The election had not gone well. That much was clear from Clanross's letters. The Liverpool ministry with its repressions and its hired informers would remain in power.

Clanross meant to escort them to London, and Maggie thought Elizabeth was cheered by the fact. Elizabeth wanted cheering, for the weather was obstinately overcast. Though she felt some guilt that her debut in society should rob Elizabeth of time with the new telescope, Maggie had begun to feel considerable excitement.

Her sniffles confined her to her room for only a few days. Then she was back in the book room, cheerfully retrieving dusty volumes for the catalogue or helping Johnny assort his work. She liked to be useful and she knew that she had eased the tension between Johnny and Owen on more than one occasion.

Johnny and Owen did not agree. At first Maggie believed that Johnny was jealous of the poet's ascendancy with her twin, but the longer she listened to the two of them brangling, the more convinced she was that their differences were philosophical, too.

Jean was so deeply in love that the poet's sentiments seemed right to her, but Maggie could not help seeing some inconsistency in his calls for revolution and his simultaneous dependence on the patronage of a nobleman. She wondered if Clanross had ever read Owen's verse. Perhaps he had.

Her brother-in-law was firmly opposed to the strictures on freedom of the press the government had enacted in the wake of Peterloo. The earl was an even-tempered man but he had looked quite fierce when he condemned suspension of habeas corpus, and he disliked the sedition laws even more. The political events of the past months were all very interesting to Maggie—like watching a history lesson come to life—and since Johnny had confided in her his political ambitions her interest had grown. Dreamily she wondered what her life would be like if she married a member of Parliament. She resolved to ask her sister Anne.

Clanross favoured reform of Parliament. That placed him among the Radicals, but he had never spoken in favour of violent action—by advocates of change *or* by the government. That Johnny agreed with Clanross's views was confirmation enough for Maggie. She did not like the thought of bloodletting, though many of Owen's causes did cry out for remedy. So, though she sympathised with Owen and her twin, her convictions placed her in the moderate camp, Johnny's camp, where her feelings also led her.

But most of the time Maggie eschewed politicks in favour of *La Belle Assemblée* whose fascinating gowns and delectable bonnets stirred her imagination. Elizabeth meant to open the town house and give a ball, unless Anne thought such an entertainment would seem disrespectful. But by May, by the twins' eighteenth birthday, the three months of deep mourning for George III would be over. Unless rioting broke out in London as it had in Glasgow, Anne would probably give her consent.

= 10 =

"WILL THEY HANG Thistlewood?"

Tom nodded. "The other poor devils, too, I daresay." The trial of the Cato Street conspirators was now in its fourth day. Tom swirled his brandy. "I wonder whether they'd have planned so extreme a course if the spy, what's his name . . ."

"Edwards." Richard Falk leaned back in the wing-backed chair, eyes half-lidded.

"Would they have planned a mass assassination if Edwards hadn't been with them from the first, egging them on? Disclosure of the plot was timely for the government. Gave 'em an excuse to crack down on journalists and stir up the voters just before the election."

"Aren't you over suspicious, Tom?"

"I don't think so," Tom said soberly. "That Cabinet dinner at Harrowby's house, the one at which the conspirators planned to assassinate the ministers, never existed."

Richard stared.

"It was a sham. Sidmouth was feeding the plotters false information for months, before the attempt was scheduled."

"I thought *I* had a Byzantine imagination," Richard murmured. "Cheer up, Tom. There'll be other elections."

Tom tossed off the last of the brandy. "No doubt, unless the ministers in their wisdom decide to suspend the whole government."

"I've never voted," Richard offered.

"You could have."

"True, but I didn't know the men or the issues."

Tom meditated. Richard's want of interest in the electoral process was common enough among army men, unless they had family connexions in office. After a moment Tom said, apropos of issues, "I don't like this business of Queen Caroline."

Richard grinned. "*I* think it's damned amusing."

A reluctant smile touched Tom's mouth. I consort too much with politicians, he thought. "The devil of it is, no one believes the queen is innocent, but the Whigs have decided to champion her cause. That diverts energy from more important matters."

Richard cocked his head. "Besides, the king is notorious for his *affaires de coeur* and has been these thirty years. 'A little touch of Hypocrisy in the night . . .' "

"Go to it." Tom rose and walked to the Adam fireplace. "Write up your satire," he shot over his shoulder, "print it, circulate it, and I'll call on you from time to time at Newgate." He kicked at the coals, not a wise action in patent pumps.

They had dined à deux and were now recovering from the chef's excesses over a decanter of brandy. Richard had been in Town several days, but Tom had only just bumped into him that morning in the street.

"Where are you staying this time—not Chelsea?"

"No. it's too far from Albermarle Street."

"Albermarle Street? Oh—Murray. You're still working on the history, I take it."

Richard set his brandy down on the occasional table. "I do not make a habit of breaking contracts," he said through his teeth. "And I *agreed* to deliver three volumes to Murray."

Tom stopped in mid-stride, surprised by the heat in his friend's voice. "I just asked."

Richard leaned back. "Sorry. Everyone seems to think I should forget about my writing . . ."

"That be damned, but I thought you wanted to give up the history. 'Tripe,' " he quoted. " 'Hackwork . . .' "

Richard flushed. "That was mostly croaking. It's dreadful stuff, to be sure—two shillings the yard—but Murray wants the book and I agreed to supply it. I don't like unfinished business."

"I see." Tom resumed his seat and eyed his friend thoughtfully. "I wish you will finish it soon."

"So do I," Richard shot back. "It's plodding work, every syllable."

"Well, plod faster. Now that you're as rich as Golden Ball."

"I am not as rich as Golden Ball and never will be," Richard rejoined, "and if I wind up in chancery I'll be as bankrupt as old Sheridan."

Tom turned that unpleasant possibility over in his mind. "Besides, after I finish the history, I must settle a few small domestic concerns," Richard went on.

Tom frowned. "Such as?"

"Such as where to set up my household." He explained Emily's remove to Mayne Hall. "It's a temporary expedient. Sir Henry and Emily go on more comfortably at a distance."

"He must be a terror."

"I like Sir Henry," Richard said unexpectedly. "Beneath the rugged exterior beats a heart of pure marzipan. He dotes on his grandchildren, and would happily take the burden of domestic decision from Emily's shoulders. Unfortunately, Emily thrives on decision making, domestic and otherwise. Therein lies the rub."

"Emily *looks* like marzipan," Tom offered. He was fond of Richard's second wife.

"An illusion. Emily could have run the regiment with a hand tied behind her back," said her doting spouse. "She managed young Matt's estate for years . . ."

Tom reached into his memory. "And increased the revenues."

"She has a head for figures and a way with Matt's tenants. Do you think I ought to purchase an estate?"

"For Emily?"

"God knows, not for me. I add on my fingers and I can't tell oats, peas, and beans from barley."

Tom poured more brandy. "Don't you object to rural living?"

"Not if Emily's there," Richard said simply. "The thing is, my mother's properties are urban—or sub-urban. I rode out today to St. John's Wood to see a villa she owned. The house is large enough, the air's clean, and the prospect is pleasant, but there's no land attached. It won't do."

"So you mean to sell off some of the houses and buy land?"

"When . . . if . . . the will is proved."

Tom brooded over his brandy.

After a pause, Richard said, "I have been trying to reach a settlement with Newsham and the other heirs, to avert a suit in chancery."

Tom sat up. "I hope you're not going to give the legacy up to that lot. They don't deserve it of you, Richard."

" 'Deserve'?" Richard's mouth twisted on the word as if he had tasted lemon. "It's not a question of deserving. If it comes to that, I don't deserve that much wealth either. No one does." He added, defensively, "You needn't look at me like that. I've turned the matter over to the lawyers. They'll drive a stiff bargain—it's in their interest to do so. I'm not a complete fool, Tom."

"No more than half." Tom was sure the wealth Richard had inherited was still a vague hypothetical figure in his friend's mind. Giving away imaginary sums was probably no more painful to Richard than discarding a botched chapter in a novel. The question was why he was ready to accommodate his half brothers and sisters. The Ffouke family, Newsham and Lord George in particular, had treated Richard abominably. The thought of Newsham profiting from Richard's scruples made Tom's blood boil.

"If you're bent on throwing the duchess's estate to the winds, give it to the Eddystone lifeboat," he burst out. "Or to our Canadian scheme. Your loving brothers and sisters won't starve."

Richard smiled. "Lord John is under the hatches, or so I've heard. Let be, Tom. Do you expect Lady Clanross and her sisters soon?"

"Next week," Tom growled. He would have pursued the matter of his friend's quixotic generosity, but Richard had given him a clear signal to sheer off and Tom was too old a Falk hand to press farther. He's more accommodating to old enemies than old friends, Tom reflected, but without resentment. The dowager's will was, after all, Richard's business. "Elizabeth and Johnny will escort the twins to Town next Wednesday. Heyday for the mantua makers."

"Does Lady Clanross mean to present the girls in May?"

Tom described Elizabeth's plans briefly, but he knew Richard's interest in the fashionable world was at best tepid, so he turned—or returned—the conversation to his earlier question.

It transpired that Richard was staying at an inn in Holborn convenient to the City and his publisher.

"You ought to come here," Tom said.

Richard laughed. "You've a large contingent arriving from Brecon. I appreciate the offer, however."

"But an inn cannot be an ideal place for writing."

"There *is* no ideal place for writing."

"Grosvenor Square is quieter than High Holborn," Tom shot back. "I'm not short of room." He cleared his throat. "And I'd like you to know Elizabeth."

Richard was frowning at him. "I've met Lady Clanross . . ."

"For ten minutes before the christening." That rankled. Richard had stopped at Brecon precisely one night to discharge his godfatherly duties, and Elizabeth had been too weak still for social intercourse. "Come, or Elizabeth will be thinking you've taken her in dislike."

After an uncomfortable pause Richard agreed. Tom wondered if the invitation had been wise, but he had come upon a brilliant idea as Richard spoke of buying an estate, and the brilliance of the idea was beside the point if Elizabeth and Richard disliked each other. No time like the present to test the waters.

As it happened, Elizabeth's mind was on her sons. She had never been separated from them, and she had felt a jolt of something surprisingly like grief as she parted from them. They were well attended, of course, and enjoyed vigourous good health. They had even taken their inoculation with the cowpox in stride. It was foolish in the extreme to feel the separation so acutely.

Perhaps if Elizabeth had liked town life, thrived on it as her stepmother had, as her sister Anne did, the prospect of some weeks in society would have turned her mind sooner from the loss of her sons' company. As it was, she missed her boys and her new telescope, in that order.

When Elizabeth and entourage finally arrived in Grosvenor Square on a rainy April afternoon, she was not best pleased to discover that Clanross had installed his old army friend in the green guest chamber. Indeed she and Tom almost came to cuffs.

"I meant that room for Johnny Dyott."

Tom said callously, "Johnny may sleep in the attics. He's a young sprout after all."

"You sound like his grandfather."

"When it comes to uncomfortable billets I *am* his grandfather. Richard needs room for thought."

Elizabeth had been lying on the chaise in her dressing room, reading an article on dark nebulae and recruiting her energies for a dinner at her sister Anne's. She sat up, laying the journal aside. "Will Colonel Falk stay through the season?"

Tom's eyes narrowed. "Do you object to welcoming my friend?"

"Not at all. I'm glad to see Colonel Falk. But I thought he lived in Hampshire."

"He's finished his history and the publisher apparently awaits each day's output with bated breath. I thought Richard might find it quieter here than in Holborn." He leaned on the mantle.

"Quieter? With Jean and Maggie in residence?"

Tom's mouth eased in a grin. "Are they aflame with social scheming?"

"I'm not sure," Elizabeth said gloomily. "Maggie is, Jean isn't."

"I thought the plan to storm London was Jean's idea."

"It was. That's what has me worried. When I suggested we visit Mme. Thérèse tomorrow to select designs for the presentation gowns, Jean turned downright snappish."

"Something's amiss," Tom agreed. "Perhaps she's off her feed."

"It's not that."

"Never mind, my dear. She'll come about." Tom drifted to her dressing table, picked up a silver-backed hairbrush and set it down. "I mean Richard to stop here as long as he likes. He has legal business to finish as well as the manuscript." He gave her the terse outline of Richard's inheritance and the problematical consequences.

Elizabeth digested the revelation. "I have every desire to accommodate your friends, Tom, but I'm no good with strangers and Colonel Falk is a stranger to me, for all that he's Dickon's godfather."

Tom moved to her side. "True, but . . ."

"I shall have to make small talk," she explained. "When I don't know a man I like to have a fund of polite phrases at the ready, and the leisure to brood about his interests beforehand. Otherwise I'm lost. I can think of nothing to say."

Tom smoothed his hands over her shoulders. "I had never supposed you shy with strangers."

"I am. Dreadfully. I have read the first of Colonel Falk's Spanish satires, however."

"And . . ."

Elizabeth smiled. "I thought it witty and good-hearted, if a trifle *warm*. I should like to congratulate your friend. But the question is, do I wish to face a satirist at breakfast?"

Tom laughed. "Richard won't eat you, my dear."

"You relieve my mind. Now, tell me, was I wise to drag the girls south when there's so much unrest? The Mob were rather thick in Great Portland Street, I thought."

"Were there incidents?"

Elizabeth looked up at him. "I kept the shades drawn. When the crowd saw your arms on the carriage doors they gave three cheers for Radical Tom."

Tom grimaced. "That should enhance my stature with the Lords." He went to the window that overlooked the square. It had gone dark. He pulled the curtain to and turned back to her, tassle in one long hand. "To answer you, I don't know what a wise course would be. The queen's business will keep the Mob stirred up all summer. Unless you can talk Jean and Maggie into making their come-out next year, you might as well present them in May. The June levee will be a crush, too, and may provoke worse demonstrations. We'll have to be careful of the girls."

Elizabeth frowned. "Keep a close watch on them, do you mean?"

He stared. "See that they're protected and amused. Do you anticipate more serious problems?"

Elizabeth rubbed her brow. "I have the oddest sensation that Jean and Davies have been plotting, but Johnny says they've not had time alone together. Johnny did me sterling service *en chaperon*, by the bye, though it went against the grain."

"So I should imagine, poor chap. At least he may relax his guard now Jean and Davies are apart."

Elizabeth murmured agreement, and Tom went into his adjoining dressing room. As she dressed, Elizabeth was still troubled by the uneasiness that had beset her since Davies had come to Brecon. It was too vague a feeling to put into words.

She was sure Jean and Owen would do nothing *wrong*, but either or both might well scheme to do something harebrained.

Jean found the map of London in the book room. It was a framed architect's plan and probably twenty years out of date, but at least it gave her an idea of the relative distance between Grosvenor Square and Greek Street.

Conveying Owen's precious manuscript to his friend had seemed the simplest thing in the world in the familiar safety of Brecon. Jean had forgotten how noisy and confusing London was.

She meant to hire a hack. That was the easiest plan, but even that would be difficult, for she was never left alone.

Until Owen swore her to secrecy, she had meant to tell Maggie of her mission. That troubled her, too—she could see that Maggie knew something was up and that her twin was hurt by her lack of openness. Jean hated hurting Maggie, though she could see Owen's logic. The more people who knew of the scheme the more likely it was to be betrayed, if only by accident.

So Jean made her plans alone and with an uneasy conscience. Her ignorance of simple things worried her. Hackneys were not numerous in Grosvenor Square where the householders kept their own carriages, but she noticed that they were thicker on the ground a few streets over. She meant to walk to Bond Street and hail a driver there. That would surely throw any lurking informers or Runners off the trail.

How much ought she to pay the jarvey? She did not know. And what if Owen's friend should be out when she called? She could not write him to warn she was coming because Owen had said his friend was closely watched. Was the address Owen had given her a private dwelling? What ought she to wear?

The last was not a frivolous question. She knew she must hide her flaming hair. Indeed, she would have tried to procure a wig if she had had any hope of doing so without being trapped in explanations. Elizabeth would have thought her a candidate for bedlam if she had tried any such thing.

Lying abed the first night, brooding, with Maggie asleep beside her, Jean decided to tuck her hair into her old grey bonnet and "borrow" an enveloping cloak from one of the servants. Not an ideal disguise, especially if the weather were warm. On the whole, though, she thought the simplicity of the disguise would work in her favour. That and the unlikelihood of a very young lady going off into the heart of London on her own.

Days passed—days full of shopping for fabrics and being poked and stared at by dressmakers, of having to choose between virtually identical hats at the milliner's, of dragging through the Burlington Arcade in the wake of Anne, Elizabeth, an enthusiastic Maggie, and three laden servants, whilst her sisters twittered over gloves and ribbands and slippers. Jean's mind was above all that. If only she could dash out, hire a hackney, deliver the poem, and dash back without being missed. The impossibility of escaping detection weighed on her spirits like a millstone.

Of course, everyone noticed her preoccupation. The gloomier Jean felt, the more anxiously Elizabeth and Maggie hovered over her. Elizabeth was sure she was sickening for something and very nearly sent for Anne's favourite physician. Maggie thought she was missing Owen—true enough—and tried to divert her. Even Clanross took time from the nation's business to sweep Elizabeth and the twins off one evening to the theatre. Jean scarcely heard Mr. Kean.

It was after the theatre party that Maggie finally forced a confrontation.

Their new maid, Lisette, left them at last, carrying their gowns over her arm. Maggie was brushing her hair.

Jean watched her. "I think I'll go to bed."

"Not yet."

"Oh, Mag, I'm tired. We can talk in the morning."

The reflected Maggie's grey eyes locked on Jean's. "I am not going to sleep until you tell me what's wrong," the image in the glass said.

"Nothing's wrong."

The reflection's mouth set.

"Oh, Mag, I'd tell you if I could but I'm sworn to secrecy!"

Maggie turned so quickly her low-backed chair almost overbalanced. "It's Owen, isn't it?"

Jean nodded, miserable but mute.

"I think you might tell me," Maggie said after a pause. "I've never betrayed a secret yet. Besides . . ."

"Besides, you're my twin." Jean shivered. "I swore, Mag."

"Then I'll swear, too."

Jean shivered again. "Do you promise never to divulge what I've told? Ever?"

"I promise."

Jean thought of informers and spies. "Even on pain of imprisonment?"

Maggie blinked. She took a deep breath. "I promise."

Jean heaved a sigh and began to describe her mission. The words tumbled out. "And I haven't been able to get off by myself long enough to do the thing. It's dreadful. At least at Brecon we can go about the grounds without a maid in attendance."

"We shall have to bribe Lisette," Maggie said calmly.

Jean stared.

"Well, it stands to reason. She's the one who walks with us. Elizabeth said we might go to the park or that circulating library in Moulton Street whenever we liked—so long as Lisette went with us."

"You're right." Jean brooded. Her pin money was re-served for paying the hackney. "You'll have to pay Lisette, then. And what if she's not corruptible?" That sounded horrid. Lisette had been with them only a week, but Jean thought she was a good maid, if a trifle haughty.

"Perhaps we can fool her—give her the slip."

"I don't know." Jean felt exhausted suddenly, but she was relieved to have an accomplice in residence and grateful that the accomplice was Maggie. More than grateful. She blinked back unexpected tears. "Let's sleep on it. Perhaps things will look clearer in the morning."

Maggie jumped up. "Of course they will, sister." She gave Jean a hug. "And when we've done it, will you promise me something?"

Jean returned her twin's comforting squeeze. "Anything."

"Promise me you'll enjoy our come-out." Maggie picked up the candle and led the way to their bedchamber. "Because *I* mean to enjoy it, and I shan't if you don't."

"I promise."

As they snuggled into the cooling sheets, Jean made a mental vow to throw herself into the coming festivities—even being fitted for ball gowns—with every appearance of enjoyment. Maggie deserved no less.

== 11 ==

"MADAM WISHES TO be driven to Greek Street," Maggie said with an artful touch of Lincolnshire in her vowels. She was dressed in a severe grey gown and plain cape they had borrowed from the chambermaid, ostensibly for a masquerade. Maggie had tied a neat cap over her tightly braided hair. It scarcely showed red.

Jean wore her old pelisse and bonnet, also grey, with black gloves and a veil rigged from a black mantilla the same maid, their sworn ally when Lisette proved deaf to hints, had found in a trunk in the box room. Jean had tucked her hair up in the bonnet, which was rather hot. She was supposed to be a widow. She clutched Owen's manuscript in her black-gloved fist.

The driver's small dark eyes appraised both girls shrewdly. He wore a battered hat and a dusty cape with a wilted posy in the lapel. Jean did not like his manner. She was glad the veil spared her direct scrutiny.

" 'Ow's that? Greek Street?"

"Number 37," Maggie said very clearly. "It is down from Soho Square."

"I know where it is, missy. Wot I don't know is why two gentry morts wants to be drove there at this hour of the morning."

"My mistress has business to transact, my good man."

The jarvey leered. "Business, eh?"

Jean felt hot blood flood her face. "Not this one," she hissed in an undertone.

Maggie bit her lip.

The jarvey snickered.

"Never mind," Maggie said with a fair assumption of hauteur. "Madam prefers a cleaner carriage. You may drive on."

"Hoity-toity." The man twitched the reins. " 'Business,' she says." He drove on, snickering.

They were attracting attention. Perhaps Bond Street had not been a good idea. Loungers from one of the coffee-houses made raucous remarks as Jean and Maggie walked past. It was early, before ten, so the raised walkway was not yet thronged, but wagons and carts and gentlemen on horseback returning from their morning rides in Rotten Row kicked up a dust in the wide street. The comments of passersby made Jean blush beneath the veil. She wondered at Maggie's composure.

Just as Jean was about to suggest that they give it up, Maggie waved energetically and a smarter carriage drew up beside them. The elderly driver, fine as fivepence in a many-caped benjamin, beamed down at them.

"My mistress wishes to be conveyed to Greek Street, sir." Maggie sounded breathless. "Number 37, and she will pay twice your usual fare if we may have the carriage to ourselves."

"Done," the man said cheerfully. "Fine day for larking about, miss."

Maggie-the-maid helped Jean up into the vehicle. It was large, made to accommodate six or seven people, and, though the leather seats were cracked with age, the driver had laid fresh straw on the floor. The brass shone with polishing.

Jean made room for her sister and settled back. As the carriage creaked into motion her apprehension began to give way to excitement. "You were splendid," she whispered.

Maggie kept her face correctly somber. "Madam has only to command."

Jean stifled a giggle. A lark. It was going to be a lark, after all. Why had she not told Maggie of her mission sooner? Since she had, everything had fallen into place. The costumes, the timing (they were supposedly sleeping late after a long evening at one of Anne's musicales), even the mistress-servant roles they were playing, all had been Maggie's invention.

Jean was used to leading. How comfortable to let her practical twin deal with details. As the jarvey negotiated a corner and made his skillful way along Piccadilly, Jean considered how often in the past she had relied on Maggie to fill in the details of her own wild-eyed ideas. Maggie seldom initiated their adventures but she always came through.

They passed Hatchard's. The traffic was much heavier in Piccadilly than it had been in Bond Street, and less genteel. Pushcarts and laden waggons jostled hackneys and tilburies, an accommodation coach, dozens of carriages and gigs, and even a shiny perch phaeton driven by a gentleman whose tiger stared at them curiously. Ahead, to the east, the crowds afoot grew thicker. The din of vendors shouting their wares and drivers bellowing at each other took on a deeper menace as the carriage approached Mr. Nash's new circus, which was still under construction.

"Bloody Mob out for the queen," the drive volunteered in a half shout.

Jean nodded. They had encountered a similar demonstration near Great Portland Street as they had first entered London in Elizabeth's carriage. Jean kept her eyes on the empty seat facing her. She hoped Maggie was following suit. It wouldn't do to respond to the remarks that were directed at them. As they drove on they were hailed by half a dozen male voices. Some of the comments were rude, other incomprehensible.

The driver was silent now, his attention given to the tricky business of threading their way through the crowd that poured among the vehicles like a liquid. Jean shrank against the seat and felt Maggie shrink beside her. The noise pressed on her ears like the roar of the sea.

"I don't like this," she muttered.

"What? I can't hear you. Madam," Maggie added in a half shriek.

Jean shook her head. "Never mind."

Then, blessedly, the roar abated and they found themselves in a narrower, quieter street. There were few pedestrians and, indeed, no raised walkway. The jarvey picked up the pace. He was a skillful whip. Twice Jean thought they must tangle wheels with passing carts but he pulled them by with inches to spare.

"It cannot be a genteel neighbourhood." Maggie craned round. A heavily rouged woman in rumpled finery blinked at them from a doorway.

Jean swallowed. "No. But Owen told me that Lawrence—the painter, you know—lived in Greek Street once, and, er, other famous artists."

"What if Mr. Carrington is not at home?"

"Then I shall leave the poem with his servants."

"What if he has no servants?"

Jean had not thought of that unlikelihood. "There's bound to be someone."

"What a lot of soot there is on that church. It must be very old. Look how the rain has washed it clean in patches."

Jean looked. "It can't be very old. London burned, after all. Perhaps it's one of Wren's churches." Miss Bluestone, their governess, though not herself artistic, had tried to teach her charges the principles of architecture. London, Jean decided, was really very dirty, principles or no principles.

The way was narrower now, cramped with a traffic of pushcarts, waggons, and shrill street vendors. The hackney crept on. Maggie gawked. Jean kept her eyes straight ahead.

"Greek Street," the jarvey announced, breathless from negotiating a tricky corner. "Wot was the number, missy?"

"Thirty-seven," Maggie said firmly. It was not a long

street. According to the map in the book room, it terminated in Soho Square on the north and Compton Street on the south. Jean thought busy Crown Street must be only one street over. That would explain the racket. Although Greek Street was relatively deserted she could hear a great deal of noise—chanting and shouting as well as the ordinary hubbub of a busy thoroughfare at mid-morning.

" 'Ere you are, ladies." The jarvey drew up in front of a soot-stained house. It was tall and narrow and distinctly seedy. The paint peeled from dirty windowsills but someone had planted pinks in a first-floor window box. The pinks were reassuring.

"It's split into rooms and let out," the driver said as he helped them down. "Most of the 'ouses is these days."

Jean's heart sank. She had been thinking that Mr. Carrington was sole tenant. He was Owen's friend, probably young, probably unmarried. Of course he would let rooms.

She left Maggie to deal with the fare and climbed the steep front steps slowly. The paint was also peeling from the door. Resolute, Jean banged the knocker.

"He wouldn't wait! He said the Mob were out and he didn't want to risk it."

Jean swallowed.

Maggie's eyes were wide as saucers. She tucked her reticule beneath her cloak, which must have been as warm as Jean's pelisse, and climbed to the step below the landing Jean stood on. Indignation had left her a little breathless.

Both girls watched the jarvey drive off. Jean suppressed an urge to call him back, to plead with him. No one was going to answer the door. They would be stranded.

She knocked again, louder.

"He's not home," Maggie said flatly.

"Perhaps not, but somebody will be." As Jean raised the knocker again, the door opened. She let the grimy brass fall with a clatter.

"Who is it?" A middle-aged woman in a mobcap peered at them through the crack.

"I should like to speak to Mr. Carrington."

"Wot? Speak up. I don't 'ave all morning."

Jean repeated her request.

"And who may you be?" The door opened wider but the woman's stout figure blocked their entry.

"You may tell your master that I am a friend of Mr. Davies. I have a message for him."

"Tell my wot? Look 'ere, Miss 'igh-and-mighty, I'm the landlady, see. I ain't nobody's blooming servant."

Jean cleared her throat. "Then I beg your pardon, ma'am. May I speak to Mr. Carrington?"

" 'E ain't in. Off with 'is Radical friends kicking up a ruction whilst honest folks work." She jerked her head in the direction of the noise, which resolved into an incomprehensible slogan followed by loud cheering.

"Then I wish to leave this for him." Jean was still clutching the slim packet of foolscap in her gloved hands. With the sinking sensation that she was making a mistake, she thrust the manuscript at the woman, who was perhaps too startled to refuse it. Jean took off her gloves and fumbled in her reticule for a coin. She came up with a half crown. Far too much, but she wasn't about to haggle. "Here. This is yours if you promise faithfully to deliver that letter into Mr. Carrington's hands, and his alone."

The woman eyed the coin.

"If you please," Jean said desperately. "You should have something for your pains."

"Well . . ."

"Please, it's very important."

The woman took the coin in one red hand. "Well, miss, if you say it's important. I don't like it, mind, and if you'd asked to see 'is rooms, I wouldn't oblige, not for nothing. Young women calling on my gentlemen in their rooms is wot I will not 'ave. I run a respectable establishment . . ."

"I'm sure you do," Jean said hastily, "and I'm sure you'll let no one but Mr. Carrington see the message. Thank you very much."

"You're welcome, miss." She was closing the door.

"Wait!"

"Wot is it?"

"My si . . . er, maid and I will be needing a hackney. Where are we likely to find one?"

"The Square, or Compton Street, I dessay." The lines of suspicion eased about the woman's mouth. "See 'ere, love, that's a wild lot out in Crown Street now. You look lively or you'll find yourself in the suds. 'Ire a jarvey, quick-like, and tell him to take you 'ome through the back streets."

Jean swallowed hard. "Thank you. That's good advice."

"Well then, good morning to you."

"Good morning."

The door closed. There was a peephole. Jean could feel the woman's eyes staring at her. "Let's go."

Maggie nodded. They regained the pavement, which was uneven and unswept. "North?"

"No, Compton Street is closer." Jean had heard unpleasant references to Soho Square. She tucked her reticule into the pocket of her pelisse. It wouldn't do to lose it to a cutpurse. "How much do you have left?"

"A few shillings. We did pay twice the usual fare for two."

Jean tried to calculate her own reserves.

"Make way!" An impatient woman in a cap and apron jostled them.

"We're blocking the path," Jean muttered. Irresolute, she began to move down the slippery cobbles in the general direction of the river. The noise of the crowd swelled. Maggie stayed at her elbow.

"I wish the driver had waited for us."

"Yes."

"Shall we find another hackney with the Mob out?"

"I hope so."

"Should we not walk the other way?"

"What . . . back towards Piccadilly?"

"Ow!"

"What is it?"

"Someone pinched me!" Maggie stopped and glowered round.

"Keep moving!" Jean ordered, grim.

They had reached what must have been Compton Street. Suddenly the crowd was thicker, and, she saw with horror, composed chiefly of men, men in mechanics' or shopkeepers' dress among what seemed like hundreds of beggars, old soldiers, and, surely, cutpurses. The girls were being pulled along, as anonymous as leaves in a flowing gutter, in the direction of Crown Street.

Other than themselves, there were no women in the press of people, not even vendors. The women had sought safety. Strangely, though, Jean heard no rude allegations. It was as if she and Maggie no longer had any identity. They had become part of the crowd, the crowd had become one enormous man, and that man was mad.

As the men about her surged forward, Jean felt her feet slip. It was like being caught in an undertow. Desperate, she clutched at an arm and righted herself. The arm pulled away. She stumbled on. For a moment she thought she had lost Maggie.

"Take my hand," Maggie shrieked, behind her.

Jean reached back blindly and her wrist was gripped. She felt as if she had been saved from drowning. Her feet in their dainty kid slippers ached from being stepped on. The stench of sweating bodies made her head swim. She was being jostled—shoved, bumped, pushed—from every direction at once, though the Mob was flowing north now, up Crown Street toward St. Giles's. Only Maggie's fierce grip kept Jean upright.

"We must make for the shops!" she shouted but she did not think Maggie could hear her above the dreadful roar of the crowd. Glass shattered in the street and a cheer went up. They were shoved against a stalled cart, almost under the wheels. As the men surged forward again, Jean yanked her sister to the tail of the cart where there was a spot of stillness. They were trapped in the middle of the sea of shouting men.

Cowering against the tailboard and still clinging to Maggie's hand, Jean tried to collect her wits and take stock. Her "veil" was gone, ripped from her bonnet in the crush. Maggie's cap hung awry and a tendril of red hair clung to her smirched cheek. Jean's twin was wide-eyed, red-faced, and panting from exertion. There was no point in trying to speak above the thunder of the crowd.

Then, horribly, their sanctuary began to move. Jean clung to the tailboard. If only they could climb up on the cart. It moved very slightly. Maggie apparently had the same thought for she jerked her head upward as if to say, shall I give you a boost? Jean shook her head. If she knew one thing it was that she did not mean to loosen her grip on Maggie's hand.

The cart inched forward and they inched with it. All about them the crowd of men shoved and hallooed and shouted. Once a clerklike fellow in rusty black stumbled against them, but he regained his feet and lurched off, apparently without noticing their presence.

All at once the press began to thin. Jean could see no reason why.

"Isn't there a bookshop along here somewhere?" Maggie shrieked. They had been pulled north on Crown Street into a region of fusty bookstalls and secondhand shops.

"I think so. Let's run for it." Jean peered round the edge of the cart. It was moving faster now, its load of corn sacks jouncing, and she had to trot to keep close behind it. "You take the lead," Jean shouted. "The shop's over there." She could see the sign.

The street was by no means deserted. Stragglers, shopkeepers, and bystanders clogged the far footpath and adventurous wagoners had already begun to push north again as well, but at least the dreadful press of people had thinned. One could see daylight. One could hear.

Jean saw her sister take a deep breath. "Now!"

They ran, still linked hand in hand, for the shop and sanctuary. Maggie's skirts were wider than Jean's and she wore stouter shoes. She leapt and dodged and bounded like a deer.

They had almost gained the safety of the footpath when Jean saw that the Mob in its mindless seeking had turned round and was heading toward them. Maggie stopped, poised on her toes, staring, then she leapt forward in a last bid for the haven of the bookshop. Jean had pulled her skirts to her calves. She leapt, too, and would have succeeded if it had not been for her foolish slippers and the treacherous cobbles. She stumbled, cracking her right knee on the stones. Maggie yanked her up and began to run again. Stones were flying through the air.

Just as the girls reached the crammed footpath, a brickbat struck Maggie a glancing blow on the head and Jean's twin fell to the street.

"Help me pull her up!" Jean screamed.

No one on the walkway moved.

Another stone, this time a cobble, struck her own arm. Desperate, she tugged at Maggie's still form. "Help me!"

And suddenly someone did help. A stout woman in a rusty black bonnet knelt beside Jean and a clerk in shirtsleeves took Maggie's left arm. Dragging the limp form, the three of them gained the footpath and Jean sank to the pavement, cradling her sister's head in her arms.

"What the devil are you doing here?"

"What?" Dazed, Jean bent over her sister.

"Is she hurt?"

Jean choked on a sob. "I think she's dead."

A man bent over her and touched Maggie's wrist. It was the gentleman who had been staying at the house, Clanross's friend, the satirist. For a moment, such was her confusion, Jean could not remember his name.

"She's just fainted," he said.

"Thank God! Colonel Falk . . ." That was his name, wasn't it?

"I must find shelter for you at once."

"What?"

The crowd was roaring again.

Colonel Falk had disappeared.

= 12 =

JOHNNY HAD BEEN following Jean and Maggie from Grosvenor Square, but always at a maddening distance. From the moment Lisette, their maid, reported them missing, and the weeping chambermaid confessed her part in rigging them out for their masquerade, Johnny knew the twins were bent on devilment. And he knew it was all Owen Davies's fault.

Hot, cross, and sick with anxiety, he finally reached Crown Street afoot because the jarvey refused point-blank to enter the thoroughfare in the midst of a riot. Throughout the entire maddening chase, Johnny had alternated between fear and guilt, and a strong desire to throttle both girls, but especially Maggie. Maggie had been his confidante. She ought to have trusted him.

He reached the edge of the crowd in time to see the girls whirled off in the vortex.

Terrified for their safety, he limped along the footpath, shoving strangers out of his way as he went, trying to keep Maggie's bright head in sight. He saw them, as he thought, trampled underfoot and poised himself to leap into the swirling Mob, then caught sight of them again in their fragile zone of safety at the cart's tailboard.

Then he, too, was swept along the street, up with the surge of the crowd and back. When he spotted the cart once more, the girls had disappeared.

Spent, his leg aching from the abuse he had given it, he

leaned against the shuttered front of a shop, caught his breath, and tried to think. Where had they gone?

The cart was moving along slowly, still headed north. They had been farther down the street when he lost sight of them. He straightened, gritted his teeth, and began to limp back down the walkway, jostled by excited onlookers as he went. When he thought he had reached the spot where he was pulled into the crowd, he began asking. Had anyone seen two young women caught up in the Mob? He described their dress, Maggie's betraying hair, the passing cart. No one had seen them.

Just as he reached the point of despair, a stout motherly woman in a drab cape and rusty bonnet—probably a procuress, in that neighbourhood, he thought sourly—gave him positive word of the girls' escape. But Maggie, it seemed, had been hit on the head and taken up lifeless.

Johnny's heart lurched. "By whom? Where was she taken? For God's sake, madam . . ."

The woman, who had been retailing the details of Maggie's injury with gruesome relish, sobered and pointed to a bookshop. It was shuttered and looked deserted.

Johnny banged on the closed door with the stick he had miraculously clung to throughout his ordeal. No answer. He banged harder.

The door opened a crack, then flung wide. "Wonders never cease," said Colonel Falk. "Come in, Johnny. We're in the devil of a pucker here and you're just the man to pull us out of it."

Johnny slipped past the older man and squinted as his eyes adjusted to semidarkness. Maggie lay on the dusty floor with her head in Jean's lap, the pop-eyed proprietor was wringing his hands beside his till, and Colonel Falk, his back to the closed door, looked decidedly ruffled.

Johnny bent over the girls. "Is she all right? That woman outside said she'd been hit by a paving stone."

"Brickbat," Colonel Falk said tersely.

Maggie moaned.

Jean had removed her bonnet and her red hair stood up in sweaty tufts. Here eyes were red with weeping, her face curd-white under a mask of grime. "Oh, Johnny, we've sent for a surgeon. She has a knot on her head like an egg and she doesn't want to wake up. What shall we do?"

Colonel Falk drew up what appeared to be the only chair in the establishment. "Sit," he said rather as if Johnny were a good dog.

Johnny sat. The relief was so exquisite he closed his eyes for a moment.

"We'll wait for the sawbones," Falk said. "Then, if he says we may move her, we'll have to find a convey-ance . . ."

"My hackney," Johnny interrupted."

"You have a carriage in this melée?"

"The driver said he would wait in Compton Street."

"Too far for Lady Margaret to walk, even when she regains her wits." Colonel Falk drew a long breath. "If you will go find the jarvey and convince him to drive here, we shall pull through this engagement after all. The thing is, Dyott, we must avoid drawing undue attention to the young ladies."

Johnny nodded his emphatic agreement. If the girls' presence in Crown Street during a riot were made known, the scandal would probably ruin them. The Duchess of Devonshire might bestow campaign kisses on the electors of Westminster with social impunity, but that had been in a wilder time and besides the duchess was a married woman of mature years. Maggie and Jean were seventeen-year-old maidens.

The patronesses of Almack's would not look with favour on the girls doing anything so indecorous as being caught up in a riot. Especially unescorted. Especially romping about in disguise like a pair of woolly Caro Lambs.

Johnny could only hope no member of the Ton had been anywhere near Crown Street or Soho Square that morning.

Or Bond Street, he thought glumly. The hope was faint and fading.

He rose, not without a twinge. "I'll be off."

Falk's eyes narrowed. "Have you crocked up your leg again?"

"It hurts," Johnny admitted, since there was no point in hiding the obvious, "but it will hold."

"Never mind. You deal with the sawbones. I'll go for the jarvey."

"But . . ."

"Your man has probably driven off. If so, I'll find another. I didn't want to leave the young ladies without an escort . . ."

A banging on the door announced the surgeon's arrival. Falk let him in. "In good time, sir."

"You can put up your shutters," the young man said irritably. "The louts have hared off toward Carlton House and good riddance. Time for the Riot Act, in my opinion. Now what is it? Ah, another whack on the noggin, I see. Fourth case I've treated this morning." He knelt by Maggie and went about his examination briskly.

Johnny and Colonel Falk exchanged glances.

"I'll hunt up a hackney," Falk said. "Do you have the wherewithal to pay the man's fee?"

Johnny flushed. His purse must have been taken at some time during his wild career up Crown Street.

Falk fumbled in his pockets and gave Johnny a sovereign and a handful of lesser coins.

"Thanks."

Falk nodded and slipped out the door.

By the time he returned Maggie was coming round, the proprietor had taken down his shutters, and some kindly soul had brought water and vinegar from a nearby shop. Jean was bathing Maggie's temples.

The surgeon seemed to think Maggie would be able to ride to Grosvenor Square without aggravating the injury— he had peered into her eyes, taken her pulse, probed the edge of the lump on her skull. He was a brusque man. Johnny did not like him. He was relieved when the surgeon departed.

Somehow they got Maggie to the carriage, which was not the seedy vehicle he had hired in Bond Street.

At Soho Square, the driver turned west and began a winding traverse of that unsavoury borough. Unsavoury as it might be, the streets were less risky than Crown Street with the mob in full cry.

Johnny and Jean propped Maggie between them, and Colonel Falk sat opposite. Maggie was still faint and her wits still wandered, a circumstance that made Johnny extremely uneasy. At Colonel Falk's direction, the jarvey drove with great care. It seemed for ever before the carriage reached the new Regent Street.

They crossed the broad avenue at Maddox Street near Hanover Square, and the way was suddenly smoother, the traffic lighter.

"Why Greek Street?" Johnny burst out. They had ridden in a silence punctuated only by Maggie's groans.

Jean, thus addressed, set her jaw. "It was a lark."

That be damned for a tale, Johnny thought resentfully. He took a calming breath. "When I reached Bond Street, the jarvey I hailed said you had given him an address in Greek Street, then spurned his services when he tried to warn you that it was a low neighbourhood."

Jean sat up. "Warn us! He insulted us . . . me. He was extremely rude."

"And extremely right," Johnny snapped. "I want to know what took you to Greek Street, of all places. If Davies . . ."

"It was my idea of an adventure," Jean insisted. "We were tired of being pent up and escorted and spied upon." Her grey eyes flashed.

Johnny winced.

"So we decided to dress in disguise and explore London."

"But why Greek Street in particular?"

"We'd never seen it."

"You've never seen Billingsgate, either. I repeat, why Greek Street?"

"Why not Greek Street? Mr. Lawrence lived there. It was very interesting." Jean burst into tears.

"Let be, Dyott," Colonel Falk interposed. "This is not the place to be cross-examining witnesses." He handed Jean a clean handkerchief.

The hackney swung onto Grosvenor Street. Jean sniffled. Johnny fumed in silence. At last they entered the Square and the jarvey drew up before the Conway town house. The butler and two footmen were at the carriage door instantly and Johnny could see Lady Clanross, her hands clasped, watching from the foyer.

Colonel Falk got out first. "Quietly, gentlemen, if you please. Lady Margaret is unwell."

The butler helped the bedraggled Jean down, then took Maggie in his arms without betraying curiosity or in any way impairing his dignity. Flanked by the two impassive footmen, he bore Maggie up the stairs and into the house in stately parade. Johnny slunk after like a dog following a regimental band.

Elizabeth sent for Anne's discreet practitioner at once and bundled Maggie into bed. Jean hovered. Maggie moaned and muttered and complained of the headache— and no wonder. The knot on her skull was large as a hen's egg.

Mercifully, Dr. Stroud responded within the half hour. He accepted Elizabeth's explanation—Jean and Maggie, escorted by Johnny and Colonel Falk on an expedition to the Tower, had been set on by the Mob. It was a thin story and Elizabeth hoped it might not embarrass the two men excessively. The physician tut-tutted and gave Maggie a paregoric draught when he had assured himself that she was not seriously concussed. Finally, sponged clean and tucked into a fresh night rail, Maggie fell asleep.

Dr. Stroud examined the bruise on Jean's arm, and the bruises and blisters on her feet, and prescribed bed rest. Jean was inclined to resist but she finally lay down on the daybed in the girls' dressing room. When Elizabeth returned from showing the physician out, she found Jean sound asleep.

Balked for the moment of an explanation, Elizabeth sought Johnny Dyott. She had not far to seek, for he was hovering in the first-floor hallway looking miserable. She led him into her small withdrawing room.

He was inclined to be remorseful.

Elizabeth said kindly, "My dear Johnny, it's not your fault. Indeed, I'm grateful to you for following after them so promptly. What a miracle you found them at all."

He explained about the spurned jarvey and Greek Street.

"I see."

"I cannot understand their presence in Soho. Unless Davies put them up to it."

"Up to what?"

Johnny buried his head in his hands. "I've no idea. Lady Jean insists they were out for a lark, that it was her idea."

Elizabeth felt her mouth curl in an unwilling smile. "The scheme certainly has the earmarks of Jean's invention."

"But why Greek Street? I could have sworn she and Davies had no opportunity to contrive a plot. I have been remiss . . ."

"Johnny," Elizabeth interrupted, "I'm the twins' sister. If anyone is to blame it is I. I should have had their confidence. Let us hear no more of your responsibility. As I know to my cost, when my sisters make up their minds to a course of action, they are neither to hold nor to bind."

"If you say so." He looked doubtful.

"I do. Now, if you please, a plain account . . ."

Johnny told his story with reasonable despatch. When he came to the point at which he lost sight of the girls in the whirling crowd, the hair stood up on Elizabeth's neck. The twins had indeed had a narrow escape.

"I couldn't reach them," Johnny concluded with obviously unfeigned distress. "I have never felt so powerless. I should have been able . . ."

"No should-have-beens," Elizabeth reminded him. "Well, Greek Street remains a mystery, but neither you nor my sisters could have foreseen that the Mob would sweep through at that moment. I am glad you were there, Johnny, and I hope your leg has suffered no harm."

He flushed. "It aches a bit but I'm sure it will be all right."

"Then go rest it and be sure. I've sent for Tom, and I know he'll want your account of today's adventure, but indeed, Johnny, you are not to blame yourself. I particularly admire your discretion."

"That was mostly Colonel Falk."

"Then I must thank him as well. Go rest your leg," she said again, rising when he showed a disposition to repeat his apologies. She hoped he would someday outgrow his exaggerated sense of responsibility. It was a trait he shared with Clanross, endearing, on the whole, but occasionally exasperating.

She found Colonel Falk in the book room.

He was stooped over the escritoire, writing, and straightened as she entered, laying his pen aside. "Lady Clanross."

"Colonel."

"I trust the sawbones was satisfied with Lady Margaret's condition." He pulled a chair for her.

Elizabeth sat. "He seems to think she'll survive. Do you always write standing up?"

"Only when I want to use my right hand as a paperweight," he said coolly.

Elizabeth bit her lip, chagrined to have been so tactless. "I beg your pardon. It must be difficult . . ." She drew a breath and started over. "I've sent for the sherry tray, sir. After the alarums of the day, I find myself in need of a composer. Perhaps you will join me in a glass."

He inclined his head, eyes wary.

"I have to thank you for your good offices today."

"Glad to be of service." He seated himself in the companion chair. Between them on the hearth stood a vase of spring blossoms. The scent was rather heavy.

"How in the world did you happen to come on the scene so conveniently?" Elizabeth asked, unable to restrain her curiosity.

"I was gawking at the rioters like everyone else." He smiled slightly. "I delivered a chapter of my manuscript to Murray in Albermarle Street, and I had some time to while away before meeting my solicitor in the City. So I decided to browse the bookstalls. When the Mob began to gather, I prudently retired to a doorway out of the range of flying brickbats."

"Then it was chance."

"The purest coincidence, Lady Clanross. The sort I shouldn't dare use in a novel."

Elizabeth smiled. "Life, being stranger than fiction . . ."

"I have often found it so."

"Well, your presence was a piece of good fortune for Jean and Maggie, and I thank you very much for the rescue."

"Strictly speaking, they rescued themselves, ma'am."

Elizabeth stared.

He was frowning. "As I said, I was watching. I noticed them at once, because there were so few women in the street."

Elizabeth grimaced.

He said dryly, "An unhappy choice of words. At any rate, they were visible but not immediately identifiable."

"Thank God for that."

"I watched as they were swept into the middle of the street and wondered if I ought to try to reach them. And whether I could do them any good if I did."

He had slipped his right arm back in the discreet black silk sling. Now he touched the fabric, adding with evident regret, "I'm not much use in a set-to these days." He flashed a grin. "There was Johnny Dyott with one good leg and me with one good arm. Between the two of us, we might have made an adequate knight errant, but I think you sisters would have been better served by a troop of Guards."

Elizabeth had to smile, too, but she said, "They were very well served as it was."

He shook his head and went on, "They kept their wits about them. They waited in the shelter of a cart that had been caught in the confusion, and when they saw a gap in the crowd they made a dash for safety. Lady Margaret's cap was torn off. That was when I recognized them. I was some way off."

"I see."

"Lady Margaret was struck as they reached the walkway and pulled to safety by her sister and two onlookers. I made my way to them at once, but I can't claim to have rescued them. Or that they needed rescue. They are redoubtable young women."

"They're a pair of pestiferous hobbledehoys," Elizabeth said roundly, "and so I shall tell them when they wake. I blush when I consider what you must be thinking of their breeding."

"I'm thinking that they have a great deal of spirit," he said mildly.

"Spirit!"

Fortunately, the butler entered before Elizabeth's exasperation betrayed her into unbecoming language.

When the wine was poured and the butler had left the room she found Colonel Falk watching her with considerable amusement in his hazel eyes. "If your sisters had fallen into hysterics or swooned in one another's arms I daresay that would have showed good breeding."

"Not being there at all would have showed good breeding." She took a sip of sherry. "Johnny says they refused to explain their presence, unescorted, in the seamiest purlieus of Soho."

Colonel Falk toyed with his glass. "Lady Margaret was

in no state to be explaining anything. Lady Jean said they were tired of, er, being hedged about by solicitous guardians. I was inclined to believe her." He took a swallow of wine. "They were looking for adventure, ma'am. An understandable impulse."

Elizabeth's wrath kindled. "Understandable in young men, perhaps, but not in well-bred young ladies."

He cocked an eyebrow. "Are young ladies immune to natural inclinations?"

Elizabeth said grimly, "They must learn to consider the consequences of heedless behaviour."

"Your sisters merely went for a little jaunt in each other's company and found more adventure than they bargained for. Lady Margaret's injury will mend. Where is the harm?"

"There might have been a great deal of harm if you and Johnny hadn't found them. I can only hope no one of note recognised them before you were able to give them respectable escort."

Colonel Falk's mouth quirked at the corners. "That's the first time anyone has ever accused me of respectability."

Elizabeth stared.

He cocked a quizzical eyebrow.

Finally recalling his scandalous antecedents, she blushed to the roots of her hair, but when he began to laugh she did, too. The situation was fraught with absurdity, after all. In her concern for the girls' reputation, she'd been in danger of forgetting that. She was grateful to him for restoring the balance of her judgement.

He was a quiet man. She had thought him colourless and unpleasantly reserved, assuming his friendship with her husband was just another instance of Tom's kindness. Tom had told her often enough that Colonel Falk was his oldest friend. She began to see why the friendship had endured.

== 13 ==

"I WANT A proper mount," Matt announced, sliding from the saddle. "Tommy can have Pie." Pie, short for Piebald Prancer, was Matt's pony, a fat, good-natured beast, and with Amy's pony, Eustachio, the universal family pet.

"Perhaps. I'll think about it." Emily dismounted with a hand from her father's head groom and gave Feather a pat on the nose. Her father had reserved the mare for her use.

It was pleasant to be able to ride again. Richard had kept neither horses nor a carriage in Winchester. The first brief rides Emily had taken after her temporary remove to Mayne Hall had left her so stiff and sore she was almost convinced that women in their thirties ought to give up the saddle and content themselves with being driven. Now she was glad she had persisted.

". . . a roan gelding just like Smithers's," Matt was saying as he led Pie to the stables. Even when Matt was small, Emily had insisted that her son see to his pony himself, though there had always been a groom to help the boy. She was glad Matt had not forgot his training.

She watched as her eldest unbuckled the girth and removed Pie's saddle, rubbing the pony down and inspecting his coat carefully before allowing the groom to lead Pie to water and the oat bag. She gave Feather the carrot she had been saving. The groom lifted the heavy sidesaddle from the mare and Matt rattled on about the superior points of a horse he had seen at the Home Farm that morning.

She and Matt had made a circuit of the Wellfield estate. It was a fine day for riding. The cherries were hung with white clouds of blossom, their annual Easter display, and everything seemed forward for the season. The bailiff Emily had hired to oversee Wellfield was a good man, no doubt of it, but she couldn't help wishing she had been able to see to the planting herself.

Emily had been homesick for Wellfield all through the winter. She meant to enjoy as much of its spring beauty as possible. She was almost certain it was her last Wellfield spring. Her melancholy sharpened the pleasure of the ride.

She watched as the groom rubbed Feather down. Then she gave the mare a last affectionate pat and followed Matt, who was still talking horse, out into the watery spring sunlight.

". . . and Grandpapa says I may stable the roan here," Matt was saying, "and Will can exercise him for me until school lets out for the summer holidays. Say I may buy him, Mama."

Emily focussed on her son. He was pink with eagerness, flaxen hair ruffling in the spring breeze. "It's too soon to decide, Matt. Your stepfather hasn't made up his mind where we're to live, and I don't want to burden Papa with another horse. He's very kind to keep Pie and Eustachio for us."

"I want a proper mount," Matt said fiercely. "I need one. You can sell Pie."

"Sell Pie? You don't mean that, Matt. Pie is a very old friend."

"I don't care."

"What would Tommy ride?"

Matt kicked a clod. "I want the roan. If my stepfather is so rich, he can buy Pie for Tommy."

Emily stared at her son in silence.

Matt's eyes dropped. He was red in the face. Shame-faced, she hoped.

"We shall keep Pie," she said carefully, "for Tommy and

Harry and Sally. Until he drops dead of old age, which will, I trust, be many years in the future. Perhaps by that time you will have learnt something of family feeling. In the meanwhile, if you insist, we shall pay you a fee every time one of the younger children mounts your pony. Perhaps you'd like to sell rides for ha'pence to other children as well. You should turn a handsome profit, enough perhaps to purchase the roan by your twenty-first birthday." Matt was twelve.

"You always take their side."

"Whose 'side'?"

"Theirs. The Falks'."

"You are speaking of your brothers and sisters."

"Tommy isn't my brother."

Emily closed her eyes briefly. "Upon my word, Matt, are you so selfish you grudge poor Tommy's existence? He takes nothing from you. To be sure, he is your stepbrother . . ." She broke off and regarded her son rather helplessly.

In the past year, since Tommy's illness, Matt's jealousy had taken to bursting forth in ugly little scenes like this one. She knew Matt loved the other children, nor did she suppose he hated his stepfather.

Matt's moments of anger, sparked by the ordinary frustrations of childhood, had been fanned to hostility by his paternal grandmother. If something were not done soon, his natural self-importance and hot temper were going to lead him into a permanent state of fancied grievance.

He continued to stare at her, lower lip jutting.

"I think we had best have a talk."

"We're always having talks."

Emily sighed. "Another talk, then. I understand that you want a more suitable mount. You shall certainly have one, though not just yet. When I'm sure we can stable it properly, it will be purchased from the income of your own estate and will belong to you alone. I'll keep an accounting for you of the price, as I have done since you were three years old of all other expenses relating to your father's estate, and when you come of age I shall turn everything that is yours over to you. I never forget what is due to you as your father's son, Matthew."

The boy's eyes dropped.

"Do you understand what I'm saying?"

"Grandmama said my stepfather was milking the estate," he muttered.

Emily drew a sharp breath. "What?"

"I think that means . . ."

"I know what it means. Your grandmother . . ." Emily broke off. Is a damnable liar, she had been about to say. Not a diplomatic utterance. "Mrs. Foster is mistaken."

"But she said my stepfather was battening on my rents."

"She may claim that, and even perhaps believe it," Emily pronounced, "but it is untrue, Matthew. Look at me."

Matt raised his head. There were tears in his eyes.

Emily melted. She bent and pulled him to her in a fierce embrace. "How unhappy you've been, Matt. I'm sorry."

Matt squirmed. "I didn't think it could be true, Mama, but she said it was." He began to cry in earnest.

Emily held him, patting him as if he were a much younger child until the first gust of tears—born of relief, she suspected—had spent itself.

How long had Matt been trying to deal with the old woman's poisonous allegations? He had spent a month with Mrs. Foster after Tommy's illness, but how long before that?

When Matt reached the hiccoughing stage, Emily released him and straightened. It wouldn't do to injure his dignity with too much babying. "Let's walk to the spinney, darling, and try to sort this out."

Matt daubed his eyes with his sleeve. "All right."

"Do you know why we closed Wellfield House and moved to Winchester?"

He sniffed. "So I could come home from school Sundays and so Amy could go to her school."

"Those were benefits of the move but not the reason. We moved because your stepfather thought it best to establish his own household. When I married Richard we continued to live at Wellfield because I wanted to oversee the estate. And," she added, determined to make a clean breast of it, "because I loved the house and felt comfortable in it. You were very young, too, and I wanted you to spend your childhood there. I thought you should know the land and I wanted your tenants to know who you were."

"The s-squire." Matt offered the old joke hesitantly. He would be the squire of Wellfield as his father had been, and one of the Wellfield tenants, an elderly farmer, had insisted on calling Matt "young squire." Emily had teased him with the nickname. The joke was stale now, but there was truth in it.

"I think my plan succeeded," Emily said cheerfully. "When you come of age, Wellfield and its people will be ready to welcome you home. That's what I wanted for you."

"But Papa Falk . . ."

"Your stepfather is a soldier and a writer. He is not wonderfully interested in agriculture."

That was an understatement. Richard listened politely enough to Emily's bucolic enthusiasms, but he had once confessed to her that when he saw a field of waving corn the words that popped into his head were "forage" and "bivouac." The revelation had shocked Emily to the core.

Matt was looking at her, owl-eyed. He had grown half a foot in the past year. The top of his head reached her chin.

She gave his shoulder a brief, reassuring squeeze and walked on. "Your stepfather had reservations about living at Wellfield, but he knew I wanted to stay on, so he didn't raise any objections until last year, when we heard of unpleasant gossip in the village. Then you began to echo some of the gossip, and we knew we'd have to find a way to set your mind at ease. Besides, it wasn't fair to Amy and

Tommy and the babies to rear them at Wellfield when it could never really be their home."

"I don't see why not," Matt muttered. "*I* don't mind."

Emily sighed. "It's too complicated. Keeping estate records and household records separate fairly addled my brain. Of course, your stepfather always paid the household expenses." Emily had thought Richard overscrupulous. He had even paid Matt a rent for the house. Now she was glad he had insisted.

Matt said nothing but she knew she had his attention.

After a moment, she went on, "When we found that Tommy was . . . had lost his hearing, we knew we should have to provide for him, something in addition to his education, I mean, and living in Winchester was less costly than running a large house like Wellfield. So you see . . ."

"But now that Papa Falk is rich we can move back to Wellfield." Matt's eyes blazed. "We can open the house again."

"Oh, Matt, no."

"Why not?"

Emily shook her head. She had tried to explain about the duchess's legacy and what it might mean. As she was not herself sure what it would mean her explanations had necessarily been foggy. Clearly Matt had not understood.

"We'll probably live in one of Richard's houses. Or he may purchase an estate. In any case, we cannot live at Wellfield."

"Where shall *I* live?"

"Oh, Matt, with us, of course."

"But I want to live at home, at Wellfield."

So do I. Emily repressed the thought. "You shall when you come of age, of course. And we'll make sure Wellfield is properly cared for."

"Grandpapa says a house that's not lived in can't be cared for properly."

Emily was silent. She agreed with her father. Only a

resident householder could see to the thousand and one small details that kept a house in prime twig.

"I want to live at Wellfield," Matt repeated mutinously.

"I wish you could, but would that be fair to Amy and Tommy and the others? Would it be fair to me?"

Matt stared.

Emily cocked her head. "Hadn't you thought of that? I've been keeping Wellfield for you, but when you marry it won't be my home either."

"You can live with me for the rest of your life, Mama."

Emily laughed, but she was touched. "Your wife would very properly object to that—and so would my husband. Besides," she added on what she hoped was a practical note, "you're in school now most of the year and you'll go down to Cambridge, too, as your father did. Wellfield will wait for you, Matt."

They had reached the spinney. Sir Henry's saplings were budding out, and the established trees made a misty show of lime green against the brilliant sky.

Matt cut a switch with his new penknife, a Christmas gift from his stepfather. His face was no longer swollen with tears or, indeed, rage. He looked thoughtful.

He took a practice slash at a tuft of winter weed. "May we still visit Mayne Hall in the holidays?"

"I'm sure your grandfather will always welcome us."

He heaved a sigh. "It's not the same as living at Wellfield, but it's better than nothing." A promising sign of mental compromise, Emily thought.

She decided to leave the discussion at that. Her own feelings were too confused to admit further probing. She did not want to live in Bath or, God forbid, London. Where Richard went she would go, but she was afraid a piece of her stubborn heart would always remain at Wellfield.

"We can't betray Owen," Jean insisted.

Maggie still had the headache, two days after her encounter with the brickbat. The physician had clipped the hair over the swelling and the lump was going down, but she was sore all over and she knew she looked a fright. She was half-glad Johnny Dyott had not seen her since the riot, though she longed to see *him*. She wondered, disconsolate, whether he would ever talk with her as comfortably as he had. She missed their talks, and she longed to ask his advice.

"I promised. I won't say anything about Owen's poem, Jean, but I hate the pretence . . ."

Jean sat on the foot of the bed. The movement sent a jolt through Maggie's skull. She bit back a groan.

"I don't like it either," Jean said earnestly, "but Clanross would dismiss Owen if he knew of the poem and I should never see Owen again."

Maggie did not particularly wish to see Owen, but she tried to enter her sister's feelings. "Did Clanross say anything?"

Jean shook her head. Because of Maggie's head injury, neither of the girls had yet been called to account. Jean, who had dined twice with the family, reported that the atmosphere was chilly. Maggie dined on invalid fare from a tray. Apart from Jean, Elizabeth had been her only caller, and Elizabeth had so far said nothing of crimes or punishments.

It was only a matter of time before the ax fell, however, and that meant the girls had to make sure their stories jibed. Jean was repeating the tale she had foisted on Johnny in the hackney.

". . . so we went to Greek Street to see Mr. Lawrence's house. Is he the one who painted Cromwell's warts?" Maggie shifted on the pillows.

"Lord, no. Mr. Lawrence is still alive. I believe he painted Mrs. Siddons. He is a member of the Royal Academy."

"It was Reynolds who painted Papa, wasn't it?"

"I think so."

Maggie brooded. "Which was his house?"

"Reynolds's?"

"No, daff-head. Lawrence's."

"I don't remember the number," Jean confessed. "Perhaps it won't come up."

Maggie closed her eyes. "Let's hope not. Have you got *Ivanhoe*?"

"Yes. Shall I read you more of it?" Colonel Falk had given them a copy of Mr. Scott's new work as a cheering up gift. It was quite enthralling, though Maggie's headache had cut the first reading short.

"Go ahead," she murmured. "I like Rebecca."

Jean had been reading for ten minutes or so—just long enough for both girls to lose themselves in the Middle Ages—when Elizabeth rapped on the door and entered.

Jean laid the book on the counterpane. "I thought you were going to the theatre."

"I decided not." Elizabeth came to the head of the bed and looked down at Maggie. "Are you feeling more the thing?"

Maggie nodded.

"Good. It's time the three of us had a talk."

Maggie caught her twin's eye. Jean grimaced.

Elizabeth touched the vase of flowers on the stand by the bed, then drifted to the window. It was dark but the street lamps made a soft glow and the reflected gaslight sparkled in the rain.

With a sigh, Elizabeth pulled the curtain to and took her seat by the hearth. In deference to Maggie's condition a small fire burnt. "I have been trying to decide what to do about your presentation."

Maggie and Jean exchanged glances but said nothing.

"At Christmas," Elizabeth continued, "you persuaded me you were ready to enter society this year. When the May levee was announced, it seemed that the Ton meant to go on much as usual despite the king's death, so I determined to do the thing properly. I spurred Anne to procure tickets for you at Almack's and I asked the housekeeper to set things in train for a formal ball. Your presentation gowns will be ready for fitting next week."

"We know we've caused a great deal of bother," Maggie muttered.

Elizabeth sighed again. "Oh, Maggie, I don't grudge you the effort. It's your due. The thing is, I can't be sure of your conduct any more. Jean is suddenly indifferent to the fripperies that sent her into transports a few short months ago, nor am I convinced *you* should be undergoing the exertion of a Season in your present state."

"I'll be all right," Maggie muttered.

"Believe me, tumbling from one ball to the next until two and three in the morning every week night and twice on Saturday can be exhausting. I believe we'd be wise to wait for the June levee. What say you?"

"May we go home to Brecon first?" Jean was white with suppressed tension.

"*I* certainly intend to. I mean to see the babies." Elizabeth gave her a searching look. "You insist that Owen Davies had nothing to do with your excursion to Greek Street. Unless Maggie offers me another tale, I'm constrained to believe you."

Jean inclined her head but said nothing. *Maggie's* head ached.

"I'll take you home with me for the rest of this month and most of May. I warn you, though, Jean, I shall watch you like an eagle."

Jean's mouth compressed.

"Maggie, what is *your* word?"

"We drove to Soho on a lark," Maggie lied glumly. "Jean thought of hiring the hackney and I came up with the disguises. We only went into Crown Street to find another hackney. We didn't mean to be caught up in a riot."

"Very well." Elizabeth stood up. "We'll return to Brecon as soon as your gowns are fitted, and delay your presentation until June. We shan't stay in London after the June levee, and I'll wait until the little season to give your ball. Perhaps by then you'll have a clearer idea of what is owing to your name."

Jean made no protest. Maggie's eyes filled with tears. She blinked them back, but it seemed unfair to her that their come-out should be curtailed.

Perhaps Elizabeth saw her disappointment, for she added in a gentler voice, "Anne and I mean to bring you out properly, my dears. You may make your curtseys to the king and try out your feet at Almack's this season. When autumn comes you may count on spreading your wings." She rose. "Now I'll leave you to your book. The new Scott, is it not? You must be sure to thank Colonel Falk for his kindness."

When she had gone, Jean made a face. "Treating us as if we were babies again. 'Be sure to thank Colonel Falk.' Good heavens, does she think we have no manners?"

"It might have been worse," Maggie said philosophically. Jean stared.

"She might have made us wait until next spring." Maggie closed her eyes. "I want to go to sleep, Jean. My head aches."

Tom poked his head in the book room. Richard was standing at the wide table at a sort of lectern, scribbling away. "How goes the history?"

"It marches." Richard scratched out a line. "Blast you, you broke my train of thought. The world has lost a masterpiece."

Tom closed the door behind him. "Sorry. I'm off to the City. Do you need a ride to the Middle Temple?"

"Not this morning, thanks."

"What the devil is that contraption?" He peered at the lectern. "You look as if you meant to deliver a sermon."

Richard set his pen aside. "Lady Clanross found me scrunched over the escritoire the other day and decided I ought to compose standing upright. So she rummaged in

153

the attics and came up with this. It does the trick very neatly. You're married to a woman of resource."

Tom inspected the lectern. "I wish I might have seen Elizabeth sweeping through the attics. The lumber up there has probably not been disturbed since the reign of George II."

"It was kind of her ladyship to think of it. I'm working faster now. How are your equally resourceful sisters-in-law?"

"Maggie still keeps to her bed. I understand you lavished Walter Scott's latest on them. Is it wise to reward felonious misconduct with three-volume novels?" He pulled a chair and sat on it backwards.

Richard looked mildly guilty. "I thought Lady Jean seemed downhearted at dinner the evening of the great debacle. Do you object?"

Tom raised his eyebrows. "I? No, though I hope the twins conduct their next adventure in a less publick arena. I wonder why they aimed for the stews of Soho? Can they know . . . ?"

"Nonsense. They're innocent as a pair of downy ducks."

"Then I fear for the nation when they feather out." He squinted at his friend who was leaning on the lectern. "I think you're taken with them."

Richard flushed. "They remind me of Isabel."

"I see." Doña Isabel was Richard's first wife.

"She was not much older than they when I wed her."

Or very much older when she died, Tom reflected. He had admired Doña Isabel. "Do you think of her often?"

"Every time I see her face in Tommy or her spirit in Amy," Richard said quietly. Both men fell silent, remembering.

"What a long time ago it seems," Tom said at last. "How do your legal affairs progress?"

Richard grimaced. "Slower than a commissary's waggon. My solicitor holds out hope of avoiding a chancery suit."

"At what cost?"

"At whatever cost. I cannot keep Emily in limbo forever." Richard's mouth eased in a slight smile. "Not that Mayne Hall is the antechamber of Hell, but she can't be comfortable sparring with her father all the time."

"Bring her to Brecon," Tom said impulsively. "Oh, not just yet. In the summer, when you've finished your history. I'd like to show Emily an estate in the neighbourhood."

Richard looked doubtful.

"If *you* don't find a place for her, your father-in-law will."

Richard grinned. "He has already found four. 'Not a day's ride from home,' " he quoted in palpable imitation of a gruff country squire, " 'and everything handsome about them.' "

Tom laughed. "Then spirit Emily off to Lincolnshire. She'll like Hazeldell—that's the estate I mean to show her—and your Harry and Sally may bump noses with my boys in the nursery."

"A brigade of infantry," Richard mused. "It's a thought, Tom, but I'd not like to burden Lady Clanross. She has her hands full as it is."

Tom rose. "She does, but as you pointed out she is a woman of infinite resource."

As he rode to the City through the noisy but no longer riotous streets, Tom wondered what he had wrought. Elizabeth would be working at her telescope. She always did so in summer and he disliked interrupting her scientific endeavours. Thrusting total strangers upon her would not be a kindness, given her uneasiness about the girls. But he thought Elizabeth would take to Emily Falk, and Emily, he was sure, would find the twins enormously entertaining. Both sets.

=14=

JOHNNY AND COLONEL Falk had been pent in the bookroom for a week, the colonel working away at his history and Johnny bringing the correspondence for the Canadian charity up to date. Colonel Falk tossed the letter he had been reading on the table and walked to the bookroom window. "Emily and her father have come to cuffs over McGrath." He raised the sash and a draught of balmy air disturbed Johnny's papers.

Johnny laid a book on the stack of letters. "McGrath? Is he drinking again?" McGrath had struck Johnny as a hardened toper. Scarcely the manservant for a genteel household.

Falk leaned against the frame of the window, staring down into the Square. The weather was exceptionally fine. "It seems McGrath and Dassett—that's Sir Henry's coachman—have been testing each other's capacity for Blue Ruin belowstairs every night. Sir Henry wants McGrath's head on a platter."

"I daresay you don't like to dismiss McGrath because of his wife." Pegeen McGrath was the children's nurse.

Falk said coolly, "I don't want to dismiss McGrath because he served me faithfully for thirteen years.'

"Oh. Was he your batman?"

"More than that." Falk sounded as if he might, for once, launch into reminiscence, but he didn't. After a moment he closed the window, turned, blinking, and came back to the table. His lectern reposed at one end and Johnny sat at the other.

The colonel began to mend his pen. He made an awkward business of it, and Johnny wondered if he ought to help.

Before he could rise, Falk had dipped the pen in the inkwell and struck out a line. "I'll have to think of something for Jerry. Have you had your fill of publick executions?" Johnny had risen at dawn that morning, which was May Day, to witness the execution of Thistlewood and the chief Cato Street conspirators. The colonel had declined to join him.

"I left before the hangman did his work," Johnny confessed.

"Wise man."

"It was shocking—the crowd, I mean. Some of them were respectable people."

Falk's lip curled.

"Well-dressed families," Johnny said indignantly, "men and women and children, gossiping and chatting as if they were at a picnic."

"I hear the more advantageous posts of observation went for half a crown."

"More. Much more."

"It must have been a great consolation to Thistlewood to know his end met with genteel applause. Such is civilisation."

"My father," Johnny offered, "says spectacles of that sort are a salutory deterrent to crime."

Falk frowned. "Have you ever witnessed a flogging?"

"No."

"I was compelled to in India. My colonel marched us out in hollow square and forced us to watch every bloody blow. It made me sick as a cat and I swore I'd resign my commission sooner than order such a punishment. Fortunately, I was not required to." He scowled at his manuscript. "In my opinion flogging and hanging are no deterrent to hardened offenders. They haven't the imagination to fancy themselves at the gridiron or they wouldn't act brutally in the first place. The others, the bystanders, are merely sickened—except for the ghouls, your respectable men and their respectable families who pay to see wretches suffer. That's a kind of sickness, too."

Johnny felt compelled to defend his father's opinion. "But the crime was so appalling . . ."

"The intent was appalling," Falk said precisely. "The crime did not take place."

"But they . . . Thistlewood resisted arrest."

"Would you not, if you knew you would infallibly be hanged and beheaded?"

There was no answer to that. Johnny drew a letter from the pile before him. For a time both men worked in silence. Colonel Falk was finally approaching the end of volume three. Heavy tomes interleafed with slips of paper covered in notes littered his end of the table.

Johnny penned four letters of thanks and set up a meeting in July between Clanross and a retired sergeant who could not find employment. The man had three children and his wife was expecting a fourth. They subsisted on a pension of six shillings a week. It occurred to Johnny to wonder if they might not starve before July. Surely not. The letter had been written by the man's neighbour, a barber-surgeon. The sergeant had friends.

"Blast!" Falk threw down his pen. "I've no head for this today. Come for a walk, Dyott. I'm sick of my own company."

Johnny did not have to be persuaded. He sealed the letters, which already had Clanross's frank, and rose from his seat, shrugging into the coat he had thrown over the chair-back.

The May air moved with enough breeze to dispel the usual London haze. The two men walked in silence. Colonel Falk had the loose stride of an infantryman used to covering twenty miles in a day's march. Johnny tried to keep up. When they had traipsed through the park—it was not a fashionable hour to be strolling along the Serpentine—they headed back to Grosvenor Square by way of Upper Brook Street. Within sight of the Conway town house Falk halted.

"There's a coffeehouse in Audley Street where I catch up on the newspapers. Do you care to take a cup?"

Johnny's leg was aching. He was ready to sit down and not choosy where. He nodded. His own coffeehouse, a club of sorts, lay in Bond Street, and he was a member of Brooks's, too, but that was too far off.

The coffeehouse proved quietly unfashionable. Colonel Falk read *The Times* rapidly, toying with his coffee cup. Johnny was content to sip and rest his leg. Beyond the plain windows, the street was almost empty. A pair of dandies minced by, one in lavender, the other in fawn inexpressibles. Half a dozen carriages and a high perch phaeton drawn by a team of matched bays rattled by. Johnny watched the horses out of sight.

Colonel Falk laid the paper on the small table and took a sip of the thick black coffee. "I was surprised when you didn't join the party at Brecon, Dyott. Gratified," he added hastily. "Relieved. Grateful. If you'd gone off, I'd be neck-deep in begging letters. Still, I rather expected you to see the young ladies safely home."

Johnny felt his cheeks go hot. "Do you think I should have?"

"Only if you meant to fix your interest with Lady Margaret," Falk said in dulcet tones.

Johnny stared. In the course of the riot, as the girls were swept away by the crowd, he had realized his preference was for Maggie, not Jean. The idea was still so new it startled him. "How the devil did you know? Am I so obviously doating?"

"No. I had the advantage of Emily's acute eye. She told me you were taken with one of the twins. I wondered which, so I watched. It's no concern of mine, Dyott, but I must say you have excellent taste. They are charming young women, high-couraged as a pair of Arab colts."

"And such speaking eyes!"

"And such flaming hair!" The mockery was kindly. "I'm bound to say I still can't tell one from the other."

"Oh . . . there's a world of difference." Johnny could have explained how unlike Maggie was to Jean, but it would have taken him the rest of the afternoon. He fiddled with the newspaper. "I daresay you think me presumptuous to hope . . ."

The colonel's eyebrows rose. "Hope is never presumptuous."

"But she . . . Lady Margaret is the daughter of an earl."

"You can't imagine Tom would object to the connexion." He finished his coffee.

"But Lady Clanross."

Falk said slowly, "I don't know her ladyship at all well, but she doesn't strike me as foolishly ambitious for her sisters. Why the diffidence, Dyott? You're well born, well educated, and reasonably prosperous, and you cut a good figure. What more could a young lady wish for?"

Johnny groaned. "Sonnets."

Falk grinned. "I thought Lady Jean was the one smitten with the poet."

"She is. But any young girl wants romance. I think I have Mag . . . Lady Margaret's friendship. Or I thought I did until I found they'd gone off to a clandestine assignation." Gloom, never far off these days, swept over Johnny again. Maggie's failure of trust had jolted him awake. Her lack of confidence in him had stunned and hurt him to a degree that caused him to examine his own feelings. He needed Maggie's trust.

Falk made a clucking noise with his tongue. "Assignation. What a word."

"It was clandestine behaviour."

"They wanted adventure. What could be more natural?"

"Perhaps you're right, but I thought Maggie trusted me!"

Johnny burst out, too distressed to notice the impropriety of referring to his lady without her style.

"If she had told you of her plans you would have prevented them. And her loyalty to her sister is surely admirable."

"Perhaps," Johnny grudged. He took a sip of cold coffee.

"Why don't you buy a seat on the next mail coach and try for an explanation? Faint heart never won a fair lady."

"I couldn't," Johnny muttered. "I'd look a fool."

"Nothing ventured nothing gained. I seem to be expressing myself in adages today. That doesn't augur well for the next chapter. I'd best stop before I say the course of true love never did run smooth." He rose. "Leg rested?"

Johnny nodded and stood up, too. He felt some resentment that Falk should be reading his mind so easily. On the other hand, it was a relief to speak of his feelings.

Outside in the bright sunlight his mood lightened. After all, the colonel had not despised his pretentions. They strolled toward Grosvenor Square.

Falk chuckled. "I'm a fine one to be spurring you into action. I was so pigeon-livered I had to wait for Emily to propose to me."

Johnny stared. "She didn't!"

"Indeed she did. She blushed like a Spanish sunrise, bless her, but she got the words out." He was back at his loping stride again. Johnny had to quick-march to catch up. He tried to imagine the sweetly conventional Emily Falk proposing marriage to her mad satirist, but his fancy failed him.

When they entered the house, they found the second post had come. Johnny had a letter from his father demanding to know, absolutely and finally, when Johnny meant to take Holy Orders. A living worth two thousand pounds a year had fallen vacant near Grantham.

Johnny's other epistle was from Lady Clanross. She asked him to come to Brecon for the twins' birthday celebration. They were still sunk in gloom, Maggie partic-

161

ularly. And their eighteenth anniversary ought to be a festive occasion. Would he bring the packet of sheet musick she had forgot? She remained his obliged servant, Elizabeth Conway.

Johnny would. He wrote her at once, and that evening he went to the book room, took out his new steel pen, and composed a careful, filial letter to his father explaining his decision not to enter the church. Afterward he felt so much better he tried his hand at a sonnet. It was not half bad.

"Johnny writes he will come in time for the dinner party." Elizabeth leaned forward and patted the new mare's neck. Her favourite mount, Josephine, had had to be put out to pasture and Elizabeth wasn't yet sure of Andromeda. That was the mare's name.

Tom held Paloma to a walk. Maggie, Jean, and the poet on a borrowed Pegasus, had gone on ahead. "Do you think Maggie's headaches are owing to the injury or to Johnny's absence?"

"A bit of both . . ." Elizabeth's smile faded as she caught sight of the rest of the party at the far end of the avenue of beeches. They had dismounted by the pavilion and Owen was reciting again. She could tell by the gestures. Maggie appeared to be examining the deep red of a rhododendron bloom, but Jean was listening to him in the attitude of an acolyte.

"It will wear off."

"Jean's infatuation? I hope it may. Her other fancies were shorter lived, except when she was in love with you." She shot him a sidelong glance.

He grinned. "I think you're trying to put me to the blush."

"Impossible!"

"Wasp!"

They laughed. "Race you?" Elizabeth challenged.

His eyes gleamed and he settled his round hat more firmly over his brow. "You're on, my lady."

Paloma was still Paloma and outdistanced the new mare easily. Tom had dismounted by the time Elizabeth reached the pavilion. The younger people gaped at their headlong elders.

"Andromeda is a slug," Elizabeth announced, a trifle breathless. She slid to the ground and Jean took her reins. "Shall I give her to Maggie?"

Jean smiled.

Maggie made a face. "I'm faithful to Joybell till death us do part. Keep your beastly slug."

That showed some spirit. Maggie was still pale, but the cropped hair suited her and a delicate pink tinged her cheeks. Perhaps she was recovering. Elizabeth gave her a sisterly grin. After a moment Maggie smiled, too.

Tom had been leading Paloma round the pavilion. Paloma, a very black dove indeed, was inclined to be hot in hand. She had been known to lash out at the end of a ten mile run; however, she looked calm enough at the moment. The girls' mounts and Owen's nag swished their tails as Tom tied Paloma to the railing. She munched a clump of harebells.

Owen watched the proceedings with the air of one who has been interrupted.

"I hope your georgics are doing well," Elizabeth said politely.

He shrugged. "Well enough, considering my heart is not in pastoral scenes. I wish I might go to London."

There was no answer to that and Elizabeth made none.

Tom said, "Richard Falk writes that he has finished his history. He is gone down to Hampshire."

"Then Johnny's alone in London." Maggie bit her lip.

"Not for long," Elizabeth said cheerfully. "He'll be here for the birthday celebration." She had meant to leave Johnny's coming as a surprise, but Maggie wanted cheering *now*.

She glanced at the girl. Maggie clasped her hands and looked agitated.

Jean said, "It's good of him to go to the trouble. I hope you don't mean to ask the little girls to dine with us."

"I thought you would prefer to take tea with our sisters and keep the dinner party strictly grown-up."

Jean nodded. "And dancing afterward?"

"If you like. Miss Bluestone will play for you, I'm sure. Willoughby and Bella have agreed to come, and the Whartons."

"Lord, Cecy Wharton can't dance in her state."

Elizabeth frowned at her. "True, but it doesn't become you to say so, Jean. Is there anyone else you'd like me to ask?"

"Let's keep the numbers small," Maggie muttered. "May we go back? I have the headache."

Elizabeth's heart sank. Perhaps Johnny Dyott wasn't the cure for Maggie's megrims after all.

Maggie's reception of the news that Johnny was coming back to Brecon baffled her twin, too.

Jean had been terrified by her sister's injury and concerned when recurring headaches kept Maggie abed half the time. As the details of the riot receded from Jean's memory, however, she was inclined to feel that the risk she and Maggie had run was well worth the prize.

Jean and Owen had contrived one brief conversation alone since her return. He was pleased that the poem had reached his friend, grateful to her. She did not have the courage to tell him she had not placed the manuscript in his friend's hands.

When she told him of the peril she and Jean had stood in, Owen was inclined to regard her as a heroine. She knew she was indulging vanity to bask in his admiration—if she was a heroine, so was Maggie—but she couldn't help herself. His praise bathed her in a warm glow. She longed to pour out her feelings to him, to reach a real understanding, but there was no opportunity.

Clanross was taking a great interest in Owen's catalogue these days. He left the two of them together in the bookroom only when Maggie, Elizabeth, or Miss Bluestone was there.

Nor could Jean and Owen walk the grounds without company. Mostly their companion was Maggie. Jean didn't have the heart to rebuff Maggie whilst her sister looked so dispirited.

After the ride to the pavilion, however, Jean felt real concern that Maggie's injury had addled her wits. So great was her concern that she spoke almost absently when Owen asked if she thought he should read the georgics to everyone that evening. Maggie and Johnny had been thick as thieves. Surely Maggie would be glad to see Johnny at the birthday dinner.

Jean waited until her sister had had time for a good rest, then entered the bedchamber. The drapes were drawn and the light dim.

"Maggie . . ."

"What is it?"

"I want to talk."

Maggie stirred on the pillows. "All right."

Jean pulled a chair to the head of the bed. "You've always liked Johnny Dyott. I thought you'd be glad to hear he was coming. What's wrong?"

Maggie flung an arm over her eyes.

"Tell me, Mag."

"He won't speak to me. Whenever he saw me after the riot, he called me Lady Margaret. He despises me." She began to weep.

Alarmed, Jean rose and bent over her. "Johnny was a little angry with us, of course, but I'm sure he likes you very much." That *she* had forfeited Johnny's esteem she knew well enough. She remembered his questions in the hackney.

"We were friends before," Maggie sobbed. "He confided in me. I love him and now it's all ruined."

"I didn't know," Jean said slowly.

"Know what?" Maggie choked on a sob.

"That your feelings were engaged."

Maggie only cried harder.

"I really didn't," Jean insisted, alarmed. "I'm sorry, Mag, but why didn't you tell me?"

Maggie was heard to mutter that it wasn't romantical.

"Like Owen, do you mean?"

Maggie gave an assenting sniff. "But I love Johnny. I want to marry him."

Jean had been leaning over her sister. Now she sat down hard on the chair. Though her love for Owen was a rare, crystalline blossom, the idea of marriage to him had scarcely crossed her mind. Marriage was something that would happen in the dim future. She would marry Owen, of course. When he was famous like Byron and ready to settle down. Settle down. The phrase weighed on her mind like lead. "Are you sure?"

Maggie gulped and nodded. "I'll never love another man as I love Johnny. I'm . . . I was comfortable with him."

Jean blinked. Comfortable? What did comfort have to do with the course of true love? "I wish you'd told me," she repeated.

Maggie hiccoughed. "I wanted to be sure. I thought we would go on as we were for ever. Now everything's spoilt. He'll be polite."

"Oh, Mag, I am sorry." Jean felt helpless to console Maggie and curiously distant from her. How could her twin, her lifelong confidante, have conceived so strange an idea of love?

They had discussed the subject at length and Maggie had always agreed with Jean's opinions. They had admired the same fictional heroes and the same love songs. Of course, Maggie was not poetic. Jean had assimilated that difference long ago. Maggie was down-to-earth, practical. But love. Surely one could not be practical about love.

Yet Maggie said she loved Johnny and her grief was a powerful argument that she spoke the truth.

"Tell me what I can do to help," Jean said humbly.

Maggie rose on one elbow. "Release me from my promise."

"About Owen's poem?" Jean licked dry lips. "I can't."

"I have to tell Johnny the truth."

"But don't you see, Johnny is Owen's enemy. He'd betray Owen."

"He would not." Maggie glowered.

"I don't mean he'd lay an information. Nothing like that. But he'd feel obliged to tell Clanross. Clanross is his employer. And Clanross would send Owen away. I couldn't bear it, Maggie." Tears blurred Jean's vision. "I couldn't."

Maggie flopped back on the pillow. "It doesn't matter. Johnny won't want to speak to me privately in any case."

Jean could think of no reply. And no solution. If only she could have a long talk with Owen alone. If he knew of Maggie's feelings, surely he would agree that she should tell . . . no. It was too much to ask.

"I'm sorry," she said again. "It's not fair."

Maggie did not reply.

= 15 =

THE DAYS BEFORE Jean and Maggie's eighteenth birthday tried Elizabeth's patience, never her strong suit, *à la outrance*.

Maggie languished. She moped and complained of the headache until Elizabeth, genuinely alarmed, sent for the apothecary and Charles Wharton of Hazeldell in sequence. The apothecary prescribed rest and laudanum. Charles prescribed exercise and fortifying broths.

Charles was a childhood friend and the surgeon who had saved Tom's life three years before. Elizabeth had a great regard for his medical opinion. He did not think Maggie was of a consumptive habit, which relieved Elizabeth's mind. Nevertheless Maggie kept to her couch.

Jean was by turns sullen and overexcited. Her desire for private meetings with Owen Davies shone out clear as day. Even with Tom's aid, Elizabeth was hard put to keep track of Jean.

Above all, the weather and the lengthening daylight frustrated Elizabeth's astronomical observations. That fact alone would have left her restive. It did not help that Tom was palpably tiptoeing about her sensibilities.

She was glad her husband was home, touched by his pleasure in his sons, and grateful that he was willing to watch over Owen Davies, but she wished he would come out forthrightly with whatever was on his mind.

Finally she took the bit in her teeth and confronted him. They had just come from a lively afternoon session with the babies. Tom followed her into her dressing room and watched as she brushed her hair preparatory to putting it up for dinner. He liked her hair, which was plain chestnut. Glossy as chestnuts, he said. He had been retailing some minor accomplishment of the Honourable Richard. She interrupted him ruthlessly.

"Dickon is clearly destined for great things. What is on your mind, Tom?"

His brows shot up. "The state of the nation?"

"Try again."

"Maggie's megrims."

She shook her head.

"You're a hard woman to please."

Elizabeth smiled. She had always liked his sparring style. "If you don't tell me what's troubling you, Tom, I shall imagine horrors." She stroked the brush through her hair and the air crackled. Electrical.

"Horrors?"

"You've sunk your fortune in shares of a steam-driven railroad and the engineer has gone bankrupt."

His grey eyes gleamed with amusement.

"You plan to leave me for Lady Holland."

"Guess again."

Elizabeth set down the brush. "I knew how it would be. You've taken up hot-air-balloon navigation and mean to cross the Channel in a wicker basket."

Tom laughed aloud. He was notoriously prone to motion sickness and would be the last man on earth to take up hot-air ballooning.

"I wish my face were not an open book," he said ruefully when his mirth subsided. "I've done an unforgivable thing, Elizabeth."

"Yes?"

"I've invited Richard Falk to bring his family to Brecon for the month of August. Well, from the end of July."

Elizabeth digested that. "Perfidy."

He was shamefaced but still amused. "I know very well

you'll be wanting to work at the telescope, my dear. It's an unconscionable imposition. Fortunately, Richard has not yet accepted. His affairs are still unsettled . . ."

"It might do," Elizabeth mused.

"I beg your pardon?"

"I meant to invite Willoughby and Bella." Watching in her pier glass, she saw him grimace. He did not like Willoughby Conway-Gore who, until the birth of their sons, had been his heir. Elizabeth was mildly fond of Willoughby's wife, but a month of Willoughby would have been more than enough for her, too.

"Why invite anyone at all?"

"I shall need reinforcements, you see, if the king goes through with his foolish divorce and you're compelled to sit in the Lords nonstop. I like Colonel Falk. He's a sensible man and I think he has a kindness for Jean and Maggie."

"Whew."

She cocked her head inquiringly.

"Not every one takes to Richard. He's an acquired taste."

"I daresay. However, he strikes me as quick-witted and commonsensical. You'll allow that anyone dealing with Owen and my sisters ought to display both qualities."

"Indeed."

"I don't know Mrs. Falk, of course."

"Emily Falk is an agreeable woman."

Elizabeth turned and faced him directly. "Will she require to be entertained? I do mean to work at the telescope. I'm sure Colonel Falk will find ways to amuse himself, but a lady who feels her hostess is slighting her can be dispiriting company."

Tom smiled. "That's the last word I'd use to describe Emily. And she dotes on children. She has five of her own to occupy her if our sons and our sisters lose their charm."

"Lord, chaos in the nursery."

"Her Sally is a trifle younger than the boys, and Harry, I think, a year older, so there are only two young Falks still in the nursery. Tommy, my godson, is six or seven. Amy is just Georgy's age, and the eldest, Emily's son, is twelve."

Elizabeth brooded. "If I were to put Jean and Maggie in charge of the older children . . ."

Tom shot her a mock salute. "Napoleonic, Elizabeth."

She sighed. "Napoleon met his Waterloo. The girls would probably balk at so obvious a diversion. However, I shall write Mrs. Falk at once and second your invitation."

He came to her, took her face in both hands and kissed her soundly. "I wish I might witness your every skirmish."

Her spirits fell. "I wish you might, too. There is an eclipse of the sun I particularly wished to observe in your company."

He took her hand in his own. "I give you my oath, queen or no queen, divorce or no divorce, I shall be with you for the eclipse of the sun."

Elizabeth pressed his hand to her cheek. "I'll hold you to your promise, sir."

Johnny reached Brecon the day before the twins' birthday dinner. During the coach ride he had rehearsed several eloquent speeches designed to restore him to Maggie's confidence. When he arrived at Brecon late in the afternoon, however, he found that Maggie was abed with the headache and did not plan to show herself that evening.

That was a facer.

The company at Brecon had swelled, and the dinner that evening stretched interminably, probably owing to the presence of the Whartons and the Conway-Gores. Mrs. Conway-Gore was witty and handsome enough to distract any man from his mutton, but her husband, a Conway cousin, struck Johnny as a coxcomb.

A waspish exquisite in very high shirt points and very tight knee breeches, Willoughby Conway-Gore soon drove the gentlemen from their port. They rejoined the ladies to discover Lady Clanross riffling through the stack of musick on the pianoforte. She was bent, it seemed, on an evening of song.

Bella Conway-Gore had a clear, well-trained soprano and an obliging temper. She sang three of the new Italian airs, then volunteered to play for the others. Charles Wharton and Lady Clanross persuaded Owen Davies to join them and the four singers were soon delighting the company with their harmonies. Owen had a true Welsh tenor and he exercised it to much applause.

Johnny no longer saw Davies as a rival but he could not help wishing the Muses' darling would strangle in his artfully negligent neckcloth. No such happy chance occurred.

Clanross listened with evident enjoyment. Once Johnny swallowed his chagrin, he might have, too, for the singers' voices blended well and he liked musick. Unfortunately, he had chosen to sit beside Mrs. Wharton, and she kept up a gentle babble of inanity that made concentration difficult. He was obliged to lend her at least half an ear.

Though it was hard to believe, Mrs. Wharton was Witty Willoughby's sister. She was a pretty woman with the remains of what must have been remarkable beauty overlaid with plumpness. She was clearly enceinte as well. Had she said anything sensible Johnny would have given her his attention, but she was as near to being witless as made no difference. She had two clever children and a clever husband and she told Johnny all about their cleverness, illustrating her tiny points with endless anecdote.

Trying to look interested, Johnny let his mind wander to the twins. Jean was listening to the singers—or possibly just to the leading tenor—with rapt attention. She had avoided speaking to Johnny at dinner though she sat on his left. He supposed she had not yet forgiven him for the cross-examination he subjected her to in the hackney.

Had Maggie forgiven him? Her absence was not a propitious omen. His spirits sank as the singers' voices rose.

How could he assure her, without offending her loyalty,

that he knew her sister had led her into the escapade in London? Maggie was by nature sweet, biddable, trusting. If only she would place her trust in him, he would wear it like a favour.

That was a good phrase. He tasted it. Perhaps he was not a wild Welsh poet, but he *could* turn a phrase. But what good would his eloquence do him if Maggie would not listen?

". . . and for bonnie Annie Laurie," Owen warbled, "I would lay-hay me doon and dee."

Indeed.

". . . oil of cloves," Mrs. Wharton was saying earnestly. "It is your only remedy for sore gums."

"Er, yes," Johnny murmured.

At that point Willoughby Conway-Gore mutinied. Though he was not so boorish as to say so directly, he made it clear he had had enough of Scottish warbling. He meant to indulge in a rubber or two of whist, if Elizabeth did not object, and where the deuce were the playing cards?

It was that kind of evening. Johnny played whist with an inattentive mind and he and his partner, the charming Mrs. Conway-Gore, were soundly trounced. The Whartons departed. The ladies retired. Mr. Conway-Gore bullied the earl into a game of piquet for chicken stakes.

That was enough for Johnny. He excused himself and went up to his bedchamber, convinced that he should have stayed in London.

He rose early with a plan of action. It had come to him in the night, as good things often do. Still in his nightshirt, he pawed through his travelling secretary, and found pen, paper, sealing wax and the not-bad sonnet. He began to write.

Possibly because she had spent the better part of two weeks lolling about in a darkened bedchamber, Maggie also woke early. Her eyes opened and would not be shut. It was her eighteenth birthday, the sun shone, and Johnny Dyott lay beneath the same roof, even if he did despise her. She stared solemnly at the canopy. Jean was sound asleep.

It was even too early for the servants to be stirring. Maggie clenched her eyes shut and willed herself back to sleep. Silently she recited five verses of "Marmion." She turned on her side and put a pillow over her head, but it was no use and her flailing about was beginning to disturb Jean.

Resigned, Maggie slipped from the bed. Jean said mmmn? and settled in like a hare in its form, but she did not wake and Maggie tiptoed into the dressing room.

As she brushed her short curls she caught a glimpse of white near the bottom edge of the door. A letter. Probably Owen plotting a tryst with Jean. Maggie rose and retrieved the envelope. It was sealed with a plain wafer. She turned it over. "Lady Margaret," it said in Johnny's neat script.

Maggie's pulse thrummed. She broke the seal hastily and a slip of lighter paper fell to the carpet. She picked it up and ran to the dressing table, both papers clasped to her bosom.

"My dear Maggie," it began.

Maggie, not Lady Margaret! She smoothed the creamy sheet, scarcely daring to believe her eyes. Her fingers trembled.

"Do daisies unclose betimes on their birthday? If I were any kind of poet, and the enclosed sonnet will show you plainly I am not, perhaps I could put into words how very much I wish you well on this bright morning. I know you have been ill and dare not hope that you may join me in the formal garden before breakfast, but, when you do read this, know that I saw the day's eye open and thought of you. The best of happy birthdays, sweet marguerite.

"Your friend and devoted servant, J. Dyott."

"Oh, my word!" Maggie whispered.

The sonnet. She had forgot the sonnet. She picked up the other sheet. The poem was called "The Pearl," another play on her name. It said pleasant, flattering things in neat iambic lines that even rhymed. Maggie had never heard of anything half so romantical—and it was addressed to her, not to Jean.

She let the sonnet flutter to the surface of the table and stared at her flushed face in the mirror. Her grey eyes shone and her mouth formed a rosy O. And she was still in her night rail and robe!

Leaping to her feet, she dashed to the window, flung it up, and craned out, but she could see only a tiny corner of the garden. Would he wait? He had to wait.

As she scrambled into her green walking dress it occurred to Maggie that she had never in her life dressed alone. Before they had Lisette's services to themselves, she and Jean had always buttoned one another's buttons and hooked one another's hooks. Probably she was putting herself together all sidewise. She swallowed a giggle.

She fastened her stockings and slid into a pair of stout shoes, smoothed her hair, and blew a kiss at her excited reflection in the glass.

She was halfway out the door when she remembered the papers lying on the dressing table. She retrieved them and slipped them into the pocket of her skirt. For once *she* was going to have a secret. Jean would have to pry it from her.

She danced down the marble stair, tiptoed through the dim salon, unlatched the glassed doors, and stepped onto the wide terrace that led down to the formal garden.

Dew still whitened the neat squares of grass and trembled on the stiff new leaves of the rosebushes. She hadn't thought of the dew when she chose the heavy walking shoes—they had merely been the first pair to hand—but she was glad of them. Her jean half-boots would have been soaked before she reached the garden. She did not see Johnny.

As she approached the still fountain, however, she found him sitting on the stone bench by the high wall, facing the sun. Perhaps she made a noise. He looked round and rose.

Maggie ran to him. "Oh, Johnny, I missed you!"

He took her hand, smiling. "Did you?"

"And I loved the sonnet. It was beautiful and . . . and very flattering."

He raised her hand to his lips. "Not flattering. Truthful."

She knew she was blushing, and looked away, unable to think what to say next.

Perhaps Johnny sensed her confusion. "Shall we go for a walk?" he asked, letting her hand fall gently.

"Oh, yes," she said. "Yes, please. A long one."

Jean thought the birthday had gone very well. Lying abed that night beside her sister, she turned the day's events over in her mind like the pages of a book of hours. Owen had discovered a gothick book of hours, writ and illuminated by a medieval hand, among the heaps of unpublished manuscripts in the library. He had saved it to show her on her birthday morning, and though the writing was in Latin the pictures were certainly very pretty. He had also writ her an ode comparing her to Jeanne d'Arc. He slipped it to her with a very significant look. The poem moved her more than the illuminated manuscript, though Owen's excitement over the gothick find interested her.

Unfortunately, Clanross had been in the book room with them all morning and the two men soon went off into a discussion of how best to preserve the manuscript. Jean supposed it must be rare.

Whilst the men talked, she slipped Owen's ode between the pages of an unexceptionable novel and read the poem through at her leisure.

She kept the book by her. She had meant to show Maggie the ode and did remember to carry the book to their room, but the excitement of the afternoon and evening pushed it from her mind.

She and Maggie, Tom, and Elizabeth had taken tea with their three young sisters at the Dower House. It was satisfying to read awe in the little girls' wide blue eyes as she and Maggie talked of the London shops. They had agreed with Elizabeth that it was better to say nothing of the riot.

Just before Jean and Maggie retired to dress for dinner, Elizabeth took them to her suite to show them their mother's jewels.

The elder Lady Clanross had died when the twins were thirteen. Jean remembered her mother well and did not need Elizabeth's reminiscences to remind her that her mother had been a very high stickler indeed. Elizabeth spoke in terms of her own gratitude and affection, but Jean read the underlying criticism. Their mother would not have approved the Greek Street adventure.

That sounded a sour note for Jean though Maggie seemed not to notice. As she and her twin pored over the trays of costly baubles, however, Jean's delight overtook her resentment. She chose a diamond hair-clip and Maggie a strand of baroque pearls, and both girls were given diamond earbobs. None of the jewellery was pinchbeck. It was the real thing, and Elizabeth gave them handsome leather cases to keep their selections in when they travelled. They wore the earbobs to dinner.

After dinner, whilst the carpet was rolled and Miss Bluestone warmed up at the pianoforte, Clanross took them to his study and presented his gifts. He had caused Rundle and Bridge to create brooches for them, each to an individual design, each quite beautiful. Maggie's centered on a perfect black pearl and Jean's on a cluster of fire opals. Both girls were struck dumb, at least for the moment, and Jean half remembered the sensations she had felt when she fancied herself in love with her tall brother-in-law. He was a very kind man. When her tongue unlocked she contrived to thank him. Maggie gave him a kiss.

Fortunately, Maggie seemed to have pulled out of the dismals. She had even gone for a walk before breakfast. She laughed and joked over a game of Fish with the little girls in the afternoon, and partnered Johnny and Owen and

Willoughby at the dancing after dinner, quite as if nothing were wrong.

Jean's conscience still pricked her when she remembered Maggie's tears, but she was glad Maggie hadn't got the headache on their birthday.

= 16 =

EMILY SET LADY Clanross's letter aside and watched as her husband concluded Tommy's reading lesson.

Richard sat opposite the little boy at the battered school-room table that had served Emily and her brothers. When Tommy stumbled, he looked up at his father's mouth and Richard said the troublesome word in a low unemphatic voice. Tommy gave a quick nod, like a robin dipping for water, repeated the word with approximately the right intonation, and went on with the story. The same process happened five times with no diminution of Richard's patience. He even contrived to look interested.

Tommy had had a holiday from reading whilst his father was in London. Though Emily felt mild guilt for neglecting the chore in the confusion of the move, she thought Tommy had needed a break from his routine. She was relieved to know that the little boy had not forgot his lessons entirely. He was also speaking more often and more easily than he had been, though he was still hard to follow when he spoke fast.

Tommy made his way to the moral of the tale—Mrs. More's tales always ended in an improving message. Emily had long ago decided she did not like Hannah More and would cross the street to avoid meeting that worthy philanthropist, but simple stories for children were rare as hen's teeth, so Tommy, perforce, read Mrs. More's tales. Emily watched as her stepson was kissed and scampered off in search of the other children.

Richard extricated himself from the low table and stretched, yawning.

"You ought to write stories for children—like the ones you writ for Amy when you were in the Peninsula. *Your* stories would not make one feel faintly ill."

He cocked an eyebrow. "I think you disapprove of moral allegory. What should I title my efforts, *Unimproving Tales?*"

"*The Phantastical Adventures of Thomas Falk*, of course." Emily brooded. "You could call yourself Charity Goodenough . . ."

Richard laughed. "Or Robin Goodfellow. Have you had another letter from your sister-in-law?"

"From Lady Clanross. She has sent me an invitation to Brecon. I discern Tom's devious Italian hand." She handed him the sheet of fine, hot-pressed paper. It smelt faintly of otto of roses. Emily favoured lavender herself.

Richard scanned the letter. "Handsomely put. Shall you go?"

"I want to know what you did to earn her ladyship's undying gratitude."

"Eh? Oh, the girls."

"What did you rescue them from, pirates?"

He explained the episode of the riot in comic detail.

"Good heavens," Emily murmured, fascinated and a trifle shocked. "They must be mettlesome young women."

"Spirited, certainly."

"Why did you not tell me before?"

"It wasn't my secret to share. Besides," he confessed, "it slipped my mind."

"Hmmm. And Johnny is in love with Lady Margaret."

"It would seem so."

"I can imagine Johnny in love with a demure miss with dimples, but a hoyden . . ." She shook her head. She liked Johnny but he was a very proper young man. That was what came of growing up in the close of a cathedral.

"I fancy the hoyden is Lady Jean," Richard said. "In any case, Cupid definitely hit the mark. Johnny spoke of marriage."

"But Lady Margaret is not yet eighteen!"

"Younger than she are happy mothers made," Richard said wryly, "though I think the twins have turned eighteen. Johnny hared off to Brecon for the birthday fete. Lady Clanross will present the girls at the June levee."

Emily rose from her chair and began to tidy the books on the schoolroom table. "Have you decided what you mean to do about McGrath?"

When Richard had returned from London the previous week he had taken McGrath off for a long walk through the Hampshire countryside. McGrath had since conducted himself soberly in Sir Henry's kitchen.

"I shall send him to Ireland."

Emily took a moment to digest that. "Oh, no! Peggy . . ."

Richard sighed. "Pegeen is McGrath's wife. If she chooses to go with him we can't stop her."

"It's not fair!"

He was still standing by her chair with Lady Clanross's letter in his hand. He took a step toward her. "Do you suppose these past years have been fair to McGrath?"

"I have made every allowance for his lapses," Emily said indignantly.

"Jerry is not used to being tied to a house. He spent fifteen years on campaign, thirteen of them in my service. He was always a man I could rely on."

"I know that . . ."

"Then you know I cannot repay him by penning him belowstairs as a sort of drunken house-dog."

Emily bit her lip.

"He's not suited to domestic service."

"God knows," she shot back, defiant.

"Jerry knows it, too. Why do you fancy he's been numbing his brain with gin?" Richard drew a breath.

"When I hadn't the means to set him up in a trade that suited him, I had to stand by and watch him destroying himself. Now I can act. He wants to deal in horses and I think he can succeed at that. I mean to send him to Cork with a letter of credit on a bank there."

"He'll drink himself into the gutter in a week."

"I think not, but if he does at least he'll know he had the choice."

"And what of Peggy and the children? Don't they count?"

He softened. "I know it's hard. Pegeen needn't go at once. Jerry means her to stay here until he has established himself, but she will go sooner or later. He's her man . . ."

"And she'll see it as her duty. Very well, but it's not fair and I don't like it."

His eyes were dark. "I don't like it either and perhaps Peggy won't, but Jerry must have his chance."

Emily stalked off to nurse Sally. She found Peggy Mc-Grath at her usual station and asked the woman bluntly if she knew of McGrath's intent. Though Peggy exclaimed and repined and shed a number of loquacious Irish tears, it was clear that she had known of the horrible plan for days and that she meant to follow her husband home to her native turf.

Emily had learnt to value Peggy McGrath in the years since the woman had first come to her with Amy and Tommy. She had thought Peggy returned her regard. She knew the nurse was attached to the children.

"How can you bear to leave them?"

"Sure, and it's a hard thing," Peggy mourned.

Sally nuzzled Emily's breast like a piglet and made quite a rude noise. "But the children . . ."

"Ah, the poor darlings."

"Peggy," Emily cried, "how can you? You don't *have* to go."

Peggy's eyes widened in honest shock. "If I didn't,

McGrath'd kill me for sure, the ould divil. Besides, he's me husband, missus."

It was no use.

In her agitation over the McGraths, Emily half-forgot Lady Clanross's letter. Richard reminded her of it that evening when they had escaped from the withdrawing room and her father.

"Do you want to visit Brecon?"

"I don't know. Do you?" Emily had ripped off her earbobs and was unpinning her hair.

"I must go, at least for a short stay. Tom wants me to look at some letters with an eye to editing them."

"Leaving *me* behind." Emily was still feeling surly.

"It's as you choose, Emily." He hesitated. "If you'd rather not go, I can take the three oldest with me."

Emily turned and stared at him.

He had removed his neckcloth and coat and sat on the bed in shirtsleeves. "Lady Clanross has a sister Amy's age, and I mean to continue working with Tommy."

"What of Matt?"

"There are bound to be horses. Tom says the lake is stocked." He undid the buttons of his shirt and pulled it over his head, muttering muffled words.

"I beg your pardon?"

"I said, it's time Matt saw a bit of the world."

The words worked in Emily's brain.

"Besides," he added, "I'd be in his black books forever if I left him behind."

"That's true."

He yanked the nightshirt over his head.

"I suppose you are trying, in your underhand way, to suggest that I, too, ought to see more of the world than my own corner of Hampshire."

" 'Thus we with windlasses and with assays of bias, by indirections find directions out,' " Richard quoted. He was quoting a great deal lately. Emily wondered why.

"I like Hampshire."

"It has its charms."

Emily's suspicion eased and she began to laugh. "Oh, very well, Richard. At least I shall escape Papa at his harvesttime worst. Must I read up on the moons of Jupiter before I meet Lady Clanross?"

"I found her conversable in plain English," Richard said seriously.

The rapport Johnny had reestablished with Maggie was a tender plant. He meant to cultivate it. He had not made her an offer of marriage. He thought that might frighten her. Colonel Falk notwithstanding, he wasn't sure he ought to be so bold so soon.

He was now in no doubt of his own feelings. He wanted to marry the ninth Earl of Clanross's fifth daughter. That was that. Every hour spent in her company deepened his conviction.

Though her headaches had miraculously vanished, Maggie was still shaken by her ordeal. She had not Jean's resiliency. Johnny found the cropped hair especially touching—perhaps because he associated it with illness. The short curls gave Maggie an elfin air he found irresistible. She looked so delicate a strong gust of wind might pick her up and blow her over the beeches into another country, faeryland perhaps.

He knew he was being fanciful. His imagination was alive with phantasies. He dreamt often and in brilliant colour, and more than once found his attention wandering from a letter he ought to be copying to daylight visions of Maggie in a rose-covered cottage with prattling infants at her knee.

Those visions led him to sober reflection on the future. He had a modest income from the Consols his godmother had left him and Clanross paid him a handsome wage. When he married, his father had promised to settle five hundred pounds a year on him—if his father were not so

offended as to cut him off with a shilling. He had not heard from his father.

He would have to find another source of income. He liked politicks but it might be years before a seat fell vacant. In any case, members were not paid. Whilst he waited for opportunity to knock, he must gain practical experience of the art and persuade Clanross that his interest was not a passing fancy. He thought of Owen's odes and Colonel Falk's history and wondered if he might not take up writing, too—political writing.

It was a difficult time to be a writer on political subjects, but Johnny thought closely reasoned, moderately expressed opinion must find a publisher. Probably the editors would be grateful to read a piece of prose that did not indulge in satirical exaggeration. Such extravagance was foreign to Johnny's temper.

In the weeks before the Brecon party were set to return to London for the levee, Johnny began to work on a temperate, well-reasoned plea for reform of Parliament. He would send it to the *Quarterly Review*. A friend from his Oxford days was the son of one of the editors.

His efforts at composition did not detract from his careful courtship. Maggie was delighted to listen to him, eager to read what he had writ. And explaining himself to Maggie helped him clarify his ideas. He was happy to instruct her when her comprehension faltered, but she understood a great deal. She came of a political family, after all. Her father had been a prominent Whig.

"Johnny and Maggie are smelling of April and May," Elizabeth said.

"Is that bad?" Tom laid the letter he had been reading aside.

"I don't know. I hope they haven't come to a secret understanding. No, Johnny wouldn't be so lost to propriety." Elizabeth paced the carpet of their private drawing room. "At least Jean is biddable these days."

"Now that I do find suspicious."

"Oh, dear . . ." Elizabeth caught the twinkle in his eyes and plumped onto the sofa beside him. "Am I fuss-budgeting?"

"I think you're making yourself more anxious than you need to."

"Perhaps," Elizabeth said darkly. "Perhaps not. I wish Owen in Timbuktu."

"I can send him to the Lothian house. Those books need to be catalogued, too."

"That's true, but he's making progress here."

"He's a good scholar with a genuine love of books," Tom said gently. "And his poetry has some merit."

"Hang his poetry. If you must be a patron of the arts," she grumbled, "take up painters. Or musicians. I know a worthy violinist."

"Bald and sixty?"

"Fat and forty with a wife and seven hopeful children."

"I'll leave the musicians to you. The truth is," he added ruefully, "I feel I should follow your father's example but I haven't his education. That exhibit we saw last autumn . . ."

"The historical painters?"

He nodded. "I remember one battle scene. Wolfe on the Heights of Abraham, I think it was. I stared at it and kept telling myself it was great art, but all the while I was seeing little puffballs of smoke issuing from misplaced cannons and thinking that the company in the middle distance would be chewed up in the first barrage."

Elizabeth laughed. "But you admired that sea battle of Mr. Turner's."

"It was very like. I felt the *mal de mer* coming on."

"You don't have to do everything Papa did, Tom."

"God forbid, but if men of wealth don't use their wealth to some purpose, what good is it?"

"Patronise the sciences, then."

"You can't want another telescope!"

Elizabeth acknowledged the hit. She was amused and rather touched by Tom's confession. She had grown up in a milieu of wealth and took its benefits for granted most of the time. She knew Tom did not. Though she honoured his sense of duty, she couldn't help reflecting that her father had not made his position such a *chore*. Certainly he had enjoyed his political duties more than Tom did.

"Does Barney have news of the divorce bill?" she asked, for Tom's letter had come from town. "Anne sent an account of the queen's triumphal entry into London, with Alderman Wood at her side, forsooth, and the Mob pulling her carriage through the City. What a scene!"

Tom shrugged. "Someone is advising the queen shrewdly."

"Brougham?"

"I daresay. Barney writes of disaffection among the Guards. One regiment wore the queen's colours on duty. The government are fools to pursue the bill. All the discontented factions in the country have taken up the queen's cause. It's a focus for them."

"Should you not rejoice?"

"The whole business is a waste of time," he said irritably. "I feel no urge to defend the queen's hypothetical honour. If I thought the opposition would gain a leader from the trial I'd accept the prospect, but such sordid revelations as we're bound to hear can only throw up a storm of muck."

"Will the streets be safe for the levee?"

He frowned. "The Mob resent Prinny's extravagance and there may be demonstrations. However, the mood in town seems good-natured enough at the moment."

"And your reputation as a Radical will insure our safety."

"Do you dislike my opinions, Elizabeth?"

"No, I'm with you." She glanced at him. He slouched in his corner of the sofa, brooding. "Perhaps the Mob will take our horses from the shafts and pull us to Carlton House in triumph."

He met her eyes and his mouth relaxed in a smile. "Your sisters would relish that."

=17=

THE MORNING OF the levee dawned clear and warm. Maggie and Jean rose well before the chambermaid entered with their hot water. Maggie could scarcely contain her impatience. Jean dawdled. Even so, they reached the breakfast table so early Clanross was still drinking coffee.

His friend, Colonel Falk, who had come up to town again on legal business, was reading *The Times*. He set it aside and both men rose as the girls entered.

Clanross inspected them. "You look as if you may be able to withstand the rigours of the day."

Jean made a face and took the chair he held for her. Waite, the butler, summoned by some obscure instinct, had come in. He held a chair for Maggie. Colonel Falk gave them an abstracted smile and returned to his newspaper.

When the girls had been served and their tea poured, Maggie said, "I shall wear your brooch today, Clanross."

"I'm honoured, my lady." He smiled at her. "Have you got the hang of walking about with a train yet? Devilish contraptions, trains. I tripped on mine and nearly fell at Black Rod's feet during the opening of Parliament."

"They've done away with hoops," Jean offered around a bite of toast. "Elizabeth said hers caught on a whatnot table and knocked an ormolu vase to the floor. It fell at the Princess Sophia's feet. Lizzie was mortified."

"Not for long, I'll wager." Clanross took a sip of coffee. He drank it black and sugarless, a barbarism Maggie had found fascinating when she first saw it. She had tried black coffee once.

She sipped her sweet bohea. "Johnny means to make his bow, too, you know."

"So I've heard," Clanross said gravely.

Colonel Falk set the paper down. "Will Dyott have to wear a train and ostrich plumes, too?"

Maggie knew when she was being twitted. She took a dignified sip of tea. "When Clanross was presented to his majesty at the pavilion he only had to wear knee breeches."

The colonel's eyebrows twisted. "I wish I might have seen him."

Clanross grinned.

Maggie tried to explain through a fit of giggles that Clanross had been otherwise conventionally attired. "Were you presented, sir?"

"Only to Bungy Louie."

Clanross looked at his friend with raised eyebrows.

"The king of the French, I should say. He was on his way to Paris, so it was a hasty affair, lasted a mere three hours."

Jean had been spreading marmalade on her toast. She paused with the knife in midair. "Three hours!"

"Waiting," Colonel Falk explained. "The audience itself lasted five minutes."

A blob of the compote dropped onto the cloth. Jean daubed at it with her napkin. "I hope we need not stand about for three hours waiting."

"I daresay you must," Clanross said sympathetically. "However, I'm told Carlton House is full of remarkable objets d'art and there will be a great many other people to quiz."

"All the ladies will be dressed alike," Jean said gloomily. "White with blue trains and ostrich plumes. Tedious."

"Don't balk at the gate, Jean. Elizabeth will disinherit you." Clanross spoke with fervour.

Jean wrinkled her nose. "Oh, I'll go through with it. But it seems a dreadful waste of time."

Colonel Falk looked up from his paper. "Ah, there you are, Dyott. I hear you mean to kiss our noble monarch's hand."

"Um, yes." Johnny blinked sleepily from the doorway. Maggie smiled at him and he smiled back.

"What news, sir?" He poured himself a cup of tea.

"Macassar oil." Colonel Falk was rereading an article on the front page of *The Times*.

"I beg your pardon?"

"Rowland and Son announce the import of a limited supply of macassar oil. Patrons may purchase it at two shillings the vial. It is said to be efficacious in the prevention of baldness."

Johnny blinked again.

Maggie grinned. The front page of *The Times* ran a great many advertisements.

Jean chewed her toast. "I don't believe you'll be needing macassar oil, sir." That was rather rude. Colonel Falk wore his hair longer than the mode decreed.

He rose. "Ah, but I may tear out my flowing tresses any day now."

Clanross chuckled. "Will the Ffoukes sign soon?"

"I hope so." Falk made his excuses and left.

"Why was *he* presented to King Lewis?" Maggie asked. She spooned a second serving of buttered eggs from the chafing dish.

Clanross rose, too. "It was after Waterloo."

Maggie resumed her seat. "Did Colonel Falk take part in that battle?"

Clanross's eyes widened. " 'Oh heavens, die two months ago and not forgotten yet?' "

Johnny had gone red. "Colonel Falk is a hero of Waterloo, Maggie. King Lewis made him a chevalier of France."

"Oh," Maggie said humbly. "I didn't know."

"If Richard felt the need to defend his honour, Johnny, he would do so himself."

Johnny lowered his eyes to his plate.

Clanross went on mildly. "He wears his forelock long to hide a scar. Not a subject for levity." He also departed.

Jean scowled after him. "How was I to know?"

Johnny glanced at the paper. "Good God, the Guards have mutinied!" He picked it up and read rapidly. "No, it is not so bad. One battalion only and they have been marched off to Plymouth."

"Shall we be safe?" Maggie's toast tasted dry. Since they had returned to town, she had wakened twice in the night to the sound of windows breaking. Lord Harrowby's house had been assailed four times since the queen's return to London. Their house had not been touched.

Johnny set the paper aside. "I daresay it's a great fuss over nothing. Don't worry, Marguerite."

The secret name reassured her. Even so, as they set out for Carlton House in the new carriage, her apprehension rose and the headache nibbled.

Bond Street was heavy with vehicles. As they crossed Piccadilly, the traffic afoot increased. The completed portion of Regent Street that led down to Carlton House was lined with troops. What if the impassive faces beneath shakoes and helmets concealed minds aflame with resentment? Would they not make their first attack on the line of glittering carriages they were drawn up to protect?

It was hot in the carriage. Elizabeth, perspiring beneath her bandeau and plumes, refused to have the shades drawn. Jean looked bored. Johnny sat beside Maggie in the facing seat and made easy small talk. She was grateful to him but she answered him at random.

The coachman inched the carriage forward. Johnny and Elizabeth bantered. Jean yawned. At long last they drew up before the colonnaded palace and the footman threw open the door. Maggie was first to descend.

Once they entered the antechamber, in line with hundreds of other sweating notables, the waiting began again. However, as Clanross had promised, there was a great deal to see and Maggie's headache receded.

Among the fashionables milling about in the first ante-chamber, Elizabeth sought out Bella Conway-Gore, who was firing off a young sister that Season. Miss Haverford was shy and rabbit-faced, so Maggie and Johnny were kind to her for awhile as Bella and Elizabeth raked the company for old friends. Jean looked cool—quite a feat in a crowded room on a warm day—and said nothing. It was as if she weren't really present. Her spirit had soared elsewhere, Maggie supposed.

The second antechamber, equally crammed with gilt chairs, porcelain bric-a-brac, and fashionable people, was even hotter than the first. No one sat in the chairs. Maggie plied her white crepe fan and hoped her face was not red as a beet.

Finally they reached the rose satin withdrawing room, a perfect cube full of royalty and their attendants in magnif-icent array. The king's equerries wore splendid laced uni-forms. Elizabeth pointed out the upright figure of Lord Uxbridge. He was quite old, fifty at least, but he was the handsomest man Maggie had ever seen. It was said he would be Lord High Steward at the coronation, if the coronation ever took place. The king meant to dispose of his turbulent helpmeet first.

Elizabeth did not point out the Marchioness of Conyn-gham, the king's current favourite, but Maggie had no trouble deciding who the fat lady was. The royal mistress was behung with precious stones, attended by a bevy of hangers-on, and clearly in the king's good graces. From time to time he cast her a look both rogueish and soulful.

"*Chacun à son goût,*" Jean hissed, elbowing her twin. Perhaps Jean was not so far away after all. Maggie hid a smile behind her fan, but the king's ponderous infatuation embarrassed her. It was one thing for beautiful young people like Owen and Jean to exchange speaking glances in publick, quite another for very fat personages in their sixties, however magnificent.

The king *was* magnificent. As Elizabeth approached the presence, Maggie heard, "Lady Clanross, Lady Jean and Lady Margaret Conway, Mr. Dyott." Then she was making her curtsey, deep and correct. She didn't wobble as she rose or step on Jean's train. The royal palm was hot and moist.

George IV, whom Maggie still thought of as Prinny, said something affable about remembering her mother, smiled kindly when she contrived to utter a strangled phrase, and turned to Johnny, who was right behind her and whose presence, Maggie was sure, had given her the confidence to bring herself off without disgracing her name. She passed on down the line without being able to distinguish one royal princess from the next. Finally the four of them escaped, and the ladies looped their trains once more over their left arms, which made walking easier. Johnny's *chapeau bras* was, miraculously, still tucked beneath his arm. He had been sure he would drop it.

"Thank heavens that's over," Jean muttered, fanning herself vigourously.

"Let's have a peep at the conservatory," Elizabeth suggested. "I doubt we'll have another chance. The king surrounds himself with Tories of the deepest dye." She led the way.

Maggie thought the gothick depths of the conservatory wonderful. In spite of the presence of several hundred of the king's guests among the towering pillars, it was a cool room, a refuge. The delicate fan vaulting of the ceiling seemed to touch the sky. Like the nave of a cathedral—not Lincoln, which was too red and real—but some phantasy cathedral. Their voices were lost in the vastness. Johnny smiled at her. Maggie smiled back.

When they had stayed a decent interval Elizabeth said they might leave. Johnny escorted them smoothly through the crowds of chattering women and uncomfortable men in knee breeches. From time to time Elizabeth stopped to speak to an acquaintance. The king's servants wore powder and the elaborate livery his majesty had designed himself. They were haughty as archdukes, every one of them. Under the murmur of voices one could hear the strains of a superb orchestra playing, though Maggie never saw the musicians. Perhaps they hung in the air like Prospero's musicians in *The Tempest*.

As their carriage swayed into motion at last and a faint breeze wafted through the open windows, Elizabeth pulled off the heavy ostrich-plume headdress. She shoved her damp hair from her brow and smiled at Maggie. "Had enough of magnificence?"

"It *was* magnificent, wasn't it?" Maggie considered. "My feet hurt."

Elizabeth laughed. Jean was yawning again. Johnny touched Maggie's gloved hand briefly with his own.

"Ready, Elizabeth?" Tom stuck his head through the doorway from his dressing room.

"In a minute." Elizabeth glowered at her reflection in the glass. She was wearing an eau de Nile ball gown with the heavy gold parure Tom had bought her in Italy. She would have preferred the peach-coloured satin Mme. Thérèse had finished only the day before, but she had decided the colour clashed with the twins' pesky hair. They were making their debut at Almack's at last and she had cast herself in the role of foil—she meant to set them off, not to extinguish them.

Well, she could consult Anne. They were dining with Lady Anne and Featherstonehaugh *en famille* before setting off for the Assembly Rooms. If Anne thought the peach would clash, Elizabeth would save it until the girls were safely launched. For tonight, the green would have to do.

"The stole, Dobbins." She wondered if Nile green made her skin look muddy. Perhaps the mirror needed to be resilvered.

Dobbins disposed the wrap about Elizabeth's shoulders and gave a brisk nod. That was as close to approval as Dobbins got these days.

Elizabeth gave the maid a relieved smile and whisked from the room.

"Why the devil are you skulking about in that rig?"

For a moment Elizabeth thought Tom was referring to her gown. Then she caught sight of Colonel Falk and gaped.

He stood by the door of the green guest chamber looking sheepish. He was wearing dress regimentals, a foreign order, and several medals. In the soft light from the hall sconces, he looked quite dashing. In fact, the transformation made Elizabeth blink. The black sling was nowhere to be seen.

He scowled at Tom. "You know very well it's not possible to *skulk* in scarlet. I'm going to dinner."

"I didn't suppose you were mounting guard at the Tower." Tom's eyes narrowed. "It's the eighteenth, isn't it? Regimental dinner?"

"Just so."

"And you mean to walk."

"I fancy I can totter as far as Stephens' Hotel without collapsing. It's in Bond Street."

"For Godsake, man, they read the Riot Act in Old Bond Street yesterday. Are you trying to provoke an incident?"

"I'm trying to go to dinner," Falk said coolly. "Lady Clanross." He inclined his head.

"Sir," she murmured, still fascinated by the alteration in his appearance. In that kind light, he looked Johnny's age, though he was Tom's.

Tom sniffed. "You reek of camphor."

Falk clucked his tongue. "Your footman aired it . . ."

"But you haven't worn it in five years."

"True."

"Then why now?"

Johnny Dyott's door opened. He emerged, resplendent

in his evening rig, stopped dead, and stared at the colonel, too.

"I'm damned if I'm going to let you go off into a riot dressed like a target," Tom muttered.

"Let me?" Falk's eyes flashed. He touched the hilt of his dress sword with his good hand. " 'By heaven, I'll make a ghost of him that lets me!' "

"Fire-eater." Tom began to laugh. "That's an abominable pun. The carriage is outside. Johnny and I will escort you—into the hotel, if necessary. Richard is bound for a regimental dinner, Johnny. Are you with me?"

"Certainly."

Elizabeth caught a flash of white and turned in time to see her sisters enter the hallway in their ball gowns. They stared, too. They looked like astonished bonbons.

"You're damned officious, Tom."

"Better officious than mad."

"We cannot be expected to disappear from sight because our existence provokes the Mob," Falk said softly. "Not all of us can emigrate to Upper Canada."

Tom drew a sharp breath.

"It isn't the solution, Tom. I'm sorry."

"I know," Tom muttered. "Elizabeth, I beg your pardon for the delay. I'll return as soon as may be."

It was not the moment to point out that Anne's dinner would be burnt.

By the time Elizabeth heard the carriage returning she was pacing the floor of the crimson salon where she and the twins had taken refuge. Almack's closed its doors to newcomers at eleven. It was a quarter of nine and Anne did not believe in hasty meals. Fortunately Berkeley Square was closer to King Street than Grosvenor Square.

"We'll be late," Maggie said for the dozenth time.

"My skirts are getting crumpled," Jean complained.

At that point the carriage drew up and Elizabeth heard Waite move to the door. Almost at once Tom stuck his head in the salon. "Shall we go?" His hair was rumpled and his cravat wanted straightening but he was still in one piece.

Elizabeth let out a long sigh. "By all means."

They heard the saga of Stephens' Hotel on the way to Anne's. Johnny had narrowly escaped being hit with a rotten orange as he and Tom walked Colonel Falk to the hotel entrance, but the real delay came because so many surviving Waterloo officers had decided to attend regimental dinners at the same time in the same place. Their equipages blocked the street.

"How will Colonel Falk get back?"

Tom shrugged. "Walk. As he meant to in the first place. I'm starting at shadows these days. Richard pointed out that the nation is in a parlous state if army officers have to be escorted about their lawful business by gentlemen-bodyguards in evening dress. I feel sure Johnny and I will figure largely in the next satire. Here we are at last. I hope Lady Anne will forgive me."

"I daresay she will in a year or two." Elizabeth straightened his cravat. "It might take *me* longer."

He laughed. Ho ho.

Except for the waltzes, Jean's card was full. She was chagrined to discover that had power to please her. Her triumph would have no lasting significance, of course, but she could not deny a twinge of satisfaction.

As the fiddler swung into a reel—most of the dances at Almack's were antiquated—she curtseyed to Johnny Dyott and bobbed to the rhythm. Elizabeth and Featherstonehaugh, at the head of the set, began their romp down the length of the line. Featherstonehaugh, a portly man, was red in the face. The rooms were hot.

If only she were dancing with Owen. He danced very well.

Johnny whirled Jean round and they, too, slid to the end of the set. As she bobbed along, she gave Maggie a quick grin and her twin's eyes sparkled. Maggie was clearly at ease. That was a little surprising. Maggie was shy of strangers and the hall was filled with the worst kind— haughty matrons and gentlemen with quizzing glasses primed to censure one's least slip.

The twins had been well coached. They knew the rules. They might not waltz until the Patronesses approved their Ton. They mustn't dance with the same partner more than once. And so on. Hedged about by rules. It occurred to Jean that knowing the rules—and knowing she knew them—had given Maggie confidence.

Jean tried to tell herself that *she* found the strictures stifling, but the musick was gay and the gowns brilliant and, if none of the gentlemen could hold a candle to Owen, their interest was flattering. Presently Jean gave herself up to enjoyment of what Owen must surely consider mere tribal ritual.

Later, as the orchestra began a waltz and she and Maggie watched Clanross lead Elizabeth onto the floor, Jean had leisure for reflection. She had promised Maggie she would enjoy their come-out. Maggie's loyalty deserved no less. Compared to the ordeal of presentation, Almack's was tolerable. At least in the Assembly Rooms one wasn't required to kiss the hand of the oppressor.

A plump gentleman who would be needing Colonel Falk's macassar oil in a few years brought her lemonade. She smiled and thanked him politely. She had forgot his name. She dropped her fan. Another gentleman leapt to retrieve it. She thanked *him*. Maggie was listening to a dandy in blue superfine and starched shirt-points who was deprecating the quality of the work hung at this year's Royal Academy exhibition. On the floor Clanross and Elizabeth dipped and whirled.

Vanity, of course. It was all vanity and would be swept away like spindrift in the coming gale. Jean allowed a pitying smile to play upon her lips.

". . .permit me to commend Mr. Holtby to you."

Jean bobbed a hasty curtsey to Lady Jersey. "Silence"

rattled on. Jean and Maggie were to be allowed to waltz, it seemed. Mr. Holtby was a bored-looking Corinthian who had been pointed out to Jean as a notable exponent of the waltz. He was reputed to spend most of his time in the gaming rooms. Jean supposed she ought to be flattered he had sought her out.

She said what was correct and allowed herself to be led onto the floor. Presently Maggie whirled past in the embrace of the connoisseur of paintings. Was he Lady Jersey's son? Jean did not remember. When she caught sight of her sister Anne among the chaperons, Anne smiled at her. They had been approved.

=18=

"HAVE THEY SETTLED with your lawyers?" Tom eyed his friend, who sprawled in a wing-backed chair by the long book room table. Tom had just returned from a walk in the park. He was surprised to find Richard back from the City so early.

Richard nodded. "Settled and signed."

Tom sat down. "Did you give it all away?"

"Don't be daft. I tossed a few bones to the hounds, that's all."

"Hounds? Jackals, more like."

"Very well, jackals."

"Tell me about it."

As Richard described the dispersal of the Duchess of Newsham's estate, Tom felt his indignation swell. When his friend wound down, he said as calmly as he could, "You needn't have been so generous."

Richard rose and walked to the window. "I kept more than half."

"Prudent of you. Does it occur to you, Richard, that you've countervened your mother's express wishes? If she had meant to divide her properties among your brothers and sisters she would have done so."

Richard turned. Back-lit by the brilliant midday sun, his face was a dark blur. "I declined to play her game."

"Game?"

"I couldn't decide, you see, whether she meant to reward me or to punish them."

Tom drew a breath.

"They are my brothers and sisters, and they were her children. Apart from Sarah, I've no feeling for them and no desire to know them, but when I found I was taking too much pleasure watching them squirm, I decided not to play the role her grace cast me in."

"Avenging Angel?"

"Her Fool, more likely." Richard returned to his chair. "I never understood her motives. So I had to consider my own."

"What of Newsham?" Tom burst out. Newsham, the eldest half brother, had persecuted Richard.

Richard's lip curled. "The duke bribes easily. I settled a house in Bath on his daughters."

"Bath!" Tom spluttered.

"I can't imagine *my* daughters wallowing among valetudinarians, so I thought his might as well. Sarah says the duchess was fond of Newsham's girls."

"Newsham is Newsham."

"Long may he rot," Richard agreed amiably. "Let it be, Tom. I'm satisfied."

"You may be, but what of Emily?"

"I shall purchase an estate for Emily where she may keep me in my accustomed style."

"You're moon-mad."

"I never felt saner."

"A common delusion of lunatics." There was no point in further protest. "Where do you mean to take your family until the will is proved?"

"After our stay at Brecon?" Richard shrugged. "A larger house in Winchester perhaps. I go down to Mayne Hall in the morning."

"Desertion! Elizabeth and the girls leave for Brecon tomorrow, too."

Richard smiled. "Not Dyott?"

"He'll ride with them as far as Lincoln. I believe his father has summoned him."

"Ah, the good dean. Probably doesn't want Johnny hanging about in a den of Radicals."

Tom cocked a snook at him. "Too late. I've already corrupted the boy's principles."

"Are your matched pair pleased with their social adventures?"

"Maggie is. I can't tell what Jean thinks these days. She affects boredom."

" 'Affects.' " Richard tasted the word. He was apt to side with the twins when Tom described their pecadilloes.

"It's certainly possible to find Almack's dull—not my idea of amusement—but I'd swear Jean was pleased with herself last evening. When she remembered to, she looked haughty but it was an unconvincing performance. *Maggie* sparkled." Tom rose. "We're for the theatre tonight. Do you care to join us?"

Richard shook his head. "The mail coach leaves at two."

"Morning dawns early these days."

"It's nearly midsummer night." He regarded the toes of his outstretched boots solemnly. "And I can't decide whether I'm Theseus or Puck."

"Or Bottom the Ass?" Tom rejoined.

Richard laughed. "Very likely."

"Sir!"

Tom started.

Johnny Dyott stood in the doorway. "The queen's business has been deferred!"

Tom said slowly, "Has it, indeed?"

"I beg your pardon for bursting in on you, but I thought you might want to make arrangements . . ."

"For how long?"

"Perhaps forever!" Johnny blushed at the verbal extravagance. "A fortnight, at least. Wilberforce means to negotiate a compromise. A handsome allowance if the queen will agree to the omission of her name from the liturgy. They mean her to live retired. The House have voted not to open the bag."

The "bag" was a green diplomatic pouch containing evidence of the queen's misconduct a commission of enquiry had gathered in 1817. Tom frowned. "If she's innocent, she'd be a fool to agree."

"Still . . ."

"Still, I shall be able to go to Brecon, too. I'm obliged to you, Johnny. I feel like a schoolboy let out on an unexpected holiday. Will you come on to us when you've seen your father?"

"If I may."

"Certainly. I'll work you like a dog."

Johnny grinned.

Tom turned to Richard, who had watched the interchange with lazy attention. "I'll see you off tonight, Richard."

"After the theatre?"

"To be sure. I'll direct my coachman to keep the carriage poled up, so don't bother to summon a hack. What inn? The Angel?"

Richard nodded.

"I'll share a noggin with you there before you go." Tom did not approve the settlement Richard had agreed to but he could see his friend was relieved. Time for a small celebration.

"Thank you. I'll take it now." Johnny paid the porter he had hired to carry his traps up the steep hill. Lincoln cathedral, its close tucked behind it, loomed over the bustling market town like a fortress, a besieged bastion of the church militant. Johnny sometimes thought the clerical inhabitants had taken on a siege mentality.

He drew a deep breath, gripped the handles of his valise, and walked toward the familiar close. Apart from the bishop's palace, his father's house was the most imposing residence in the precinct, as his father was the most imposing personage. Johnny hoped the dean would not reduce him to stammering incoherence. That was what usually happened.

His mother's greeting was sufficiently subdued to tell him he was for it. Mrs. Dyott submitted to her husband's judgement in all things as a matter of principle. She was a woman of principle and not subdued by nature.

Johnny washed the dirt of the journey from his person and dressed in garments suitable to bearding deans in their dens. His father meant to grant him an audience before dinner, and Johnny had no desire to be cut down for slovenliness. He intended to enter the study well armoured.

By the appointed hour, his palms were sweating and his throat clogged. The butler announced him and held the door open.

When the ceremony of greeting was over and the dean had permitted his son to sit, he took out a paper and tapped it. Johnny recognised his own handwriting. "I should like an explanation of the meaning of this . . . this outrageous defiance."

Johnny cleared his throat. Ha-hmmm. "Sir, it wasn't intended as defiance. Indeed, I'm grateful for your, er, attention to my future."

The dean tugged at his bands and settled in behind his wide mahogany desk. "You have an odd idea of gratitude."

"I cannot take Holy Orders, sir. As I writ in my letter, I have doubts and scruples a clergyman ought not entertain."

The dean's lips pursed. "You subscribed to the Thirty-nine Articles when you went up to Oxford."

"I didn't question them." Johnny had no wish to be trapped in theological debate. His father was a leading defender of dogma, impossible to best. "Merely I cannot see myself as incumbent of a parish. I haven't the pastoral temperament."

"Temperament!" If so dignified a person could be said to snort, the dean snorted. "I have no patience with such notions. You were bred for the church, sir, and we have already indulged your quirks of 'temperament.' "

That was an allusion to the ill-fated army commission. Johnny gritted his teeth.

"When you went up to Oxford you meant to take your degree and enter the church. It was a settled thing. I cannot ask Sir Edward Hollins to hold the living for you indefinitely. You will take orders, settle into your parish, and do your duty."

Johnny steeled himself. He thought of Maggie and the article he had sent off to the *Quarterly Review.* "No, sir, I will not. With all due respect."

"Respect!" The dean's rather red face darkened to purple. He launched into a denunciation that took into account all of Johnny's shortcomings from the moment of his first word ("pudding") to the latest evidence of insubordination. The speech was laced with general comments on the depravity of the present generation, and the likelihood of Judgement, both personal and global, sitting not far off.

The dean's words had a curious rehearsed quality. Perhaps he writ them out, Johnny reflected, as he writ out his sermons. Johnny was surprised by his own detachment. It was as if the dean were describing some other miscreant.

". . . well, sir? Well? I am waiting on your word."

"I mean to pursue a political career," Johnny said politely.

The dean stared at him, goggle-eyed. "Then I wash my hands of you."

"I'm sorry to disappoint you, sir."

"If you were sorry," the dean said majestically, "you would not persist in your ingratitude. Leave me. I am not well."

Johnny went. He was trembling as he reached his room. He was not so innocent as to take the dean literally and went down to dinner at the usual hour. It was an unpleasant meal. Prudence and Egeria, his unmarried sisters, reproached him with their eyes. His mother uttered careful commonplaces. His father ate in silence and retired to his study as soon as the covers were cleared, taking the port with him.

Johnny caught the coach to Earl's Brecon next morning. He had astonished himself by sleeping the sleep of the just.

"I cannot delay showing you this, Lady Jean." Owen thrust a printed sheet into Jean's hands. Maggie peered, too. They had been walking by the lake and now stood on the ornamental bridge.

" 'Anthem for the Ploughmen of England.' " Jean read the title aloud. "Oh, Owen, how splendid! It's in print!"

Owen's mouth twisted. "Without my name." The poem was signed "A Patriot."

Jean was a little disappointed at that, though it was probably a wise precaution. Also, the broadside printing did not please her. Owen's poem ought to have been bound in a tasteful pamphlet.

"It must be gratifying to see it in print, all the same," Maggie offered. "My congratulations."

"Thank you. Lady Jean . . ."

Jean cocked her head.

"I've had a letter from Carrington."

Her stomach knotted. "I thought he said you couldn't trust the mail."

"It was delivered by messenger to my parents' house." A breeze lifted Owen's fair hair from his brow. His eyes were intensely green. "He says he did not see you, that you gave the manuscript over to his landlady."

Jean swallowed. "Well, yes. He was off with the rioters and we had no time to wait."

Owen's eyes went dark with reproach. "You should not have shown it to anyone but Carrington."

Jean bit her lip. "But I told you we were hard-put to get away long enough to deliver it. If I hadn't given the manuscript to that woman, it wouldn't have seen print at all. After the riot we were too narrowly watched. And Maggie's head . . ."

"The landlady might have informed on me. Carrington writes she is not to be trusted."

Jean blinked back tears. "I'm sorry. I did my best."

He took her hand. "Pray don't cry. Indeed I'm grateful to you, but I wish you had told me how it was."

"I meant to," Jean mumbled.

"I'm a cad to reproach you." He raised her hand to his lips. "Forgive me?"

Jean gave him a watery smile. "Of course."

"I'd sooner be transported to Van Dieman's land than cause you a moment of pain."

Jean's heart contracted in a love pang so sharp she nearly gasped. He was so noble, so forgiving, the prospect of Van Dieman's land so appalling. "It's a fine poem, Owen. Worth any risk."

His eyes shone. "My dear, gallant lady . . ."

"I say!" Maggie interrupted. "Isn't that Johnny?" She pointed to a small figure trudging up the long carriageway.

It was indeed Johnny Dyott. Jean and Owen exchanged glances. Owen grimaced.

"Let's catch him up and walk with him." Fresh colour brightened Maggie's cheeks and her eyes glowed. "I hope his father was not too harsh. Oh, I am glad he's come." She danced down the bridge to the lake edge. At the gravelled path she turned back and said impatiently, "Come on or he'll reach the house before we do."

Jean cleared her throat. "Go ahead, Mag. We'll follow you."

Maggie hesitated, then began to run. The two setters, who had been waiting by the water, chased after her, yelping with excitement.

"We cannot lose this moment," Owen said in an urgent undertone.

Jean blinked at him. "What is it, Owen?"

"Too long have I held my tongue." He retained his grasp of her hand. "You must permit me to tell you how very much I love you."

Jean's pulse hammered. She could not have spoken for a thousand guineas.

"I know I've no right." Owen dropped her hand and turned, leaning on the rail. "I know what the world will say. I have no right to love you, but a kindred spirit leaps over false barriers of rank and wealth. Dare I hope? Tell me, I pray you, whether I may live or die."

Jean gulped. "Oh. Yes, of course you may hope. I admire you more than any man of my acquaintance."

"Admire me? I adore you." He clutched at his disordered locks. "You may walk on my heart."

"Oh, Owen, my dear, do not. I cannot bear to see you unhappy. I love you."

He turned back to her, his vivid features alive with hope. "Do you say so?"

"Yes. Yes, I do," Jean said firmly. "You are my lodestar." She heard Maggie calling in the distance. "I love you," she repeated desperately, "but do you not think we should rejoin my sister? If we don't, they will part us." "They" were Clanross and Elizabeth, Maggie, Johnny, society, the stars—all the forces bent on prudence and caution. Although she could not quite throw caution to the winds, Jean yearned for Owen, longed to receive his homage.

It was not to be. When Johnny saw Maggie, he dropped his portmanteau on the carriageway and waited for her. Although Jean and Owen still stood on the bridge, he saw them, too. Jean was almost sure of that.

"We must join my sister." She tucked the printed sheet in her reticule. "For now."

"Yes." Owen's voice throbbed with emotion. "Yes, we must go. Perhaps we may not have many such moments. I shall cherish them, my lady. My consolation must be that when you look at me, your eyes speak of love."

"Oh. Yes, they do." Jean choked on tears. It was so sad, so romantic. She would love Owen till the end of time.

Coming back to Brecon was far more like coming home than visiting the cathedral close had been. Johnny settled into the Conway circle happily. The warmth and spontaneity of the earl and his lady among their family contrasted sharply with the severe formality of the dean's household.

Johnny respected his father. He knew some part of him would always hold the dean in awe, but he no longer felt he must submit to his father's judgement. He would make his own life and hope someday that his father approved it. If not, well, there were others to applaud him.

This mood of self-confidence lasted until the first week of July. At that point the editor of the *Review* returned his manuscript with a polite letter saying he was sorry they could not make room for it. The note gave no indication why the article had been rejected and Johnny didn't know what to think.

He had been so sure of a favourable response he had begun another piece on repeal of the Corn Laws—very scholarly it was, full of references to utility and the political economists.

Bewildered as much as hurt, Johnny took his manuscript to Clanross and sought his opinion.

They sat in the earl's private study, a snug room apart from the main traffic of the house. Clanross read slowly. Johnny held his breath. At last the earl set the paper aside.

"It's well reasoned, Johnny, and clearly worded."

"Then why did they not want it?"

Clanross frowned. "I don't know. Perhaps . . ."

"Perhaps what?"

"Journals are strange organs. Mind you, the only writing I've published has been scientific in nature and the reasons for selection may be different. I'd guess the *Review* sent this back because you say nothing very surprising."

"Nothing of a sensational nature?"

Clanross smiled. "I don't think you ought to strain after sensation." He came from behind his desk and returned the manuscript to Johnny, gripping his shoulder briefly. "The man you should be asking is Richard Falk."

"But Colonel Falk is a satirist. That is, the history was not satire, but . . ."

Clanross interrupted him. "Richard is a writer. He has been publishing his work since he was twenty years old. You say you wish to write for money."

"Not just for money!" Johnny protested. "I should never sign my name to ideas I thought were false or . . . or depraved."

Clanross's eyebrows rose. "Do you find Richard's ideas depraved?"

Johnny was horrified. "No, no, of course not, but I'm sure I couldn't write satire. I'm not witty or fanciful. I just want to tell the truth."

Clanross regarded him for a silent moment, then nodded. "Well, my advice is to show this piece to Richard, and your next, when you've finished it. Meanwhile, recast the first in the form of a speech. I need an all-weather oration on the subject of Reform and I'm fresh out of phrases."

Johnny stared.

Clanross's eyes twinkled. "I'll probably change it in delivery. My ideas are rather more extreme than yours, but I like your line of reasoning."

Johnny swallowed. "I'd be honoured."

"Nonsense, My speech-making talents have been compared unfavourably to a creaking gate."

Johnny rose, feeling lighter of heart.

"Come to London with me."

The queen had refused Wilberforce's offer and the House had finally brought in a Bill of Pains and Penalties. Although the trial would not begin until August, Clanross felt obliged to spend a week in town consulting with Featherstonehaugh and other like-minded politicians.

"Do you need my services in London, sir?"

Clanross frowned. "Not necessarily. The thing is, you

211

could visit the offices of other journals and talk to men who make a profession of political writing."

Johnny swallowed hard. "Oh, sir . . . my lord. Thank you!"

=== 19 ===

"Good heavens, Johnny, where did *you* spring from?"

"London. Is Colonel Falk at home?"

A home question. I think like Richard, Emily reflected. In fifty years shall I look like him? "In a manner of speaking," she said vaguely. "Do sit down. I'll call for sherry. Tell me what you've been doing."

Johnny sat on the edge of the withdrawing room sofa. He looked as if a loud noise might propel him ten feet in the air. "I must see the colonel."

"You shall, of course, but he's out riding with Amy and Tommy. You're agitated, Johnny. Has something happened?"

"I . . . I want Colonel Falk's advice on a delicate matter."

The idea of Richard dispensing delicate advice tickled her. She bit back a smile and rang for her father's butler.

Johnny was so distressed his manners had flown out the window. Emily made soothing remarks, poured sherry, asked after Tom, offered small family anecdotes. Johnny began to look less harassed. He even gave her a few connected answers. When she asked how the Brecon ladies did, however, he lapsed into lip-chewing silence. Richard's entry was a relief.

The two men shook hands. When Emily excused herself, neither objected. They wanted her to leave. She wondered what would happen if she continued to sit obstinately between them.

Johnny was so relieved to see Colonel Falk he could not immediately order his thoughts. When Mrs. Falk had left the room and both men were seated once more, he burst into an account that sounded confusing even to him.

"Start over, Dyott, from the beginning." Colonel Falk took a sip of sherry. "You discovered what the young ladies were doing in Greek Street."

Johnny pulled the crumpled poem from his coat pocket. Mute, he handed it over and watched as Falk read it through, eyebrows raised.

"Heady stuff."

"I found it in a Crown Street bookshop. It's bound to be labelled seditious."

"No doubt. Almost everything one thinks these days is seditious."

"You do see that?"

The colonel's eyebrows twitched.

"That the abuses the author attacks are real."

"Oh, yes. 'A Patriot,' " Falk read. "An ambiguous nom de plume. You didn't write this?"

"Certainly not!"

"Then I gather Tom's librarian did. He knows his Burns."

"Eh?"

" 'Scots Wha' Hae wi' Wallace Bled,' " Falk said impatiently. " 'Lay the proud usurper low,/ Liberty in every blow/ Let us do or dee.' "

"Oh." Johnny was briefly consoled to know Owen had plagiarized his best line. That was beside the point, which was Maggie's safety. "I think the twins took the poem to Greek Street to friends of Owen's who saw it into print."

"Sounds likely. How did you recognise the poem without the author's name?"

"I heard it," Johnny said grimly, "at every stage of composition. I believe I have it by heart. Ought I to tell Clanross?"

"Why not? It summarizes Tom's feelings. Some of his

feelings." He frowned. "A trifle bloodthirsty for Tom, of course."

Johnny drew a breath. "If such a poem were to come into the hands of an informer . . ."

"The ladies might find themselves in the suds and so might their guardian." Colonel Falk completed the thought for him. "Tell Tom."

"If I betray Maggie she'll never forgive me."

To his relief Falk did not laugh. "You'd run that risk."

"I can't do it!" Johnny tumbled into an account of his courtship of Maggie, how important it was that she trust him.

"Why don't you explain that to Tom?"

Johnny swallowed. "I can't ask Clanross for her hand until I've the means to support her." He went on to describe the quarrel with his father and the sad business of the article. A week in London haunting coffeehouses patronised by journalists had not shed light on the rejection.

"Did you bring the article with you?"

"I . . . as a matter of fact, yes. It was in my coat and I forgot to remove it."

Falk held out his hand.

Reluctant, Johnny dug out the paper and turned it over to him. "It has nothing to do with Owen's poem."

The colonel smiled briefly. "I might as well advise you on something that lies within my experience." He read it through. "Not bad. Rather dull."

"Dull! Reform of Parliament?"

"My dear Dyott, interest, like beauty, is in the mind of the beholder. You've done almost nothing to stir your reader's sympathy."

"I won't make extravagant emotional appeals!"

"I don't suppose you'd consider collaborating with young Davies? Forget I said it," he added glancing at Johnny's face.

"What am I to do about the poem?" Johnny uttered through clenched teeth.

Falk leaned back in the chair and closed his eyes. After a considering pause, he opened one eye. "Has the author been identified? By government spies, I mean."

"Not yet. I hope not."

"And the twins have escaped detection?"

"No hint of scandal has appeared in the newspapers."

"Ride up to Brecon and ask Lady Margaret to tell you exactly what happened. Tell her you must inform your employer, then go to Tom and lay the matter bare."

"It sounds simple."

"We already agreed you would be running a large risk," the colonel said patiently. "Lady Margaret is not stupid. You say she likes you and trusts you. If you're open with her she'll feel obliged to reciprocate."

Johnny brooded. "All right."

"You must tell Tom."

Johnny rubbed his forehead.

"If you don't I shall."

Johnny stared.

Falk met his eyes. "Tom and I have been friends too many years for me to connive at a deception that could embarrass him. He's a publick man with a reputation for honest dealing. The government won't charge a peer of the realm with sedition, but they might try to discredit him. Forewarned is forearmed. Let Tom decide what to do."

When Johnny did not reply, he added, "I'll give you a week."

Johnny rose. "I'm obliged to you, sir."

Falk got to his feet, too. "I doubt it. I merely clarified what you were already thinking. About the article, Johnny."

Johnny turned in the doorway.

"There's meat in it."

"Thank you."

"What it wants is a daub of mustard."

Johnny stared.

"Good luck," Falk said gravely.

Johnny rode off as precipitously as he had come. That evening, when Emily and Richard had retired to their bed, she decided to pry.

"I daresay you can't tell me what Johnny wanted." According to Emily's brother, James, a statement like that, if couched in Latin, would begin with the particle *num* and expect a negative answer.

"No," Richard said predictably.

Emily sniffed. "Can you tell me whether his concern had to do with the Nation or the ladies at Brecon?"

"Both."

"We could play twenty questions."

Richard chuckled.

"You won't tell me?"

"My lips are sealed."

"Oh, very well." She turned away from him and punched the feather pillow with her fist.

"We may have an entertaining time at Brecon," he murmured. "What an earnest chap Johnny is."

"Is that bad?"

"No, but there are more and more like him. That doesn't bode well for satirists."

Emily propped herself on one elbow and squinted at him. "Do you mean to write another satire?"

"Yes," he said drowsily. "If need be, I'll publish it myself."

Maggie was dawdling up the hill from a visit to her young sisters at the Dower House. She heard the horsemen before she saw him, and stepped onto the grass verge.

It was Johnny. She recognised him at once. Her heart leapt and she found she was grinning foolishly.

When he came abreast of her, Johnny reined in and slid from the saddle. "Thank God I found you alone. We must talk."

"Of course." He had ridden *ventre à terre* to be at her side? Really, Johnny had a great deal of romance in his make-up. "You're covered in mud." Alarm sharpened her voice. "Is anything the matter?"

He drew her off behind a screen of trees and tied his nag to a low branch. "I've found out what you and Jean were doing that day in Soho."

Maggie went cold.

"Quite by accident." Johnny drew a breath. "I wasn't trying to spy on you, truly." He described how he had found Owen's poem in the bookstall, his cruel dilemma, and his hasty journey into Hampshire to seek Colonel Falk's advice. Johnny looked tired. If he had ridden to Hampshire, turned round, and come directly to Brecon without pausing to rest, it was no wonder.

Maggie could think of nothing to say. He must despise her.

"I would not have forced your confidence for the world." His eyes were so dark with distress, she had to look away. "For God's sake, Maggie, speak to me."

"I couldn't betray Jean," she mumbled, "and she made me swear."

"Of course you couldn't." The warmth in his voice gave her the courage to look at him again. "She's your twin, your oldest friend."

Maggie blinked back relieved tears. He understood!

"I'll never come between you and your sister, Maggie. I promise."

She smiled tremulously.

"But I have my loyalties, too. Clanross pays me a wage. Even if I did not like and admire him, I should still be obliged to inform him. It's too dangerous a matter to leave undisclosed." He twisted his hat in his hands.

"Must you? He'll send Owen away, punish him . . ."

"Look at me, Maggie."

She obeyed.

His brown hair ruffled as the breeze touched it. "Do you think Clanross would act unjustly?" His eyes were grave.

She raised her hands to her face. "I wish I knew what to do. We must warn Jean. At once."

"Where is she?"

"In our room, I think. She meant to read Colonel Falk's novel."

He gave a hollow laugh. "Let's find her, then, and talk it over with her."

"She'll want to inform Owen, too."

"Owen should be hanged by the thumbs," Johnny said bitterly.

"He was worried when he found out we left the poem with his friend's landlady." Maggie untied the horse and handed him the reins.

"You did what?"

Frightened, she repeated what she had said.

Johnny groaned.

Maggie was having trouble breathing. "I'll find Jean. Do you find Owen, and we'll meet in the book room in half an hour. It's empty. Lizzie is with the babies."

"Oh lord, Lady Clanross!"

"She won't find out," Maggie said without conviction.

But Elizabeth did find out.

Scarcely had the four of them got past the first explanations and recriminations when Elizabeth entered the book room, looking puzzled.

Maggie and Jean froze. Johnny made an odd noise in his throat, and Owen edged toward the open window as if he might cast himself from it.

"Johnny? Fisher told me you'd come on horseback. Is anything wrong? Tom . . ."

Johnny cleared his throat. "His lordship is very well and still in London."

"Then that's all right." Her eyes narrowed. "You look guilty, all four of you. What's amiss?" When no one answered, she said impatiently, "You might as well open your budgets. I'll find out sooner or later."

Maggie and Jean launched into simultaneous protest. Johnny overrode them.

"I came to warn Lady Margaret that I had discovered the reason for the twins' visit to Greek Street."

" 'Tell me that. That do I long to hear,' " Elizabeth quoted dryly.

Maggie writhed. She had hated deceiving Elizabeth only a little less than deceiving Johnny.

"Well?" Elizabeth tapped her foot.

Johnny launched into a partial explanation. When he had got as far as his hasty flight to Hampshire, she interrupted him.

"Why did you not tell Tom?"

"I thought I ought to warn Lady Margaret first." He looked at the toes of his boots. "And Lady Jean."

Elizabeth's mouth set. "You must inform Clanross at once."

Johnny met her gaze. "I mean to return to London at first light."

Elizabeth turned to her sisters, unsmiling. "How you must have enjoyed your come-out—frolicking at Almack's, kissing the king's hand. Tschaa!"

Maggie squirmed.

"Clearly you have depths of character I've never plumbed. As for Owen . . ." She took a step forward.

Owen stood by the window with his chin up. Maggie, from the pit of her humiliation, had to admit he looked heroick.

"It's a fine poem," he said, defiant.

"It's a skilful pastiche of half a dozen works I could recite for you if I had the stomach. I acquit you of malice and ingratitude, Mr. Davies. You are merely a reckless fool."

"I shall remove from Brecon at once."

"Oh, no, you shall not!" Elizabeth in a fury was not to be trifled with. Maggie took a step backward and bumped the bookcase, but Owen held his ground. "You will remain here under my guard until my husband decides what's to be done with you. I know you for a coward, sir . . ."

"By God, ma'am, if you were a man . . ."

"If I were I man I'd call you out. Puppy! Poltroon! Allowing girls of seventeen to run your risks for you! You sicken me."

"Owen is *not* a coward," Jean said passionately. "It was all my idea. I insisted."

"That I can believe." Elizabeth gave her a look designed to freeze her marrow.

Maggie was glad Elizabeth's glare had not fallen upon *her*. She had not felt obliged to defend Owen but she felt she ought to defend Jean. She cleared her throat. "I thought of the disguises and worked out the details of our venture, Lizzie. It was *not* all Jean's idea."

Elizabeth closed her eyes briefly. "Very well. You're to blame, all three of you. Johnny I acquit of everything but confused loyalties."

Johnny winced.

Elizabeth glowered from one to the other. "Does none of you have common sense? Sedition is not a game. Men have been transported for less than that poem. Yes, and women, too."

"The cause of liberty . . ."

"Fustian, sir. If you cared tuppence for Liberty, you would not have placed Clanross's credit in the Lords at risk."

"The Lords . . ." Owen's lip curled.

Elizabeth said in a shaking voice, "Be still, jackanapes, before I do you a mischief."

Owen's eyes dropped.

Elizabeth raised a hand to her brow and brushed back a strand of hair. Maggie saw that her sister's hand trembled. "I must write Tom at once—and think what to do with you all meanwhile. You had better go to your rooms until dinner."

No one moved.

"In God's name, go!" Elizabeth roared, echoing an ancestor of the maternal side.

They went.

By the time Elizabeth had writ Clanross and dressed for dinner, the first surge of her wrath had spent itself. She knew she had spoken with more heat than was becoming or, indeed, just. She felt rather sick.

As she paced the floor of her dressing room she turned the facts over in her mind another time. What kept her anger at a simmer was the recollection of how long the government had toyed with the Cato Street conspirators. Lord Sidmouth had known of the plot for months before his agents acted. Maggie and Jean were still in jeopardy. So was Tom.

She did not suppose Tom would be charged—or the girls—though Owen might. What troubled her was the possible effects on reputation—the girls', for they risked ostracism, and Tom's.

Her husband was a reluctant politician, but he was a sincere one. He not only favoured extending representation to the manufacturing towns, he also wanted annual Parliaments and a wider suffrage. His opinions were heard because he spoke carefully, without threatening bloodshed and revolution. His critics might think of him as a blue-blooded sansculotte, but his integrity compelled their respect.

If he were accused of harbouring an out-and-out revolutionist . . .

A knock at her door startled her from her nightmare phantasy. "Come!"

Johnny Dyott entered looking like one who has steeled his nerves to storm a bastion.

Elizabeth sighed. "Come in, Johnny. I was wanting to talk with you in private."

He entered. Though the whites of his eyes did not show, his apprehension was clear enough.

"I ought to apologise for my intemperate language this afternoon," she said glumly. "I was startled as well as angry. I had nearly tucked the twins' misconduct in the back of my mind as just another escapade I'd laugh at in ten or twenty years."

He ventured a faint smile. "What you said to Davies was mild to what I've been thinking. I'm sorry to cause you distress."

"You didn't."

"Not directly, perhaps . . ."

He was bound to blame himself but Elizabeth was in no mood to be Johnny's hair shirt. "It's I who should apologise for placing you in an impossible dilemma. You're in love with my sister Margaret, are you not?"

He nodded, wide-eyed.

"I ought to have seen how torn you would be. She didn't tell you why they had gone to Soho?"

"She couldn't betray Lady Jean. I saw that clearly enough."

"So you were caught between your loyalty to Tom and your affection for Maggie. I am sorry, Johnny."

He cleared his throat. "How did you know? I've tried to be circumspect. I don't want to frighten her—she's so young."

"Too young," Elizabeth rejoined, "as this harebrained episode proves." His face fell and she added, hastily, "You must know I have no reservation about *you*, Johnny. I cannot agree to Maggie's marriage at eighteen, but if you're of the same mind in a few years, and if she consents . . ."

He spoke several disjointed but grateful phrases. His surprise and relief were evidence of the sincerity of his feelings. If Elizabeth's exasperation with Maggie had been a shade stronger she would have thrust her sister at him. Take her, she's yours.

When joy left him speechless, Elizabeth said wryly, "I wish Jean showed a little of Maggie's discernment. Will you carry my letter to Tom, Johnny?"

"Of course."

"Meanwhile, what am I to do with the poet? Keeping in mind that I'd like to shove him down an oubliette."

Johnny hesitated. "He's not such a bad chap, you know. Merely impractical."

"And egotistical."

"You could lock him in his chamber with bread and water."

"He'd probably write dithyrambs on the moulding."

Johnny grinned. "Only think what he'd write in an oubliette."

=20=

"RICHARD!"

Richard Falk stepped down from the hackney into the rain. It had been pouring for two days.

Tom, muffled in round hat and greatcoat, was about to leave the house. His butler held an umbrella over him.

"Never mind, Waite. Hold it for the colonel." He ducked back in the foyer and removed his hat. Richard entered, damp but not soaked.

When the two men had retired to the bookroom for a glass of brandy out of earshot of servants, Richard said, "I've come about this business of Johnny's. Has he told you?"

"Of the twins' Soho adventure? I believe I have you to thank for advising him."

Richard flushed. "I gave him a week's grace."

"Because of Maggie?"

Richard heaved a sigh of relief. "Then he's made a clean breast of it. Good, because unless you understand his attachment to Lady Margaret his conduct is inexcusable. And mine. I ought to have writ you at once."

Tom rubbed his forehead. "He spoke to you in confidence. I'm sorry Johnny and the girls fancied me such an ogre they couldn't confide in me."

"It wasn't quite that, Tom. When you were a subaltern did you tell your captain everything?"

"No, though I was trying for a less military bond with

the girls. I daresay with Johnny it was inevitable. I *was* his captain."

Richard swirled the brandy absently in the glass. "How grave a matter is it?"

"If I knew I'd be at Brecon right now. At least Davies wasn't fool enough to sign his name. Discretion is called for, but the danger may blow over."

"Can I be of use to you?"

"Do you have connexions in Bow Street?"

Richard took a warming sip. "In the dock, more likely. I was thinking of my connexions with publishers, writers, and other seditious types."

That had not occurred to Tom, though it should have. "Will you find out whether the printer knew Owen's identity?" He had ascertained the printer's name through Sir Francis Burdett. He gave it to Richard, adding, "The man was a jobber."

"I'll try."

"And you might question Davies's friend, Carrington, for me. I sent Johnny back to Brecon to reinforce Elizabeth, and my presence at the Radical Poets' Club might cause remark . . ."

"Whereas I am known for my outrageous opinions. I thought they called you Radical Tom?"

"That may be but no one has ever accused me of poetry." He met his friend's amused eyes over the rim of the snifter.

"Is there such an establishment? I rather fancy masquerading as a Radical poet. Mind you, I've not writ so much as an iamb since I was eighteen and in love with the colonel's daughter."

"Coffeehouse in Rose Street."

"I'll test the waters."

"Emily will be wishing me in Hades."

"For dragging me from Mayne Hall? Nonesense, she's being spared nightly skirmishes in the drawing room between Sir Henry and his freakish son-in-law. Besides she's packing for Brecon. She says all three boys need new shirts. I left her to it."

"Well, I'm glad you've come."

"Er, speaking of wives. Lady Clanross . . ."

Tom groaned. "She's wonderfully restrained in her letters."

"But she wants your guts for garters?"

"Lord, you're vulgar."

Richard grinned.

"Something along those lines," Tom admitted. "Richard, what the devil shall I do with this poet?"

They discussed Tom's choices, which were limited, and Tom began to feel less harassed, though he knew Owen Davies was going to be a knotty problem to solve. The mood in London was strange. On the one hand, the Mob continued its noisy support of the queen. On the other, the government were perplexed by the king's insistence on a divorce and well-nigh hysterical with fear of the Mob. The servants of Tory MPs set up makeshift barricades of chiffoniers and ironing boards nightly in elegant town houses. The Tories expected the revolution at any moment. The Duke of Wellington had been jeered in Hyde Park.

From Tom's viewpoint their terror was foolish. So far the Mob were good-natured enough. Caricaturists were enjoying a heyday. The queen's cause was a publick entertainment, no more. Still, it could not be pleasant to have one's windows broken every time the Mob wished to express itself. Tom had some sympathy for his neighbour, Lord Harrowby, but if Harrowby and his friends insisted on stifling lawful dissent what more could they expect? The people, in Tom's opinion, would always find a way to be heard.

The trouble was, the penalties attached to publishing material the government considered seditious were extreme. If the men in Westminster were frightened enough to pursue a caricaturist for portraying the king as a grossly fat man—which was true—God knew what they might do to a poet whose figures of speech were a little intemperate. Tom did not want to see Owen Davies languishing in custody. Boiling in oil, perhaps, but not stewing in prison.

Whilst Clanross and Colonel Falk were attempting to find out how far the damage had gone, the party at Brecon held its collective breath.

Jean's devotion to Owen burned with a fierce flame. He was by turns defiant and melancholy. If Elizabeth had chained him in a dungeon (there were no dungeons at Brecon but it did boast extensive wine cellars), Jean would have moved mountains to rescue him.

Apart from maintaining an icy civility toward Owen at dinner, however, Elizabeth did nothing untoward. It was true that Jean and Owen were never left alone together, but they had not been before Johnny's revelations either. Nothing had changed but the climate.

Jean had begun to look on Maggie as her gaoler, too, though she knew the feeling was unfair. Maggie had not betrayed her and swore she would not, but Jean knew there had been a shift of allegiance. It galled her that Maggie's attachment to Johnny was acceptable whilst hers for Owen was not. She wanted to attribute the persecution of Owen to his comparative poverty, but neither Elizabeth nor Clanross was mercenary. They objected, she thought with resentment, because Johnny was dull and conformable and Owen was colourful.

That Maggie didn't find Johnny dull Jean knew very well. The sonnet he had writ for Maggie shook Jean's conviction when she finally read it, and she had to admit Johnny was well-looking and knew how to make himself agreeable, but he was not romantic. If Maggie had spurned Johnny he would have been unhappy, perhaps even taken to drink, but he would not have died for love.

Owen's more sensitive nature led him into an observable decline. His eyes grew heavy, shadowed with sleeplessness. He took long solitary walks. Jean saw him brooding by the waters of the lake. Several times he was so unwell he could not come down to dinner. She worried that he might be consumptive.

She smuggled notes to him to cheer him. It was no easy matter to do so unobserved, but she didn't grudge the effort. She had to wake herself at three in the morning to slip out into the hall with her letters, and then she ran the risk of bumping into Elizabeth, who was working at her telescope again and apt to be up at strange hours. Owen's first note to Jean—a tragic epode called "Frost in Spring"— came by the way of Polly, the chambermaid who served all the bedrooms in that wing. Thereafter Polly was their courier.

Twice Owen suggested secret meetings and twice Jean attempted the tryst but was foiled by the vigilance of her wardens. Miss Bluestone on the first occasion and Elizabeth herself on the second appeared as if by magick as Jean tried to make her way outdoors unnoticed. 'Going for a walk? I'll join you.' How could they be so unfeeling?

She was balked, stymied, frustrated at every turn. Finally her frustration led her to confront her twin.

"I want to see Owen alone."

"But Elizabeth . . ."

"Does Elizabeth put an armed guard on your visits with Johnny?"

"Well, no, but . . ."

"How would *you* feel, Maggie?"

Maggie was neck-deep in soapsuds. She flapped one hand delicately and made a small wave of soapy water. "I shouldn't like it."

"Then help me meet him."

Maggie submerged, sloshing water on the rug, and surfaced. She mopped her eyes with a cloth and began soaping her hair. "No. It wouldn't be right. Rinse please."

After her own bath, Jean had sent Lisette, whom she trusted not an inch, from the room. So she hefted the can and poured warm water over her twin's head. Maggie spluttered.

"What did you say?"

"I like my cropped hair. It's much quicker to wash. And I needn't brush it forever."

Exasperated, Jean watched as her twin climbed from the tub, towelled dry, and slipped into nightrail and robe.

"You meet Johnny alone," Jean accused.

"I've met him alone twice." Pink spots burnt on Maggie's cheeks. "On our birthday and when he rode up from Hampshire last week. The second time was an accident. Otherwise we've been chaperoned—by you or Elizabeth or one of the maids. Besides, you know Johnny wouldn't do anything improper."

"And Owen would?"

Maggie sat at the dressing table and brushed her damp curls. "His language makes me blush."

"He says what his heart tells him to say." Maggie couldn't have heard Owen's avowal of love. She'd been too far off.

Maggie daubed lotion on her nose. The twins were subject to freckles. The lotion was supposed to bleach them but Jean had never noticed dramatic results and had given it up.

At last Maggie said, with an air of grave deliberation, "I think you ought to wait until Clanross comes before you try to meet with Owen."

"Why?"

"Because, if you see Owen alone now and you're found out, Clanross will be twice as angry with all three of us. He's probably very angry already."

"We won't be found out unless you peach."

Maggie went white. She turned. "I've never broken your confidence, not even to Johnny, and I don't think it's fair of you to suggest I may."

Jean's eyes fell. She was rather ashamed of the impetuous remark but she had thought Maggie would be easier to persuade. "I'm sorry."

Maggie rose. "All right." She walked to the window and looked out at the starry night. "I won't help you meet Owen, because it's underhand dealing. I don't like sneaking about deceiving people. It made me sick in London." Maggie turned to face her. "And I won't deceive Johnny again. That's flat."

Jean gaped.

"Don't bully me."

"I don't bully."

"Yes, you do. You poke and poke and I give way because it's easier. Well, I won't this time."

Jean's eye welled tears. If Maggie was against her the whole world was.

They made up the quarrel after a fashion. Their quarrels never lasted long. But Maggie would not be swayed. When Jean raised the subject again, Maggie gave her a long, unsmiling look. "You're bullying again," she said, and Jean had to give it up.

When Tom finally came from London, Elizabeth had gone from outrage through gloom to honest anxiety. Why didn't the man come.

She was with the babies in the nursery and hadn't heard the carriage, so he startled her when he came into the sun-filled room at the top of the house. "Tom! Thank God!" She thrust Dickon at the nursemaid and ran to her husband.

He kissed her cheek. "Are you all right?"

"Am I well, do you mean? Of course, though I'm near distraction." She touched his face. "Why didn't you come sooner?"

"I had to find out the consequences of that poem's being published." He looked grim. "I've summoned Johnny and the three conspirators to the bookroom in half an hour. I should like you to be present, Elizabeth."

"What is it?"

He glanced at the head nurse and her assistant. "It will keep."

"All right."

He went to the boys who had recognised him and were making importunate noises.

Elizabeth wondered if Tom had chosen the library for its air of courtroom gloom. The withdrawing room would have been a friendlier arena, but it did not take long to see that Tom was in an unfriendly frame of mind.

When the brief courtesies were done and everyone but Tom was seated, he said, without preamble, "The Runners have identified you as the author of that poem, Davies."

Jean gasped.

Elizabeth stared at the poet. He had been unusually pale when he entered the room. Now his eyes darkened.

"There's little doubt that you'll be charged," Clanross continued. "They're building a dossier. The only question is when the warrant will be issued."

Johnny shifted in his chair. "Do they know of the girls' role?"

"Not yet, according to my sources."

Maggie raised her clasped hands to her mouth. Jean set her jaw.

Elizabeth said quietly, "How good is your information, Tom?"

He frowned. "It's not official, if that's what you mean. I was constrained to ask through friends, and friends of friends." He turned back to Owen. "I understand you'd already published a piece calling for revolution under your own name."

"It was published privately." Colour returned to Owen's cheeks. He sat straighter on the stiff chair. "How did they connect the 'Anthem' with me? Carrington wouldn't betray me."

"I've no idea. The point is you'll have to leave the country or stand your trial."

Owen's lip curled. "Let them charge me. I shall not be the first martyr . . ."

"Save your oratory for the dock, you . . . you poetaster." Johnny clenched his fists on his breeches-clad knees. He had come in from riding and not had time to change. "Have you no thought for Lady Jean and Lady Margaret? If you're tried, the Runners will make every effort to identify the young women who brought the poem to London."

Owen blinked.

"Johnny's right," Tom said heavily. "I've booked passage for you on the *Urania* packet bound for Halifax at the beginning of September."

Jean made a noise.

"He ought to leave at once!" Elizabeth protested. Her heart was thumping.

"He may have to make a run for it yet." Tom paced to the cold hearth. "I'm gambling that they won't act so soon, and that his departure will appear to be a mission I've sent him on. I meant to send Barney Greene. Owen will take his place." He raised his head and looked at Owen directly. "Once the river freezes, you may travel by sledge to Montreal and Kingston. My agent there will employ you . . ."

"I prefer to stand my trial."

"I can't allow it."

Owen threw back his head, flipping the fair hair from his eyes. "You can't stop it."

Tom said coolly, "I've no doubt you'd enjoy the notoriety. The Radical press would make a hero of you and you'd swank it in prison like Leigh Hunt, receiving callers and sending out your latest incendiary thoughts to the journals. You'd probably get two years or less and you'd leave gaol a famous man. I daresay that's what you were aiming for when you suborned Lady Jean to run your risks for you."

"He did not s-suborn me. It was my idea!"

Tom's face softened. "My dear, he could have prevented you easily enough by withholding the poem. And how should you have heard of his friend in Soho if he hadn't told you?"

Jean's eyes dropped but her jaw set in a mutinous line.

"I won't go into exile," Owen exclaimed. "I've done nothing wrong. It's the laws that are unjust. You said so yourself, my lord."

"I did." Tom leaned against the long table, arms folded. "I believe they are wrong. If you'd acted openly and honestly, on your own, I'd swallow the embarrassment of your being in my employ when the Runners came for you. As it is, I'm afraid you'll have to forego the pleasure." He spoke almost mildly but Elizabeth perceived he was very angry indeed.

"Pleasure!"

"Sensation, if you prefer."

The two men stared at one another and Owen's eyes dropped first.

Jean said hysterically, "You cannot exile Owen, Clanross! I love him!"

Oh, Jean, Elizabeth thought. Don't be a fool.

A long silence ensued, broken only by Jean's sobs. At last Tom said carefully, "If your feelings are engaged, Jean, I'm very sorry for you."

"They are, they are!"

"Elizabeth."

Elizabeth started.

"Will you and Maggie take Jean from the room and see to her comfort? I'll come to you later."

Elizabeth rose. Eventually she and Maggie, who had begun to weep in sympathy, led the sobbing girl from the book room. Elizabeth wanted to console Jean, then strangle her and throw her body to the ducks, but that was an impractical course of action.

If Clanross had not been in the room Johnny would have milled Owen Davies down. Fury cramped his muscles and hazed everything in red. He sat in his chair and seethed.

For a while no one moved. At last Owen rose and made his way to the window, which was open. "I know what you're thinking, my lord," he said in a muffled voice.

"I doubt it."

"You accused me of seeking the notoriety of a trial. I did not. I writ the poem. What I writ needed writing. It's a good poem, whatever her ladyship may say."

"What does her ladyship say?"

"She accused me of plagiarisms!"

Clanross said in less frigid tones, "That was intemperate of her. I daresay she spoke in the heat of the moment."

Owen clutched at his forehead. "What does it matter? I'm done for. If you had not forbid it, I'd have gone down to London myself. When Lady Jean suggested that she convey the poem, I was at my wit's end. Perhaps it was weak in me to agree. Certainly I didn't foresee that she would give the poem over to anyone but my friend."

"Why did you not foresee it? You must know young ladies are not allowed to roam freely through the stews of Soho in search of young men."

"Is it a low neighbourhood?" Owen asked with such palpable surprise that Johnny's red haze began to fade. Surely the man could not be that naive.

Clanross explained how very low the neighbourhood had sunk, adding, "I daresay you don't know London well."

Owen groaned. "Since I came down from Oxford I've spent a year in Wales writing and a year as secretary to a gentleman resident in Bath. I've never lived in London."

"Then perhaps your mistake was an honest one. Since my expressed opinions led you to imagine I would not object to your poem, I can understand your trying to see it into print without consulting me."

"You said you favoured a free press."

"I do." Clanross sighed. "I know my sister-in-law's impetuous nature, and I can believe you were caught up in her enthusiasm, though the fact that you're five years older than she makes that hard to credit. What sickens me,

Davies, is that you used your presence in my household as an opportunity to trifle with Lady Jean's feelings."

"I do not trifle!" Owen held out an imploring hand. "Upon my honour, sir, we could not help ourselves!"

"And the thought of Jean's blood and wealth didn't enter your head?"

"No!" Owen cried passionately. "It did not! She was so kind, so beautiful. When I perceived that she was not entirely indifferent I could not forebear to speak. My feelings burst forth. I shall worship Lady Jean forever."

Johnny heard this speech with considerable confusion. It was just possible Owen was sincere.

"I honour her," Owen was saying in a low, trembling voice. "I would cut off my hand sooner than hurt her."

"An impressive declaration," Clanross said dryly. "Then you can have no objection to leaving for Upper Canada."

Owen sank onto the nearest chair. "What?"

"You claim you don't want to hurt Jean. Surely you must see that being called as a material witness in a criminal case would harm her."

"And what of Mag . . . Lady Margaret?" Johnny's voice sounded hoarse in his own ears. "She would be called, too, subjected to the insinuations of counsel in a publick court. The two of them went, unescorted, to seek out a man in his private quarters. Are you so high-minded you don't know what would be said? For Godsake, they'd be ruined. Both of them."

"You must go, Davies," Clanross said heavily. "It's a bad business and I'm sorry for it, but there it is."

Owen looked from one to the another. "Must I?"

"You needn't imagine you'll be exiled for ever. In a year or so the prosecutions will ease and you may return without penalty." Clanross touched his shoulder. "I'm aware of my own responsibility in this. I'll send for you as soon as may be."

"Very well, I'll go." Owen buried his face in his hands.

= 21 =

A FORTNIGHT PASSED in wretched inaction. The weather was hot and mutinous, like Jean's mood. Maggie felt her twin's anguish deeply, and, worse, her twin's withdrawal of confidence.

The most dramatic development was Owen's removal from Brecon to the rectory. Clanross had called on the rector and his wife to explain that Owen must leave the country. Once Clanross made it clear that the alternative was a trial, Mr. Davies resigned himself to his son's exile. His wife proved less persuadable. Owen was her favourite and she let her feelings be felt. Prudence had so far prevented her from spreading her outrage abroad among her friends and neighbours, but she blamed Clanross for leading her son astray. She insisted that Owen live at home until he was compelled to leave for the wilds of Upper Canada. She was said to be knitting warm things.

Maggie grieved for the mother deprived of her child, but she mourned the effects of Owen's removal on Jean more. Although Owen continued to ride up to Brecon every morning, he worked in the library only a few hours each day and that was all Jean saw of him. Everyone else felt the advantage of Owen's absence—the level of tension at dinner lowered noticeably—but Maggie's twin withdrew into brooding silence.

When Jean requested a separate bedchamber, Maggie was stricken. She had done nothing to cause Jean's grief, yet Jean was treating her like a stranger. Maggie's resolve not to abet a private meeting between Owen and her sister wavered.

Clanross and Johnny went down to London again, something to do with records of the charity Owen would be carrying to Clanross's agent. They returned within three days, however, and both men took to joining the girls and Owen in the book room as they worked on the nearly completed catalogue. Maggie could not help thinking Owen's despair was less black than Jean's.

"Have you read this yet, Davies?" Clanross handed the poet a slim volume.

In the previous days Owen had read all of the American voyages in the Brecon first edition of Hakluyt's *Principle Navigations*. He exclaimed over Frobisher, Cabot, and Hudson, and sketched out a verse-drama of discovery. He also went about quoting such references to North America as he had unearthed in the works of other poets. "Oh, my America, my New-found Land," was a line Maggie remembered because it seemed to refer not to the continent but to the poet's lover, an unsettling thought.

Owen took the volume from Clanross and leafed through it. "Cartier's account of the Iroquois! I've been looking for it. By Jove, they're fierce devils. I'd like to see an Iroquois warrior." He went to the window and soon lost himself in the book.

Jean watched him from somber grey eyes. Maggie watched Jean.

"Jaysus!"

Emily started. "What is it?" She had been dozing off and on since they left Chacton.

Peggy's head blocked Emily's view from the window of Sir Henry's carriage. "Jaysus, it's the Prado," the nurse muttered.

"Do move over, Peggy. Are we in sight of Brecon?" Emily eased the sleeping Harry onto the seat, half rose, and peered around Peggy's shoulder. Persuaded by a jab in the ribs, Peggy made room.

Ahead of the two carriages—far off and well above them—floated an enormous ice palace. Emily blinked. It did not vanish. Tom's travelling carriage, which contained Richard, Matt, Amy, and Tommy, momentarily blocked her view. Again the vision appeared. The arrogant Palladian facade was broken by a double flight of steps, curving out to embrace the carriageway that swept up to it. The afternoon sun glinted from an acre of tall windows, two tiers of them. A balustraded parapet in the doric mode masked any hint of chimneys. Emily could make out a tiny figure at the head of the stairs, but that was the only sign of humanity in the entire neoclassical expanse. Then the carriages entered a gracefully placed wood and the house was lost to view. Emily sank back on her seat, her stomach in a cold knot. She had been told that Brecon was not as vast as Blenheim. In all conscience it was vast enough.

Peggy and Phillida burst into excited questioning. They woke Sally, who wailed to be fed. Harry also woke and Peggy and Phillida were distracted into answering his questions. It was clear that the Earl of Clanross's principal seat lay still some miles off, so Emily attended to her daughter's appetite and tried not to give way to panick. The journey from Mayne Hall had been accomplished in great comfort—and at great expense. Travelling was a costly enterprise, especially for a large party. Tom had sent his carriage and Emily's father had also insisted that they employ *his*, so Richard had engaged to keep the three oldest children out of mischief in one, whilst Emily and the two servants dealt with the babies in the other. McGrath had gone off to Cork the week before and Emily determined to revel in Peggy's services. Phillida was an afterthought, probably a mistake, though she could be trusted to hold Sally occasionally without dropping her.

They had stopped one night at the Conway town house in London. By dint of imagining herself in Grillon's Hotel,

Emily survived the shock. It was not like the house in Winchester. Richard took her to a play at Drury Lane. She enjoyed the novelty of an evening in her husband's sole company—they occupied the Conway box and were ogled—but she couldn't help noticing she was dressed like a provincial dowdy. Her gown was new. Mme. Hebert in Winchester had assured her it was à la mode. Mme. Hebert had lied.

Emily hoped she was not vain or unduly concerned about appearances but now, brooding over the looming ice palace, she couldn't help wishing she had accepted Richard's offer of a week's shopping in London before the journey.

Sally lapsed into contented sleep. Peggy and Phillida held Harry to the window. The carriage lumbered on. *If I were a great lady*, Emily reflected, tidying her blue travelling dress, *I would be preparing witty bons mots for the amusement of my hostess and her fashionable, if mettlesome, sisters.* Unfortunately, nothing came to mind.

There was a lake. The carriage slowed from the long pull up the slope upon which the palace sat and Emily had leisure to consider which child would drown him or herself in the ornamental water. Harry espied ducks and commented at length. Peggy and Phillida exclaimed.

When the carriage drew to a halt at last Emily was full of dread and foreboding. A footman in livery opened the door and pulled down the steps, assisting Emily at alight. Perhaps the figure she had spotted on the stairway had been a sentinel. Since she had first glimpsed Brecon, a large party had assembled at the front entrance. Among them she recognised only Johnny Dyott and Tom.

Tom came down to her, hand extended. She took it and held her face up to be kissed. "Snug cottage you have here, my lord."

He laughed and led her up the stairs to a tall woman with chestnut hair and brown eyes, who held out her hand, too.

"I'm glad you've come in spite of everything," Lady

Clanross said warmly but obscurely. "I've been wanting to welcome you and your children to Brecon for a long time now."

Emily murmured something she hoped was appropriate and was introduced to two red-haired damsels in spotted muslin. It was fortunate Lady Margaret wore her hair short. Otherwise, Emily would have been unable to tell the two young ladies apart. They had freckles and Tom's grey eyes, and Emily remembered they were his remote cousins. Lady Clanross resembled neither her sisters nor her cousin-husband, but she was a handsome woman and, of course, handsomely gowned. Emily's blue travelling dress was crumpled, grimy, and five years out of date. Mme. Hebert had a great deal to answer for.

In the bustle of greeting everyone, Johnny and a phalanx of footmen had handed down the older children, Richard, Peggy, Phillida, and the babies. Emily was relieved to see that the magnificence about them had subdued Matt and Amy. Tommy clung to Richard's leg.

It was clear that Lady Clanross had given considerable thought to their reception. Emily, escorted by the obliging Lady Margaret, saw the babies safely to the nursery—and Amy and the boys to the reopened schoolroom in which three still younger Conway sisters and a competent-looking governess awaited them. Then she was guided to the room she and Richard were to share.

Guided was the operative verb. She would never have found the door. The long hallway was full of doors, all exactly alike. Nor was "room" the right word. She and Richard had been given a suite with a vast dressing room and, in the bedchamber, a huge four-poster swagged in new satin. The dressing room was pink, the bedroom ivory with framed watercolours the chambermaid said had been executed by the twins' mother. A vase of damask roses reposed on the dressing table.

The maid had unpacked Emily's trunk. She laid out a fresh muslin gown, announcing that her name was Polly and she would be at Emily's service during her sojourn at Brecon. The girl had also brought hot water for washing, and fresh towels. She curtseyed when Emily thanked her and sent her off. Although the maid seemed obliging and not at all haughty, permitting a stranger to undress and dress her at that juncture would have been beyond Emily's powers.

Before Emily could climb into the enormous armoire and hide with her thumb in her mouth, Richard appeared, looking cheerful.

"Lord, Richard, why did I agree to come? I'm terrified!"

He removed her bonnet, laid it on the dressing table, and kissed her soundly. "Nonsense, you've taken the citadel by storm. Is Tommy frightened?"

"I think not. I told Amy to stay with him. The governess seemed kind and very interested in him."

Richard expelled a sigh. "Good. Tea in half an hour, madam. Shall I undo your buttons?"

Emily submitted. She told him of the maid and her own confusion and he made small jokes that cheered her sufficiently to wash and dress. He had engaged a footman to leave a trail of crumbs, he said solemnly, so they could find their way to Lady Clanross's withdrawing room.

Elizabeth awaited her guests behind a battery of tea things. Maggie came in full of laughter. She had revisited the schoolroom and found their sisters and the three new inmates absorbed in a marathon of spillikins at which young Tommy seemed especially adept.

"It's kind of you to see to the children, Maggie." Elizabeth was amused. Something was bringing out Maggie's domesticity with a vengeance.

"Matt and Amy want to go riding in the morning and my sisters have promised to join them. I may have Jem saddle Joybell, too. A sedate plod round among the ponies would suit me."

Elizabeth touched the brewing teapot. Still very hot.

Fisher and a footman were waiting her call for hot water. "Be sure to ask Jem Fosse to accompany you, at least until he can form a judgement of the other children's skills."

"May I ask Johnny?"

"Certainly. And Jean."

Maggie nodded, resigned to be tactful. Elizabeth did not really object to Johnny and Maggie taking a morning ride round the park together, but neither she nor Maggie wished to offend Jean's sensibilities, which were still tender.

As if cued, Jean drifted in looking vague.

Elizabeth greeted her in tones she knew were over-hearty. "You may take charge of the bread and butter."

Jean sighed. "Very well."

Elizabeth was about to favour her sister with a crisp lecture on the perils of self-induced melancholy when Tom entered followed almost at once by the Falks and Johnny. She saw everyone seated and served, and set herself to make Mrs. Falk feel at home.

Emily Falk was prettier than Elizabeth had expected her to be, small-boned and only a little plump. She had speedwell blue eyes and a humourous look about the mouth that promised tolerance.

"Maggie says your three eldest and my sisters have taken to each other."

"That's a comfort." Mrs. Falk smiled at Maggie, who blushed and offered her a plate of cakes.

"What think you of Brecon?" Elizabeth ventured. This question was her private test of a guest's mettle.

Emily Falk took a sip of tea. "I was thinking I'm happy not to have charge of the servants. You must keep a regiment."

Elizabeth smiled. Not a witty answer but commendably frank. "Thirty-seven, indoors."

Mrs. Falk shuddered.

"However, I'm fortunate in my housekeeper. Mrs. Smollett was trained by my stepmother, and *maman* was both exacting and experienced. I daresay Mrs. Smollett will desert me someday to open an hotel in London."

"Like Grillon's?"

Elizabeth laughed. "In that rococo style, yes. I'll show you the Dower House one of these days. I daresay you saw it as you passed the gate house."

Mrs. Falk admitted to having dozed as they passed the lodge.

"Then I shall certainly show you the Dower House. My father left me the use of it, and it's much more to my taste than Palladian palaces. Before Tom and I went to Italy I thought we might live there and close Brecon. However, that was not practicable. My sisters and their governess are happy there."

"I'd like to see their establishment. Tom tells me Miss Bluestone is a notable educationist."

Elizabeth leaned toward her. "And a delightful woman. I wish she might stay here forever . . ." Her voice trailed. She had meant to produce a schoolroom of misses for Miss Bluestone.

"She's a first-rate botanist," Tom offered. The men had been talking politicks. "Keeps the gardeners on their toes."

Maggie said boldly, "And she never fusses one about one's failures. Jean and I think she's splendid, don't we, Jean?"

Jean deigned to agree.

"She's the only one of our governesses to make real use of the bookroom," Elizabeth added. "I wonder why."

That led to a discussion of governesses who looked upon learning as an unnecessary encumbrance to young ladies and thence to the general state of education (deplorable) and what could be done about it (very little so long as the Church and the dissenters disagreed).

"Is the bookroom catalogue finished?" Colonel Falk asked in a lull.

"My word, I've not met the poet!" Mrs. Falk exclaimed. "I should like to. I thought he was living here."

Her remark, which was grossly tactless or wholly innocent, had the effect of a brick crashing through a window.
A silence fell.

Jean leapt to her feet and ran from the room.

Elizabeth jerked her head at Maggie who excused herself
and followed her twin. "I beg your pardon, ma'am. Jean is
not usually so rag-mannered. The thing is she feels she has
formed an attachment for Owen Davies and now that he
must leave the country . . ."

Mrs. Falk's wide blue stare persuaded Elizabeth that the
colonel's wife had not been told of recent developments.
Richard Falk, it would seem, had strict notions of honour.
She glanced at him and he rolled his eyes heavenward. His
ears were red. Elizabeth did not envy him. If she had been
his wife she would have dissected him before dinner.

"It's rather late for discretion, Colonel," she said dryly,
"though I thank you for it. Ma'am, a double apology. For
Jean's manners and for leaving you in the dark. I ought to
have writ you of our political adventures but I couldn't
trust the mails." And she launched into an account of the
smuggled poem.

She made no attempt to conceal her sisters' infamous
conduct, though a mild protest from Colonel Falk caused
her to soften her language. It was clear that Mrs. Falk was
appalled by the danger the girls stood in of being called as
witnesses, perhaps even as accessories, but she did not
seem disposed to make harsh judgements.

If she had been, Jean and Maggie had able defenders.
Johnny and Colonel Falk praised their spirit and excused
their naiveté until Elizabeth wanted to shake the two men.
Tom said little. In the long run, *he* would probably be the
chief sufferer. When she considered that Owen's poem
might undercut Tom's political efforts, Elizabeth's blood
was still inclined to boil. However, Maggie returned before
she could express herself forthrightly.

It was clear from Maggie's blushes that she knew her
conduct had been under discussion. Everyone rushed into

speech with alternate topics of conversation and Maggie's blushes faded. Nevertheless Elizabeth was glad when the tea was cold and the cakes a few scattered crumbs.

As she rose to leave, Elizabeth turned once more to her bemused guest. "I go up to the nursery every day at this time. Do you care to join me?"

Mrs. Falk agreed. She was nursing the infant, Sally, herself, and had been afraid she would wander for hours vainly seeking her child.

Elizabeth was a little surprised to hear that her guest did not employ a wet nurse, though she knew quite respectable ladies sometimes preferred to nurse their own babies. That led to a discussion of the nursing of infants, tooth-cutting, and the colick which continued up the stairs and down the long corridor to the wing that housed both the nursery and the schoolroom. By the time the babies had been bathed and fed, Elizabeth felt almost at ease with Colonel Falk's wife. She even offered to show her guest the new telescope.

"Time to dress for dinner."

"I can't, Maggie!" Jean lay facedown, so her wail was muffled.

Maggie sat on the bed. "I know it's hard, but you ought to. The sooner the better."

"But that dreadful woman . . ."

"Mrs. Falk is not dreadful," Maggie said firmly. "She's a pleasant lady and you embarrassed her horribly. She knew nothing of Owen's exile."

Jean sat up. She looked crumpled but her eyes were only a little red and not swollen at all. "Truly? Then Colonel Falk . . ."

"He didn't tell his wife. I think he's on our side."

Jean cocked her head, considering.

Maggie wondered if she ought to explain that she hadn't meant Colonel Falk would connive at private meetings between the lovers.

Jean slid from the bed. "I daresay I ought to get it over with. Lisette . . ."

"I'll help you dress. Like old times."

Jean gave a wavering smile. "All right."

As they were leaving to descend for dinner, Polly, the chambermaid Elizabeth had delegated to wait on Mrs. Falk, burst into the room. "Oh, my lady . . ." She broke off when she saw Maggie.

Maggie raised her eyebrows as she had seen Elizabeth do any number of times. The maid blushed.

Jean said casually, "I shan't need you until after dinner, Polly. Thank you."

Polly stared, then bobbed a curtsey and vanished.

Maggie said, "Lisette will be glad to wait on you, Jeanie. It's her duty."

Jean bit her lip. "If you must know, Polly carries messages for us."

"For you and Owen?"

Jean nodded, defiant.

"I wish you wouldn't," Maggie said unhappily.

22

"IT's MY TURN to sit by Amy!" Georgy had tied the bow of her bonnet unevenly. A great loop hung on one side.

Fanny's lip trembled. She was a weepy child. "No, it's mine."

"She wants to sit by *me*." Caro sniffed. She was the eldest of what everyone thought of as the Three Little Sisters. The Three Bears, Maggie reflected, listening to the girls bicker. Maggie's sisters had taken to Amy Falk. After two weeks' constant companionship, the girls were inseparable.

"Amy and Matt will sit between Mr. Dyott and me," Maggie said. "You may sit with Jean, facing us so you can talk to Amy."

Grumbling, the girls permitted themselves to be handed up into the first of the two carriages that were bound for the church in Earl's Brecon. Amy gave Maggie a saucy grin. Her elder brother was inspecting the horses.

"Can you deal with them?" Elizabeth smoothed her gloves.

Maggie nodded. "I think so. Johnny will sit on anyone who misbehaves." Giggles from the coach told her the girls had heard. Elizabeth smiled.

Jean was handed up, then Maggie. When she had tidied her skirts, Maggie patted the place beside her and Amy settled in. She was a bright-eyed child, much prettier than the Conway sisters, but she seemed unconscious of the fact.

Johnny persuaded young Matthew to leave off admiring the near leader's gleaming coat and they, too, climbed in.

A footman closed the door. Gravel crunched as the heavy equipage began to move. Clanross's carriage would pull up before the main entrance to load the rest of the party.

"Where's Tommy?" Amy piped.

"He decided to ride with your papa."

The little girl nodded, satisfied. She was protective of her small brother, but in other ways a compleat minx, full of mischief. She made a comic face at Fanny. Fanny giggled, and that set the others off. Jean looked resigned.

Johnny was describing for the enthusiastic Matthew a pair of matched chestnuts Clanross had lately acquired. Johnny was wholly at ease with children, a quality Maggie thought suitable in husbands. Smiling to herself, she settled back for the ride.

As it had the previous two Sundays, the size of the Brecon party would cause a stir at church. The little girls and Miss Bluestone usually walked to church from the Dower House, no very great distance, and Elizabeth ordered the carriage for such of the party at the great house as were churchgoers. She and the twins attended regularly. Clanross did not. *His* presence for the first time in months would cause a real stir. A number of the neighbouring gentry were convinced he was an atheist. They didn't like his Levelling tendencies, either.

The weather threatened rain, but it had been lowering for a week. Maggie hoped the expedition to Hazeldell Clanross had planned for the afternoon might not be rained out. He wanted to show Mrs. Falk the house and lands once more, before he had to go down to London to attend the queen's trial. Charles Wharton meant to break the entail and move his family to London where he had the promise of a lucrative surgical practice. Colonel Falk apparently wanted to purchase an estate. He and Mrs. Falk had already inspected Hazeldell twice. Maggie thought they would prove good neighbours, though she would miss the Whartons.

"I don't think I'll come to Hazeldell this time," Jean said

over the hubbub. Sometimes their minds ran on the same subject at the same time.

"Why not? There's Cecy's baby to admire, and we haven't seen Mary Wharton in an age. She's back, you know."

Jean made a face. "I don't feel up to it."

Maggie sighed and decided not to try wheedling in a carriage full of giggling brats. Later.

Although Mrs. Davies glowered at Clanross throughout the opening hymn, and Jean and Owen gazed at each other and sighed during the collect, the service went smoothly enough. Mr. Davies's catarrh made itself heard in the homily.

Maggie was conscious of being watched. At first the sensation was satisfying. She knew she looked handsome in her chip-straw bonnet and ivory muslin, and Johnny's presence beside her gave her confidence these days. She no longer shrank from publick view. During the latter part of the service, however, as the handful of communicants approached the altar, she sensed rather than saw that someone was staring at her particularly, and that was discomforting. So discomforting the hair prickled on the back of her neck.

The concluding hymn came to a full-throated close and everyone began groping for prayer books, reticules, hats, and gloves. As they started to file out, Clanross and Elizabeth first as became their rank, Maggie turned to view the congregation.

She spotted the stranger immediately. He was a small man, soberly dressed like a clerk or a shopkeeper, but he had overgrown side-whiskers and sported a flashy stickpin, and his face was a map of London. He was staring directly at Maggie. His small, shrewd eyes did not blink.

She lowered her gaze and poked Johnny in the ribs. "Who's that?"

Johnny sometimes took a glass of ale at the inn when he had been out riding in the countryside, and he had been at

Brecon long enough to recognise the locals. He drew a breath. "I don't know but I'll find out."

She nodded, smiling at old Mrs. Pollard and the Higginses, and took young Amy's hand.

Outside, the air pressed down and the sky darkened. Everyone had to shake hands with everyone else and hear about the haying and the coming crop of corn. Clanross drew the rector apart and spoke at length, whilst Elizabeth and the Falks made conversation around the unresponsive Mrs. Davies. Owen and Jean gazed at each other. The little girls twittered like birds among the gravestones and Matthew tried to climb the monkey-puzzle tree some Conway, home from a voyage, had planted in the last century. Johnny plunged into a group of farmers by the lych-gate.

The churchgoers had begun to disperse and the Brecon carriages had drawn up when a sharp clap of thunder and a simultaneous flash of lightning hastened the pace of farewells. Fat drops of warm rain pelted Maggie's chipstraw bonnet as she and Amy scrambled into the carriage. The girls and Jean followed. Matt, his fair hair stuck with needles, jumped in. Finally, Johnny climbed in and slammed the door behing him. He was out of breath and rather wet. The carriage swayed into motion. Lightning flashed and another clap of thunder pealed overhead.

"I didn't hear you," Maggie half shouted.

"I said no one knows the man. His name is Pickens and he's stopping at the Ross Arms. I think he's a Runner."

Maggie gasped.

Johnny, notwithstanding the proprieties, reached across the two Falk children and took her hand. "Don't worry. It's Sunday. He won't act today, and in any case I may be wrong."

Jean sat up straight. "Do you mean a Bow Street Runner?"

One of the girls gave a nervous giggle. The rain was coming down in sheets.

Tom had also spotted the stranger. An occasional chandler or pedlar drifted through Earl's Brecon, but this man was no bumpkin. "Runner" was the first thought that popped into Tom's head.

It rained hard for perhaps ten minutes, and the Falks and Elizabeth began to consider the pros and cons of abandoning the Hazeldell expedition. The roads would be heavy for carriages.

After some discussion Elizabeth suggested that the adults ride over on horseback for a briefer visit. The entire party had meant to take dinner with the Whartons, but trundling two carriages through the mud seemed tempting fate. The children would be disappointed, but they had the picnic at the Weeping Cave on Tuesday to console them.

By the time they reached the lake, the rain had stopped and Elizabeth had settled everything. She determined to send a messenger to warn Cecilia Wharton of their decision. Tom listened to her plans with half an ear and brooded about the stranger in church. When the carriage reached the house at last, Tom sent a footman to fetch his man, Sims.

Johnny drew him aside in the foyer as everyone else headed upstairs to change into riding gear.

"What is it, Johnny?" Tom hoped Sims was not off courting the Falks' housemaid. Though it seemed unlikely, Elizabeth had reported that Mrs. Smollet thought Sims was smitten with Phillida.

"There's a Redbreast in the village."

Johnny came into focus. "Are you sure?"

"No, sir. I asked several of the farmers, though. The fellow's a Londoner, says he's looking for horses. He's stopping at the inn. He keeps standing the locals to drinks and trying to pry information from them. He's interested in Owen."

"And the girls?"

Johnny said slowly, "I'm not sure. One of the ploughmen

said the man was curious about the Brecon household. That may mean the girls."

Tom nodded. "Owen had better leave at once. I've sent for . . . ah, Sims. I'm glad you're here. We're in a fix." He explained rapidly and Sim's eyes, in their rolls of fat, brightened. He liked a bit of action.

"To Bristol, eh?"

Tom grasped the newell. "Yes. I've money for you, and I'll write a note to Davies and a letter to the captain of that ship Barney said was bound for Quebec. You may take the gig."

"And the new chestnuts?" Sims fairly licked his lips.

Tom grimaced. "If you lame them I'll have your ears. Wait for the letters—it may take awhile. I must think this through."

"Wot about Lunnon?" They had meant to leave for London the next morning.

Tom looked at him. "You'd rather go to Bristol, I think."

Sims grinned villainously, sketched an impudent salute, and vanished into the domestic offices. Not for the first time, it occurred to Tom that his man was equal to anything.

Tom took the stairs two at a time, Johnny at his heels. In the hallway, Tom turned. "We've decided to abandon the carriage ride to Hazeldell. The Falks, Elizabeth, and I will ride over for a brief look at the house after we take some refreshment. I think you and the twins ought to come, too."

"I'd be glad to escort Owen to Bristol, sir."

Tom had to smile. "Eager to see the last of the poet, or just eager?"

Johnny flushed.

"Never mind. Sims will do the job handily and I need you and Maggie to keep Jean under surveillance."

"Shall you tell her Owen's leaving?"

"I must. I hope she'll take the news sensibly." Tom rubbed his forehead. "In fact, a council of war is called for.

Richard and Emily ought to know what's happening, too. Will you ask them to come to my study? I'll send Elizabeth for the girls. I need hardly mention that the servants shouldn't hear of this."

"But Sims . . ."

"Sims is my right hand," Tom said impatiently. "I mean the Brecon servants. The less they know the better for them."

Johnny nodded. "I'll tell the colonel."

The adults assembled in Tom's study as he was finishing the letter of instruction to the master of the Quebec-bound packet. He rose and seated the ladies—there were too few chairs for the men. Richard was watching him with a familiar wariness, alert for any action. Maggie looked pale, Jean agitated. Elizabeth and Emily exchanged puzzled glances.

Tom addressed Richard and Emily first. "You're in for a flurry of melodrama. I hope you won't object."

Richard's eyebrows rose and Emily's blue eyes brightened.

Tom turned to Jean. "There's no way to make this easier for you, Jean. Owen Davies must leave for Bristol at once. There's a Runner on his heels."

Jean's hands flew to her mouth.

"I'm sorry, my dear."

She bit her lip. At least she did not burst into tears. "I must tell him good-bye!"

"That won't be possible, Jeanie."

"Oh, you are cruel . . ."

"Jean," Elizabeth snapped. "Be still."

Tom drew a breath. "I shall send Sims in the gig. He'll pull in behind the rectory and make the situation clear to Owen. If we time our arrival, we may create a diversion that will permit Owen to escape undetected. That's my aim, Jean, and it requires your cooperation."

Jean's lip trembled. "He does not wish to go. He wants to stand his trial."

"I think you'll find he has changed his opinion. When I last discussed the matter with him, he was eager to leave."

"He is not eager! His letters . . ."

Tom stared.

Her chin went up. "We have corresponded. His feelings—all his feelings—are unchanged."

Tom wondered which of his servants Davies had bribed to carry messages. A maid or footman, no doubt. "I won't contradict you, Jean, but he has agreed to go. If you value his liberty and your reputation, yours and *Maggie's*, you will cooperate."

"I want to make my farewells."

Elizabeth said in gentler tones, "Pray hear Tom out, sister. If I understand what he's suggesting, the Runner will be drawn after our party."

Tom nodded. "He won't expect Owen to travel on Sunday, and any movement the girls make will interest him. We'll ride through the village at a leisurely pace. I may even stop in the taproom for a word with the landlord. When we've stirred this fellow up, we can continue to Hazeldell, and I trust he'll follow us. By the time he returns to the inn, Sims will have spirited Owen away. With luck Owen's absence won't be discovered until he's safely in Bristol."

"Shrewd tactics." Richard sounded amused. Tom had not doubted his cooperation, but Emily was another story. Tom regarded her with some anxiety.

"I have never had the opportunity to abet an outlaw's escape." Her eyes glinted. "Of course, Matilda Mayne-Wilkins assisted Charles II, but I daresay *our* adventure will be tamer."

"A pity." Tom suppressed a relieved smile.

"We shall be accessories," Johnny said thoughtfully.

"Does that give you pause?" Tom put the dean of Lincoln cathedral guiltily from his mind.

"No, for the warrant must *not* be served." Johnny and Maggie exchanged meaningful looks.

Ah well, Tom thought, plenty of time to deal with that.

As they rode slowly back from their visit to Hazeldell, Emily decided that a life of crime suited her. Though she felt some sympathy for Lady Jean, Emily had seldom enjoyed an afternoon more. A life in the shadow of Brecon, however, still gave her some pause. Did Richard really mean to purchase the Hazeldell estate? She was not sure.

"What think you of the house?" he asked, reading her thoughts with husbandly ease. They had fallen behind the company. Johnny Dyott and Maggie flanked a stiff-backed Jean. Tom and Elizabeth had taken a long lead.

"I like it very well. Who would not?"

"But?"

"The land is not in good heart. Charles Wharton does not understand agricultural improvement."

Richard grasped the reins more firmly in his left hand. He was a good horseman, but his disability made it wiser for him to ride a biddable horse. The bay gelding was rather frisky. "I thought that might suit you."

Emily blinked. "Good arable fallen to seed, tumbledown outbuildings, decayed cottages . . ."

"I thought you liked a challenge."

Emily patted the neck of her mare and brooded.

"But you're homesick," he added in tones of resignation. "You prefer Hampshire."

"I'm used to Hampshire. You're right, though. I do like a challenge. It gave me great satisfaction to make Wellfield pay. Edward didn't try. He was a lawyer through and through." Her first husband had continued his practice of the law even after he inherited Wellfield. It was she who had made the land productive, after his death. The effort had taken nearly ten years. Ten good years. If Richard would allow her to manage the land . . .

"You're your father's daughter."

Emily swallowed.

Richard cocked his head. "Don't look so downcast. It's a very good thing to be, my love."

Emily forced a smile. "But you don't go on comfortably with Papa . . ."

"I didn't say you *were* Sir Henry, merely that you had inherited his talents."

That judgement was more to her liking. "Shall you buy Hazeldell?"

"Not unless I'm sure of your feelings."

"I wish I could be sure of them myself. But should you not be consulting your own feelings?"

He reined in. She did, too, and sat looking at him inquiringly.

"I thought I was."

"But you're not agricultural!"

Richard smiled. "No, but I am Emily Mayne's husband and I like to keep her happy."

Emily melted. "Richard, you must not put my odd quirks before your own wishes . . ."

"Before *my* odd quirks? It doesn't matter where I live. I like Hazeldell because I enjoy Tom's company, but I'll see him in London, after all. You've been driving me mad, Emily, with your little deferential phrases." He pursed his mouth and quoted in a genteel falsetto, " 'I shall live where Richard takes me. I'm content in Winchester and would be content in Bath or London.' "

Emily felt herself blush.

He said gently, "That's cant, Emily. Where you live matters to you—a great deal. You hated living in a town. You were homesick for Wellfield. I appreciated your restraint, but I'd appreciate the truth even more. What do you want?"

"A place to raise the children comfortably. I don't wish to be a fashionable lady or a town matron." She took a gulp of air. "And I'd hate London. The air crawls in one's lungs."

"So it does."

"I thought you liked London!"

Their mounts ambled along, stopping to chew a tasty

clump of greenery as the spirit moved them. The rest of the party had disappeared from sight.

"London's no place to raise children. I'll probably take rooms or join a club so I can go to Town when Murray beckons or my man of business requires my signature, but I've no intention of living there." Richard paused. "I never allowed myself to become attached to a place, Emily. It wouldn't have been wise. I'll admit that I'm sometimes restless when the after-dinner talk turns too often to cows, but that's not a serious consideration." He urged his mount to a stricter walk and she followed suit.

"So the decision is mine?"

"You sound appalled."

"I am," Emily wailed. "What if I make the wrong choice?"

He clucked his tongue. "Where is that spirit of daring and defiance I married you for? A little risk . . ."

"You married me to be a mother to your children," Emily mumbled.

"What!" He stared, then began to laugh. In fact he laughed so hard he startled his horse into gyrations that took several minutes to control.

When they were once more moving along the deserted lane at a steady pace, he said, laughter still close to the surface, "But Emily, you were a mother to my children well before I married you. Or so I tell my friends."

Emily raised her crop. "Devil!" She had taken on the care of his two older children after his first wife died.

"And only today you abetted the escape of a felonious poet. Admit it, my dear, you're a pirate at heart."

"Only under your influence," she said darkly.

"You were the one who proposed marriage."

That was true—one of her great triumphs. Emily savoured the moment in her mind.

"Do you regret your choice?"

Her eyes flew to his. He was in earnest.

"Not for a minute."

"Nor do I. Ever."

A vast happiness stilled Emily's tongue. They rode side by side in silence. Finally Richard said, "So, you see, I'm inclined to trust your choices."

Emily smiled at him. "And I yours. Shall I be frank?"

"Please do!"

"I'd like some time to think—about Hazeldell and Hampshire."

"The will cannot be proved in less than a sixmonth. You've plenty of time."

"But where shall we live meanwhile?"

He started to say something, but bit off the words. "I've an idea about that but I must take advice before I mention it."

Tom, she thought. Of course. Perhaps there's a house in Chacton we could let on a short lease.

"Shall we try to catch up with our accomplices?"

"Lord, yes. Poor Lady Jean." As they set their horses to a canter, Emily reflected guiltily that the unhappy child had behaved very well throughout the entire trying episode.

Emily greatly preferred Maggie, who was cheerful and helped with the children, to her melancholy twin, but she couldn't help sympathising with the young lovers. However, they were *very* young lovers and a few years' waiting would prove their attachment. She had waited three years for Richard, after all.

23

By the time she reached the Brecon stables, Jean had begun to think again. The speed with which Clanross effected Owen's escape had left her numb.

She watched Johnny dismount and help Maggie from Joybell's saddle, then climbed down herself with Jem Fosse's help. Jem had been her ally in the past, but he was Clanross's servant. Everyone was against her. Except Polly.

An idea surfaced. Polly's cooperation could be purchased, not with money but with intrigue. Life in service bored Polly. She wanted romance, adventure. She had served as Owen's messenger eagerly and taken very little by way of payment.

Well, Owen was gone. There were no messages to be sent. Watching her sister feed Joybell an apple, Jean felt a sudden rush of inspiration. Good, biddable Maggie, Maggie whom everyone trusted. Maggie could leave the house, and even, perhaps, the grounds without arousing suspicion. Maggie and Polly.

Before she reached her solitary bedchamber Jean's plan had come into full flower. Determination buoyed her steps. Life surged in her veins. She felt so transformed she was sure Elizabeth would smell a rat when she announced she did not mean to come down to dinner, but Elizabeth merely nodded understandingly. Everyone was terribly understanding.

Polly entered the room with hot water as Jean was

sending Lisette away to help Maggie dress for dinner. Lisette closed the door with neat precision.

Jean saw that Polly's eyes were red with weeping, and felt a stab of fear. Had Elizabeth uncovered Polly's role in the exchange of clandestine messages? "What is it?"

"Mr. Davies is gone, so they say," Polly mourned.

"No one is supposed to know!"

"That man from London won't find out." The sky had clouded over again and it was quite dark. Sniffing sadly, Polly lit a branch of candles. "Nobody would betray a Brecon man to one of them Runners."

"Are you sure?" The Brecon servants, now Jean came to think of it, usually knew everything.

"Certainly. Mr. Sims made off this afternoon in the gig, clever as paint, and no one peached. I dessay Mr. Davies is safe aboard ship by now."

That was unduly optimistic. However, Jean's heart lightened. "Did you see Mr. Owen before he left?"

"Only at church, me lady." She gave a gentle sob that would have been appropriate if Owen had died. "Such a handsome man as he was and so kind."

"I must go to him," Jean interrupted. "I must follow him to Bristol, Polly. They cannot separate us."

Polly's eyes widened.

"And you shall help me."

Polly's face paled but her eyes lit as they did when she was carrying secrets. "I couldn't, me lady. I'd be found out. Smollet would sack me for sure, and me dad'd beat me purple." Her father was a gamekeeper for the estate, rather an idle one since Clanross did not hunt. Her mother was dead.

"You won't be found out. You shall come with me—to Upper Canada."

"Lord a mercy!" Polly's eyes glittered.

The promise was rather grandiose. Jean had the remains of her quarterly allowance—generous as pin money but perhaps inadequate to buying passage for two on a ship bound for Quebec. However, Clanross had supplied Owen with moneys for the journey. Owen would see the justice of taking Polly with them. The trick was to reach Bristol before the packet sailed on Wednesday.

Jean drew a breath. "Do you want to come? It will be hard, I daresay, and dangerous."

"Oh, yes," Polly breathed.

"Splendid. When my sister has gone down to dinner, the first thing you must do is bring me Maggie's habit and a pair of scissors. And tomorrow morning, at first light, we shall make our escape."

"That Lisette'll take Lady Margaret's habit away to brush it."

Jean's heart sank. "Do you know where?"

"A course."

"Then when Lisette has finished and gone down to the servants' hall, you must bring me the habit. I can wear my own hat and boots, and you shall cut my hair."

Polly's eyes narrowed. "So's you'll look like your sister?"

Jean nodded.

"What if Lady Margaret or Lady Clanross come after dinner to see how you go on?"

Jean hadn't thought of that. Two heads were definitely better than one. "Then I'll cut it myself when they've all gone to sleep."

Polly pursed her lips. "And when I bring up the water in the morning . . ."

"That will be too late. You must come to me at first light. Bring your cloak and bonnet, and we'll slip out to the stables before the others rise."

"I dunno, me lady. His lordship's off for Lunnon in the morning." The queen's trial would commence on Thursday.

"Blast, then we'll have to wait a day. Owen's ship sails with the tide Wednesday . . . stay! How far is it to Bristol?"

"I dunno, me lady. Two day's ride?" The clock on the mantle chimed. "Lord a mercy, I mun' see to Mrs. Falk!"

"Then come back to me when they've gone down to dinner," Jean said imperiously. "I shall work this out yet."

In the interests of verisimilitude, Jean washed and donned her night rail and robe. Then she sat at her dressing table and brooded.

A footman brought in a tray of choice delicacies. He looked as if he might offer his sympathy, given the chance, but Jean decided one ally was enough. Trying to look melancholy, she waved him away and tucked into the meal.

Maggie was not an early riser most days. Clanross would leave early. Why should not Jean, in disguise, see him off, then go for a quiet ride? Breakfast with Clanross would be a test. Then, in Maggie's character, she could ride off, escorted by Polly, to do what? Aha, Mrs. Pollard. Maggie had always had a kindness for old Mrs. Pollard. Really, it was a good plan and would work very well unless Maggie should be so perverse as to rise early. Surely she would not.

An hour later Polly scratched at the door and entered with the scissors and Maggie's habit.

Jean waved at the wardrobe. "Hang it there, Polly. We go tomorrow!"

"Lord a mercy," said Polly.

Jean was visited that evening by Elizabeth and Maggie. Elizabeth spoke gravely about Jean's secret correspondence with Owen and sympathetically about one's feelings on being separated from one's friends. Friends! Before Jean burst into an ill-considered defence of her devotion to Owen, Maggie entered. Presently Elizabeth left. She had not made a serious effort to find out which of the servants had carried Owen's letters. That was fortunate. Jean had never been able to withstand Lizzie when her elder sister was really determined.

Jean and Maggie talked, or rather Maggie talked. She even wept a little, and she offered to spend the night with Jean if that would be of comfort.

Jean felt the tears sting her own eyes. It might be years before she saw her twin again. She wanted to pour out her feelings, take Maggie into her confidence, but she knew she must not. At last her silence drove Maggie off, but not before Maggie kissed her. Jean clung to Maggie and wept, but she did not give way to betraying speech.

Alone at last, Jean took her bedside candle back to the dressing room and found the scissors. Two snips persuaded her that the cutting of hair was a rare and difficult art.

She packed a cloak bag with such items as she thought might be useful, and tucked a string of pearls and Clanross's brooch into her purse. When she had laid out the purse, boots, and riding hat, Jean hopped into bed and composed herself to sleep. Sleep did not come.

She thought of Owen, alone and dreaming of her. She thought of Upper Canada, turning over in her mind such facts as had come her way. Very cold winters, very large mosquitoes. She had no desire to see an Iroquois warrior but she thought she might like to see the Great Falls of the Niagara.

Maggie appeared in her mind's eye, and Elizabeth. She wept a little. Still, the time came when a woman had to leave her family and cleave to a man. It said so in the prayer book. She was ready to cleave. Owen had taught her to despise the trivialities of rank, to value ideas of real worth. She would go with him to the wilderness and he would write an epic so powerful it would set London on its ear. The king would beg him to return.

Birds chirruped in the bushes before she drowsed off.

"Me lady!"

Jean started awake. Polly was shaking her shoulder. "What time is it?"

"Gone seven, me lady. You did say first light."

Jean scrambled from the bed. "I overslept myself. How could I?"

"They're up."

"Who?"

"His lordship," Polly said tersely, "the colonel and his lady, and Mr. Dyott. Her ladyship's up but won't come down until nine."

"Maggie?"

"Not yet."

Jean gulped. Her hair was cut, her bridges burnt. She splashed cold water on her face, gave her teeth a hasty scrub, and scrambled into her undergarments. Maggie's habit fit perfectly, of course. Jean did not like the frogging. She sat to pull on her boots.

"Let me help you . . ."

"Did you say Johnny was up?"

"Yes, me lady. They're at breakfast now. Cook's grumbling." Cook thought persons of quality should not take solid nourishment before ten o'clock.

Jean groaned. "If Johnny's up I daren't go into the breakfast room. He'd know me in an instant."

Polly brought her hat and gloves. "We could go out to the stables and hide in that nook behind the tack room till it's safe."

Polly was a superior accomplice, no doubt of it. Jean eyed her gratefully from under the brim of her riding hat. "Yes, the stables will be safe enough. Clanross means to take the curricle, and Jem will drive it to the front entrance for him."

"Peter," Polly blushed, "that's the new undergroom, he'd saddle Lady Margaret's horse for you . . ."

Jean was conscience-stricken. Polly and Peter had been walking out together. "You won't want to leave Peter!"

"Ah, he's a good enough lad, but I don't mean to wed him. Shall I ask him?"

Jean contemplated Maggie's Joybell. A worse slug did not inhabit the stables. "Would he pole up the old gig for us, do you think? You can't want to ride pillion on Joybell."

Polly nodded and poked her head out the door. "Do be quick, me lady!"

Jean grabbed her purse and the cloak bag.

Polly led her through passages Jean did not know existed. From time to time they halted as voices neared and passed, but no one saw them. At last they emerged from a dark corridor that smelt of cheese. The stables, unfamiliar in the early light, lay beyond a stiff hedge and a brick court-yard.

Polly found Peter as soon as Jem had left with the curricle. When Jean, trying to sound like Maggie, asked him to pole up the old gig, he looked doubtful.

"I dunno, me lady. Mr. Fosse didn't give no orders . . ." Jem was Mr. Fosse now, a dignity her old ally had achieved when Clanross made him head groom.

Jean gritted her teeth. "Mr. Fosse couldn't know. Mrs. Pollard is ill. Polly and I mean to take her . . ." Her mind groped feverishly. ". . . uh, these fresh linens and a potion Miss Bluestone recommends." She indicated the cloak bag. "Do hurry, Peter. She's in pain."

Peter allowed that he was sorry to hear it, his granny would be sorry to hear it, too, being a good friend of Mrs. Pollard from way back, and wasn't it hard how old folks suffered. However, he did move slowly toward the stalls. Jean began to hope.

Half an hour later they were off. In fact they followed in the wake of Clanross's curricle. Jean held the bay in check until she could see that the last of the well-wishers had gone into the house, then she set off down the carriageway at a smart trot, Polly twittering beside her.

They reached the gate house. Jean, in her Maggie-role, smiled at the lodge-keeper, whose breakfast they had clearly interrupted, and saw that the curricle had passed from view. Clanross's team, though not so swift as the pair Sims was driving to Bristol, moved faster than the sedate bay Peter had chosen to draw the gig. The bay was defi-nitely a Maggie-horse.

Jean feathered a corner neatly and entered the single street along which the trim cottages of Earl's Brecon had been built. She trotted the bay past the church and the rectory, eyes straight ahead, slowed for a cart near the inn, and caught sight of old Mrs. Pollard tending to her flowers. Mrs. Pollard gave her a cheery wave.

Jean waggled the whip in response. She hoped the news of Mrs. Pollard's miraculous recovery would take some hours to reach Brecon.

That was the only mishap. Jean reached the newly metalled road to Lincoln, remembered the toll in time to hand Polly her purse, and trotted the bay gently onward. She supposed she would eventually have to change horses, but she meant to conserve the bay's strength as long as she might. All her funds would be needed for the journey.

Maggie slept until half-past nine. She had mourned for Jean, and more for herself, because Jean had spurned her sympathy, until nearly one. Even so, she slept later than she might have. Polly had not brought her hot water at the usual hour. That puzzled Maggie. She stuck her tousled head out the door and asked a passing footman to bring water.

Briefly she considered slipping into Jean's bedchamber, but if her sister had contrived to sleep late, too, she ought to be left in peace. Maggie brushed her hair, thanked the footman sleepily when he brought a cannikin, and asked him where Polly had got to. He seemed as puzzled as she.

When she had dressed in an old blue muslin, Maggie drifted down to the breakfast room. Elizabeth was still there, though she was bound for the nursery.

"Is Jean awake?"

"I think she's still abed." Maggie dropped two lumps in her tea and stirred, suppressing a yawn. "I decided not to disturb her."

Elizabeth frowned, abstracted. "I'm troubled for her, Maggie. She was too quiet yesterday."

"She's sad."

Elizabeth sighed. "Of course she is. I hope . . . well, do what you may to comfort her, my dear. I'll come to her when I've seen the babies." She left, and Maggie munched cold toast and drank sweet tea, and stared vaguely at nothing.

She returned to her own room, set out several items for Lisette to mend, considered seeking Johnny out in the book room for a stroll in the garden, wondered if she ought to look in on the schoolroom, and heard the clock strike the half hour. Half-past ten. Jean had still not come out, or she had done so without the usual good morning greeting.

Maggie rose. She was about to go to Jean's room when Lisette knocked and entered the dressing room, looking as disturbed as her smooth facade permitted.

"What is it, Lisette?"

"Lady Jean is not in her chamber, my lady, and your habit is missing from the press."

Maggie's heartbeat quickened. "Are you sure?"

Lisette almost wrung her hands. "It's very strange. Please come, my lady. Something must be amiss."

Maggie needed no urging.

Jean's bedchamber presented the picture of hasty ablutions. Her nightcap lay on the floor and the bed was unmade.

"That Polly," Lisette grumbled, but she looked worried.

Polly. Maggie ran back into the dressing room. Again signs of haste and, carelessly tossed on the cold and garnished hearth, snippets of red hair. Maggie knew herself to be slower-witted than her twin but she was no dunce. Jean had run off. It did not take genius to guess where.

Maggie cleared her throat and forced herself to speak calmly. "Desire Lady Clanross to meet me in the book room at once, Lisette, if you will be so kind." Johnny would be at work in the bookroom. She needed Johnny.

Lisette dipped a quick but correct curtsey and hurried off. Maggie abandoned her false serenity and dashed to the library.

Johnny was there and Mrs. Falk. At her entry, Johnny leapt to his feet. "What's wrong, Maggie?"

"Jean has eloped." Maggie clung to the doorknob. "There's no other explanation. I think she must have persuaded Polly to help her. Ma'am, did Polly bring your water this morning?"

Mrs. Falk laid the slim volume she had been holding aside. "No, and she didn't come to help me dress, either." She rose. "Are you sure, Lady Margaret?"

Maggie was sure as death. "Jean cut her hair off, you see." Her voice broke and she took a deep breath to compose herself. Not the time to be falling into the vapours. "When we were younger we sometimes tried to fool people into thinking one of us was the other." She gulped. "It was a game. Miss Bluestone cured us of it. I think Jean must have passed herself off as me in the stables."

Elizabeth came in, out of breath. "Lisette says Jean has run off!"

"She's gone and she didn't tell me." Maggie flung herself into her sister's arms and burst into tears.

Elizabeth hugged Maggie fiercely and tried to think, but fear and anger made her head whirl.

Johnny and Emily Falk exchanged glances. "Find Richard," Emily suggested. Johnny yanked the bell-pull, and Fisher himself appeared with suspicious alacrity.

Servants, Elizabeth reflected with some bitterness, always know everything.

Maggie shuddered with sobs. How could Jean have been so unkind to her twin? Elizabeth patted the girl's shoulder. And for what? A tweedling poetaster with the spine of a boiled leek.

Emily Falk was saying, "The colonel was out on the lake with Matthew, Fisher. If he's come in, he's with Tommy in the schoolroom."

Fisher bowed and retired.

Maggie's sobs had begun to ease. When Elizabeth thought the girl might reply coherently, she said, "Tell us what you know, Maggie, and for the love of heaven hold nothing back. Did she have help?

Maggie's sad tale tumbled out.

Emily was frowning. "I cannot believe Polly . . . such an obliging girl . . . but she didn't come to help me dress this morning."

"She was supposed to wait on you," Elizabeth blurted, almost as shocked to know that her guest had been neglected as that Polly was corruptible.

Emily made a moue. "I usually send her off once she's laid out my gown, and I surmised she'd given up on me this morning. I didn't think twice about it, Elizabeth, but I see now that I should have. I beg your pardon."

Johnny had been working things out in his head. "If Jean passed herself off as Maggie in the stables, then she'll be riding Joybell. I can overtake her . . ."

Colonel Falk entered still wearing buckskins and boots, and everyone burst into speech at once. Elizabeth overrode the babble and gave him a terse summary.

He looked thoughtful. "As we came in from seeing Tom off, I caught a glimpse of a gig driving away at a smart clip. Does Lady Jean drive?"

"Jem taught both of us," Maggie said, hiccuping. "J— Jean's a capital whip."

"Then she probably took the gig so the maid could ride with her."

There was some slight comfort in thinking that Jean was not galloping about the countryside alone, though in the circumstances Polly could scarcely be considered a respectable escort.

"And she's making for Bristol." Colonel Falk turned to Johnny. "Set for action?"

Johnny drew a long breath. "Certainly, sir."

"If you will trace the gig's progress, I'll try to overtake Tom. He means to stop the night in Huntingdon."

Maggie straightened and drew away from Elizabeth. "I'm going with Johnny!"

"My dear, you can't." Elizabeth tried to keep her voice calm but the effort showed. "A young lady . . ."

Maggie turned on her. "Pho, we can take Lisette with us in the barouche. Johnny and I can lend Jean countenance, and she's more likely to . . . to cooperate if I persuade her."

"The barouche," said Elizabeth, "is probably the only vehicle left on the estate."

That provoked constrained smiles from everyone but Maggie.

"On mature thought," Elizabeth continued, "you may be right. She will need the comfort of a female of her own blood. I would go myself, but I clearly don't have Jean's confidence."

Maggie's mouth trembled. "Nor do I."

Although Elizabeth felt another pang for Maggie, there was no point wallowing in sympathy. "But she *will* listen to you, and someone must stay here to prevent chaos. What of the Runner?" She looked at Colonel Falk.

"He's bound to follow the girls." Falk frowned. "If Lady Jean drove through the village he probably caught the scent and has gone after her."

"Lord, what a mull. Tom . . ."

"Perhaps he can forestall the Runner—send an emissary to the magistrate's court, or some such thing. I'm no lawyer," he added apologetically. "Tom should be informed, however. I'll catch him up at Huntingdon tonight, and go directly to Bristol if he thinks I ought."

"Then there's a chance you may reach Owen before Jean does. She won't know the route," Elizabeth mused. "Once she leaves the Great North Road, she'll be asking her way."

"Grantham," Johnny said decisively. "She'll turn west at Grantham. I'll go out to the stables, sir, and see what Fosse has to say for himself. Maggie . . ."

Maggie gave him a look of such obvious reliance he blushed. "I'll have a footman pack your things," she offered.

Johnny looked alarmed. "Er, a cloak bag merely. And

for yourself and Lisette, Maggie, only such items as may be necessary. We shall be four in the barouche coming back."

That was the most reassuring thing he could have said. Maggie beamed at him. Elizabeth thought him overconfident but she was not about to cast doubts.

Maggie and Johnny went their separate ways, and Elizabeth regarded the Falks rather helplessly.

"I'm obliged to you again, Colonel. Jean is . . ."

"Hot in hand?" He smiled.

Elizabeth sighed. "Just so. Pray don't judge her too harshly."

Red tingled his cheekbones. "I'm the result of such an elopement, so I'm the last man likely to hold her up to censure, ma'am."

Elizabeth bit her lip. "I . . ."

"However," he added thoughtfully, "we had probably better try for a rescue. Young Davies appears to be even less reliable than my father, if that's possible. I shall leave at once." He executed a crisp bow, kissed his wife on the cheek, and went off, leaving the two women to stare at each other.

Elizabeth ran her hands over her face. "I beg your pardon, Emily, since it's too late to beg the colonel's. That's the second time I've spoken to him with gross want of tact. I don't watch my words with him."

"He's oversensitive on the subject," Emily said calmly, "because he avoided thinking about his mother for years. Her death forced him to brood a bit. It's probably good for him. In fact, I find his admiration for Lady Jean most encouraging."

"Admiration?"

"He speaks highly of her spirit."

Elizabeth gave a hollow laugh.

"I find Lady Margaret more agreeable myself." Emily tidied her skirt. "But Richard, you see, needs to forgive his mother."

"And helping to rescue Jean would be an act of approval?" Elizabeth heaved a sigh. "I wish I had your understanding of people's motives. Clearly I don't even understand my own sister, and Jean, of all my sisters, is most like me in temperament."

"I daresay that's why her conduct annoys you."

Elizabeth stared. It was all too true.

"But now is not the time for philosophizing. Tell me what I may do to help."

Elizabeth blinked back tears. "Keep me company, Emily. I hate waiting."

"So do I," Emily said, giving her arm a gentle pat, "and I've had a great deal of practice. Let us go oversee Lady Margaret's preparations."

= 24 =

"WHAT THE DEVIL brings you 'ere, me lady?"

"Sims!" Jean pulled at the job-horse's stubborn mouth. Conflicting feelings brought her to a halt.

On the one hand she hadn't expected to find Sims still in Bristol. He was Clanross's valet and ought to have followed his master to London once Owen was delivered to his fate. Sims's continued presence at the port was a blow to her plan.

On the other hand, it was past nine o'clock at night, the horse and Polly were nearly dead with fatigue, and Jean had not yet found Owen's inn. She was beginning to wonder if she would find a room at any hostelry. Land-lords, she had discovered in Warwick the previous night, did not want the patronage of young women travelling without male escort.

The night before, she had wheedled and bribed a room at a shabby inn after being turned away twice from more respectable establishments. The place had been dirty and noisy, and only the sight of a gold guinea produced a private parlour. Although she had pawned the pearls in the morning, she had had to hire the nag. She wasn't sure she could pay for a room and parlour in Bristol, and for her passage, too. Sims looked like rescue, and Sims, like Jem Fosse, had been her ally in the past.

Indecision—and weariness—held Jean still.

Sims's heavy body tilted the gig sidewise as he climbed

up beside her. "Move over, me lady." He took the reins from her nerveless grasp.

"What are you going to do? You can't stop me, Sims. I mean to join Owen aboard the *North Star*."

"If I can't stop you," Sims growled, "the master can. She don't sail till the evening tide."

"Tomorrow?"

"Aye. 'Is nibs and me 'as rooms at the Crown and Anchor."

"I know. Someone, Elizabeth I think, mentioned the inn, but I can't find it."

Sims's mouth compressed. "It's in the Welsh Back, of all the 'eathen names. I'll take the pair of you there."

The Crown and Anchor was bound to be costly. Jean sighed. At least she would see Owen. "I have some money."

" 'Ave you now? That's a wonder, me lady. D'ye 'ave common sense, too, by any chance? 'Ere's a fine kettle of fish . . ." And he went on scolding as he turned the gig and headed the shambling job-horse down a wide waterfront street toward the inn. She could make its sign out by the light of torches. She'd been looking in the wrong street.

The moon was up and nearly full, but the flaring torches dimmed her night vision. Her eyes hurt, and her back and wrists and arms. She wanted to fall onto a feather bed and die. She'd even stopped wanting to eat.

Beside her, Polly moaned. "I'm hungry, me lady."

"A bit less free with the 'me ladies,' girl," Sims said with magnificent inconsistency. "We don't want that Redbreast to find 'er la'ship, now do we?"

Polly straightened. "I want to eat."

Sims drew up at the inn and handed the reins to the ostler. "Stable 'im, lad."

"On you reck'ning, zur?" People in the west had strange accents, Jean thought sleepily. Was the Runner in Bristol, too?

"That's right. These ladies is kin to the lad."

The ostler winked. "Prime articles, zur."

"Mind your tongue," Sims roared.

The man ducked his head, grinning, and Sims descended. His weight shook the flimsy vehicle. He handed Jean down tenderly and Polly less tenderly, and took their cloak bags, which he gave to a florid man who appeared at his elbow.

"Miss Carter and her maid will be wanting a bedchamber, Mr. Oates. I 'ope you ain't going to tell me you're out of rooms."

"No, sir, Mr. Sims. We've one room left should suit . . . what did ye say the lady's name was?"

"Carter," Sims said firmly. "Miss Jane Carter. Of the Lincolnshire Carters. Swells, Mr. Oates. D'ye understand me?"

The man had disposed of the cloak bags to a slatternly maid who scurried off with them. Now he rubbed his hands. "Any kin to your Mr. Evans?"

"First cousin," said Sims. "Come to bid 'im farewell. The ladies is famished, Mr. Oates. You may bring meat and bread to me parlour in a quarter hour. I'll see the ladies to their room. Can't be too careful, can we, with the riffraff as 'ang about the docks."

Hand on Jean's elbow, Sims surged into the crowded ordinary of the inn like a ship under full sail. Polly and the host followed in his wake, the host promising culinary miracles despite the late hour and Polly whimpering.

The room was cramped but clean and the bed looked like heaven. The chambermaid had brought water. She pulled a truckle for Polly. Unpinning her hat, Jean washed the dust of too many miles from her face and hands. She looked at the crumpled muslin gown the girl had laid out and decided she hadn't the strength to change from Maggie's travel-stained habit. That would shock Owen, she supposed. She ran a comb through her hair—it looked as if mice had been gnawing at it—and sat on the room's sole chair whilst Polly made herself tidier.

What was she going to say to Owen? Jean's tired mind

groped for the eloquent speeches she had been rehearsing along the way, but she could think only of bed.

Sims knocked and Polly unlatched the door. Jean had forgot how fond of Sims she was. He had once given her a looted ribband of the Legion of Honour. Well, he would be awarding no medals tonight.

Stifling a groan at the stiffness in her limbs, she rose and followed him to the parlour. "Where's Owen?"

"Out. 'E wanted to catch the moonlight on the tower of some big church. St. Mary's I think 'e said. Aye, St. Mary Redcliffe. Famous place," Sims added, massively unimpressed. " 'E's writing a pome."

It was a relief not to find Owen waiting. She wanted to see him, talk to him, go with him, but not in her present condition.

Sims carved ham and cut off slices of bread. The waiter had brought ale and fruit. Jean swallowed a draught of ale and Sims fed her like a bird. Polly wolfed down meat and bread and drank off a tankard of ale in no time at all.

"I want to go to bed," Jean announced. "We'll discuss . . . talk 'bout . . . g'night, Sims." Her eyes drooped. She pushed herself to her feet. "I forgot to say thank you."

"You're welcome, I'm sure," said Sims. Polly burped.

Jem Fosse had insisted on driving the barouche himself. Johnny had not objected. He was no whipster. They followed the scent as far as Coventry, then lost it in the confusing splay of streets. It was late. Maggie drooped beside Johnny and even the iron Lisette showed signs of fatigue. He found an inn, took bedchambers and a private parlour, and attended to his lady. There had been no sight of the Runner, though necessity had forced Fosse to drive through Earl's Brecon to the Lincoln road.

Next morning things looked brighter. Johnny gambled that Jean would have headed for Warwick and Gloucester, and found clear evidence of her presence in Warwick. She had pawned a string of pearls.

"They were a gift!" Maggie's hands twisted. "How could she?"

"She had to change horses." Johnny was glad Jean had funds. He was well-inlaid with cash himself thanks to Lady Clanross. He would have redeemed the necklace but he didn't have the ticket. He paid the ostler a small sum to keep the horse Jean had left until a groom from Brecon could be sent for it, then directed Fosse to set the barouche on the road once more.

With Lisette riding guard, it was a little hard to carry on an unconstrained dialogue with Maggie, but Johnny was pleased to see that she did not indulge in endless repining. She was anxious for her sister, true, but she kept the "if onlys" and "what ifs" to a minimum.

Warwick was a pretty town, but there would be another time to show Maggie the castle. They pushed south, through Stratford and the vale of Evesham. Gloucester, famous in story, gave no hint of Jean's passage, but Johnny had gained enough confidence to press on to Bristol by moonlight. In the outskirts, he found a pleasant hostelry, saw to the ladies, let Fosse see to the horses, and retired for a short night's rest.

He rose at the maidservant's knock as dawn silvered the eastern sky. He had hired a horse the night before. He meant to ride into Bristol to the inn where Sims had taken Owen and roust Sims out. Between them they should be able to find Jean. It sounded simple, but time pressed. Under strong protest, Maggie had agreed to wait at the suburban inn with Fosse and Lisette.

Johnny found Owen's ship moored at the floating dock, quite near the cathedral. Owen had not yet boarded. Discretion prevented Johnny from asking whether a young red-haired lady had boarded. Surely the mate would have commented if Jean had created a dramatic scene of reunion. It seemed that Owen still awaited the boarding call at the Crown and Anchor in Welsh Back. Johnny decided he would find Owen, knock his teeth down his throat, throw

Jean over his shoulder, and carry her to her sister. He was smiling as he read the inn's sign.

Tom and Richard had spent a comfortable night at the White Hart in Bath. Richard had reached Huntingdon as Tom was retiring the first evening. When Tom climbed down from the rafters, he decided there was no point trying to drive all night. Next morning they cut southwest through Buckingham and Bedford to Oxford. From Newbury, it was a straight shot on the Bath road to Bristol. Tom thought they might as well have a snug dinner and an early night in a Bath inn. He wasn't sure when the ship would sail, but he was too disgusted with Jean to tie his back in knots jouncing into Bristol at midnight. He and Richard set off at daybreak and reached Sims at the Crown and Anchor as breakfast was brought into Sims's parlour. Jean was safe. Owen had not yet been arrested. The lovers had not yet seen one another, both being asleep in their separate rooms. Tom complimented Sims on his tactics and called for coffee.

It was full morning before Jean woke. The slatternly maidservant knocked at the door with hot water for Miss Carter.

Jean, muscles twinging, rose to let her in. She was about to tell the maid to go wake Miss Carter with her blasted water when it occurred to her that she *was* Miss Carter. "Er, thank you."

"The gentlemen be waiting in parlour, miss."

"Tell them I'll come to them directly."

The maid bobbed a curtsey and left.

Anticipation drove Jean's aches from her mind. She scrubbed in the deliciously hot water and even washed her mouse-eaten hair, though that left little water for Polly who stirred and groaned but did not waken. Someone, surely not the slattern, had ironed Jean's sprigged muslin. It hung, crisp and pretty, from a peg in the wall.

Jean dressed, approved the result in the tiny looking glass, and composed herself to meet her beloved. Her haphazard curls were still damp.

Polly eyed her sleepily from the truckle. "What's the time?"

"I don't know," Jean said blithely. "Time to see Owen. We've done it, Polly. He's here, and I'll get round Sims. Sims likes me. We sail for North America on the evening tide!"

Polly made a noncommittal noise and dragged herself from the tangled quilt.

"You'll take forever to dress, at that rate. I'm going to the parlour to see Owen."

"Will there be breakfast?"

"I daresay. I shan't forget your help, Polly," Jean said generously, "and neither will Owen." Polly's usefulness had vanished once they left Earl's Brecon behind. She had never travelled farther than Lincoln in her life. Still, she had helped when Jean needed help.

Jean left Polly staring into the soapy basin and danced down the uneven floor of the hallway to the parlour Sims had hired. The power of speech that had forsaken her the night before returned as she walked. Her mind spun off eloquent phrases. She rapped once and grasped the door handle.

On the threshold she stopped short, "Owen" dying on her lips.

Clanross rose. "Good morning, Jean." The remains of a plate of roast beef lay before him. "I hope you slept well."

Colonel Falk, Johnny Dyott, and Sims had also risen at her entrance. Her eyes flew to Sims's.

"Morning, me lady," said the traitor.

Her first thought was flight, but where should she flee? There was no escape. "Where's Owen?" she asked, numb with defeat.

" 'E come in late," Sims said with no sign that he

recognised his own perfidy. "Still abed. 'Ave a chair, Lady Jean. I'll serve you."

Still numb, she sat in the chair Colonel Falk held for her.

Clanross addressed the beef and mustard. Colonel Falk drank his coffee. Sims cut bread. Johnny glowered at her and seemed on the point of speech several times.

At last the men's silence penetrated Jean's awareness. She clenched her fists. "I shall join Owen aboard the *North Star* this evening, Clanross. You cannot prevent me!"

Clanross laid down his cutlery and took a sip of coffee. "I could, if I chose to. Persuade me to change my mind."

Jean blinked. "I . . . Owen . . . we love each other."

"I congratulate you, but that is not a conclusive reason for you to abandon your family and take to the woods."

"We wish to wed!"

"Has he proposed marriage?"

Jean glowered. "He has not had the opportunity. Thanks to you and Elizabeth, we have been constantly spied upon, constrained . . ."

"Tyrants that we are," Clanross murmured. "Then I daresay Owen ought to be given the opportunity to make his feelings clear."

Jean gaped. So did Johnny, and Sims made a strangled noise he converted to a cough. Only Colonel Falk seemed unsurprised.

Jean swallowed. "Shall you permit us to meet privately?"

"I think a meeting can be arranged. Sims . . ."

Sims rose, his broad face red but impassive. "Me lord."

"Summon Mr. Davies. He was not informed of her ladyship's arrival, was he?"

"Not unless one of the inn servants told 'im. 'E come in late. I was already on me couch of ease."

"Lady Jean went to considerable pains to surprise Mr. Davies. It would be a shame to spoil the, er, happy conjunction."

" 'Appy? Look 'ere, me lord . . ."

Clanross raised his eyebrows. He did not smile and his grey eyes were cold.

Sims departed, grumbling.

Clanross stood up. "Gentlemen, let us retire to the ordinary and leave her ladyship to her breakfast."

Jean could scarcely believe her ears. "Oh, Clanross, thank you . . ."

"Don't thank me yet." He bowed, still unsmiling, and the three men filed out.

Jean jumped to her feet and began pacing the polished boards. On the mantel a nautical clock ticked away the minutes. Noise from the street, the kitchen, the taproom filtered through the shut door. Her mouth was dry. She poured herself tea and swallowed the unsweetened liquid.

There was a scratch at the door. Her hand shook and the teacup rattled in the saucer. "Come!"

It was Polly, still blinking sleepily. Everyone had forgot the maid's existence. Jean sent her, protesting, down to the ordinary, and resumed pacing. Owen was taking a long time. He had been asleep. Probably he had lain awake, brooding over his exile, thinking of her, until dawn.

Finally, when Jean's overstretched nerves had almost driven her to seek Sims, the valet opened the door and announced, "Mr. Davies," and Owen entered.

He stopped in the doorway, staring.

He was so beautiful with his fair flowing hair and his wild green eyes, Jean's hands reached out of their own volition. "Owen . . ."

Sims gave him a shove from behind and shut the door.

"Mag . . .L–Lady Jean! How the . . . I'm, that is, I am amazed. I had not hoped see you here. How do you, my lady?"

Jean gave a tremulous smile. "Very well now I see you. I have come to you, Owen. They would have prevented me, but I escaped them and drove at once to your side."

Emotion seemed to have deprived him of his wonted eloquence. He cleared his throat. "But I sail this evening!"

"Oh, my dear Owen, only say the word and I shall sail with you!"

"Impossible!"

"What?"

"I mean, surely your guardian . . ."

"Clanross is here. He permitted us to meet alone."

"He did?" His light tenor rose almost to a squeak. "He's here?"

"In the ordinary with Colonel Falk and Johnny," Jean said, suppressing impatience. "Owen, we must make haste . . ."

"Were you followed, Lady Jean? That is, you say you escaped the confines of Brecon and drove to Bristol."

"To be at your side."

"Yes, yes, but the Runner!"

Jean had half forgotten the Runner. "I saw no sign of him."

Owen closed his eyes. "I must think. It's too much for me to take in."

Poor darling, Jean thought tenderly. He's overwhelmed, and no wonder. Few women would show so much enterprise.

When she thought he had had sufficient time to collect his thoughts, she went to his side.

He took a step backward. "Lady Jean, you do me great honour, but you must see it's impossible. A gently bred young lady in a wilderness? No, you *shall* not come. It would be unfair."

"But Owen, you don't understand. I'd be your bride!"

He took another step backwards and bumped the closed door. "I shall worship you forever, my lady. Our souls are wed, certainly, but . . ."

The tea Jean had drunk churned acidly. "But what?"

"I am in no case to be married!" he exclaimed. "I've no means to support you. My parents . . ."

"What have they to say to anything?"

His eyes widened. "They would not approve my marriage to you, my lady."

"On what grounds?" Jean cried, stung. Who was a country rector to be objecting to an earl's daughter for his son?

"My mother dislikes the connexion," he muttered. "It won't do, my lady. You are too much above me, too young . . ."

It was Jean's turn to back away. Confusion and hurt warred with pride. "But you said you loved me!"

Owen ran a distracted hand through his fair hair. "I do. I adore you. I worship you as men worship Truth . . ."

"But you don't want to marry me."

"Marriage is for fettered souls, men like Dyott with no dream and no mission. I cannot marry—I must be free to serve my country's liberty!" His eyes took on the glow that meant he was off on a flight of lyricism.

Before he could unloose his muse, Jean said in a hard voice, "If your words of devotion to me did not bespeak marriage, Owen, did you perhaps intend to give me a slip on the shoulder?" She chose the crudest phrase she could think of.

His mouth gaped.

"Never mind. I can see I misunderstood you. Forgive me for causing you embarrassment."

Owen flushed a deep, unbecoming red. "Forgive you? My lady . . ."

"I'd esteem it a favour if you left me alone."

"But Lady Jean . . ."

"Go!" she whispered. "In God's name."

He fled, leaving the door wide behind him.

Jean did not bother to close it. She sat slowly on the nearest chair. Her eyes felt as if someone had sprinkled sand in them, but she had no tears. Instead she felt a strong urge to cast up the tea. She shut her gritty eyes and clenched her teeth. Presently the nausea passed and she felt cold, though the day was warm and the morning sun shone merrily through a tall window. What a fool she had been. No wonder Clanross was willing to risk the meeting. He must have known Owen had no real desire to marry her. Fury—at Owen, at Clanross, mostly at herself—drove the cold away. What had she left? Pride and her name. Well, she would hold to both.

= 25 =

WHEN SIMS STUCK his head in the door half an hour later Jean was sitting at the table making a good pretence at eating breakfast and never mind that everything was cold.

"Are you all right, me lady?"

"Perfectly." She raised her chin. "You may tell Clanross it's safe to return."

"Safe . . ." Sims's shrewd eyes regarded her without expression. "As you say, me lady."

Her brother-in-law came in almost at once.

Jean set her teacup down because her hands were starting to shake again. "Mr. Davies and I have decided we shall not suit." She didn't look at him.

"Very well," he said quietly. "I'm sorry, Jeanie." He was alone, and he looked underslept and far from happy.

Jean shut her eyes. She would not cry in Clanross's presence.

"What do you mean to do about Polly?"

Jean's eyes opened. "Polly?"

"Your servant. You must know that Mrs. Smollet will be unable to give Polly a good character after this episode."

"Hang Polly," she said bitterly. Her heart was broken and he was prosing on about servants.

Clanross drew a chair. "One of the first things I learned when I took up my commission—I was about your age—is that an officer must take care of his men."

Jean stared.

His grey eyes met hers gravely. "The analogy may seem

286

strained, but you should be able to see the parallel. You've involved Polly in an independent action, against orders. Is it right that she should suffer for your misjudgement?"

"She was willing to come."

"She admires you, Jean."

Jean swallowed. "What must I do?"

Clanross smiled a little. "Ask Elizabeth's advice, and ask Polly what *she* wants to do. The consequences could be graver for her than they will be for you, and it's her life, after all. *I'm* satisfied so long as you understand your responsibility to her."

"I'll see to it."

"Has Davies gone out?"

"I don't care where he's gone," Jean muttered. "I told him to leave me." That sounded too much like a confession. "I needed time to think," she amended.

"I see." He looked down at his hands, which were clasped on the table. "I ought to leave you alone, Jean, but the blasted trial begins tomorrow and I must leave in an hour or so." He glanced over at her and smiled slightly.

She forced a smile.

"If things had gone as I meant them to, Owen would have sailed and you would have writ him."

She drew a breath.

"I fancied you'd find a way to correspond, Jean. I trusted your ingenuity."

"Much good it's done me."

He touched her hand but she wasn't ready for comfort and drew back. He sighed. "You'd have writ him and he'd have replied—it sometimes takes three months for a reply to come from America—and you'd have writ again. His next letter, or ode, or jeremiad, would have taken longer to reach you. After awhile you would have understood what you discovered so cruelly today. If I'd seen any other course, I'd not have exposed you to that . . ."

"He doesn't love me!" The words burst out.

"Owen loves his idea of you. After you made your avowal

that day in the Brecon library, I charged him with trifling with your feelings. He was honestly shocked. He believes his words, Jeanie. Some men have a gift of words so intoxicating they seduce themselves."

Jean said nothing. It was easier to hate Owen than to try to understand him.

After a moment Clanross pushed himself up. "*I've* no gift for words, unfortunately, or I'd find some comfort for you."

"I've learnt a lesson." She knew she sounded sullen.

He said wryly, " 'Keep you in the rear of your affection, out of the shot of danger . . .' "

" 'And desire.' " She completed the quotation for him and made herself meet his eyes. They were kind and troubled. She forced another smile. "Don't worry so, Clanross. I know I've been a fool."

"We're all fools for love, my dear."

"Not I. Never again." She bit her lip.

"You've always had courage, Jean. Judgement will come when you've seen a bit of the world, but don't harden your heart. That's the worst kind of cowardice, being afraid to feel."

She digested that, or tried to. "Don't go yet."

"All right."

Slow tears began to leak from her eyes. "I love you, Clanross. Oh, I don't mean romantically, though I once imagined I did. I mean as I ought, as your sister."

He said nothing, but came to her again and held her while she cried for her own folly.

When the worst storm was over he handed her a large lawn handkerchief. "Blow."

She gave a damp giggle and blew. "Tell me what I must do now."

"You know what to do."

"Maggie." She swallowed hard.

"Maggie, certainly, and Elizabeth. She loves you, too, Jean, for yourself and because she loved your mother."

"Lizzie will flay me!"

He laughed. "She'll ring a peal over you. She's concerned for your reputation—as I am. People tend to judge a pretty young woman . . ."

"I beg your pardon, Tom," Colonel Falk said from the door, "but I think the second act of the drama is about to begin."

Clanross took a step toward him. "The Runner?"

Falk glanced round the room, nodded to Jean. "Sims and Johnny are trying to forestall him, but I'm afraid . . ."

Sims's massive form filled the doorway. "Begging your pardon, sir, Miss Carter, there's a person 'ere won't take no for an answer." He stepped aside.

The stranger everyone had noticed in church ducked under Sims's arm. "I'll 'ave you for obstructing an officer of the court, my man. See if I don't."

"Wotcher," said Sims.

The Runner advanced into the room, bristling with truculence. "Me lord, I 'ave reason to believe you're 'arbouring a wanted man."

"I?"

The man flushed.

Clanross said icily, "I don't believe I've had the honour."

The man gave a stiff bow. "Samuel T. Pickens, of the central criminal court, Bow Street, at your service." He handed Clanross a card.

Jean had risen at his entrance. She began to edge away from the table.

"Well, Sergeant?" Clanross sounded lordly, for once. Jean hadn't believed he could.

"I 'ave with me a warrant for the arrest of one Owen Talbott Davies for seditious correspondence and inciting to riot."

"Do you see your man?"

"No, sir, but I've reason to think your servant," he jerked

his head at Sims, "has been 'arbouring the fugitive under an assumed name."

"Owen Davies is my employee," Clanross said coldly. "So is Sims. It's natural for Sims and Davies to associate. There can be no question of 'harbouring a fugitive' until it's known that a crime has been committed. The charge is absurd."

"That's not for me to say, me lord. A warrant was sworn out against the said Davies on information received, and it's me duty to serve it. Anyone 'indering me in the exercise or me duty is liable to charges, as your lordship well knows."

"Then serve your warrant."

"Where is the miscreant?"

"I've no idea."

" 'E was 'ere last night. I followed him into the taproom. When 'e went upstairs the waiter said 'e was stopping at the inn."

"Then find him and serve your warrant. You're intruding on a private conversation between me and my ward."

Jean had edged as far as the sideboard. The man's shrewd eyes fell on her. She gave a smile that felt like a grimace.

The man laughed, a barking sound like a seal. "Madam led me a fine chase."

"I thought you'd a warrant for Davies's arrest," Colonel Falk murmured. He was leaning on the doorjamb. "What has his lordship's ward to do with anything?"

"Ward?" the man snorted. "She's 'is sister-in-law, and it's my belief she's 'and-in-glove with the aforesaid Davies. If you don't produce the fugitive, me lord, I mean to take 'er ladyship in for questioning. As a material witness."

"I think that would be unwise," Clanross said mildly.

"Where's Davies?" Pickens looked from one impassive face to the other. No one spoke. Johnny Dyott bit his lip.

"Very well," the Runner said heavily. "Lady Margaret Conway, it is my duty to . . ."

"Stay, you shall not!" cried a voice from the hall. "*I* am Lady Margaret Conway!"

Three hours later Tom and Richard had almost sorted things out.

The Runner, unable to say absolutely which twin was Lady Margaret Conway, at first threatened to take both girls into custody. A very young "widow" had delivered the seditious poem to a house in Greek Street. He would lay odds the widow was one of the girls.

"But you don't know which," Richard observed, "and your witness can't swear . . ."

The man growled like a baited bear.

Keeping his face as blank as he could, Tom turned to Sims. "Sims, you can identify Davies. Go with Sergeant Pickens. He will be wanting to find Owen and serve his warrant."

Sims's eyes, nearly invisible in their rolls of fat, didn't blink. "I understand you, me lord."

Tom was in dire peril of falling into the whoops. That would have been a fatal error, offending both the Runner and the twins beyond apology. He avoided Richard's eyes and turned back to the Runner. "I daresay you're aware that the queen's trial begins tomorrow."

"Aye, me lord."

"If I do not attend, for whatever reason, I shall be fined a hundred pounds. You'll understand why I must start for London within the next few hours. Even driving all night, flat out, I'll be cutting it close."

"Yes, sir."

"Go with Sims and find Davies. Serve your warrant, if you can. If not, come with me in my curricle and we shall both go to your superiors and seek their advice."

A flicker of relief in the small eyes told Tom the man was looking for a way out of what had to be a discomfortable duty. He felt sorry for Pickens. The law was an ass, but its officers were sworn to uphold it, however foolish and impossible to enforce it might be.

He added what he hoped was the clincher. "I'll guarantee, on my word as a peer of the realm, to produce Lady Margaret Conway at any time the court wish to hear her testimony."

"I dunno, me lord."

"Your warrant is for Davies, is it not?"

"Yes, but I'm allowed to take material witnesses."

"I shan't deter you from interviewing Lady Margaret once you've arrested Davies. Perhaps you ought to go about it." He hoped Owen had lost himself thoroughly in the back streets of Bristol, or stowed aboard the *North Star*, preferably in the scuppers. Well, that part of the operation was in Sims's hands, and Tom knew his man's ingenuity.

The longer the Runner stood arguing the greater Owen's chances of eluding him. Pickens knew it. It took a bit more persuasion, but the man left at last, in Sims's safekeeping, to inspect Owen's room. Tom hoped the poet's fear of matrimony had driven him far afield.

When the Runner had gone, the twins flew into one another's arms and engaged in an affecting reunion. Tom knew from Richard's rapt attention to the scene that his friend was busy composing the next satire.

Tom sat and poured himself a cup of cold coffee. What he wanted was a tumbler of brandy.

"Sir!"

He looked up. Johnny Dyott, eyes blazing, had finally broken his heroick silence.

"My lord, may I have your permission to ask you sister-in-law to marry me?"

Which sister-in-law? Tom left the frivolous response unspoken. "Now is not the time, Johnny."

"If she is to be hailed away to prison, I want her to know she shall have my protection."

Tom said gently, "It won't be necessary. Trust me."

The boy flushed and looked down at his shoes. He burned to do *something*.

"I have a high regard for you," Tom continued, a trifle oppressed by his marathon of tact, "and I shall certainly permit you to speak to Maggie. But you must wait to marry until you've sold an article to a respectable journal and she's turned nineteen."

Johnny's solemnity split in a wide grin. "Truly, sir?"

"Truly. But it's as Maggie wishes."

"Do you object to a formal engagement?"

Tom threw up his hands. "Ask Elizabeth. If she says yes, I can't say no."

Johnny's gratitude, though profuse, was premature. Maggie was still sobbing happily in Jean's arms, oblivious of Johnny and everyone else. Tom had no doubt she would eventually hear a formal proposal of marriage.

With a reluctant but happy sigh, Richard got to business. "You think Davies will avoid the embrace of the law?"

Tom said, "Sims can do anything."

Sims and Richard did not love one another but Richard nodded. "*Capable de tout*. And you mean to carry the Runner in the curricle, posthaste as it were, to London? I thought you'd pay the blasted fine and stop here tonight."

Tom grimaced. "I don't look forward to the drive or the company, but I can think of no other way to convince Pickens of my patriotic devotion."

"And no other way to save his face," Richard said shrewdly.

"I shall abase myself before the Bow Street magistrate, confess all, and trust that no one, not even the present government, could want to conduct two trials in the House of Lords in one short year."

"If I start laughing," Richard mused, "I shan't be able to stop. Has it occurred to you that someone will have to drive the gig back to Brecon? I can't do it."

That was true. Driving a gig one-handed would be foolhardy. "Jem Fosse drove the barouche." Fosse and

Lisette, who had brought Maggie into the town, were below in the ordinary instructing Polly in the error of her ways.

"I rather think the ladies would be safer with Fosse driving the barouche again."

"And you accompanying?"

"I engage to tell them the adventures of Don Alfonso." Richard placed his left hand on his lung, being unable to place the right on his heart. "That should keep them out of mischief as far as Coventry. Johnny may drive the gig ahead of us."

"You don't object to intruding yourself into love's young dream?"

Richard eyed Johnny, who was approaching the ladies. "I shall relish every moment."

"You'll have to change the names when you write it up."

Richard smiled. "Lady Rosalind and Lady Viola."

"And the heroes?"

"Romeo and Hotspur?"

"Doesn't ring right."

"I'll come up with something."

Tom expelled a long breath. "I wonder how Sims is faring with the Runner?"

"Splendidly. Should you object to my calling for a bumper of ale?"

Maggie beamed from Jean to Johnny. "Clanross!" she called, "may we go for a walk on the quay?"

"With my blessing." Tom turned back to his friend. "A bumper of ale? I may dive into it."

=26=

Four days after Colonel Falk and Johnny returned the fugitive twins to Elizabeth's custody, Sims, too, came home to Brecon. He rattled up in triumph, driving the matched chestnuts, and delivered a letter Clanross would not trust to the mail. From the expression on Sims's broad beaming face it was clear he had contrived Owen's escape. Colonel Falk and Johnny bore him off for brandy and interrogation in the bookroom, and Elizabeth took her letter to the withdrawing room. Maggie waited with barely concealed impatience for her to finish reading. Jean sat quietly. She was still penitent. Emily Falk knitted.

". . . so I slept through the prosecutor's opening remarks in the trial of Queen Caroline," Tom wrote. "In fact, I slept through the entire session and relied on *The Times* to tell me what to think.

"As I had promised the Runner, I spoke with the Bow Street magistrate the next morning. He dismissed the charges against Owen, trembling at the thought of two innocent (*n.b.* I embroidered the truth) damsels of high birth held up like torches by the Whig press. As a martyr to the cause of liberty, Owen couldn't hold a candle to the twins. I assured the gentleman that questions would be asked in the Lords if the twins were arrested, interrupting the queen's trial if need be, and that Sir Francis Burdett would himself speak in their behalf before a giant Radical rally in the

Haymarket that would make Manchester look like a picnic. (Sir Francis had agreed to the use of his name. He was a trifle disappointed when I assured him no such rally would ever occur.)

"I also pointed out that my attempt to help a fugitive from justice evade arrest made me an accessory and that I would welcome a trial in the Lords. The magistrate blenched and sent for a clerk at that point. The queen's trial keeps the town in such a stir that the thought of another cause célèbre shook him to his already shaky foundations.

"I'd never have used my name and influence in such a cynical way had it not been for the peril the girls stood in, but once I swallowed my scruples I rather enjoyed what amounted to political blackmail. The Runner was not a bad chap. I bought him a glass of gin afterwards. He appeared to think his career would not suffer for my interference.

"As it turned out, Sims did not have to diddle the Runner, who had misconstrued Owen's character so thoroughly he visited every grog shop, tavern, and gin parlour in the port without result. Pickens gave Sims a bad moment when he insisted on directing the local magistrate to continue the search, but Pickens's information was so vague it was clear he had not discovered which vessel Owen was booked to sail on. Sims had taken the precaution of enrolling Owen on the passenger list under the name of Wilkes, not Evans, the name he had used at the Crown and Anchor. That being so, Sims decided it would be unnecessary to have Owen rowed to Avonmouth to board there.

"The Runner and I left Bristol. Johnny and Richard had removed the girls earlier. There remained the task of finding the wandering poet. Unlike the Runner, Sims did know Owen's character. Even so, he searched five bookshops and a circulating library before he remembered that Owen had been writing an "Ode to Freedom Penn'd in the Shadow of St. Mary Redcliffe" the previous evening. Sims dashed to the church, found Owen deep in composition among the tombs, hired a boat at the foot of the bridge across the floating harbour, and spirited Owen aboard the *North Star* without interference from the Bristol constabulary. It was half past six. When the tide reversed, and it reverses at Bristol with a vengeance, the vessel swept down the Avon to the Severn and, we devoutly trust, out to sea.

"My efforts at Bow Street rendered Owen's exile unnecessary. I have sent a letter by the slowest possible means to tell him he may come home. My hope is he will be deep in the interior by the time the letter reaches Quebec City. Even if he is not, he will probably have to winter in Quebec. As I recall, the cold in those parts comes early. Pray inform his worthy parents he is no longer in danger of trial and incarceration (unless he has committed another sedition en route).

"Well, my dear, I have done my best for your sisters. I wish I might act as effectively in behalf of reform of Parliament. (I am scribbling this in pencil at Westminster whilst the evidence against her licentious majesty mounts. The peers of England believe I am taking notes.)

"The queen has twice been seen sleeping during witnesses' testimony. The weather is hot and the procedure dull so one cannot blame her, but her drowsiness has resulted in a joke of the sort Willoughby Conway-Gore enjoys: "She sleeps *not* with servants—She sleeps with the Lords." By the same token, I may be said to have slept with the queen. She was present in the hall whilst I was snoring away on Thursday.

"Elizabeth, my dear, pray suppress your natural inclination to sororicide and deal moderately with Jean. She has suffered a blow to her self-

297

esteem, if not to her heart. Maggie is quite the heroine. Boldness becomes her. I thought the Runner would swallow his back teeth when she leapt onto the stage in defence of her sister.

"You may tell Richard I shall sue him for traducing the family honour if that dramatic moment appears in the next satire. Sims is the hero of the hour, but Richard did yeoman work, and so did Johnny, who finally overcame his diffidence and asked me for Maggie's hand. I told him yes but not yet. I hope that was the correct answer.

"The prosecution have just called an Austrian housemaid. The testimony in this trial is giving a new, literal meaning to the idea of airing one's dirty linen in publick. If that's the nature of politicks, I may come home and cultivate my cabbages.

"I *shall* come home for the eclipse of the sun even if I have to pay the fine. Shall we observe it privately or do you wish to give an eclipse-watching fete? I could hire the Pandaean Pipes.

"My love to all the right people and my chief love to you.

"Your still somnolent spouse, Tom."

This missive Elizabeth handed to Emily Falk who read it with starting eyes. Elizabeth felt it was too spicy to read Jean and Maggie, so she summarized, assuring them Owen was safe. Owen's fate left them unmoved.

When Emily asked about the eclipse, Maggie burst into spontaneous plans. Elizabeth had rather fancied celebrating the event in Tom's sole company, but she decided not to be selfish, and told the girls they might hold an alfresco party by the lake. Jean made a timid suggestion for refreshment. Elizabeth complimented her sister on the idea. Jean gave a tentative smile. Within days, Jean was her wonted self.

She had decided, with Elizabeth's permission, to send Polly to Anne's chef to be trained as a cook-housekeeper. The idea of the apprenticeship appealed to Polly, and London appealed even more, so Polly rode off to town with Sims. Mrs. Smollet sniffed, but everyone else approved.

Johnny remained at Brecon. Elizabeth wondered if he had yet proposed marriage. Surely not. Surely, if he had, Maggie would have come to her in high excitement. Perhaps he had decided not to ally himself with a nest of Radicals after all.

August passed faster than Elizabeth would have thought possible with Tom in London. The Falk children and the Little Sisters romped about the grounds, rode their ponies, and played battledore and shuttlecock on the fresh-rolled lawn. Matt broke a window demonstrating his prowess with the cricket bat to an admiring female audience.

Richard Falk finished the book room catalogue, a makeshift, he said. Elizabeth was sure it was excellent and said so, but he was not an easy man to compliment. He lost himself in the letters of one Hercules Conway, a captain in Marlborough's army, bringing in some of the less shocking anecdotes to amuse the twins and Johnny. Emily and Elizabeth enjoyed their babies. In short, in a fair approximation to paradise, nothing of significance occurred during the rest of the month.

Tom arrived late on the eve of the eclipse looking wilted. He revived like a thirsty plant in a rain shower when Elizabeth bore him off to their suite for a private celebration.

"We shall observe the moon's shadow as it passes between us and the sun, the penumbra first, then the umbra. Umbra means . . . ?"

"Shadow!" a chorus of piping voices answered Miss Bluestone. The children were ranged on one of the cloths the servants had spread in a half circle facing the lake. Each child held a painfully constructed box of stiff paper—a camera obscura for observing the sun's reversed image without damage to the eyes. The notion came from Lady Clanross, though Johnny, Maggie, and the still subdued Jean had helped in the construction of the boxes.

Miss Bluestone beamed at her charges. "And if umbra means shadow, then penumbra is . . . ?"

"Come with me, Maggie," Johnny whispered. He felt he had done his possible for the advancement of science. He had other, long-delayed intentions for the climactic moment.

Maggie glanced up at him, wide-eyed. "But the children . . ."

"I'll stay with the children and Miss Bluestone," Jean said absently. She was helping Fanny position the pinpoint in the top of the box so as to catch the sun's image.

Maggie looked from Jean to Johnny. Johnny held out his hand.

Maggie smiled. "All right. Has someone let the dogs out, Jean?"

"Yes, yes, go on."

Johnny led Maggie along the grass until they came to the beech avenue.

"Where are we going? We'll miss the eclipse!"

"No, we won't." Anticipation was making him giddy. "It's not for half an hour. We can reach the pavilion."

"Oh." Maggie gave him a sly look as if to say "what have you in mind, sir?" but she walked along with him in peaceful silence. They held hands.

The sky darkened so gradually they did not notice the change until the foolish birds began tweeting and chirruping in the beeches above them. "It's coming!" Maggie began to run. They reached the pavilion in twilight and sat on the steps.

Or rather Maggie sat. Johnny stood before her, hat in hand. "Will you marry me, Lady Margaret?"

"Good heavens, yes." The grey eyes twinkled. "What an age you've been. Were you waiting for the eclipse?"

"No." Johnny drew her to her feet. "I was waiting for this," and he kissed her full and lingeringly on the mouth. It was quite dark. No one saw them.

The children and the birds twittered as the sunlight dimmed. Jean's setter gave a confused yowl and ran in search of his mistress.

Some yards from the schoolroom party, Emily was seated on another of the picnicking cloths. She patted the place beside her. "Join me?"

Richard sat and drew Tommy onto his lap. Tommy gave a small bounce, then watched wide-eyed as night came in the middle of the morning. The leaves rustled and somewhere a cock crew, but Tommy was watching the racing shadows. He looked up and touched Richard's face.

" 'Sdark," he said quite clearly.

"So it is." Richard kissed the top of his head.

Emily leaned against her husband and they watched the children watching the eclipse. Tom and Elizabeth had gone off to the telescope platform.

All too soon umbra and penumbra passed and the world emerged into the common light of day. Tommy jumped up and ran off shouting. Emily sighed.

"What is it, dear heart?"

"The magick always goes away."

"Not always. Shall we go home, Emily?"

"To Mayne Hall?"

"To Wellfield."

She drew a sharp breath. "But I thought you meant to ask Tom's advice . . ."

"Not Tom's. Matt's."

Emily sat very still.

Richard regarded her with quizzical hazel eyes. "It won't be forever. I mean to purchase Hazeldell, but that will take some time. Even then, if you like, you can place a bailiff in charge of the land. Tom has a lad his agent has been training . . ."

"But you can't want to live at Wellfield," Emily said, distressed and hopeful at the same time.

"My dear, wherever we go there will be gossip. I thought you understood that."

"I do, but . . ."

"Then let's go home and ignore the tabbies. Matt rowed me around the lake three times explaining why we should live in his house. He plans to charge me an enormous rent and buy a roan gelding that runs like the wind."

"The little devil!"

Richard laughed.

"You don't mind? Truly?"

"I don't mind. But I said I'd give you time to reflect. Instead, I've forced your hand . . ."

Emily touched her fingers to his lips. "Hush. It's exactly what I want to do. Live at Wellfield and visit Hazeldell at first, then, as the children grow older, live here and visit Hampshire. When Matt comes of age . . ."

"And his roan wins the Derby . . ."

"Hush."

"But . . ."

She hushed him with a brazen daylight kiss. It was probable that everyone saw them, including Miss Bluestone.

Tom and Elizabeth wandered back. Maggie and Johnny, flushed with their not-very-secret engagement, trotted up hand in hand. The servants spread the alfresco meal. The children abandoned their boxes and dashed off to the lake, shrieking.

After the picnic, when the children had at last been herded off to their quarters for a wash and the babies bathed and admired and fed, Tom and Elizabeth led the Falks to the withdrawing room for a glass of restorative sherry.

They talked, lazily, agreeably, of the Falks' plans. Elizabeth was a little disappointed that they would not be removing at once to Hazeldell, but she could understand how Emily's attachment drew her new friend back to Wellfield.

They were about to go up to dress for dinner when Sims, who had never quite fathomed the uses of a great household, entered the drawing room.

Elizabeth and Tom exchanged glances.

Sims went straight to Emily. "Ma'am, pursuant to instructions, I'm asking you for the 'and of Miss Theale."

Emily's mouth formed a silent O.

"He means Phillida," Richard said helpfully.

"Oh heavens, Sims, are you sure?"

Sims's face was red. "She 'as done me the honour to agree to me proposition."

Emily gave an audible gulp. "She's a very good girl, Sims, but you'll have to take care of her. She's not . . . that is, she . . ."

"I shall clasp 'er to me bosom with 'oops of steel," Sims said firmly. " 'Is lordship don't mind."

"Then *I* can't very well object." Emily cleared her throat. "And of course I wish you well. I shall miss Phillida."

Sims beamed benignly. "That's all right, then."

He left.

Emily gave Tom a sorrowing, reproachful look.

"Don't blame me."

"I should have known the eclipse portended some kind of doom. I shall have to find a nursemaid *and* a maid-of-all-work. How did it come about?"

"I'm not sure," Tom said with evident caution. "I think Sims fancies himself as Touchstone to Phillida's Audrey."

Richard gave a crack of laughter. " 'Trip, Audrey, trip.' "

"Just so."

Elizabeth thought it was time to turn the subject. "Of course, being a purely natural phenomenon, an eclipse portends nothing, certainly not doom. It's easy to see how the superstition arose, however. I felt quite a chill when that rooster at the home farm began to crow."

Tom stood, stretching and yawning. "I know what *I* hope it portends."

She smiled up at him. "What?"

"The end of the queen's trial. I can't afford very many two hundred pound interludes."

Richard rose. "I thought the fine was one hundred pounds a day."

"It is. I intend to stay the week-end."

Emily stood, straightening her skirts. "Was it worth the cost?"

Tom smiled at Elizabeth. "Absolutely."

Epilogue

As it turned out, the eclipse portended a recess. The trial was adjourned on Monday. Tom had paid two hundred pounds for the privilege of not hearing the prosecutor's summary.

When the trial resumed after Michaelmas, the defence began calling the queen's witnesses. The goverment's majority in the Lords, never firm, had already begun to erode. Though it was wonderfully seamy and sold a great many newspapers, the evidence against Caroline of Brunswick was circumstantial. No one could prove anything. The Lords were restive and so was the Mob. After the second reading, the Bill of Pains and Penalties was withdrawn.

> "Our gracious queen, we thee implore
> To go thy ways and sin no more.
> Or if the effort be too great,
> To go away at any rate."

The queen's qualified victory provoked demonstrations wherever there was discontent, and especially in London. Once more the houses of ministers and government spokesmen lost windows. Whig houses were illuminated as a sign of victory, or, as in the case of the Earl of Clanross's town residence, out of prudence. Elizabeth was giving a ball the next evening.

All day Tory servants swept glass and Whig servants spread straw in Grosvenor Square. By eight Elizabeth's dinner guests were arriving. By ten the carriages were lined up past Lord Harrowby's house and around the corner. It was going to be, as Jean put it, a famous crush.

Jean glittered. Maggie, clinging happily to Johnny's arm, glowed. There was no doubt they were going to be the talk of the Little Season.

"I believe you saved this one for me."

Elizabeth smiled at her husband. "The dinner waltz? Yes, indeed." He led her onto the floor. "Have you danced with every notable old cat in the room?"

"Except you." They swooped. "I wish you wouldn't provide me with an easy target, darling. Are you off your feed?"

"Preoccupied."

"With the girls? Never mind. They'll do. The gossips are calling them Fire and Ice and predicting great things."

"A comfortable irony. Mmm." She closed her eyes and let the musick take her.

"Jean will eventually thaw."

Eyes still closed, Elizabeth smiled. "That's what I'm afraid of."